WORST NIGHTMARE

THE AL ANDALUS OPERATION

STEPHEN R. FIELD

D1225850

FORTIS
PUBLISHING

Jacksonville, Florida ♦ Herndon, Virginia
www.Fortis-Publishing.com

WORST NIGHTMARE
THE AL ANDALUS OPERATION

By STEPHEN R. FIELD

Worst Nightmare is a work of fiction. Names, characters, places, and incidents are the products of the author's imagination, or are used fictitiously. Any resemblance to actual locales or persons, living or dead, is purely coincidental.

ISBN 978-0-9845511-8-7 (Trade Paperback)

Published by Fortis Publishing
Jacksonville, Florida—Herndon, Virginia
www.Fortis-Publishing.com

Manufactured in the United States of America

Cover art by Karen Lowery

All statements of fact, opinion, or analysis expressed are those of the author and do not reflect the official positions or views of the publisher, or any U.S. Government agency or personnel. Nothing in the contents should be construed as asserting or implying U.S. Government agency or personnel's authentication of information or endorsement of the author's views. This book and subjects discussed herein are designed to provide the author's opinion in regard to the subject matter covered and is for informational purposes only.

DEDICATION

To my children
C and S
whom I love deeply

ACKNOWLEDGEMENTS

For a while, I have wanted to write and publish this story as a cautionary tale. I give thanks to those who have helped me accomplish that goal.

I am extremely grateful to ER for her excellent editorial assistance, support and guidance over countless hours reviewing my manuscript. I also received excellent editorial assistance from Dennis Lowery, who arranged for the publication of this book. In addition, I warmly embrace my dear friend of many years, Stephan M. Minikes, Ambassador (Ret.), who was instrumental in helping me find the publisher. My hat is off to each of you.

CHAPTER 1

LAYING IN WAIT OFF THE NORTHEAST COAST OF SUMATRA

August 10, 2006

From his boat, Hamad saw his prey: a large oil supertanker bound for Europe, moving slowly in the quiet waters of the Strait of Malacca at a distance of about 4,000 meters. For over a year, he had been trained arduously by Al Qaeda in a remote tribal area of northwestern Pakistan and in northern Indonesia for this mission, to attack and seize the liquid gold carrying vessel for the Al Qaeda cause. As his reward, he now commanded a sleek heavily armed black patrol boat, and its crew of 14 well-trained dedicated Muslim warriors—mujahedeen willing to die for Allah. The boat carried a mounted 50-caliber machinegun as well as a separate 20-millimeter cannon. The crewmembers, each outfitted with a Kalashnikov, wore black, tight fitting suits with detachable ski masks.

It was a perfect night for the attack –a half moon, but the cloud cover effectively eliminated almost all of its potentially revealing light. At the evening prayer, Hamad had wished for such a heaven-sent gift. Now he was sure that his attack vessel, which moved at a speed of up to 60 miles per hour and boasted a custom-designed silencer to block the engines' powerful roar, could intercept the tanker without detection.

Hamad al-Ibrahim and his band of pirates knew all of the features of the supertanker by heart. They had studied the blueprints of the Japanese and Norwegian shipbuilders. Capable of carrying 2 million barrels of oil, the tanker was lightly armed with a machine gun placed mid-deck and up to five members of the crew might have assault rifles or submachine guns. At over 300 meters long and the superstructure holding the bridge and living quarters at the back of the vessel, an assault from the front was too risky. The captain had a clear view of the entire deck of the ship. Based on data obtained from various oil shippers' international trade association meetings, the pirates knew that more than half of the tankers crew of 15 slept at night. They would attack from the vessel's rear between 1:00 a.m. and 3:00 a.m.

Hamad turned to a trusted lieutenant, Abdullah Abu Hassan, who sat at the wheel of the attack boat, and said:

"We're 80 kilometers from the Indonesian coast and have the cloud cover we need. If we move at 65 kilometers an hour, we should be able to intercept the infidel target in about 15 minutes. Let's go."

Abdullah gunned the powerful engines and the boat leapt forward in the quiet waters headed for its target.

The rest of the crew waited for the leader's final countdown. They knew the drill: make sure your weapon is locked and loaded; take the safety lock off your Kalashnikov immediately before you leave the boat; check your night-vision goggles; make sure your mask covers your face; move in two squads of six; and make sure the grappling ropes land quietly on the rear deck. They heard these commands in their dreams.

CHAPTER 2

STRAIT OF MALACCA

August 10, 2006

The *Argus*, a Panamanian-registered oil supertanker, had left Singapore over 20 hours earlier. The port had been bustling. Over the past five years, ship traffic had increased steadily in order to satisfy the increasing appetites of China to the north and Europe to the west. From the bridge, the Norwegian captain, Christian Johannsen, counted more vessels than he had ever seen in the past. Sturdily built, dressed in a tan short-sleeved uniform, at 56 the Norwegian looked youthful and healthy. Years spent in the sun at sea had added lines to his round face, but they did not mar the cheerfulness of his expression or the sparkle of his intensely blue eyes heightened by a ruddy complexion. Looking back at the harbor wistfully, he could clearly see the silhouettes of the ultra-modern skyscrapers against a rainbow-hued sunset that so pleased him. He and his Norwegian and Dutch crew generally spent two to three days ashore, carousing in seedy smoke-filled nightclubs, sleeping in rooming houses that catered to itinerant sailors and their special needs and occasionally consuming gourmet meals at first-class restaurants.

The loading of the tanker took longer than usual because of mechanical difficulties in the housing mechanism. Once completed, the harbormaster gave approval for the tanker to leave and, at the same time, radioed one of the Singapore destroyers on duty that the tanker was leaving.

It was clear why the tanker needed an armed escort. Like other vessels headed toward Africa, Europe or the Middle East, it had to travel through the Strait of Malacca, the shortest sea route bridging the Pacific and Indian Oceans. This second busiest commercial shipping lane had become a feeding ground for pirates.

The destroyer escorted the oil supertanker from the main harbor toward the Strait. The crews in both vessels knew that the destroyer would only act as an escort until about 75 miles outside of the harbor. Afterwards, the tanker would be on its own without a safety net. Although the Indonesian, Malaysian and Thai navies routinely patrolled the Strait near their territorial waters, there would be a gap in armed protection.

When Captain Johannsen gathered his 12-man crew (two less than the ship's normal compliment) as they left the safety of the Singapore harbor, he gave the following instructions:

"There have been no recent attacks of late in the Strait. Obviously, the tsunami may have played a role here since it struck northwestern Indonesia heavily. But we still have to be on our guard. As soon as we clear the port area passage, here's what I want you to do:

Joachim, you check the mid-deck machine gun to make sure it's ready and fully loaded. Hans, you test the searchlight at the bow and the stern. Gunter, make sure that the rifles and machine guns are ready to go. OK. No screw-ups here, guys!"

At about 7:00 p.m. the crew gathered in the ship's dining room for rijsstafel. Everybody agreed that it made sense to have an Indonesian dish as they approached that country. A rib-filling dinner that everybody enjoyed and the Heinekens boosted their mood. After a good meal with excellent brew, the crew relaxed for two hours.

Several hours later, the destroyer signaled it was ending its escort by using coded fluorescent cards, visible for at least a mile away. The tanker acknowledged with a similar response. It was now on its own. There were at least eight hours to go before it would run into a Malaysian patrol and over 20 hours before it would approach Thailand's territorial waters.

Every two hours an armed crewmember walked the perimeter of the ship to check that all was in order—no items loose on deck and all hatches secure.

The first day passed without incident. At midnight of the following day, Joachim, Hans and Gunter reported to Captain Johannsen that they had finished their duties, adding that six crewmembers were now sleeping.

The tanker proceeded through the Strait at a speed of between 20 to 25 knots; the sea air was a balmy 70°. The reflection of the moonlight on the water faded, as heavy clouds crept across the half moon. All seemed peaceful. Just about 2:00 a.m., another crewmember, Olaf, reported to the Captain, "Everything on the deck is fine, Captain. Anything on radar nearby?"

"Nothing within 40 miles of us, some large ships, probably freighters at that range," the Captain answered authoritatively and confidently.

They were 45 miles from the Indonesian coast and proceeding west northwest.

Gunter, Hans and Joachim were in Johann's cabin playing poker and boasting of their exploits in Singapore. All three were in their late twenties and shared a love of the sea and the pleasures it afforded. They worked hard, played hard, and felt secure in their profession. Little did they realize that great danger lurked nearby.

Hamad left the pirates' hideout in northern Indonesia at Pangkalansusu about 24 hours after the Al Qaeda operative in Singapore sent an encrypted email informing him of the exact time of the supertanker's sailing. Finally, they would be carrying out a mission on their largest target. Their previous successes with a small freighter and a large yacht last year in the Strait were child's play. Still, those actions boosted their morale, making them feel like seasoned veterans.

Hamad and his crew marveled at the stealth quality of their vessel. Made of Kevlar and several additional necessary components, it could not be detected by radar, as was true of the Great Satan's stealth bomber.

The attack boat headed due north towards the approaching tanker, now approximately 1,000 meters away. Despite the absence of moonlight, the target was visible to the crew when they put on their night-vision goggles. To them the target looked like a big, slow-moving animal—one they planned to devour.

As they moved swiftly and steadily toward the point of interception, water splashed some crewmembers. In their black tight fitting waterproof suits, they paid no attention.

The men faced each other on two 20-foot cushion-covered seats with weapons cocked, masks on and ammunition belts worn in an x-pattern across their chests. Two of the crew also held grappling hook ropes to throw over the stern of the target. Their outfits were especially designed to strike fear in the minds of their adversaries. The dress code of the 21st century Al Qaeda pirates was as somber as the black outerwear and veils of the women in those countries where Islamic law prevailed.

When they were 75 meters from the stern of the tanker, Hamad commanded Abdullah to slow gradually. 40 meters, 30, meters, 20 meters, 10 meters. Now they were at the attack point.

Awad Zahali, the leader of the first squad, shot one of the grappling hook ropes over the left half of the stern, while simultaneously Mirza Abu el-Shami, the leader of the second squad, shot his over the right. Within 10 seconds, Awad nimbly climbed over the 30-foot stern of the tanker and quietly pulled himself over the top, dropping to the deck like a cat. The other five members of his squad and Hamad immediately followed him. Mirza's squad moved rapidly, athletically, skillfully and silently. In less than a minute, all 13 pirates had boarded. Only Abdullah, the vessel's driver, and one other crewmember remained on the attack boat awaiting their commander's next instructions.

Meanwhile, oblivious to the presence of intruders, Captain Johannsen and his Dutch first mate, Hendrik Feliks, a 41-year old from The Hague, sat at the tanker's wheel, their eyes fixed ahead of the ship's bow, awaiting the rendezvous with the Thai Navy in a few hours. Feliks rose to stretch briefly, stroking his unkempt wavy long blonde hair.

In the rear cabin below the bridge, six crewmembers slept peacefully. The other four were engrossed in a poker game, their fully loaded weapons left unattended near the entrance to their cabin.

Hamad, Awad and his squad moved in a crouched position slowly towards the staircase leading to the bridge from the rear deck and ascended noiselessly. When he was near the top step, Awad saw through the eight-foot square side window of the bridge that there were only two crewmembers there, that the captain had only a pistol and that the mate had a machine gun.

Hamad earlier had told his crew: "We must capture the captain of the tanker alive. We need him to communicate with the Thai naval representative as we approach Thai waters. If he does not personally communicate with the navy, the Thais will think something has gone wrong - and then they'll want possibly to board the ship and check it out. We cannot let that happen. Is this clearly understood?"

Hamad, Awad and three members of his squad quickly entered the unlocked door to the bridge. Caught by surprise at the reality and overwhelming force of an enemy in their presence, Captain Johannsen and his mate immediately dropped their weapons and surrendered. At Hamad's command in English, they put their arms behind their backs and sat on the floor, where two pirates tied up their hands and feet with rope and taped their mouths shut. Hamad then barked at the Norwegian captain:

"Captain, I have simple rules. If you follow them, you and your mate might live. If you don't, we'll behead each of you, a fate you deserve in any case. One of my crew will steer the ship through the Strait and thereafter to our final destination. When I need you to communicate with any person, including the Thai Navy, I will let you but under my instructions. You see this gun. It will be right next to your head when you communicate. One slip and you and your first mate are both dead."

"I understand what you want me to do," Captain Johannsen replied somewhat timidly. "But if I do as you say, I expect you will let my crew and me live and let us off at your final stop."

"I make the rules," Hamad answered coldly. "As the Spanish say: 'Que sera sera.' Forget the rest of the crew. They're dead or will be soon."

Captain Johannsen looked away, knowing that his chances of survival, and that of any of his crew, were highly unlikely. But he had one glimmer of hope - he could not identify the pirates because their faces were covered and maybe they would let him go. That hopeful thought faded immediately. He was thinking much too rationally. Pirates clearly operated on different principles; rationality was in all likelihood not their strong suit.

While the bridge was taken, Mirza's squad quietly descended the stairs to the deck below undetected. They saw the four sailors playing cards and drinking beer in the first cabin. Crying "Allah Akbar" (God is Great), two of Mirza's crew opened up with their Kalashnikovs killing the four of them. The firing was so heavy and intense that the heads of Joachim and Gunter were cut in half as they fell to the floor dead. Hans' body was riddled with 40 bullets. No warning, no request to surrender, only brutal death.

Moving silently and quickly to the rear cabin, Mirza and the other three members of his squad kicked in the door. Aroused by the sound of gunfire, the six sailors had just jumped out of bed to be machine-gunned down. Mirza fired a bullet in the head of one sailor who was still moving slightly.

Mirza's squad searched the rest of the ship and found no one else onboard. The intelligence that Hamad had received from Singapore was accurate - there were only 12 crewmembers. Ten were now dead; the remaining two, including the tanker's captain, had been captured.

Mirza's squad then returned to the bridge. Mirza looked at Hamad and said excitedly "You did it, Commander. The plan worked perfectly. You are a genius!"

"My brother, this was a team effort," Hamad replied softly. "We Muslim brothers did it together as a well-trained unit. I commend you and each of the crew. Allah Akbar!"

The entire crew of pirates responded with laughter and cried, "Allah Akbar!"

The tanker was now entirely under the pirates' control. But Hamad knew that much peril still lay in front of them before the mission was completed - unloading the oil at the Pakistani port of Karachi without any outsider's knowledge.

CHAPTER 3

DISGUISE STRAIT OF MALACCA

August 10, 2006 3:30 a.m.

Hamad ordered his crew to move into their sailor operation, the second phase of the pirates' plan. Hamad signaled Abdullah in the attack boat to send the maritime working clothes hidden in the duffel bags below deck to the tanker. Abdullah's assistant then lifted one of the hatches, grabbed both 20-pound bags, climbed the grappling rope with them and gave it to one of the crew on board the tanker.

Before putting on their new disguises, the pirates attended to the gruesome task of disposing of the victims. They gathered the 10 slaughtered men one by one, a bloody trail revealing the fatal carnage. The crew placed each of them in two metallic storage bins large enough to hold more than six adult men, which the pirates kept in semi-assembled pieces on their attack boat. They sealed the bins permanently with screws. Using the gangway as a plank, they lifted each bin separately on it and then let the bin slide into the cool waters. They were sure that the bin, which was full and weighed close to 800 pounds, would sink to the Strait's bottom, bury itself into the ocean floor and remain undetected - an unmarked water grave.

Once done, some of the crewmembers removed all evidence of the slaughter from the two cabins. To many of the pirates, this task was no different than cleaning up after the ritual of sacrificing sheep on various holidays in commemoration of one of the 12 imams that were sacred to them. Some gathered the torn and discolored bloody remains, others hosed down the walls and floors and then scrubbed them clean, eliminating the foul odors of blood and the stench of death. They destroyed the bloodstained bedding in the incinerator below deck.

Afterwards, all of the pirates put on their assorted maritime outfits. Those assigned to the engine room wore assorted T-shirts of single colors - with dark blue preferred - and with trousers of different colors. Those assigned to maintain the crew's cabins wore long-sleeved shirts with blue work pants. The deck hands' light blue long-sleeved shirts were rolled up to the elbow, worn over dark brown or black khaki-style pants. Hamad switched into an outfit typically worn by first mates assigned to tankers - a light tan outfit.

It was still the middle of the night but soon dawn would come and with it the possibility of close observation. He ordered Abdullah to return to the secret base in Pangkalansusu, about 90 kilometers from their current location.

Normalcy was the key to the success of the operation. If the tanker were closely observed by air or by an onboard inspection, the crew had to appear to be veteran seamen doing their normal tasks. Training at the terror camp supplied all the skills needed - and the pirates absorbed them well. The ruse had to work or else the mission might fail.

Interception had occurred in the Strait about midway between the Indonesian coastal town of Kualalangsa, and Georgetown in Malaysia. As they continued north northwest at about 25 knots, the crew was aware that they would soon approach the area where the Thai Navy had undertaken aggressive patrolling and the Thai Air Force dispatched an occasional reconnaissance plane in areas beyond which the Navy patrolled.

The Indonesian Navy also posed a threat. Hamad knew that until the enormous tsunami of December 2004, they tended to focus their patrols more heavily on the 150 to 200 mile area between Banda Aceh on the northwestern tip of Sumatra and Lhokseumawe and in the area between Pulam Rupat off the coast of north central Sumatra and Medan. Hamad surmised that since over 7,000 pirates have died in the devastating tsunami (with Banda Aceh at the earthquake's epicenter); the Indonesian Navy probably switched their heavier patrolling activities to the second area. He smiled and mused to himself: "Allah must be on our side; the earthquake may actually help us."

He was proud to have Awad and Mirza at his side, knowing they were extremely reliable and experienced fighters. As he glanced at Awad, a 35-year old from a Peshawar slum who had six siblings, he could see the strength and confidence the six-footer exuded, the fire from his large, dark brown eyes, which stood out against his heavy beard and bushy, brown hair. A smaller man with a wider girth, Mirza had a less menacing appearance, which belied the many tough years he spent as an angry boy growing up in the port city of Aqaba. Of the two, Awad was more introspective and more familiar with the Koran, having spent many years at a local madrassa.

Hamad addressed Awad and Mirza in a strong voice:

"I know from the start of our training that we had to have an international mix of operatives, just like a well-blended couscous. I insisted on it. Now with two from Holland, three from France, two from Germany, five Pakistanis, a Moroccan and a Jordanian, we have the right blend. Of course, add my Lebanese background, and we have seven countries here just like many other vessels working this part of the world."

"When a Commander, like you, is both a wolf and a fox at the same time, he can achieve much." Awad smiled knowingly. "A wolf is an able hunter and can be very independent. But the fox adds craftiness. You are blessed with both traits, Commander, and we would gladly follow you anywhere and give our lives for the cause."

Awad chose his words with great purpose. His commander was a man of great determination, possessed uncanny leadership ability and was extremely cool under pressure. While only 40, he had spent many years as a warrior, leading treacherous missions and rising in the Al Qaeda ranks. He had an olive complexion and piercing brown eyes, made more prominent by the extensive crow's feet that surrounded them, a result of the many years spent in too harsh conditions. Hardened by years of service, his body was muscular. Most disturbing to any outsider was his sinister appearance and an unspoken hardness.

"We will have many tests of our skills along the way." Hamad replied, looking directly into Awad's eyes. "This attack was the first. The future ones can prove equally, if not more, dangerous. The Thai naval security force is one example. Crossing the Indian Ocean in presence of the infidel United States Navy is another. Let us not overlook the prying eyes from overhead."

Mirza who was standing nearby added:

"We know what to do. Our crew will be up for the task. Some may be nervous, but we are all very disciplined."

Hamad looked toward the northwestern horizon and said pensively:

"I know that. But there is always the potential for the unexpected. We drilled on all the risks we thought we might face, such as a well-armed tanker crew that could defend well. But maybe there is a communication from the tanker's agent that contains a secret code that we're not aware of but Captain Johannsen is. Then what? The prying eyes could then become tiger's teeth, rip our legs off, and make us helpless. It is the unknown that could endanger even the wolf/fox."

Awad frowned slightly and, facing Hamad, replied quietly:

"Yes, it is true. There are potential unknown risks we face. But you, Commander, are the master of response. You saved us on the retreat from the caves of Tora Bora for three days as we fled to the safety of Pakistan. Afghan troops were in hot pursuit of the fleeing Taliban and Al Qaeda bands. One night, our good fortune almost ran out. It was about 10:00 p.m. when we arrived at a deserted mostly bombed out compound several miles west of the Pakistani border. While we briefly rested and ate some of our meager food portions, Afghan troops emerged from the darkness. When the Afghan troops surrounded our compound, you convinced them you were the local Afghan commander. Allah be praised. Since they outnumbered us by five to one, they clearly had the upper hand. The Afghans left. We all smiled. I knew this was a sign from the Almighty. We would go on because we were needed. So I feel confident now we'll overcome any danger. I know, Commander, you will devise a plan that works."

"I respect your confidence in me," Hamad replied softly. "Our Commander of Piracy Operations handpicked all of the crew, but I had the right to strike a name or two if I didn't feel the person was right for the mission. So, you see, Awad and Mirza, I have with me the men I want. As you know, each crewmember has had extensive battlefield or intelligence training. We all know how to use our weapons, machine guns, knives. Some of us know the ways of the infidels well. Some of us even worked in the Western intelligence service, to learn how they think to track us and pursue us. You don't think Ismael bin Azal from Amsterdam and Masur el-Rami from Bonn are here by accident. Our leadership groomed them for years and correctly devised ways to get them inside. They had the right backgrounds. They are university graduates having majored in Islamic studies. They speak Arabic excellently. Ismael became a translator in Amsterdam; Masur became a low-level analyst for the German counterterrorism work. With this inside knowledge, we hope to rebuff their efforts to capture us. We are not fools. We're smart."

Lost in thought for a moment, Hamad paused and added:

"Enough of this chatter, we must now focus on our Thai friends. We'll be approaching Thai naval patrol perimeters within an hour."

Awad and Mirza immediately assembled their respective squads below deck.

"All of you actually look like seamen," Awad spoke loudly. "I know you don't like T-shirts, jeans, khakis, but we have to blend in and look like a mixed international crew." He smiled admiringly at Omar Rumallah. Omar, a Moroccan with dark skin, faded overalls and partly stained long-sleeved but rolled-up shirt, appeared as if he spent years in the sun and wind aboard ships; the long lines on his face attested to an earlier outdoor existence. Similarly, he nodded approval at Masur's sweatshirt advertising a German soccer team worn over dark khakis.

"You would all fool me," Mirza quipped.

Awad and Mirza sent two crewmembers to patrol the main deck and instructed only one of them to carry a Kalashnikov.

"We can't look like an army up there, you know," Mirza said.

Awad instructed the rest of the pirates to stay below deck, only three of them were to show their weapons, the others were to hide them under the mattresses in the crew's quarters.

Daybreak was still two hours away.

Hamad knew it was important to have any initial contact with the Thai Navy before that time. Based on the intelligence reports given to him, he believed that the Thai crews on night patrol would be less likely to entertain unwanted encounters. Theirs was a long vigil of over six hours and they would be anxious to get some well-deserved sleep by 6:00 a.m. He also knew that their navy had become more vigilant of late. The recent spike of piracy takeovers of several fancy yachts and one small freighter by criminal thugs might be was the primary reason for this increased security level.

Hamad looked at the radar screen, noticing two dots moving slowly in the direction of the tanker's path.

"Captain Johannsen, come here quickly. You see that movement. How far away are they? When do you think we can identify them? Of course, I have my own thoughts on these matters, so don't try to fool me."

The Captain got up from a chair, with his hands and feet still bound, and slowly approached the radar screen:

"We were told when we left port in Singapore that a Thai naval unit would, in all likelihood, make contact as we moved near the perimeter of their patrol area, just as an added security measure. Although no supertanker had been hijacked before, the criminal pirate activities stirred up some extra concern. The Thais are not interested in having piracy occur on their watch. From what I was told, they would view such an event as being highly embarrassing. So, that's why they have stepped up their vigilance."

After peering through the bridge window, Hamad stared at the Captain:

"I'm glad you're being truthful. Our Singapore unit gave me the same report. Now, what about those moving dots?"

"At this hour of the night, there could be some freighters' activity and generally not much else. I passed through this area often enough to know that. But, if you look closely, you see that the dots are moving at about the same speed and keeping about the same distance between them. It would be highly unlikely that two freighters would be moving as a unit with the same speeds."

Hamad smiled:

"Good observation, Captain. My reading is the same. We have studied traffic patterns in the Strait for over a year. We realized that few pleasure craft ventured this far out and alone at night. We know the U.S. Navy passed through here, but usually they had a least three vessels moving in tandem, as a show of force, we thought. We also noted that freighters typically didn't pass through in convoys or even as twosomes. That narrows the current choice. I think we have two Thai vessels and I believe they may want to check up on the *Argus*. They routinely receive daily updates on maritime traffic that will pass in their waters or outside of their perimeter. I'm sure they know of the tankers' schedules, including ours."

"I agree with you, so what do you want me to do now?"

Hamad looked at him sternly:

"I'll remove the ropes from your hands and feet because I know you will cooperate with me. While I speak both Arabic and English, my English is a bit rusty. Besides, our studies did not find any captain of a supertanker or another tanker who was Lebanese. I know there may always be a first, but I don't want to arouse any potential suspicion on this score, especially when there is a Norwegian captain in charge of this ship. Your ship agents typically select Nordic types for these ships: Swedes, Norwegian, and Danes. Arabs? Forget it!"

"I understand your point," replied Johannsen quickly. "A Lebanese captain would definitely be out of place here. As for the two moving dots, I think our company will arrive in about 15 minutes."

"An accurate assessment, I believe," said Hamad in a relaxed tone. "So please make sure you answer any Thai signal or request as you normally would. Of course, I'll be watching you and your mate very closely. Remember, no games, please. I may be a patient man, but I get extremely upset if my instructions are not followed exactly to the letter. You understand, Captain? You understand, mate?"

Each nodded. At that point, Awad removed the first mate's bonds. Mirza stood on guard near the door to the bridge.

Hamad now put on his specially crafted long distance night goggles, which had a range of up to five miles and acted as a pair of binoculars. He scanned the horizon slowly. As he did, he saw a destroyer with its Thai flag and a support tender also with a Thai flag approaching at a speed of about 30 knots, which he estimated would put them within a half-mile of the *Argus* within five minutes.

"Mirza, go below deck and tell the crew to be especially vigilant. At least three men should be in bed feigning sleep. The rest should appear to be ready to start the day shift."

As Mirza moved down the steps from the bridge, he replied:

"I'll take care of it immediately."

From the bridge, Hamad could barely make out the silhouettes of the Thai vessels. With his special nighttime goggles, he could see that the destroyer was a formidable adversary, armed with three nine-inch guns, at least four heavy 50 caliber mounted machine guns and a crew of about 40, each with a weapon. The tender following in the destroyer's wake carried about 25 armed sailors in addition to its regular crew.

The radio crackled. Hamad motioned for Captain Johannsen to answer. "Hello, Captain, this is First Lieutenant Noon Ashtong of the Royal Thai Navy. We're just checking up on your vessel and its cargo. This is merely a routine precaution. Is all O.K.?"

"Yes, Lieutenant, all is normal here."

"Excellent. I'm glad to hear that. We're just keeping a watchful eye on the traffic in this area. We have our concerns, as you may be aware."

"Yes, Lieutenant, I received a briefing on the stepped-up piracy activities in the Strait. Fortunately, we're fine. Besides, no one would think of trying to capture our ship."

"I agree, Captain, such a step would be a highly unlikely scenario. I don't see any need to board you. Besides, it is late and I'm about done with my shift. Anyway, I'll file my report about you after I get up in the afternoon. Over and out."

Hamad smiled happily at the Norwegian.

"Captain, you did a first-class job. I don't need to send you to study theatre. I think you're a naturally good actor. You passed your first test. This I'm sure is only the beginning."

About five minutes later, Hamad motioned for Mirza to tie up the Captain and his first mate. He again bound their arms and legs with rope separately to their chairs.

Peering at the horizon, Hamad knew that within six hours they would be in the Indian Ocean, a vast area that he knew posed additional dangers. It was 5:30 a.m. and dawn began to break in the east, as the sun's rays reflected on the white cumulus clouds, giving them a pink color. He knew already the temperature would rise considerably during the day. He hoped there would be a sea breeze to provide some relief.

As the sun began to rise higher over the horizon, Hamad saw that there were several freighters about 10 miles away, headed down the Strait toward Singapore, and two other freighters headed on his course, seemingly bound for the Indian Ocean - which he hoped, because of its vastness, might serve as a sanctuary.

CHAPTER 4

U.S. NAVAL PRESENCE

August 11, 2006 7:00 a.m.

The United States Navy Fifth Fleet headquarters at Bahrain was bustling at 7:00 a.m. All key personnel had their pre-assigned orders for the day. Many had already started to implement them at this hour.

Bahrain served as the principal United States Naval command center for operations covering both the Gulf of Hormuz and the Indian Ocean, including the eastern coast of Africa. This independent state had allowed the United States to build a major naval base and operations center there, in part with the hope of adding stability to the volatile Middle East. Years later, Bahraini clairvoyance proved extremely farsighted. The Shiite expansionists from mullah-ruled Iran, and their allies, the Hamas in Palestine and the Hezbollah in Lebanon, and the insurgents in Iraq provided by the United States invasion all contributed to the region's unrest in 2006.

A week before, there had been a high-level meeting with Admiral Jason Flood, the Commander of the U.S. Navy Fifth Fleet, his deputy, Captain Frank McLoon, and Admiral Thomas Wade, the Commander of the fleet in the Indian Ocean. The meeting focused on naval and maritime threats in the region, including the threat of piracy and the potential risks posed by the recent escape from a Yemeni jail by Jamal al-Badawi, the Al Qaeda mastermind of the *USS Cole* bombing in a Yemeni port in 2000 which killed 17 U.S. sailors. The parties focused on the need for increased vigilance, greater patrolling, and heightened security measures for ships at sea and in port.

Meeting in Admiral Flood's secure conference room at the Fleet's Bahrain headquarters, Admiral Flood warmly greeted his two visitors. The threesome brought with them over 70 years of combined naval experience. Admiral Flood, a wiry 55 year old with closely-cropped graying hair, was a graduate of the U.S. Naval Academy having over 30 years of wide-ranging experience, including tours in Washington D.C. and at sea. Unflappable by nature, a born leader, he had risen steadily in the ranks to become the Fifth Fleet Commander. Admiral Wade, a youthful looking 50 year old, had over 25 years of service, including several stints in the Mediterranean and the Indian Ocean. His wide-ranging service had made him a prime candidate for a position at naval headquarters in Washington. The junior attendee, Captain McLoon, a short, bespectacled 37-year computer whiz, had served extensively in the Far East and the Atlantic sectors. Highly sought after for his analytical and programming skills, he was a welcome addition to the Fleet Headquarters staff.

After an exchange of recent naval gossip and a light lunch of sandwiches and soft drinks, the participants turned to serious business.

Presiding at the meeting, Admiral Flood took the lead role and said:

"I was not in the region when the bombing of the *Cole* took place but I can assure you that I will not let another attack like that occur on my watch. So here is what I have in mind as far as security is concerned:

- Let's set up a 750-meter no-approach zone around all our naval vessels while they are in port.

- Let's also put in place a one-mile no-approach zone while any of our vessels are at sea.

- If any one violates these rules, we will give the intruder one warning to leave the area, and, if the warning is not obeyed, we'll fire to destroy the intruder."

- We should also increase security around our bases, by building more barriers, adding more guards, checking for tunneling and, if possible, by trying to clear a 200-meter perimeter around each base. The latter may not be possible if the base is next to a built-up area.

Your thoughts, gentlemen?"

After reflecting on his superior's vision, Admiral Wade replied thoughtfully:

"I agree with most of what you say on beefing up our security. Implementing these steps is another, and perhaps more difficult, matter. Posting prominent warning signs in several languages on buoys in port areas is clearly possible. On the other hand, giving warnings at sea is a far more complicated matter. A publication of our rule at the United Nations and with each of the governments around the world won't help much. Besides, there may be a language barrier at sea. We probably wouldn't have a linguist at hand to communicate in the intruding vessel's language, but we may be able to rely on a standard international radio link, found on most commercial vessels. Sure, we could post an international warning sign on our vessels, but it'll not be visible a mile away. As for the on-land measures, what's your opinion, Captain McLoon?"

Captain McLoon, who felt completely at ease in the presence of these high-ranking superiors, now replied candidly:

"Gentlemen, we can certainly try to implement the on-land heightened security measures you think will help. I think some countries will strongly object to the 200-meter security perimeter around our bases. They certainly may not go along with destroying fixed business establishments or fancy apartments that may exist near our bases. So we'll have to see how that plays.

But let's not overlook the human element here - our use of local residents who cook our meals, serve in our offices, and help bring supplies to the base. We can screen these people to a degree, but it will be almost impossible to catch a turncoat, or someone who is able to breach our security by bribing a guard. Look at what happened near Mosul: some local dressed in an Iraqi Army uniform came into a mess hall and blew our guys to smithereens. Obviously, the bomber had been allowed onto the base. This is where our weakness is."

Intrigued by the Captain's remarks, Admiral Flood replied:

"Good point, Frank, I knew I could count on you to focus me in ways I may have overlooked."

"This is a team effort," replied the Captain deferentially.

"Let me continue, Tom," said Admiral Flood. "The local residents issue is a big problem. But we need them because we don't have all the folks who can do the tasks they do. We certainly need Arabic-speaking workers as part of our headquarters staff to deal with many of the local issues that come up. And in the maintenance area, we need local labor. Besides, there are not so many available crews from the U.S. who want to do that type of work. It makes sense that offloading oil in Bahrain is done by Bahrainis who then help us move it to our base. In each of these areas, there is potential vulnerability. I think we should have another meeting in about a week to focus specifically on that issue."

Admiral Wade and Captain McLoon nodded in agreement.

Admiral Flood continued:

"Keep in mind that another Yemeni escapee was Fawaz Yahya al-Rabeei, who was considered by Interpol to be one of the persons responsible for the attack on the French tanker off the Yemen coast in 2002. That attack caused the loss of some life and caused an oil spill in the Gulf of Aden. He's now on the loose and we must get in touch with naval headquarters in Washington, D.C. to find the latest tracking reports on both Fawaz and Jamal. Our port facility in Bahrain may be far more secure than our much smaller facility in Yemen, but we can't be too smug on that point."

"Tom," Admiral Flood added, "I know you wanted to address the piracy issue, so go ahead now."

Admiral Wade looked down at his notes:

"As you both know, we've been doing extensive patrolling throughout the Indian Ocean. However, this is a huge area, and it's impossible to be in all places at all times. So we have to pick our spots where we make our presence known. Since you, Admiral, decided not to run any naval exercises in the region because of the cost and the commitment of our existing resources, we haven't done any. On the other hand, we have tried to convince some of the countries bordering the Strait of Malacca to allow us to run joint patrols with them in the area, pursuant to Washington's instructions which were relayed by you."

"What's the latest on that idea?" asked Admiral Flood, as he leaned closer to his fellow Admiral.

"We explained to the folks in Indonesia, Thailand, Singapore and Malaysia that we thought that the increase in piracy had to be dealt with aggressively," said Admiral Wade. "And we even pointed out that some successes with the pirating of yachts and other smaller vessels might tempt other criminals or terrorists to attack other larger vessels."

"So what did they say to that?"

"They said 'no,'" replied Admiral Wade in an angry tone. "Each said it had the capability to protect its own area, and, therefore, they didn't need any outside help from the United States on this score."

"Why do you think they reached this decision?" asked the Captain politely.

"Because each of these countries has a strong sense of pride and is highly nationalistic," said Admiral Wade. "I think the idea of a joint patrol implies the host country is weak and not capable of handling its problems by itself. Take Indonesia, for example. Even after the December, 2005 tsunami hit with catastrophic effect, the Government imposed limits on the number of American military and naval personnel allowed to help in the rescue and rehabilitation area."

"Nonetheless," said Admiral Flood, "it seems to me that we may have to pursue that proposal again and soon with just one of these four countries, perhaps Singapore. I'm concerned that, with these escapees on the run in Yemen, we could find ourselves with a potentially large problem in the Strait. And I certainly don't want that to happen."

"I share your concern," Admiral Wade said as he moved a bit restlessly in his seat.

"Frank," said Admiral Flood, "I think I might get in touch with the brass in D.C. to see whether I can get their approval to push this joint patrol idea in the Strait by using the two escapees as an alarm bell. Once I get some word on that front, I'll immediately get back to you."

"That sounds like a plan," the Captain replied.

"But, I have some other thoughts," Flood continued. 'There isn't any reason why we cannot run a few extra vessels in that direction on a sporadic, but regular, basis. Ostensibly, a vessel or two might pass through the Strait to the east for a little rest and recreation for their crews in Singapore. Maybe we can do some more refueling there too. What do you think?"

"Admiral," said Tom Wade, "there are some destroyers and cruiser crews who actually do need a few days off in Singapore. Many of our vessels have been at sea for months. Perhaps now would be the time to schedule a period of necessary relaxation for several of them."

"The key here, Tom, is to make sure these movements appear normal. We don't want to upset our friends in the region, especially in Indonesia, a country with the largest Islamic population."

"Admiral, I assure you that all will appear normal," replied Admiral Wade. "Perhaps, with some further prodding, Washington may alternatively be able to convince one or two other countries to agree to our joint patrol proposal. The presence at large of two seasoned escaped Al Qaeda operatives may help decide this issue."

After the meeting ended, both Admirals felt uneasy. The tasks confronting them were enormous and the stakes were very high. Admiral Flood lamented to himself that his fleet simply didn't have all the resources necessary for him to cover all of its needs. He called his deputy, Captain McLoon:

"Frank, I'm deeply troubled. We are so multi-tasked. As part of this spectrum, we have the Al Qaeda potential threat to our naval units and those of our friends. We have to deal with the ultra-nationalists in Iran who are increasingly eager to spread their Shiite gospel. Years ago, we worried about Cuban expansionism in Central and South America. Now we have that Iranian concern, a big picture issue. Lastly, we have piracy threats that could escalate. We simply don't have enough resources to defend ourselves against each of these threats."

Over 2,000 miles away, Admiral Wade felt equally uneasy following the meeting in Bahrain. As he sat in his room on his flagship, a U.S. carrier located 500 miles off Diego Garcia in the Indian Ocean, he looked at a map covering the Indian Ocean and its nearby environs, including the Strait of Malacca. He realized that his group's operational directives were enormous. He knew he had the most advanced fighter aircraft on board - 45 F-18 Phantoms, with a range of 1200 miles fully loaded with air-to-ground and air-to-air missiles. He knew he had at least five cruisers and 25 destroyers that could deter most enemies by providing huge firepower, speed and direct gun support for a military operation on land, if necessary. The destroyers could also protect against submarine threats. In addition, the four AWACs had been assigned to give the group a continuous stream of data that was constantly updated, through use of their revolving radar, sonar and telecommunications capabilities to cover all movements in the air or at sea within range. He even had access to satellite tracking data received from United States satellites to various military headquarters, including Fleet headquarters at Bahrain and thence on to his group.

Still, he was troubled. Something could happen. Something that, despite all his resources, he would be unable to stop.

CHAPTER 5

INDIAN OCEAN CROSSING

August 11, 2006 5:00 p.m.

The *Argus* crossed into the Indian Ocean on the afternoon of August 11, 2006. From the bridge, Hamad surveyed an endless horizon to the west and southwest that stretched for miles over the vast calm blue waters. He saw no ships in his immediate vicinity, except for a small freighter some seven miles ahead of another ship headed for port. The day was balmy, with a light sea breeze from the puffy cumulus clouds drifting by quietly against an azure sky.

He relished this momentary isolation, aware that he had succeeded in implementing the initial phase of the Al Qaeda plan. He knew very well that what lay ahead was risky and that one minor mistake could be fatal. But given his extensive training and discipline combined with his deeply felt belief in the purity of the Koran, he had faith in his ability to overcome any adversity he might encounter. He believed his was the "winning side:" the establishment of a new caliphate that he and his brothers-in-arms hoped would reign over a vast kingdom ranging half-way across the world from Pakistan and Afghanistan through the Middle East, from North Africa to Spain. The successful completion of this mission would hasten the achievement of that goal, another step in Allah's ordained plan. These thoughts brought him back to the next steps of his plan.

Summoning Awad and Mirza to join him outside on the bridge – far from Captain Johannsen and his first mate - Hamad put his arms on the shoulders of his two squad leaders and spoke to them softly:

"My brothers, we're now starting our Indian Ocean crossing phase. Our destination is over 4,000 miles away, which will take at least eight days if we have good weather; but if we have storms, we could be delayed several days. The ocean is patrolled by Western naval vessels and the Indian Navy, which sometimes undertakes missions far beyond its recognized boundaries. The United States Navy is engaged in air reconnaissance missions and we know they also get satellite data. Obviously, our ship will be tracked. If it varies from its planned course, prying eyes will be suspicious."

"If I remember correctly," Awad said, "our plan calls for the ship to head due west southwest to the southern coast of India and then proceed northwest toward the Gulf of Hormuz where we will dock at Bandar-e-Abbas in Iran to unload the oil."

"You remember well, Awad," Hamad replied gently. "But some disinformation was given out at the time. We did this on purpose to ensure that only my commander and I knew our true destination. There is a saying: 'Loose lips sink ships.'"

Awad smiled. "I have always assumed that you hold your tongue for good reason, Commander. Why tempt fate? One of our brothers could, in a moment of weakness or forgetfulness, let slip a few errant words that might be overheard by an interested outsider."

"Exactly, Awad. I trust our entire group. But, above all, we must protect ourselves against any possible failure. The stakes are high."

"Commander, what is our true destination?" asked Mirza. "As I recall, this tanker was bound for Rotterdam via the Cape of Good Horn and its oil was to be unloaded there. Where are we headed now?"

"I'll tell you soon enough, my brothers. But let's first consider what unforeseen act or event could cause a change of plans. Any ideas?"

"A typhoon or major storm would make us change course," replied Mirza quickly.

"True," Awad interrupted, "but that's not within our control."

"We could have a fuel leak or engine failure," Mirza went on. "We could also collide with some smaller vessel, although that seems unlikely."

Hamad smiled at both of them.

"Yes, an unfortunate accident would force us to go to a nearby port. Even a fuel leak or an engine failure might suffice. However, an oil leak could be too messy and would precipitate unwanted publicity. No. We need something quieter but equally plausible."

"So," said Awad, who was listening closely, "engine failure?"

"Precisely."

"Engine failure will occur off the west coast of India some 750 miles northwest of Goa," Hamad answered. "After that I'll give you our final destination. For now we must proceed full speed ahead and try to average at least 25 knots. May the Great One, praised be he, help speed our way."

Their conference over, the group went inside the bridge. Hamad instructed Awad, Mirza, and two other guards to untie the Captain and his mate. Hamad knew that the Americans made good use of their specially crafted long-distance photographic technology. A passing reconnaissance helicopter or AWAC might be able to see two persons being held captive, a message the pirate group surely did not wish to convey. On the other hand, Hamad knew that the electronic bracelet worn around each captive's ankle to shock the wearer into immediate submission was not visible. Mirza went to get the ankle bracelets, which he put on both captives once they were untied.

Hamad walked over to Captain Johannsen.

"Your Norwegian seafaring skills are needed now," he said. "We have to go at full speed, at least 25 knots per hours. You know your route and your directions. I expect you to make sure we follow the intended route. Do you understand?"

"Yes, I do. But I'll need someone down in the engine room to make sure all of the settings are in order and are maintained."

"That won't be a problem, Captain. Three of my crew are experienced engine experts. I'll send them below immediately to check out the engines. If maintenance is needed, they'll know exactly what to do. Anything else?"

"No, Commander. If I have any further thoughts, I'll let you know."

The next two days passed without incident. Captain Johannsen and his first mate, Feliks, alternated eight hour shifts sleeping on a small well-worn couch in the corner of the bridge. These days were hot, with temperatures rising to the high 90's. A piercing sun made deck-duty impossible for more than an hour.

On the third day, the weather began to change, as threatening thunderhead clouds began forming late in the morning. Small whitecaps started to appear as the wind began to pick up. Within a few hours, those whitecaps became ocean swells, cascading over 10 feet in height. From meteorological readings on board and from the weather messages, Hamad immediately understood that the *Argus* was heading directly into a major typhoon, which was impossible to avoid because of the storm's huge width that covered several hundred miles.

A bit nervous, Hamad went to consult Captain Johannsen.

"You have been through this type of storm before, I assume?" he asked.

"Yes, I have had my fill of at least five in more than 35 years at sea and I've been lucky to come through each one without any loss of life or damage to my ship. True, several of my crew were seasick for days and I lost some items on deck. Fortunately, I never capsized, but one of my ships, a 250-ton freighter, almost went under. Usually I have been on larger vessels which can handle a storm like this well."

"I'm glad to hear your tales, Captain. I have never experienced a storm like the one that's about to hit us head on. I trust your judgment and your skills."

"Commander, if I potentially save us all here, I hope you will consider freeing us when you reach your destination. After all, one good deed deserves another."

"Ah, yes, that lovely Western golden rule. I'll consider it."

"Thank you, Commander."

As the storm began to intensify, the ship felt its full force. Huge waves smashed against the *Argus* repeatedly, rolling continuously over the deck. The 1,000-foot long ship rode the swells up and down. At times, the bow disappeared below the massive surf only to reappear shortly thereafter. The wind increased in intensity to over 100 miles an hour. Those on the bridge hoped the glass enclosure would not give way. At least four pirates below deck became violently seasick. Hamad was also nauseated, but managed to overcome that feeling after several hours. The Captain and his mate felt no physical upset.

The storm continued for at least 15 hours, during which there were several highly perilous moments that threatened everybody's life. The greatest menace was a massive 80-foot wave that approached the ship, clearly visible in the gray afternoon sky. It smashed the deck and the bridge with tremendous force before rolling off the ship.

Everybody on the bridge ducked except for the Captain, who gripped the steering wheel tightly, knowing that the ship might sink if he lost control of the steering.

In the end, the Captain's steering skills and experience, together with the vessel's size and sturdiness, saved the *Argus* and everyone on board from certain death.

During the raging storm, the Captain had slowed the ship's speed down to about 15 knots an hour. Despite the loss of time, the vessel safely passed the southernmost point of India, heading northwest in the direction of the Suez Canal.

It was on the sixth day in the Indian Ocean, when the *Argus* was about 750 miles from Goa, that Hamad instructed Captain Johannsen to change direction:

"Captain, I want you to follow my exact instructions. Advise the harbormaster in Rotterdam that the vessel suffered severe engine damage because of the typhoon. Then head directly north to our new destination, Karachi, Pakistan."

"I'll do what you say, but you know our engines are fine."

"I know that," replied Hamad. "But we'll proceed as if two of our six engines are down. So slow our speed down to about 17 knots an hour."

"O.K."

After five hours, the ship's radar picked up several approaching dots in the area. One dot was moving much faster than the other three, almost six times faster. Hamad sensed the immediate danger these dots represented: a possible U.S. naval patrol with a lead helicopter doing advance reconnaissance. The dots continued to close in, in the direction of the *Argus*.

"Captain, I think our American friends are about to pay us a visit. First, they'll do a fly-by. Then, depending upon the report given by the reconnaissance helicopter, the navy might give us a very close look."

"Commander, you can't be sure it is the Americans out there. Although it's unlikely that the Indians would patrol this far out, the Indian Navy has conducted some training exercises in this part of the Indian Ocean. In fact, I saw one about three or four years ago. Still, I have to admit that the Americans, not the Indians, are in the habit of using helicopters in front of their naval vessels."

"I have some doubts myself, but I agree with your assessment," replied Hamad.

"What do you want me to do, Commander?"

"Proceed exactly as we planned before. If the intruders try to communicate with us, tell them about your engine problem and that you are heading to Pakistan for repairs. I'm sure they're aware of the fact that a devastating typhoon passed through the Indian Ocean."

"I'll act accordingly."

"Good, Captain"

Hamad turned to instruct Mirza.

"Put Henriks on the deck now," he said. "Awad, join Henriks there. I want both of you to swab the deck and pick up the debris from the typhoon. When the helicopter comes near us, I want both of you to give a friendly thumbs-up gesture and wave happily.

The Americans will like those friendly gestures. I will be watching the scene very closely, Henriks."

Awad and Henriks left the bridge and took up different positions on the deck, each armed with a mop and a pail.

Within 15 minutes, a helicopter appeared on the horizon and approached the ship's port side rapidly. As it came closer, Hamad could feel his heartbeat quicken, knowing another test was at hand. The helicopter swooped in and passed so low that its U.S. insignia and aircraft number were clearly visible to those on the deck of the *Argus*. Henriks and Awad waved at the helicopter and gave a thumbs-up sign.

Five minutes later, Hamad looked at the radar screen. The three dots had changed direction and were now moving south-southeast, away from the path of the *Argus*. The ruse worked; the helicopter pilot must have cleared the ship.

Thirty-five miles away, a U.S. cruiser, the *Chotah*, together with its supporting attack destroyers, the *Naples* and the *Highridge*, headed toward the Strait of Malacca before docking at Singapore. No one on board these naval vessels gave further thought to the tanker limping northward.

CHAPTER 6

KARACHI

August 21, 2006 10:00 p.m.

After four more days at sea, the *Argus* was about five miles from the port of Karachi, Pakistan's largest seaport. Hamad chose to arrive under the cover of darkness, in part because the port was usually less busy at night. But there were several other crucial factors that underlay the arrival time.

At sea, Hamad had communicated by satellite phone with Hajib Abu Zussa, his area's Operations Commander, based in Lahore, to arrange a time to begin the unloading of the ship's 2 million barrels of oil - a process that would take at least a day and a half. He received instructions that the *Argus* should aim for an 11:00 p.m. berthing at the offshore unloading facility on August 21, 2006.

Most importantly, at least three Pakistanis who belonged to Al Qaeda worked at the port. Concealing their political beliefs, each had risen to prominent positions in the port facility. One held the third highest position - supervising the log register which recorded all the arrivals and departures of vessels and overseeing the documentation of all inbound and outbound goods. A second held the position of superintendent in charge of the oil unloading facility between 8:00 p.m. and 6:00 a.m. daily. The third was in charge of supervising the transportation of goods to their intended destination. Recruited about four years ago, this sleeper cell finally had a mission to undertake.

Slowly the *Argus* approached its intended unloading facility, which extended at least a mile into the harbor. Long pipes ran from the offshore hook-up point to the storage facilities on shore. These were used to unload oil from the supertankers which were too large and had too much of a draught. A crew of six men from the unloading facility began the hook-up to the *Argus*, and its cargo of oil began to flow through the pipes at around midnight.

Before the arrival of the *Argus*, Hajib alerted the members of the port cell. Each was well versed in his duties. He also instructed them to follow the orders of Commander Hamad.

With the hook-up started, Hamad met with Awad and Mirza outside the bridge.

"My brothers, we're now in the next phase of our operation - the disposition of the oil," he said. "Everything has been pre-arranged, and I'll handle that matter. You will take care of our two prisoners, the Captain and his mate. There are several safehouses randomly located throughout the city, safely nestled among the millions that live here. Awad, here is a map showing the route to safehouse # 3. Take your crew of six and the Captain there. Make sure his ankle bracelet is secure and keep him blindfolded. Mirza, gather your six other crewmembers and take Henriks to safehouse # 4 and secure him as well. Plan to stay in these houses for a while, at least a week or more. I'll get in touch with you before then and tell you what we'll do next. Any questions?"

"Your instructions are clear, Commander," Awad replied. "But there are a few details I want to go over with you based on prior experience in this country. I assume that only one or two of us should be sent out to get food and other needed items - and the rest of us should stay indoors."

"Yes, exactly. People in the adjoining buildings typically know the comings and goings of their neighbors. They can easily recognize outsiders because of language, dress or other reasons. So we have to keep a low profile. Obviously, it would be wise to use your Pakistani mates to do outside errands. They would be the least likely to arouse suspicion."

"I agree with you, Commander," said Awad, looking directly at Hamad.

"Commander, I too will follow these precautions," added Mirza. "But what happens if you don't come by when you say?"

"In that case, which is highly unlikely, you two will receive word from another operative or from a person at the Operations Commander's headquarters. I am sure you will recognize the code words. We all spent days studying and memorizing them."

Awad and Mirza nodded in agreement.

They gathered their crews below deck, and gave them their orders. Their relief at being on safe ground, away from the perils at sea, was evident. Each crewmember gathered his duffel bag and put his weapon in it. Awad and Mirza put a 9-millimeter Glock in holsters underneath their jackets.

In the midst of all this activity, Awad pulled Mirza aside and said:

"We will leave in two groups. My squad and I'll leave first with the Captain. The oil facility night superintendent, Abdul Hussein, will take us in his van to our designated safehouse. Since the guards at the entrance to the facility are his friends, there should be no problems. In any event, a number of us will crouch on the van's floor, so it will seem that only four people are leaving. The superintendent will then return to the port facility."

"And then what?" asked Mirza.

"After the superintendent leaves at the end of his shift at 6:00 a.m., you will take your crew and Henriks to his van. The superintendent will drop you off at the second safehouse. Understood?"

"The plan is clear," Mirza replied. "I assume we can trust the superintendent completely."

"You can, Mirza. I have been assured of his complete loyalty."

Hamad went to the bridge to speak to the Captain.

"Captain, we're leaving now. You will be our invited guest for a few days. Then we'll see what happens."

"Look, Commander, I played my role. I saved you and your men during the typhoon. I want to leave now. I have a wife in Oslo waiting for me. I have two children and three grandchildren whom I would like to see. I sense you have great respect for your kin, whether they're family or tribe. I'm sure you understand that I deserve to be let go."

"Yes, yes," replied Hamad hurriedly. "But you know too much. You have seen our faces. You know where we landed. If I let you go, won't you go first to your home and then to the authorities? Soon someone will ask questions about your crew and the cargo. They'll expect you to talk, or they could drug you and make you talk. What then? Our risk becomes greater. That's a problem. Maybe your knowledge will become relatively unimportant after the passage of time."

"If I'm to be held by your group, I know it is highly unlikely you will let me go. I appeal to you now to free me. I feel you can decide my fate, that you have the power to do so."

"Even if I have the power and let you go, Captain, my chief will surely ask me difficult questions and will be very unhappy with my make-shift answers. He certainly will not understand that I let you go so that you could be reunited with your family. He's inclined to more radical solutions, like the Pearl beheading. But I think there may be other ways to deal with you and Henriks." Hamad stared at the Captain with a sadistic smile.

"Commander, my ship's owner and agent will know the *Argus* docked in Karachi," the Captain replied testily, gazing back into Hamad's eyes. "They'll alert my embassy in Islamabad, which in turn ask the Pakistani authorities to look for me. The Americans and the CIA may take an interest in pursuing a group holding a Norwegian captain hostage. That should pose an even greater risk for you."

"What you say may be true, Captain, but no one can ever be sure that you actually made it here," said Hamad coldly. "Maybe the ship's crew manifest got lost. Who knows? Or perhaps you were lost at sea after your last communication with the port operator in Rotterdam. The bottom line is that you will stay with me at present. If you try to escape at any point, we'll know we can never trust you - and you will meet a gruesome death."

At that point, one of the men in Awad's squad pushed Captain Johannsen toward the door of the bridge. Awad, the Captain and six squad members left the ship and immediately went to a green Toyota van that was parked nearby. The superintendent, Abdul Hussein, was at the wheel. Awad put a hood over the Captain's head covering his eyes and made him sit down behind the third set of seats together with three of his men. Once he was settled, Abdul drove along the paved driveway that ran along the water's edge, passing numerous modern storage facilities that stood out like sentinels against the night sky. Turning 90 degrees, he drove past some older warehouses and office facilities and arrived at the main gate of the oil facility. Leaning out of the window, Abdul advised the guard, an old friend from the neighborhood, that he was taking a break and would return shortly. Smiling at Abdul, the guard opened the gate without hesitation.

The superintendent knew the route to the safehouse well. Over four years ago, he had driven five Al Qaeda members there when they were on the run from the Pakistani

Inter-Service Intelligence agency, the ISI, and the CIA. They had crossed into Pakistan from Afghanistan when the Taliban regime fell. One of them had been a high-ranking Al Qaeda member whose face was well known in certain intelligence circles. These fugitives had to be hidden while they were in Karachi - thus safehouse # 3, became available. Eventually the five men boarded a small freighter bound for Morocco via the Suez Canal; the ship's captain was well paid for taking on a few extra passengers.

Located in an older residential neighborhood about three miles from the port's main shipping terminal, safehouse # 3 was a small light brown three-storey apartment building owned by a wealthy Pakistani exporter. The building had fallen into a state of modest disrepair but neither the tenant nor the owner seemed to care. The owner rented it to a Hong Kong corporation that used it for its employees and guests when they were in Karachi. As long as the tenant paid on time, the owner was pleased - and didn't ask questions. If he had probed, he might have learned that the Hong Kong corporation was owned by a Pakistani, a militant Islamist who believed in Al Qaeda.

The safehouse consisted of six apartments, two per floor; windows faced the front and rear of the building. The building was wedged between two eight-storey apartment buildings, typical of housing projects for the poor, where whole families were typically crammed into a small apartment.

The drive to the safehouse passed without incident. Several police cars passed, but their occupants had no interest in a non-descript green van. City life still bustled at that hour in the summer. Sweltering temperatures prompted many without air-conditioning to flock to late night restaurants, cafes, bars and nightclubs that were air-conditioned or were cooled by the breeze that came in from the Arabian Sea. As Abdul drove along the street, he could hear a mixture of noise, laughter and music.

When the van stopped, Abdul gave Awad the keys to the apartments. Awad motioned for his men to leave the van with their hostage but without his hood. The group entered the safehouse quickly, splitting into two segments. One group occupied an apartment on the ground floor and another took an apartment on the second floor. In this way, the ground floor crew could act as an advance guard for those on the second floor, including Awad and the Captain. Awad's crew bound Captain Johannsen's hands and feet again. After that, they settled in, awaiting word as to the arrival of Mirza's squad with Henriks at safehouse # 4. Awad's squad had to remain on full alert until then.

That morning when Abdul's shift ended at 6:00 a.m., Mirza's crew, along with Henriks, ran into the waiting Toyota van. Even though the streets were more crowded, Abdul navigated them easily. He knew the morning rush hour would not start for another hour. A resident of Karachi for all of his 35 years, he knew the city very well, its seedy as well as its modern side. Safehouse # 4 was about a mile away from safehouse # 3 in another poor section of the city. The two safehouses were similar in appearance, except that safehouse # 4 had only two floors, with four small apartments per floor. Once the van arrived, Mirza and his crew with Henriks quickly entered the empty building and split up. Henriks and two of the crew went into one apartment and Mirza in the other.

Abdul left for safehouse # 3 and arrived without being followed. He went directly to Awad's apartment.

"The other squad is now secure at safehouse # 4," he said. "I saw no one follow us or take any interest in us."

"Excellent, Abdul," replied Awad quickly. "You have done your job well."

Pleased, Abdul drove home to his apartment several miles away in the northwest part of the city. He was proud to be part of a major plan, an event he awaited for what seemed like an eternity and a useful member of the team.

Meanwhile, back on the *Argus*, Hamad was supervising the unloading process. Two of Mirza's crew stayed on board to adjust the valves for the release of oil and deal with any emergency that might arise. It was now 10:00 a.m. and the sweltering heat felt like a hot oven blast.

Hamad's mind was occupied by several worrisome tasks. Besides unloading the oil and completing its sale, he had to initiate steps to ransom the ship.

He had spoken to Hajib about the problem of finding the right type of buyer. Such a person had to have a penchant for dealing with smuggling or the black market. It was impossible to give any buyer good clean title to the goods, since the oil was stolen from its rightful owner. The buyer had to accept that risk. He also had to pay the cost of transporting the oil from Karachi to some ultimate port, unless, of course, he traded the oil to a third party or sold it in Pakistan. Moreover, the buyer risked being considered an aider and abettor of a terrorist organization or somewhat involved in the financing of terrorist operations, which would prove troublesome if he were to deal with the United States, Canada, Europe and many other countries.

These considerations narrowed Hajib's options. After careful deliberation, he came up with an answer: Syria. It was generally believed that Syria participated in the smuggling of Iraqi oil out of the country during the period that sanctions on the Saddam regime were imposed by the United Nations. The Syrian Government also knowingly harbored members of organizations on the terrorist list, such as Hamas and Hezbollah. In his view, the risks that normally would eliminate almost all potential buyers would not necessarily deter the Syrians.

Several weeks before the capture of the *Argus*, Hajib, a balding professional-looking 44-year-old Syrian national, had traveled to Damascus where he met with the third ranking person in the Oil Ministry, Omar Dashan. A native of Damascus, Hajib immediately felt at home in the city, although he had been away for years. That night, he and Omar dined at the Syrian's luxurious two-storey modern residence on the outskirts of Damascus. Over a delicious dinner of a spicy lamb stew with grilled eggplant and rice and scrumptious desserts, they covered many hot Muslim topics of the day – Palestine, Iraq, Lebanon, Iran and Afghanistan. Both were well versed in political matters.

Towards the end of the meal, Hajib posed the hypothetical question - if he had a certain quantity of oil for sale, regardless of the validity of its title, would the Government or a "dummy entity" acting on its behalf be willing to buy it at a discount of

10% from the posted price for such crude. Displaying more than 25 years of experience in the oil industry, the Syrian smelled an attractive business deal in the making. He pressed Hajib for a 15% discount, to make the deal more attractive. Hajib agreed. Omar told Hajib he would receive his answer the next day.

Hajib received the news he hoped to hear the following afternoon. Yes, a certain entity controlled by the Oil Ministry would be willing to buy such oil at the port of its initial unloading at a 15% discount from the posted price.

Familiar with these events, Hamad awaited the arrival of the Syrian representative, who would first verify that the oil in question had been pumped into the storage tanks and that the bill of lading reflected the buyer's purchase of 2 million barrels of oil. The representative, Hassan bin Abdul, a middle-aged overweight Syrian dressed in a light tan suit, showed up in the late afternoon a day after the unloading was completed.

After he inspected the storage tanks, he wiped his brow with a white handkerchief and turned to Hamad:

"Hamad, I'm delighted to meet you here," he said solemnly. "The port facility superintendent was kind enough to give me a tour of the storage facility. I brought certain measuring instruments with me to check the depth of the tanks and to test the grade of the oil. I'm satisfied on both counts. So let's proceed."

"Fine. Here are our bank account instructions," Hamad replied quickly. "Deposit the sum of $110 million in cash, whether in U.S. dollars or Euros, in our account at our designated bank, the Islamic National Bank, at its headquarters in Tehran. Please don't wire the funds. Have the bank send me written confirmation of the receipt of funds first via fax to the superintendent's office and later by sending me the original bank receipt by courier at this office or to your hotel."

"I'll take care of it immediately," answered bin Abdul, smiling weakly. "I will stay in Karachi at the hotel until our transaction is finished, which I think should be done within three days. Is that satisfactory?"

"Yes," replied Hamad. "We'll both wait in Karachi until my conditions are met."

At Hassan's urging, the Syrians acted swiftly. A captive Cyprus corporation with bearer shares acted as the buyer. The Syrians had plenty of cash on hand offshore because of prior dealings with the Saddam regime and others. Three days later a courier came to the hotel where bin Abdul and Hamad were dining. Hamad thanked the Syrian for his swift action. The transaction was now complete: Al Qaeda was now $110 million richer.

After dinner, Hamad shared this success with his crew at the safehouses.

"All of you are my brothers," Hamad said with great joy, embracing several of them at once. "Without your help and your belief in the Praised One, this could not have happened. May Allah be with all of us!"

"Allah Akbar, Allah Akbar!" shouted the squad members.

Hamad felt a deep sense of accomplishment. Thus far, he had succeeded without mistakes. He sensed what use was to be made of these funds, a secret he kept to himself. The next step was to secure a ransom for the *Argus*.

The Syrians were equally delighted with their purchase. They immediately resold the oil to the Iranian Government at a discount of five percent off the posted price for that blend pocketing the 10% spread. The Iranians, in turn, resold the oil in place to the Pakistani Government at market price. Since the price of oil had spiked by $2.50 a barrel due to the seizure of certain British Petroleum oil platforms and properties by Nigerian dissidents, the Iranians received a greater profit than they originally anticipated.

CHAPTER 7

RANSOM ROTTERDAM

August 24, 2006

When the lanky scholarly-looking Dutchman, Luks Brinhoff, opened his email at 8:40 a.m., he expected to find the usual daily management issues that confront a maritime agent specializing in oil tankers. After glancing at a few messages randomly, his eyes roamed to the heading on the next email – "S.O.S. *Argus*". Soon his glance turned to shock. The message was short but clear:

"Gentlemen:

We will sink the *Argus* this evening at 6:00 p.m. unless you pay U.S. $75 million immediately per our further instructions.

I expect a reply email from you within two hours informing us whether you will comply with this request. Send your reply to holywarrior_77@hk.net.

If we do not receive your reply by then, the ship will be destroyed an hour later.

If you go to the police or any other similar authority, the vessel will be destroyed. We are watching you.

The Holy Warrior."

Horrified, the young Dutchman sat back in his chair at his desk as he overlooked the Rotterdam harbor. He knew action had to be taken immediately. If the *Argus* were lost, a new replacement tanker would take at least two years to build and complete. Given the spike in oil usage worldwide, the Norwegian shipyards were completely booked. Also, he was aware that his agency might have a major fight with the ship's Luxembourg-based insurer to recover the ship's insured value. Since there were well-crafted exculpation clauses, any recovery might prove difficult, time-consuming and potentially unsuccessful.

He printed the email, rose from his chair and went into the president's office, a well-appointed corner office filled with dark sturdy German furniture and expensive richly colored oriental rugs.

Sitting comfortably behind his desk, the President, Pieter Remlant, saw that Luks was extremely agitated.

"Pieter," said Luks handing him the printout, "I just received this shocking email. I don't think it's a prank. I sent an email to the Captain of the *Argus* but received no reply. When I checked the ship's schedule, it was headed through the Indian Ocean en route to Rotterdam via the Cape of Good Horn. But I don't know where it is now."

The president read it twice.

"This could be a real disaster for the owner," he said tersely. "The loss of the ship might be considered an act of war or some other exclusion under the insurance set-up. We must protect the loss of the ship. Wait half an hour. Then reply. Show me your draft before sending it."

"I'll get it to you as soon as possible."

"Also, Luks, you must keep this quiet. We manage the ship owner's contingency fund, set up years ago to cover possible uninsured losses. When I last reviewed the financial statement as of March 31, 2006, there was over U.S. $2 billion invested, primarily in European governmental and corporate bonds. We just might have to tap those funds. In the meantime, I'll check to see how much of that fund is immediately liquid."

"What about going to the police or Interpol, Pieter?"

"I don't think there is enough time for any authority to react immediately. We don't know where the ship is at present. You know the red tape involved. Besides, if the persons holding the *Argus* see any police or SWAT team appear, they'll probably destroy the vessel. In any event, if the intruders are heavily armed, a police raid may not be effective.

"I agree," said Luks nodding his head. "We cannot rely on the police or Interpol here."

Luks left the president's office quickly to draft a reply to the so-called pirate. In 10 minutes, he returned to Pieter's office and gave it to him to review:

"'Holy Warrior:
We will cooperate. However, we are prepared to pay only U.S. $15 million.
Please reply by email with further instructions.
Remlant & Sons

"So you want us to negotiate the price," said Pieter, turning to him. "You assume the pirate is reasonable. He could take this reply as an insult. On the other hand, if he's anxious for a reasonable sum, this might test his resolve."

"Exactly," replied Luks. "Let's try to smoke him out and reveal his hand."

Luks emailed the reply to the Holy Warrior's email address. Twenty minutes later, he had his answer.

"Gentlemen:
You must think we are fools. You pay all U.S. $75 million or you lose the ship. The choice is yours. You offended us with your reply; the destruction time is now in one and a half hours.
Send us acceptance within the next 30 minutes.
If you do not, we will cease communication at once.
Use our new email when replying, holywarrior_79@hk.org
The Holy Warrior"

Pieter and Luks looked at each other. The pirate had called their bluff and time was running out. Further negotiations seemed risky. They considered whether they should make one further effort before capitulating and decided to try it. This time Pieter prepared the reply:

"Holy Warrior:

There are limits as to what we can do immediately. We offer U.S. $40 million, if you destroy the ship, you will get nothing.

Remlant & Sons"

The firm received an answer from the pirate 10 minutes later:

"Gentlemen:

When we state a position, we do not change it. We are a mere instrument of a higher power.

Again, we reject your Western form of negotiation. U.S. $75 million.

Reply within 20 minutes to our new email address for further instructions – Holywarriors_80@hk.link. This is your last chance to save your precious ship.

The Holy Warrior"

Pieter and Luks tensely faced each other. They had no options. After a brief discussion, Pieter dispatched the following reply.

"Holy Warrior:

We will pay U.S. $75 million.

Give us your further instructions and assurances you can provide regarding the present condition of the ship and its return to us without harm.

Remlant & Sons"

Fifteen minutes later, they received their reply:

"Gentlemen:

Follow these instructions precisely:

1. Hire a private corporate jet with a range of 7,500 miles.
2. Pack U.S. $75 million in 10 suitcases of U.S. $7,500,000 each.
3. Do not tell the pilot what is in your baggage.
4. Bring only two representatives of your company.
5. Neither the pilot nor you can carry any weapons on board.
6. You will fly first to Cairo and arrive there by 3:00 p.m. local time tomorrow.
7. You will refuel in Cairo.

8. When you arrive at your final destination, you will use a rented white Toyota van to transport the money. One of your representatives and our representative will remain in the van.

9. You will have the opportunity to fly over the ship and one of your representatives can physically inspect the vessel under our supervision.

10. Once your representative returns to the rented van and reports to your associate that the vessel is in good order, my representative will take control of the van and your representatives will leave the van.

11. You can hire a new crew no earlier than five hours after our representative leaves.

12. You will acknowledge receipt of these instructions, and furnish your aircraft's coordinates and flight path within one hour from now via email to– Holywarrior_81@hk.skytel.

The Holy Warrior"

The two Dutchmen now realized they were dealing with highly trained professionals. The clarity of the instructions, the safeguards taken and the protection supplied all spoke of a thoroughly executed plan.

Sitting on the couch in his office, Pieter looked around the room as he thought of a plan.

"I think that you and Theo Ringen, should go on behalf of our company," he said finally. "Ringen as a senior vice president has an intimate knowledge of the layout and working mechanics of an oil supertanker, having served on tankers for years. You, Luks, are our most skilled employee for dealing with this type of situation. With your background in the Dutch Special Forces, you have the nerves needed for this assignment."

"Of course, I'll do it, Pieter. Others here can do the job as well. But if I'm your choice, I'll go."

"Good. I'll work on the money issues. You line up the corporate jet but be discreet. I'll take care of telling Theo. You will leave as soon as I have the money on hand, packed and ready to go. Let's meet within the next 45 minutes. Bring me your draft email reply. That must be sent within the hour."

"Fine."

Within half an hour, Luks had chartered a 10-seat Bombardier jet with a range of 8,000 miles. The plane was in Brussels and would arrive in Rotterdam within two hours.

Meanwhile, Pieter worked feverishly on assembling the needed funds - no small task given the time constraints. He learned that the ship owners' contingency fund had over U.S. $150 million in ABN-Amro Bank and Fortis Bank certificates of deposit as well as U.S. $10 million on hand. Citing an emergency need, he instructed ABN-Amro to redeem U.S. $75 million of the certificates of deposit immediately for Remlant & Sons. The bank's representative did not ask questions. Remlant had been a trusted and valuable client for almost 50 years, directed almost all of its business and referred many clients to the bank; there was not a need to pry. Fortunately, ABN had vast amounts of cash on hand, since it recently closed a U.S. Dollar bond offering. Normally, such an undertaking could have taken days. And many questions might have been asked as well. Per Pieter's instructions, the bank did not use an armored vehicle. The funds were sent to the firm packed into suitcases as instructed in a discreet security van.

Pieter arranged for the company's limousine to meet them downstairs. He watched as Luks placed the suitcases in the car, and stood forlornly on the sidewalk as Luks and Theo left for the Rotterdam airport.

Luks and Theo arrived at the airport at 9:00 p.m. They managed to get their suitcases through security without any problem. Because of their heavy travel schedules, they were well known by the airport staff. Half an hour later, they were on board the Bombardier jet. That left 18 hours to get to Cairo, at least a seven-hour flight from Rotterdam. Luks planned everything very carefully. The rendezvous deadline at 3:00 p.m. the following afternoon was crucial. He wanted to leave extra time in case the plane ran into bad weather or developed a malfunction that might force it to land for emergency repair.

Once airborne, Luks and Theo settled in their luxurious leather seats. After an excellent meal, they tried to sleep, but were too wired to do so. About an hour later, they finally managed to fall asleep.

The plane landed at 5:00 a.m. local time, well before the 3:00 p.m. deadline. The pilot taxied to the refueling facility and arranged to refill the jet's fuel tanks.

While there, a swarthy, tall, solidly built man in a dark blue business suit approached the aircraft, came on board and introduced himself as Mahmoud el-Abadi, an Egyptian businessman.

"Gentlemen," he said, speaking English with a faint Arabic accent, "I am here as your host until we arrive at our final destination. You will be so kind as to follow my instructions. If I'm unable to give a personal report to my superiors when we arrive, the *Argus* will be destroyed. So in case any of you want to try to make me your prisoner, that will not work. Do we understand each other?"

Luks and Theo nodded.

"Good. First, I want to inspect the suitcases to make sure the money is there."

Luks led Mahmoud to the rear of the aircraft, out of view of the pilot, and began to open the bags. After taking a $100 bill from a stack, Mahmoud poured a few drops of a chemical from a small bottle he held onto it and was satisfied that the bill was authentic. The Egyptian began to count the money in one bag. After actually counting several stacks of bills in their entirety, he motioned for Luks to close the suitcase. He directed Luks to open the next one, where he followed the same counting procedure. Finally, he came to the last bag and was satisfied.

"O.K., gentlemen, the funds apparently are in order. I can now give you our flight plan, which you will provide to the pilot."

Luks and Theo both looked at it. They were headed toward Goa in southern India.

"Is that where the *Argus* is?" Luks asked gently.

"Be patient, gentlemen, you will see soon enough."

The refueling was completed, and after studying the flight plan to Goa, the pilot radioed the Egyptian air controller and received clearance for take-off.

The flight proceeded without incident. Luks and Theo drifted off to sleep easily realizing that little was expected of them until they landed. Mahmoud did not sleep. He kept a watchful eye on the pilot and the two Dutchmen. He knew that neither of them posed a threat. He carried a 9 mm semi-automatic revolver, hidden in a holster concealed under his upper left arm. In addition, with a black belt in judo, he felt confident that he could easily overpower anybody on board.

When about 1,100 miles west of Goa, a few hours of flight time away, Mahmoud told Luks and Theo that a new flight plan had to be followed and again Theo took it to the pilot. The pilot immediately turned the aircraft northwest. They all realized that-- they were now bound for Karachi. The pilot estimated that he would arrive there in about in about five hours, or at about 7:00 p.m. local time, and knew he had sufficient fuel to get there. The Dutchmen realized that these pirates were being extremely cautious and were taking every safeguard to accomplish their mission.

Luks knew that they would be able to fly over the *Argus* during daylight, if they arrived on schedule, since the sun would not set before about 9:15 p.m. at this point of the summer. Looking out the window, at the vastness of the Indian Ocean, he felt isolated and helpless, a mere puppet in a play with a possibly disastrous ending.

After hours in the air, the pilot announced:

"We're about 50 miles south of Karachi and should arrive in about 15 minutes. We're cleared to land at Karachi International Airport. Do you have any special instructions for me before I land?"

"Yes, I do," Mahmoud, replied. "Fly over the supertanker oil facility. It is located about 10 miles southeast of the airport. There is enough daylight left to see it."

"Will do."

About 10 minutes later, Luks and Theo looked out of the port side of the jet. They could see a huge supertanker next to the oil facility. Looking through his binoculars, Luks clearly could make out the name of the ship. It was the *Argus*.

When the aircraft landed, it taxied to a small hangar. Once inside, the baggage handler, a young Pakistani whom Mahmoud recognized, came alongside the aircraft, unloaded the suitcases and took them to the customs area. Mahmoud knew that he could rely on the handler; he was an Al Qaeda member.

The Pakistani customs officials did not bother to inspect the foreigners' baggage. They appeared to be ordinary business people. Each of the foreigners said they were there on business and showed their visas, which Mahmoud pulled out of his pocket. Although false, they proved effective. The officials stamped their passports and let them pass without any further inquiry. The baggage handler followed the group.

Once outside the main terminal building - a newly built, mostly glass edifice - the handler led them directly to the white Toyota van that had been rented for the mission. He put the suitcases in the van. While Luks and Mahmoud stayed in the van, per the pirates' precise instructions, the handler and Theo got into an old gray Honda parked nearby, and drove to the port's oil unloading facility, a 20-minute ride at this time of night.

Since the night superintendent loyal to Al Qaeda was on duty, they gained entry to the facility without being questioned. The Pakistani drove through the facility and parked near the *Argus*, and Theo left the car to inspect the ship.

As he ascended the long gangplank, Theo felt very vulnerable. He was unarmed, alone and no one, except for Luks, knew where he was. It became clear that he could be entering a trap cleverly set by the pirates - and could possibly be killed and disposed of easily.

Once on board, he surveyed the scene. The *Argus* appeared empty, and he had an eerie feeling that danger lurked below deck. He decided to inspect the bridge first and examined it thoroughly. He tested the radar, the sonar and the main computer. Everything seemed in order; he did not find any hidden bombs anywhere.

Now came the true test - below deck. First, he had to check the oil storage tanks to make sure they were in good working order. Then the engine room and last he would inspect the crew's quarters. Going below deck, he followed the well-lit main passage to the storage tanks. He saw no leaks and found all the tanks in reasonable order. While he was looking at the last one, he thought he heard a noise, maybe a footstep, about 100 meters from him. He stiffened, feeling vulnerable and overwhelmed.

He proceeded cautiously toward the engine room, and descended the access staircase. The engines were enormous and thankfully quiet since he had forgotten his earplugs. He went from engine to engine and up to the control station. Outwardly, the equipment seemed in good working order, although he had no idea what would happen if he started an engine. He realized he had to take that chance, and switched one engine on. It roared to life and its noise was almost unbearable. Five minutes later, he turned it off. Again, nothing appeared out of the ordinary. Still he sensed he was being observed.

Reluctantly, he approached the crew's quarters. There he noticed several mattresses were missing. In the dim light, he could also see many small marks on the walls. When he examined them more closely, he realized these were bullet holes. While the floors were recently washed, he detected that some parts seemed more heavily scrubbed than the rest of the floor, but he did not find any telltale signs of blood. Nevertheless, he knew that a slaughter had occurred where he now stood, and again wondered whether he would be the next victim. But, again, he saw no plastique or other hidden bombs.

He ascended to the bridge and came down to the main deck where the gangplank was located. The bridge cast a long shadow over him and almost made it appear as if two people were present. He did one last 360-degree survey of the deck, the bridge and the rear of the ship but he saw no one. Then he rapidly descended the gangplank, breathing a sigh of relief once he was finally off the ship. The inspection had taken about two hours.

The Pakistani was waiting for him, casually seated in the driver's seat of the Honda. He looked at the driver warily. He certainly did not trust him. The man seemed very confident, almost arrogant. He got into the car and they drove off rapidly. The guards at the front gate let the car pass without question. The night superintendent had made sure that the car exited without a hitch.

En route to the airport parking lot, neither Theo nor the Pakistani spoke. The tension between them was palpable.

The drive back was quicker than the way out because there was hardly any traffic at that hour.

At the terminal lot, Theo left the Honda and approached the white Toyota van. He motioned for Luks to get out.

"Luks, I made as thorough inspection as I could under the circumstances. Obviously, I didn't have an engineer with me. From what I saw, the *Argus* seemed undamaged. If there was a bomb on board, I certainly could not locate it."

"You're satisfied that the vessel is seaworthy."

"Yes, I think the ship is in good shape. It is possible that a bomb could be timed to explode in several days. But we don't have the time or the personnel to check further now."

"O.K. Then we'll tell them that they kept their side of the deal."

"Agreed."

Luks turned toward the Egyptian, who was standing nearby.

"We're satisfied with the condition of the *Argus*," he said.

"Excellent, gentlemen. I had no doubt you would find it in good condition. When we do business, we keep our word. Now that the last condition has been satisfied, we'll say good-bye to each other. You are both free to go, but remember don't contact any one for at least five hours, and do not try to arrange for a new crew during that time either. I'm sure you realize that you will be closely watched until then. So, for your own sake, please make sure to follow my instructions."

"We understand," Luks, replied, "The five hours ends at 7:00 a.m., correct?"

"That's correct," said the Egyptian.

As the Pakistani and Mahmoud drove off in the white van with $75 million dollars, Mahmoud wore a great smile. He immediately pulled out his cell phone.

"Commander, we have the money!" he said excitedly to Hamad at safehouse # 3.

"My brother, you have done a fantastic job. I salute you, Mahmoud. Our leader will be very pleased."

When the call ended, Hamad closed his cell phone.

"Praised be the Great One!" he exclaimed loudly. Now, Allah, lead us to the next phase."

Mahmoud and the Pakistani continued driving towards the northwestern outskirts of the city. There the car stopped in front of an elegant private residence, a two-storey Spanish Mediterranean style structure, with a security gate at the walled entrance. This was the southern Pakistani headquarters of the Al Qaeda, a place unknown to the Pakistani police or the Americans.

CHAPTER 8

SECRET COUNTERTERRORIST OPERATION

August 23, 2006

The house looked like all the other Victorian townhouses on Pont Street. It was made of mottled reddish-brown brick with a gabled roof that came to a peak at the center – just like all the other stately, four-storey brownish-red brick houses that faced each other on this quiet street in south central London. About a mile away from Buckingham Palace, not far from Harrods and the high-end shops of Brompton Road, Pond Street was the personification of the Victorian era, a semi-residential oasis that turned its back on the hubbub and bustle of the 21st century. Flanked by houses on either side, Number 42A was right in the middle of the block, and only the names discreetly placed beside the bell-system (located within the house) indicated that more than one tenant occupied the premises. On the ground floor, the solicitors, Grenson & Sons, plied their trade with dignity. On the second floor, Worldwide Associates, S.p.a., a business consulting firm based in Luxembourg, purported to deal with multinational corporations involved in international matters of high finance.

In the City of London registry, Worldwide Associates was listed as the owner of the building. In fact, Worldwide was a fictitious business name for a clandestine counterterrorist center made up of MI6 and CIA operatives that focused on terrorist activities outside the UK. The tenant/owner was really MI6. Since the center most often focused on highly sensitive counterterrorist operations, only a handful of the principal deputies at MI6 and at CIA headquarters in Langley, Virginia had firsthand knowledge of its activities.

The center began its operations after the September 11, 2001 attack on the World Trade Center. Until then, both MI6 and the CIA had been protective of their respective turfs. The magnitude of the threat posed by Al Qaeda in Europe and the United States prompted both agencies to pool their clandestine forces to thwart terrorist activity effectively. It was no longer thinkable that a request from a sister intelligence agency be pigeonholed or subject to a slow bureaucratic waltz. Serious and immediate response was needed in the face of terrorist threats.

Although the CIA had begun exploring ways and means of greater cooperation between itself and various clandestine agencies throughout post 9/11, such feelers did not yield the type of fruitful relationship it was seeking. Petty jealousies and mutual suspicions, coupled with CIA intransigence and lack of cooperation during certain European terrorists' trials, made for sullen partnerships. Against this frustrating result, CIA decision-makers opted for close cooperation with their English counterpart, MI6. Given their common language and similar cultures, they considered MI6 far more trustworthy than the French *Deuxieme Bureau,* the German *Bundesnachtrictendienst* or the Italian *SISMI* – to mention but a few European intelligence agencies.

40

As a result, the deputy in charge of counterterrorist operations at the CIA in Langley proposed the creation of a joint operational force under the direction of MI6 combining the intelligence resources of both agencies. The center's primary mission was to disrupt terrorism outside of England. They had many target groups on their agenda, but the highest was al Qaeda.

Roger Dunleavy was the deputy in charge of his CIA counterparts in London. Six feet tall and wiry, Roger possessed enormous energy, reflected in his penetrating brown eyes. A 40-year-old Afro-American Harvard graduate, he had attended the Fletcher School of International Relations and served in the U.S. Special Forces, where he saw action in Bosnia and other areas. A skilled martial arts expert, Roger was also fluent in four languages, including Arabic. As a bachelor, he could devote whatever time was needed to his profession without concern for family.

The head of the center's MI6 had impressive credentials as well. Nigel Thornton, a Thornton from Newcastle Upon Tyne, read history at Oxford and served in the British Special Forces for almost 18 years before he was recruited by MI6 when he was 42. Tall and sandy-haired with shrewd blue eyes, Nigel possessed all the chameleon-like qualities characteristic of his profession: with family and friends, he was charming, affable and somewhat absent-minded. With his fellow-officer and peers, he was precise and cool. These qualities, combined with good judgment, keen intelligence and a lack of pretension, made him a natural to run the new joint counterterrorist center. Although he had to report "upstairs" occasionally to those in command, he had great latitude and a sizeable budget to conduct the center's day-to-day operations.

Roger's chief assistant, Gregory Markel, had spent years as a deputy chief in the Federal Bureau of Investigation's domestic security branch, charged with deterring foreign operatives from carrying out terrorist missions in the United States. A graduate of UCLA, Gregory was 42 years old and had worked for the FBI in Washington, D.C., New York and Los Angeles. He had served in the U.S. Army for six years in the Army Rangers' Airborne Unit based in Ft. Bragg, North Carolina. Born and bred in Brooklyn, Gregory had big city street smarts and spoke Spanish fluently.

Roger's second assistant was Anne Brix, whose sharply honed analytical skills at the agency made her a great asset. Prior to joining the center, she had spent 15 years with the CIA, mostly at Langley, but also served long missions in North Africa and the Middle East. She enjoyed an informal liaison relationship with Israeli intelligence and had coordinated activities on various missions of interest to both the CIA and Israeli intelligence. Although Anne was seven years older than her boss, her youthful appearance and compact, muscular body was a product of years of skiing, running and summer sports. Anne was also fluent in French.

Thornton's two principal deputies added invaluable experience to his group. Timothy Wentwood, just shy of 50, had been with MI6 for almost 20 years and had risen to first deputy in charge of Western European operations. Highly skilled in the pursuit and capture of targeted individuals, he had unlocked many leads ignored by other analysts. After graduation, he had served in the British Army as part of a swift response team, and had left the ranks as a Captain. A Scotsman, Timothy spoke French and German fluently.

Clifford Roberts was the third in rank in the British unit. Born in Liverpool, he spent his childhood on the street and had many a scar to show for it. After graduating from the University of Liverpool, he enlisted in the British Army, where he became an expert marksman as well as a communications expert, eventually joining an elite Special Forces unit. During his first year with the Special Forces, he saw action in Afghanistan and distinguished himself by killing 20 Taliban in Konar Province almost single handedly and at great risk to himself, when his platoon's position was about to be overrun by enemy forces. The fact that several members of his platoon owed him their lives did not pass unnoticed by MI6 who recruited him for Worldwide, where his skills would prove to be an invaluable asset for certain clandestine operations.

The remaining 19 members of the center, including two additional CIA representatives, carried out a variety of administrative, analytical, security and logistical duties and a limited amount of translation. These added personnel gave the center the necessary backup to make it an independent functioning body.

Although the center had undertaken some important missions by the summer of 2006, its effectiveness had not been fully tested. A year previously, Gregory Markel and Clifford Roberts had provided useful information to the Belgian police in connection with their prosecution of certain terrorists in Brussels, who had provided false passports and other material aid to a terrorist cell plotting a bombing in Italy during the summer of 2005. The two were able to connect some of the missing dots in Brussels based on data they had previously received from Italian investigators. Fusing their own data with the sensitive information gleaned from their access to the database of both countries, they were able to see a broader picture and to trace the movements of the terrorists between Belgium and Italy, as well as the cell phone calls between both countries. Similarly, Gregory and Timothy Wentwood had given the Dutch police vital data that helped the Dutch prosecute several Moroccans accused of giving false Dutch passports and explosives to an Al Qaeda cell in Casablanca.

The six senior officials at the center met together at least weekly, for about three hours, usually on Monday afternoons. Typically, Nigel chaired the meeting and prepared the agenda with Roger. In preparation for the August 28, 2006 meeting, Nigel invited Roger into his office the previous Wednesday and showed him the draft agenda,

"Agenda – Meeting of August 28, 2006
    1.   Discuss Western Europe operations
         (a) United Kingdom
         (b) Belgium
         (c) Netherlands
         (d) Spain

2.   Review Middle East issues
     (a) Syrian assistance to Al Qaeda
     (b) Hezbollah threat to Lebanon
3.   Analysis of African operations
     (a) Morocco
     (b) Yemen."

"What do you think?" he asked. "Any additions or deletions?"

"It looks like you've covered most of the areas we should go over," said Roger. "I'll have Anne and the others in my group prepare two-page summaries of the issues in items two and three for further discussion. Obviously, Anne will check in with Langley to get an update before preparing the summaries. But the agenda is so broad we may want to have a follow-up meeting or two to get into further detail. Let's see how the meeting goes before we decide how to proceed."

Nigel nodded,

"I agree. I'll get Tim to prepare a similar summary of item one on the agenda. I think it's important to cover the current landscape first and then, if necessary, spend more time together going over several of the agenda items. For example, Yemen may require a separate focus. The Al Qaeda terrorist who masterminded the bombing of the *USS Cole* is now on the loose, along with about 22 other terrorists who broke out of that Yemeni jail in January, 2006."

"Absolutely," Roger said, nodding in turn. "I'm sure we'll want to spend a good deal of time on the Yemeni situation. I know the President has quietly offered our country's help behind the scenes to pursue the escapees. I'll be getting an update on the status of that offer very soon and will inform you immediately."

"Sounds good to me, Roger. And, by the way, would you please tell our four other colleagues what time we're meeting on Monday, the 28th?"

"Sure."

Roger went off to find Gregory, Anne, Tim and Clifford to tell them about the next meeting and agenda. Anne was engrossed in reading something on her computer monitor, but got up quickly when she saw him.

"I'll be speaking to our top analysts at Langley tomorrow by secure telephone link to tell them what I need on the African and Middle East agenda items," Anne said quietly. "Their analysts have the most current assessment on these and other topics, since they continually update the latest information they receive at Langley from multiple sources."

"Anne, please remember to ask Tim to give you MI6's assessment of our agenda items to see whether our view of the situation dovetails with theirs. If our view is different, we'll explore the issue further. In any event, you can mention their assessment in your summaries."

"That makes sense," said Anne.

"Then we understand each other?"

"Yes, we do, chief," said Anne as she gave him a quick smile, before turning back to her monitor.

Roger went back to his own office on the third floor of the townhouse. Like those of his colleagues, his office was furnished in a style that resembled top London boutique law firms – a large Biedemeyer-style brown desk with an adjoining computer workstation, two comfortable leather chairs facing the desk, a small round conference table in the corner that could sit four and several Oriental rugs of Bukhara or Persian design. Unmarried, and currently uninvolved, Roger felt lonely in his personal life. But he filled this void with the camaraderie of his colleagues at the center. As he considered the day's events, he realized that service to his country left him little time to develop long-lasting relationships. He smiled ruefully, hoping that side of him could flourish later. For the moment, that had to wait—there was just too much to do.

He then began to review his own thoughts on the subjects his team had to assess for next Monday's meeting. He knew that each agenda item was complex and hoped that the center's resources were adequate to the missions he sensed they might have to undertake.

CHAPTER 9

NEWS OF THE ARGUS INCIDENT SPREADS

August 24, 2006

Once the pirates took off with the money, Luks and Theo decided that the safest course to follow was to stay at the airport until 8:00 a.m. the following morning. Each understood his own life was at stake.

"I've given some thought to our alternatives," Luks said. "We could check in at a hotel in the city. But that worries me. We don't know who might follow us there, and it would be easy for some terrorist to attack us once we go to our rooms."

"I agree."

"We can't call our consulate in Pakistan to seek help," Luks continued. "We've been warned not to seek help and I don't want to cross the line."

"Neither do I," Theo replied.

"The airport scene makes the most sense. We can be very visible sitting in a restaurant or coffee shop for hours. Then we can wait at the gate for the morning flight to Frankfurt at 10:00. I saw a fair number of security guards and at least 15 armed Army soldiers on duty at the airport. Although I can't be sure, they must make occasional rounds. The Pakistanis don't want an unpleasant international airport incident broadcast round the world. So I think we'll be safe there."

"I'm dying to get some sleep," said Theo, who looked exhausted, "but that will have to wait. I think you're right. The airport seems the safest place to be. Let's go back inside the terminal with our bags. O.K.?"

"O.K."

They picked up their bags and reentered the main terminal. There was hardly any activity in the terminal at 1:00 a.m., but at least three restaurants were open, two coffee shops had customers, and the maintenance crews were busy sweeping the floors and cleaning the bathrooms. Soldiers patrolled the area in twosomes, highly visible in their dark khaki uniforms. Civilian security guards in white outfits also roamed around the premises; several sat in one of the open restaurants.

Surveying the scene, Luks and Theo headed for the restaurant with the security guards. Once inside, the Dutchmen intentionally sat far away from them, making it clear they were not seeking contact, just in case anyone was watching. They were very hungry and ordered a chicken a piece with couscous and a salad of chopped tomatoes. The coffee, from Brazil, was surprisingly good. Each took turns picking up magazines from a nearby newsstand and leafed through them over coffee.

They left the restaurant at about 6:30 a.m. heading to the gate for the flight to Frankfurt. Apart from a few early arrivals, the area was deserted. Theo thought he saw a male figure dart behind a pillar about 40 meters from where he and Theo were seated. He decided to keep an eye on that area, but there was no further movement. Eventually a young man emerged from behind the pillar, but it turned out he was an off-duty security guard who had been told to watch the passengers as they lined up for the Frankfurt flight. Luks struck up a conversation with him when he asked for directions to the nearest men's room. The Pakistani proudly revealed some of his exploits as a security guard, which seem odd to Luks, who felt he should have kept that information confidential and certainly should not have revealed it readily to a foreigner at an airport. No, Luks thought, this was very strange. The plan he and Theo had adopted might have to be changed.

Over their meal, the Dutchmen seriously considered the next few steps. The most important issue was their personal safety. Should they stay in the country or leave immediately? They both felt they were at greater risk if they stayed in Pakistan. They could be tracked and easily followed, and it would be difficult to detect if they were being followed. In addition, they did not have great faith in Pakistani police protection.

"We could go to our Dutch consulate in Karachi, if there is one," said Theo, as he assessed various alternatives. "If we made it there, they might give us asylum of some sort so we can implement our plans from the safety of the consulate. This would give us time to locate a crew for the *Argus*, do a thorough inspection of the ship and arrange for a new oil pick-up.

"Going to the consulate might be helpful in terms of safety," Luks replied, careful to keep his voice down, "but I'm not sure we'll be able to conduct business from the consulate, even if we use our own cell phones. Remember consulates have their own rules - they perform limited functions as representatives of their governments."

"You may be right, Luks, but maybe it's worth a shot to find out. No doubt, we can only get an answer on the business issue if we go there. I'll call information from that local phone over there," he gestured at a telephone booth about 50 meters away, "to find out whether we have a consulate here."

"Theo, you can't use the local phone here. It could be tapped or watched."

"Then I'll use my cell phone."

"O.K. Give it a try, even if we are under surveillance."

Theo made the call and found out there was a Dutch consulate in Karachi.

"We can go there in about two hours Luks, when the consulate opens."

Luks eyed Theo directly.

"The safest course for us is to get on the 10:00 a.m. flight to Frankfurt and leave this country now," said Luks. "Once we arrive in Germany, we can take care of our business. I have an uneasy feeling that the consulate will not let us do what we want to do, even after we explain what happened to the *Argus* and our adventures."

"I guess you're right, but I think we should go there."

Two hours later, the Dutchmen took a taxi to the consulate on Chaudhry Khaliquzzaman Road. As the taxi pulled out, Luks looked into the driver's mirror to see if they were being followed, but he couldn't decide yes or no. Both men were also nervous because they were Westerners who clearly were not welcome in some quarters of this port city.

Traffic was heavy at about 9:00 a.m. The streets were clogged with compact Japanese and Korean cars and the sidewalks along the main avenues were mobbed with people heading for a variety of shops, food stores, cafes and office buildings. Along the way, they also passed police cars on routine patrol. After 30 minutes of wandering around, the taxi pulled up across the street from a three-storey modern office building displaying the familiar coat of arms of the Netherlands. Several uniformed security guards stood inside a booth behind a 10-foot steel gate, which served as the outer entrance to the consulate. As Luks crossed the street to the entrance, he noticed a four-door brown Nissan with two youthful Pakistanis that came to a stop 50 meters up the street from the consulate, and that one man got out and headed towards a convenience store nearby, while the other waited behind the wheel. Was this a tail, he wondered? But he quickly dismissed the idea, thinking he might be overreacting. Soon he and Theo would be safely inside the protection of the consulate.

As they approached the entrance, a guard came out of the security booth.

"We're Dutch citizens and seek help from one of more of the consulate's personnel," said Luks. "Here are our passports." He held them up in his right hand.

"Gentleman, the consulate is closed today," he said smiling politely. "There was a major protest demonstration at the British and American consulates last week. The crowd turned ugly and stoned the windows, threw firebombs and tried to storm the gates. The guards were only able to dispel the crowds using tear gas and firing bullets in the air. As a precaution, the Netherlands staff decided to close the building for the first three days this week. So we will not be open until Thursday."

Greatly disappointed, Theo and Luks looked at each other. Theo was the first to speak:

"Let's go back to the airport immediately and book the next available flight to Europe."

"Yes. The *Argus*, its inspection and a new crew will have to wait. But first we have to find a taxi."

The two Dutchmen started down the street towards to an intersection about 75 meters away. Luks knew they would have to pass the brown Nissan, which, to his surprise, was still there with the two Pakistanis in the front seat. Luks spoke quietly to Theo, while laughing loudly:

"I think we're being followed," he said. "Don't look left, but there's a brown Nissan parked about 25 meters up the street on my left. It may be wise to split up. Go back to the consulate entrance. I'll look for a taxi around the intersection and pick you up."

"Good idea," Theo said, laughing aloud uproariously as he turned towards the consulate.

Without turning his head, Luks eyed the two Pakistanis seated in the car across the street and continued toward the intersection at the corner. When he arrived, he crossed the street in the direction of the Nissan and turned into a food store 30 meters away. Inside the store, he moved quickly to the rear in apparent search for bottles of water and sandwiches. He waited several minutes behind stacks of boxes filled with cereal and rice before he approached the register, where he paid for the goods. Surveying the scene closely from the doorway, he spotted an empty taxi a block further, ran towards it and hopped in.

The taxi driver drove immediately to the Dutch consulate. They passed the brown Nissan with its two occupants still in the front seat. Luks assumed they were watching the consulate entrance where Theo was standing. As the taxi came to an abrupt stop, Theo entered the cab quickly. Without missing a beat, the driver drove rapidly to the airport.

They arrived at the Karachi International Airport's main terminal within a half hour. Looking into in the driver's mirror, Luks could see that the brown Nissan had followed them to the airport, keeping a discreet 40-meter distance behind the taxi.

"We're definitely being followed, Theo," said Luks as they exited. "The same brown Nissan with the two Pakistanis that was parked across the street from the consulate. It could be a coincidence, but I don't think so. Someone is very interested in our activities. Once we get inside the terminal, we must melt into the crowd, and stay on guard. Keep an eye on where the armed soldiers are standing. O.K. let's go."

Inside the main terminal, the Dutchmen immediately found a monitor showing a departure schedule that covered the next eight hours. Scanning the monitor, they saw a 1:00 p.m. flight to Budapest. The two looked for the Malev ticket counter, and, after a fast walk, found it about 80 meters from the main entrance door. Theo bought two coach seats after learning that the business class section was completely sold out.

With about three hours left to kill, Luks and Theo returned to the same restaurant where they had hung out for almost six hours, their home away from home. Although they were not very hungry, they acted as if they were ravenous and ordered a tremendous lunch. They talked quietly as they ate. Luks kept an eye on the other customers in the restaurant and on the front entrance.

Time passed slowly. This was always the case, Theo thought, when he was desperate to go somewhere. After about an hour and a half, Luks recognized a familiar face. It belonged to one of the Pakistanis who had been in the Nissan. He was bearded and could not be more than 25 years old. He some coffee and a sandwich and sat down at a table near the first entrance to the restaurant. Looking around casually, Luks could also see that the other Pakistani was seated some 25 meters away in a waiting area, leisurely reading a local Pakistani newspaper.

Luks looked at his watch. He knew that the flight to Budapest would not start boarding until 12:30, about a half-hour later.

"We're definitely being followed," Luks said quietly. "The guy near the entrance here I recognize from the car. There's a bulge inside his left breast pocket. It could be a wallet or it could be a gun. Listen carefully. When we leave the restaurant in about 20 minutes from now, you take the lead. I'll follow you. This will give me an edge in case the Pakistani tries to stop us."

"You said there were two fellows in the car," Theo said nervously. "Where is the other one?"

"He's sitting to the right of the front entrance, about 25 meters away reading a newspaper. Keep your bag in your right hand so that you can use it to hit someone if necessary."

"O.K., Luks, you decide when we're ready to leave."

Fifteen minutes later, the two Dutchmen walked toward the restaurant's entrance casually, passing within 10 feet of the young Pakistani. They immediately turned left toward the Malev gate, away from the other Pakistani, as they walked rapidly down the corridor towards the counter at the gate. The two Pakistanis followed, picking up their pace and were only 30 meters behind Luks and Theo. Heading rapidly to the gate, the Dutchmen showed their boarding passes and walked quickly down the ramp into the plane. Once inside the plane, they exhaled deeply.

"I don't know what those Pakistanis were up to," Luks said, smiling with relief, "but they were certainly interested in us. Maybe they wanted to capture and kill us. I'm sure they were working with the pirates' group because no one else knew we were here."

"You're right," Theo replied softly. "We're lucky to be on board. I can't wait to get out of this place."

The flight to Budapest took about eight hours and was uneventful. Unlike the luxurious wide leather seats on their flight to Cairo aboard the corporate jet, the seats in coach were narrow and did not provide much legroom for the weary twosome. But such discomfort and inconvenience seemed far less important than the ordeal and close brush with possible death they had just been through. Although they were cramped and the Russian-built Malev jet was noisy, nothing bothered them.

Upon landing at Budapest International Airport, they hailed a taxi and went directly to the Four Seasons, a luxury hotel Luks had frequented on his recreation breaks while working with NATO in Bosnia. The hotel was an historic landmark, a former palace that once belonged to the Hapsburg family. The hotel had preserved its landmark exterior and palatial entryway, while creating beautiful rooms from the former palace drawing rooms and apartments. Luks asked for two rooms with a view of the Danube and the Chain Bridge while facing the Royal Palace in Buda on the other side of the river.

Now they turned their attention to the tasks immediately ahead of them. Luks called several agencies in Norway, Holland, and Germany trying to find a crew capable of handling a 350-metric ton oil tanker. Within two hours, he had his answer. A Dutch captain and his crew of 11 had just disembarked from a cargo vessel at Gwadar in Pakistan, a port facility newly constructed and financed by the Chinese. The Amsterdam agency advised Luks that the crew could board the *Argus* within 18 hours and that the

Dutch captain had served on large oil tankers before. Luks finalized these arrangements immediately - and emailed details concerning the tanker to the provider.

While Luks was focused initially on finding a crew, Theo was busy looking for a first rate firm of ship inspectors. He succeeded with his first call to Oslo, where the ship's builder provided the coordinates of an engineering firm that had made the final inspection of the *Argus* after its construction. Theo contacted an executive in that firm who agreed to fly a team of four engineers to Karachi to do a special inspection of the *Argus*, including the elimination of a bomb, if one existed.

These two actions buoyed the Dutchmen's spirits. They knew they had to locate a new cargo, but left that assignment for the morning. Happy to have made some headway, they decided to review the next steps - perhaps contentious ones - over a late dinner in one of the hotel's well-appointed dining rooms. With relief and a feeling close to joy, they settled down to a delicious meal of veal medallions, shrimp risotto and haricot verts and consumed a bottle of Croze Hermitage.

Going over the day's events, they discussed how they would disclose the hijacking of the *Argus*.

"I don't think the hijacking is simply a police matter," said Luks, taking the initiative. "The pirates played for extremely high stakes and won. We must assume they sold the oil. We also know they received a wad of ransom money from us, all in cash. I think their professionalism and the nationalities of the two we negotiated with suggest we were not dealing with any ordinary multi-national ring, but some other, larger group. I could be wrong but I don't think so. What's your opinion?"

"I know of no other incident involving the hijacking of a supertanker," Theo replied quickly. "We don't know exactly where it happened, although we know the ship was headed north northwest out of Singapore, through the Strait of Malacca. It could be that the pirates were criminals based on Indonesia. Remember before the tsunami, there were close to 8,000 pirates there, almost all of them based on, or coming from, Sumatra. In short, it's hard to judge who is responsible."

"There's another new element that may provide some clues, Theo. We don't know what happened to the crew. Formerly, when pirates attacked yachts or small freighters or travelers, they held the crew hostage until they left the scene. But with the *Argus*, no member of the crew was left on board and there was no hint whatsoever that the crewmembers were being held hostage."

"So where does that difference lead you?" asked Theo.

"I think we should first report the matter to the Dutch police since the owner of the tanker is Dutch, although the vessel was registered in Panama. But I also feel we should contact Dutch intelligence, either directly, or via the Dutch police in Rotterdam."

"I'll go along with your suggestion," Theo agreed. "It's clear we need the help of an agency with expertise in terrorist matters to solve the mystery of the hijacking."

"Let's work on this approach first thing tomorrow," replied Luks.

The following day, refreshed, but still weary, Luks called Jürgen van Strident, the police chief in Rotterdam, to provide a detailed description of the entire incident, including the ransom payment made for the ship. Noting the huge ransom and the nature of the threat, he urged the chief to attach great importance to the matter. Van Strident said he would assign one of his best squads to the case. He also told Luks he would personally call a colleague he knew in the General Intelligence and Security Service (or AIVD) in Amsterdam and send him a copy of his police department's preliminary report on the incident.

"I'll call you back in several days to get a status report," Luks persisted.

"That's fine, Mr. Brinhoff. I'll be happy to do that. Hopefully, I'll have some preliminary input from the intelligence agency, although I know they usually don't share the results of their investigations with us, unless they want our continued involvement."

"When I return to Rotterdam, Mr. van Strident, which I plan to do by tomorrow, I will email you a written summary of the events I just described."

"Anything you can provide may be useful, Mr. Brinhoff. My email address is vs_rotter.pol.@neth.org. One last precaution. The AIVD often focuses on domestic non-military threats to national security in the Netherlands. Since this occurred overseas, it is possible they may not want to jump into this matter. In any event, I'll let you know."

Luks was far from satisfied with this conversation, but he did not consider pursuing any other alternative at this point. He also wanted to speak with Peter Remlant before even deciding whether to disclose the matter to one of Rotterdam's daily newspapers or the maritime news agency, since such a step might undermine an investigation. Upon further reflection, he thought it best to act prudently and patiently.

The Dutchmen left late that afternoon on a non-stop KLM flight to Amsterdam and then took a train from Schiphol Airport to Rotterdam. Luks called Peter Remlant at home that night and suggested the three of them meet the next morning.

Luks did not sleep peacefully that night. His mind was too active. He tried to find clues involving the hijacking of the *Argus* that could provide useful information or unlock part of the mystery. But he could not fathom the identity of the pirates or what actually happened at sea.

Arriving first at the office the following day, Luks immediately examined the monthly crude oil loading and unloading schedules. A large supply of crude oil under a spot contract was available for pickup at the Indonesia port of Surabaya in two weeks. He decided this could be the new cargo for the *Argus* to take on board. He sent an email to the Indonesian oil ministry with a copy to the port operator advising them that the *Argus* would be available to pick up the oil. The Indonesian oil ministry emailed the terms of the spot contract, including the date of loading and the port of delivery, which in this case was to be Antwerp, on a c.i.f. basis. Although not entirely certain that the *Argus* would be available for that pickup, Luks accepted the proposal on behalf of his corporation as agent for the ship owner.

CHAPTER 10

THE DUTCH INTELLIGENCE PROBE

August 26, 2006

The Dutch police in Rotterdam received a follow-up email from Luks Brinhoff the day after he spoke with them. In it, he disclosed the date and time the *Argus* left Singapore, its cargo of 2 million barrels of oil and the location of the ship when it was found, 10 days later, in the port of Karachi, with no trace of its stolen oil. Luks also included a copy of the manifest from the Singapore harbormaster showing when the *Argus* departed. He theorized that the pirates probably seized the vessel in the Strait of Malacca or in the Indian Ocean or possibly even in the Arabian Sea. Of course, Luks had no idea that Thai and American naval patrols encountered the *Argus* and that each believed the vessel was functioning normally.

After reading Luks's email, Jürgen van Strident invited Luks to a meeting the next day at police headquarters several blocks from the Maas River. Luks made the half-hour trip by taxi, which gave him time to think quietly, if briefly, about the events he was going to describe.

Upon arrival, an attractive blond policewoman escorted Luks to the office of the chief, where he saw a heavy-set man seated at his desk in a crisp, blue outfit. His closely cropped, white hair stood out against his clear, blue eyes. The chief's broad, easy smile immediately put Luks at ease. Over excellent Dutch coffee, the two had an in-depth discussion concerning the mystery of the *Argus*. In a friendly manner, Captain van Strident, who had over 20 years of experience on the force, invited Luks to describe what happened as precisely as he could.

"We don't know much, Captain," Luks started. "The *Argus* had loaded its oil at Surabaya in Indonesia and had stopped in Singapore for a day because one of its engines needed an emergency repair. Once it left Singapore, it proceeded up the Strait of Malacca toward the Indian Ocean en route to Rotterdam. As you know, most of the oil tankers that move eastward to Japan, Korea or China or westward to Europe pass this way. We next saw the *Argus* in Karachi. By that point, its cargo had been unloaded. We aren't sure where that happened; it could have taken place in Thailand, India or Pakistan." Luks signed and smoothed back a lock of his wavy blond hair. "That's all we know."

"There are a lot of details that have to be filled in," said the Captain authoritatively, sipping his coffee. "As you know, we only involve ourselves in domestic matters, crimes committed on our soil. Since the hijacking of the vessel occurred thousands of miles away at sea, I think this incident is outside our jurisdiction."

"I expected you might say that," replied Luks. "But you also said you might try contacting Dutch Intelligence. Did you get in touch with them?"

"Yes, I did. Two representatives from the Service will meet with us this afternoon at 1:30. I suggest you join us so that we can explore the matter in greater detail."

After leaving the building, Luks walked along the wide river walk next to the Maas for about five blocks, in the direction of a new restaurant near a barge on the water's edge. Sitting outside in the strong noon sun, the breeze from the river provided some relief and cooled him. Distractedly, he finished his potato soup, and filleted, tasty grilled salmon a la Florentine, one of his favorite dishes, all the while preoccupied with the saga of the *Argus*. Although he felt more at peace for the first time in days, secure in his own homeland, he shuddered briefly, when he thought of the flight to Karachi and the ordeal there. However, he felt some relief in telling his tale freely to others who might unravel the mystery of the *Argus*'s hijacking. Glancing at his watch, he realized it was time to return to police headquarters.

The meeting with AIVD took place in an inner conference room adjacent to the police chief's office. There he met Amrit Friesen and Hans Kramer, two serious-looking Dutch intelligence officials whom he guessed were in their late forties or early fifties, together with the chief, van Strident. The Dutch agents wore new gray business suits, which appeared a bit baggy and seemed overly large for their size.

Luks repeated the story he had told the Captain a few hours before.

"Mr. Brinhoff, can you give us some of the details concerning your flight to Karachi and the Egyptian who boarded the jet in Cairo?" Mr. Friesen interjected.

After telling them about the flight, including its change of plan over the Arabian Sea, Luks added:

"The Egyptian was a well-built man in probably his late thirties. He had dark brown hair, brown eyes but no beard. He wore a blue pinstripe suit and I assumed he was armed. And, oh yes, he also spoke English fluently. I would certainly recognize him if I saw him again. Another thing: he brought a device to chemically test the authenticity of the U.S. Dollars we carried."

"I think, Mr. Brinhoff, we may want to check that Bombardier jet to see if we can pick up any clues or some matter on which we can get a DNA reading. Did you bring with you any information concerning the jet and the pilot?"

"Yes, I did," Luks, replied, handing Friesen a copy of the confirmation of the rental he had received from the jet rental agency in Brussels.

"Also, we'll want to do, or arrange, a thorough inspection of the *Argus* to see if we can pick up any leads, such as fingerprints or some DNA evidence," continued Friesen.

"The vessel is still in Karachi," replied Luks. "A Norwegian engineering firm we hired will be completing its inspection within the next several days. Perhaps you can have a representative join them."

"We'll try to get someone there immediately," said Friesen, writing a note to such effect.

"You said that your group met a Pakistani at the Karachi airport who handled your suitcases with the money and who drove your colleague to the oil unloading facility. Describe him to us, please."

"The Pakistani was about five feet nine inches tall," Luks replied eagerly. "He was about 30 years of age. He wore a gray-T-shirt with dark khakis and black sneakers. He had very curly bushy dark brown hair, and a beard that covered a good part of his face. I think he spoke Arabic and another language. I heard a few strange words when he spoke briefly on his cell phone. It was a native language - it could have been Punjabi, Urdu or Pashtu. But I don't know."

"Did he know the Egyptian?"

"I'm not sure, but I think they knew each other. I can't be sure of this point."

"Do you remember what kind of car they rented at the airport?" asked Kramer.

"Yes, it was a white Toyota van, maybe one or two years old."

"Do you remember the plate number, Mr. Brinhoff?"

"No, I don't."

"You said the Pakistani drove your colleague, Theo Ringen, to the oil unloading facility in the evening. Do you remember the time?"

"Yes, it was about 9:30 p.m. It was almost dark."

"And they returned about 1:30 a.m.?"

"Yes, that's correct."

"Before the Pakistani and the Egyptian drove away with the van and the ransom money, did they give you further instructions?" continued Kramer, rising from the conference room table.

"Yes, they said we shouldn't contact any authority or any person for at least five hours and that we would be watched during that time."

"Did you believe him?"

"Yes, we did. In fact, we were watched by two other bearded young Pakistanis in their twenties, both near the Dutch consulate in Karachi, and at the airport. Again, these guys wore casual clothes, a tan t-shirt with wide khaki pants and sandals. They drove a brown Nissan."

"Did you hear them speak?"

"No, we didn't."

"Do you remember the license plate number on the Nissan?"

"No, not really. I think it had the letters 'N' and 'L' on it, but that's all."

Satisfied with Luks's responses, Friesen began to focus on the money his firm used for the ransom payment.

"Which bank provided the money?"

"ABN-Amro, at its main branch in Rotterdam."

"Who was the bank officer that handled your firm's request?"

"A senior vice-president by the name of Sven Wiegen. We have dealt with him for many years."

"Did the bank tell you whether the bills were marked in any special way?" said Friesen smiling, as if remembering a successful case.

"No, he didn't. I suspect the bank has ways of checking on that."

"I agree," replied Friesen. "I'm sure they have a record of the serial numbers of the money in question. We heard of one case where the money was coded with a hidden electronic signal so that it could be followed as it was moved. We doubt the bank had time to do that in this case, but we'll check on that angle. As for the suitcases the bank used, I don't think we'll be able to find them. I am sure they were either destroyed or well hidden. In any event, the bank should have a sales slip or other record for the suitcases."

"Let's go back over the ship's route," continued Friesen, turning to the page of notes he had prepared for the meeting. "At which port was the oil loaded and on what days did the loading take place?"

Looking through his briefcase, Luks found the relevant information.

"The *Argus* loaded its oil in Surabaya, Indonesia," he said. "That took two days. The tanker then stopped in Singapore for repairs on August 8, 2006 and left the following evening at about 6:00 p.m. We think it traveled through the Strait of Malacca in a day and a half - beginning on the night of August 9. It arrived in Karachi on August 20, 2006."

"As you know, Mr. Brinhoff, since the Strait is so narrow, no wider than 20 miles at some points, it's likely that a hijacking could have taken place there," said Friesen authoritatively. "It might have taken place later, say in the Indian Ocean, but that seems unlikely. Pirates need a base nearby since the small boats they use typically have a very limited range. Theoretically, a group could operate out of Meulaboh, on the northwest coast of Sumatra, but it might have to travel over 100 miles to intercept a vessel coming through the Great Channel directly north of Banda Aceh. We'll consider that possibility, but we doubt the boarding came from there."

"You may be right," exclaimed Luks, moving to the side table to pour himself another cup of coffee.

"Also, as you know, the tsunami of December 2005 wiped out almost all of the pirates from Banda Aceh," said Friesen. "So we don't think the piracy came from there either."

"O.K."

"Of course, we have to consider whether this group came from Malaysia. We're familiar with reports of piracy of small yachts that may involve Malaysian pirates. We discount those reports because we have heard that the Malaysian Government has almost zero tolerance of incidents of piracy that might taint its international standing. Also, we think the Malaysian Navy patrols the Strait more aggressively than the Indonesians do. But these impressions don't tell the whole story. In any event, one or more groups of pirates might well escape detection from the authorities, either because they keep below the radar - operating in a very professional and clandestine fashion - or work in cooperation, secret or open, with the authorities. We know there's a lot of corruption in many quarters there."

"Do you have any more questions for me at this point, Mr. Friesen?"

"Yes, I do. But I have another thought concerning the passage of the *Argus* through the Strait."

"What is that?" said Luks looking at Friesen, not knowing what to expect.

"Satellite data may exist showing movements of vessels through the Strait on the night of its capture. We know there is technology available that can enlarge the images of movements through the waterway. In this way, we just might get lucky and be able to see what happened. Getting such information, however, is no easy feat. If the Americans have such data, they will not make it readily available. But we shall see what can be done. On the other hand, the Russians and the Chinese may also have such satellite data. However, we have not experienced or heard of their sharing such information with Western intelligence agencies."

"You said you had some remaining questions for me, Mr. Friesen."

"Yes, let me get back to that. Do you have, or do you know, of any communications the ship may have had immediately before or after its capture? We could get a possible lead or two from that source."

"I'll check our office files," replied Luks. "We also may be able to check with the port authority in Rotterdam, where the vessel intended to unload its oil."

"If you find something on that front, contact me," said Friesen, adding that item to his notes. "Here is my telephone number, Mr. Brinhoff, but keep it confidential."

Luks studied the card before putting it in his breast pocket.

"One more thing," said Friesen, by way of conclusion. "We don't know who the pirates might be. But the stakes are high, for sure. At his point, the pirates not only sold the oil for probably over a $100 million, but also pocketed another U.S. $75 million in cash, a tremendous haul. That money can be used for many sinister purposes. If the pirates are not caught soon, they may feel emboldened enough to try to duplicate this hijacking. And I must add a word of caution: do not disclose the piracy to anyone. If you have a potential insurance claim, don't file it until immediately before the final deadline, and, if you file it, tell the insurer to keep the claim confidential."

"I'll follow your request," said Luks obediently.

As they shook hands, the Dutch intelligence agents told Luks they were pleased with the preliminary information he had provided and that they would begin an initial investigation of the matter. Luks reiterated that he would furnish them with any additional information he might have within the next few days.

After the meeting broke up, Friesen and Kramer decided to convene a meeting of the three senior members of the Dutch counterterrorist group as soon as possible to consider the piracy of the *Argus*. They were aware that they would have to act swiftly to try to prevent another hijacking.

Luks left the meeting partially satisfied. On the one hand, he was pleased that he had initiated an investigation by the Dutch intelligence service. Also, he was relieved to have transferred the primary responsibility for the investigation to a group of professionals and away from himself. On the other hand, he was uncertain where the investigation would lead or how long it might take. He also had a sinking feeling that recovering the oil and ransom loss via insurance would be an extremely difficult matter. Most disquieting, he had a lingering fear that he and Theo might be potential targets for the pirates since the Dutchmen had met at least two of those associated with the group.

The AIVD convened a meeting of the counterterrorist services the next day. They realized their information was, at best, fragmentary and they did not know where an investigation might lead. They also instantly recognized the need of other intelligence agencies to come to their aid.

CHAPTER 11

PIRATES' SECRET CLAN

August 26, 2006

After a well-deserved sleep, Hamad woke in time for the early morning prayers. Throughout these parts of Karachi, where Islamic militancy was especially strong, the sounds of the muezzins could be easily heard. The faithful performed their prayer ritual at the time wherever they were, at home, on a street or in a mosque. Hamad felt the kindred spirit of his fellow Muslims most deeply often at this early hour, when a new day had just begun. He sensed that this was no coincidence. He believed that the Al Qaeda movement represented the dawn of a new age, one blessed with the purity and sanctity provided by a literal interpretation of the Koran and devoid of the decadent features of Western culture that he found appalling.

Once the prayer session concluded, he informed Awad that he had to leave safehouse # 3 for a meeting and that, depending upon the outcome of it, he might have to travel for several days. Hamad trusted Awad completely, knowing that he would protect the safehouse and its current occupants at all costs.

Before leaving, Hamad, who was always very careful, looked up and down the street from the second floor window. The street was quiet. A car or two drove up the street, and no person was in sight, except for an elderly man limping up the other side of the street. Since he sensed he and his crew were safe and apparently not under surveillance, he left by the front door, entered his car which was parked a half a block down the street and drove off. He did not tell Awad where he was going or the names of the persons he would be meeting. He had been thoroughly trained only to share that information which his crew absolutely needed to know. Compartmentization of information and cells, an old Russian NKVD trademark, served Al Qaeda well. In case a cell was uncovered, its link to the whole cell network could not be unraveled. The Commander knew that this theory usually worked in practice. However, even he knew that such attempted isolation of knowledge might not be foolproof. Some unexpected circumstance might occur that could create unwanted problems or crises.

He drove about 25 minutes to the proposed meeting place, an isolated and gated residence of the Al Qaeda leadership in southern Pakistan, which lay on the outskirts of Karachi. After stopping about 150 meters from the house, he waited in his car for 15 minutes. When he saw that no vehicle had followed him, and that there was no person visible on the street to his naked eye, or that he could detect with his small, high resolution Japanese binoculars, he got out of his car and walked to the compound gate. There he uttered the password "Caliphate" and the two armed guards then unlocked the gate and let him enter.

The exterior of the residence bore a weathered and partially rundown appearance, as if the repeated downpour of the heavy monsoons had taken their toll. Yet over the years the inner walls throughout the house were heavily fortified, reinforced with steel and Kevlar and could not be penetrated by rifle and machine gun fire (even that of a 50 caliber machine gun) or by rocket propelled grenades. Whether armor piercing rounds could penetrate the walls was unknown. Construction had taken place over close to two years to make the work appear as a long-term interior masonry project. Because of the fortification, the armed militants who were on duty regularly at the house could easily hold off most police attacks from their protected berths on all the floors. There were two smaller one-storey buildings behind the main house that served as a second conference center and a storage area, respectively.

The meeting had been scheduled for 7:00 a.m. that day. Hamad arrived about a half hour early; he could be counted on for being punctual, a characteristic of his discipline and training. After he was led into the house, a bearded and black turbaned man led him into the dining area, almost 20 feet in length and 18 feet wide, and festooned with colorful cushions from the Kandahar region of Afghanistan atop several Bukhara rugs. The shades in the room were drawn. Light came from the old sconces on the brown walls as well as an overhead fixture.

There were five men present for the meeting. Hamad, Hajib, the Al Qaeda Commander of Piracy Operations, and the Egyptian, Mahmoud el-Abadi, all of them directly participated in the piracy of the *Argus*, its ransom or the sale of its oil. The house's principal occupant, Zafir el-Amin, a 45-year old Karachi native who had fought for 10 years in Afghanistan with the mujahideen, served as the host. The last guest had traveled many miles from his home in a village, Miran Shah, near the Afghan border in northern Waziristan to attend the meeting. As a tribal elder, Muhammed bin Halem, commanded great respect in his village and the immediate surrounding area.

Zafir had grown up in a poor section of Karachi. Schooled at a madrassa, he became a dry good tradesman, buying and selling textiles, threads, buttons and belts in a local market. He married a local woman when he was about 30, and had three children, who were now teenagers. Hoping for a better way of life, he met a wealthy Saudi businessman, who recruited him for al Qaeda. His piercing brown eyes, creased-lined face and bushy beard made him an imposing figure, although he was only five feet six inches tall.

Muhammed had always lived on a family farm. His all white hair and beard, grey eyes and wizened face reflected the many years spent outdoors in harsh conditions.

After his guests were seated and introduced to each other, Zafir addressed the group:

"Commander Hamad, you undertook a perilous mission and accomplished it so successfully, with Allah's help. May the Great One continue to lead us on. We owe you an immense amount of gratitude. When your mission was planned, we thought you might succeed, but we were all aware of the great risks involved. The capture of an oil tanker had never been carried out. Running the gauntlet of foreign navies and getting to a friendly port had also been untested. The result – U.S. $185 million – is now in our hands, the first step in our long-range plan."

"I thank you for your generous praise," Hamad interjected. "It was a team effort and my men performed like clockwork. Their hours of training were worth it. The mission further bound us together, like brothers. We're now ready to move on from what we have done."

"Yes, Hamad, your whole crew is to be congratulated. As you know, each person will be personally rewarded," continued Zafir.

"Do you know the details of our long-range plan?" asked Hamad.

"Hamad, I know it will involve your crew and all of us in this room. The plan is to deliver a devastating blow to the Great Satan, one that will cause great damage to its people and its economic infrastructure. The details of the nature of the plan, the timing and how it is to be carried out must come from elsewhere."

"So, Zafir, where do I learn of them," said Hamad. Zafir then pointed to Mr. Muhammed, who, in turn, said:

"I have traveled a long distance from my village near the North Waziristan border with Afghanistan as a courier and a guide. There are very important people in Al Qaeda who live nearby. The number three man, a Saudi currently in charge of operations, instructed me to tell this group that there is a plan to be carried out, another high-risk mission, and that he will give you your instructions in person. I'll lead you to him."

"Do you know the area that well, Muhammed?" asked Hamad politely.

"I do. I know that area as well as my own backyard, since I have traveled through our tribal region for years, first as a young boy tending to some herds of goats and later as a loyal warrior against the Russians. We trained in different parts of my region after those Russian beasts invaded our Muslim brothers in Afghanistan in 1979. I'm well-known in the area and can move through it easily and securely, knowing that I will be protected by the many other members of my tribe."

"Muhammad, have you considered how we'll travel back to your area?"

"Yes, I have. I have been instructed on this point. We must first travel by car to Quetta, about 600 kilometers north of Karachi. We should appear to be ordinary businessmen from Karachi who are selling spices to the local markets there."

"And what happens at that point?"

"We try to sell our spices there. Afterwards, at a militant's house, we change our clothes and dress as farmers, country folks who have just come to the city and now are homeward bound. Then we travel by bus to Wana, a journey of at least 500 kilometers, carrying the goods we purchased with us. From there a truck will take us the rest of the way."

"To the meeting place for my important face-to-face meeting?" asked Hamad.

"Yes. Remember, you are an outsider to this area. If you come into our village alone, we may think you are a government agent or foreign spy. We can clearly recognize our own neighbors and tribesmen. People from outside the area are suspect."

"Yes, I know that," said Hamad.

"For years, we have been isolated, leading our way of life as my father, grandfather and great grandfather did before us," said Muhammed. "When our country was born, the Government in Islamabad left us alone. This continued for many years. Little by little, the Government began giving us some assistance, some loans, some equipment and even paved some of the roads. Almost all of us didn't want the Government help. We relied on our fellow tribesmen for our own protection, a pattern followed by the other tribes throughout the territory. So, you can see, outsiders generally are not welcomed."

"Then, Muhammed, I am obliged to follow in your footsteps and be guided by you on this path," said Hamad deferentially.

"Excellent," said Zafir. "I can vouch for Muhammed; he is loyal to us and can be trusted to the grave."

"I'm sure, Zafir, that he would not have been entrusted with this mission to take us to his village if he were not deeply committed to our cause."

"Hajib and Mahmoud, you have not been forgotten," continued Zafir. "Once Hamad receives his further direct instructions of the plan, return hereand then he'll brief you on your role in the next part of the plan."

"I recognize that it would be far too dangerous for all four of us to travel there and then return," Hajib said in his high-pitched voice.

"Yes, that's right, Hajib," said Zafir as he rose from the table. "The Pakistani military and intelligence services, I understand, were recently given orders to step up their activities against Al Qaeda. You all know that President Bush visited this country in the spring of this year. Our president, in an attempt to show his good ally stripes, ordered a step-up in the attacks on foreign militants and their Pakistani supporters in the Northwest Frontier area and further south along the Afghan-Pakistani border in the Waziristan region. This means there is a much heavier Pakistani Army presence there."

"There's a greater Pakistani intelligence presence in the area as well," Muhammed added. "Again, anybody who is not known to one of my fellow tribesmen is suspect, and with good reason."

"My brothers, you know now what is to happen in the near future," Zafir concluded. "Hajib, Mahmoud and I will wait here until you two return."

After leading Muhammed and Hamad to the second floor, Zafir opened a large closet and asked the two of them to select the business outfits they would need and for Hamad to select suitable farming garb. He also gave them several small bags or pouches to use for what they had to carry. Zafir recommended they each carry a five-inch knife for their protection.

Zafir had decided that Hamad should drive his car to Quetta. He was more familiar with the roads than Muhammed and was highly trained in escape and evasion maneuvers.

About two hours later in the late afternoon, Hamad and Muhammed left the compound. Since they were already on the outskirts of Karachi, they left the city easily. Following the main highway through Baluchistan toward Quetta, they made good time. The blazing sun beat down on the car as they traveled north. The sky was a light blue; a few cumulus clouds could be seen to the north. They passed many trucks headed north with the goods imported at Karachi as well as numerous crowded buses, some so dilapidated that they appeared ready for an immediate breakdown. To the west they could see the mountainous areas of first the Kirchar range and then of the Central Brahui Range. They were also imposing mountains nearby, some of which ranged from almost 2,000 meters to about 3,275 meters high. After many hours on the road, they pulled off at an exit and, after finding a quiet spot, Hamad napped for several hours while Muhammed kept watch.

They shared one great fear as they drove north, a surprise army roadblock, and with good reason. The next day when they were about 30 miles southeast of Quetta on the route north, three army trucks about a mile ahead of them suddenly stopped. About 15 soldiers then pulled out several wooden barriers, stopping the traffic in both directions, while armed soldiers stood nearby with their Kalashnikovs ready. When they were about five cars away from the roadblock, several soldiers ordered a driver out of his Honda van, and threw him into the back of an army truck under the watch of two armed guards.

"Muhammed, I have been through this before in Indonesia and Afghanistan. We have to be calm and relaxed. Maybe you'll tell a short local joke to the two soldiers who will examine our papers, as if we have nothing to worry about. If need be, we can show them our supply of spices in the trunk and the backseat."

"Commander, I will be glad to follow your lead. Besides, as a village elder, these youngsters should have some respect for me. I know our papers are in order. I have my legitimate papers, my resident card from the mayor of my village. I cannot show a passport or a driver's license because I don't have either of them."

"My papers look fine," said Hamad. "I'm from Gwadar and have a fake Pakistani passport. To me, it actually looks more real than a genuine Pakistani passport."

As Hamad's car stopped nearest the barrier, two armed young Pakistani soldiers approached the car, one on each side; one asked for Hamad's passport and the other for Muhammed's passport. Each soldier showed his no-nonsense training; they both looked somber, serious and intended to conduct a thorough search. One soldier looked at Hamad's passport, saw it was in order and returned it to him. He then asked:

"Where are you headed and state why."

"We're spice merchants and plan to sell some goods in Quetta to the vendors at the main market and to several large trading houses," replied Hamad calmly.

"Did you pick up your companion on the road or did you start your journey together?" the soldier asked.

"We work together and started out from Karachi together," Hamad replied.

"Is this your car?" the soldier continued.

"Yes," said Hamad, "I bought it in Karachi." He then showed the soldier a car ownership certificate.

Satisfied with Hamad's answers, the soldier motioned to his younger compatriot to question Muhammed.

"Where is your passport?"

"I don't have one," Muhammed answered in his gravelly voice. "Where I live in North Waziristan, we don't travel outside the country, so I don't need one."

"I have never seen these other papers you have shown me," the young soldier replied in a suspicious tone. "Your village certificate could have been made up by any one. And we certainly don't recognize your tribal card."

"That's all I have where I come from. We don't abide by all of the government's rules in Waziristan. Generations of my tribe have lived there for years, my great grandfather, my grandfather, my father and so on; we don't want the government there. We don't need its medical help or financial resistance. We certainly avoid its paperwork too. We're very independent by nature and have avoided the burdens that come from accepting government assistance. So I don't have papers that you normally see."

"What you say may be true." the younger soldier persisted: "I don't know. There are foreign militants nearby, in your area, and in North Waziristan. They are troublemakers that we have orders now to root out. You could be helping one of them," he added in a threatening tone. "Wait here."

At that point, the younger Pakistani approached a nearby officer, a Pakistani lieutenant who was in charge of the roadblock, relating the conversation he just had with the elder traveler. After thinking for a moment, the officer approached the car to question Muhammed further:

"Do you have any other way to prove who you are?"

"Officer, I'm a respected village elder in Miran Shah. I preside over our monthly tribal meeting. I have lived there all my life. My dialect is from there. I have a wife and five children. Here, see this photo. It may be old, but is shows us standing in front of our humble home with the mountains in the background."

The officer looked closely at the photograph and then at Muhammed:

"There is definitely a strong resemblance here. Your hair and your beard are obviously much grayer now."

The officer thought further for a moment, looked away and then continued:

"How else can you convince me of who you are?"

"Smell my hands and you will see."

Sniffing near his hands, the officer clearly smelled the aromatic multi-spice scent on them from the handling of the spices. As the officer started to examine the spices in the back seat and the trunk of the car, Muhammed began to tell a joke about goat herders and their special love for their animals. With raised eyebrows and a few hand gestures, Muhammed conveyed the raunchy part of his joke.

The officer laughed loudly and then said:

"Only a native from that area would know that joke. We city-types tell something like you did about sheep, but it is different. O.K. I'm convinced for now. I'll let you pass and I hope I'm not wrong. You are both lucky. We're going to take the other guy we threw in the back of our own truck to our army base. And he will regret that."

"We may be more lenient here, a big distance from your home area," continued the officer. "Up there, our soldiers may not be so easily convinced. You will see when you return home."

The officer allowed Hamad's car to pass through the roadblock. Hamad smiled at the officer as the twosome drove off toward Quetta. The future threat was clear; getting to Muhammed's village could be treacherous.

They finally made it to Quetta almost an hour later. Hamad remembered the route to the designated safehouse easily. He had used it at least four times in the past. As he approached the apartment house located in the northern part of the city, he shivered slightly. He remembered that the Pakistani intelligence service had learned of another safehouse in the southern part of the city, staked it out for four days and then launched a surprise 1:00 a.m. raid. Four Al Qaeda members were captured alive, while two were killed. Hamad had learned from his cohorts there that the designated safehouse he now sought was still a well-kept secret and unknown to Pakistani intelligence. Still he decided it was best for Muhammed and him to go first to the local market to sell their spices and then to decide where to change their outfits and to leave the car.

The central markets were still busy at this late afternoon hour. The merchants were selling their chickens, fruits, vegetables, spices, fibers and other products to an unending line of would-be buyers and various onlookers. Many of the stalls were covered in case it rained; others were out in the open and defenseless against a deluge. Hamad knew which vendor to approach and which trading agencies to visit, based on the information his Quetta colleagues previously gave him. The spice merchants drove a hard bargain. They had their usual suppliers of spices. Still they were willing to pick up additional quantities if the prices were low enough. Hamad and Muhammad smiled happily after making one large sale of about half of their spices on hand.

After leaving the teeming market, they went into a small office building nearby. While they were not successful at first, they finally made a sale of the other half of their spices on hand at the last office they visited.

As they returned to the car, Hamad made a decision:

"Muhammad, I feel it is too dangerous to go to the safehouse. We don't know if our captured brothers spoke too freely to the intelligence agents or, if in the raid, the agents grabbed one of our computers, which might have revealed the existence of our designated safehouse. We can't risk going there."

"I trust your street smarts," replied Muhammed.

Hamad drove to a parking garage about a mile away from the market and managed to find a distant corner spot. Hidden by the other nearby cars, they both took off their business suits and changed into the farmers outfits they previously put in the trunk, wrapped in an old blanket. Muhammad changed first while Hamad kept watch. Afterwards, Hamad changed quickly as Muhammad kept guard. They felt fortunate; no one appeared to see their city-to-country transformation.

Leaving the garage on foot, each carried a pouch with some fabrics for sewing at home. Hamad also carried several small wooden storage boxes to hold spices and herbs during the winter, suitable purchases which, in his view, should arouse no suspicion if examined.

After walking about two kilometers to Quetta's main bus terminal, they bought one-way tickets to Wana in South Waziristan on the 8:30 p.m. bus. The bus they boarded looked weathered but it proved serviceable. The route took them into the nearby mountains and along winding and bumpy mountain roads, filled with hairpin turns. The passengers of the half-filled bus knew the driver could handle these roads; he had driven them some many times in the past. The bus made innumerable stops at one small town after another, finally pulling into Wana at about 7:00 a.m. the next morning. Hamad and Muhammad even slept for several hours, although Muhammad's dozing was much more peaceful than the Commander's, since he kept on alert in case the army, police or intelligence agents boarded the bus.

After a quick breakfast of coffee and some sweet cakes at a local café near the station, they boarded another bus for Miran Shah. Since the sun beat on the metal roof of the bus without mercy throughout the journey, all the passengers sweated heavily. After a seven-hour trek, the bus reached its destination.

One of Muhammad's sons, Abdul, a lean bearded 25-year old, came to pick them up and drove them to Muhammad's house. There Hamad was treated as an important guest and he felt the warmth of their hospitality as well as their protective embrace. Muhammed's wife, Azila, served them a filling lamb and vegetable stew and baked bread. Hamad finally relaxed, feeling safe for the moment. Two of Muhammed's four sons, armed with Kalashnikovs, kept watch outside, alternating their duty with their two other brothers. After a delicious coffee and some quiet conversation, Hamad and Muhammed went to sleep. Knowing they were in the presence of an important guest, the sons kept up an all-night vigil, determined to protect Hamad in all events.

At about 6:00 p.m. the next day, Hamad and Muhammed left to attend the long-awaited meeting with the Al Qaeda leaders. Three of Muhammed's sons joined them for about three quarters of the two-hour journey in a small black truck. Muhammed drove the rest of the way, another half hour, and then proceeded by foot to a seemingly abandoned farm compound nestled high in the mountains. When they arrived at the gate entrance, they could dimly see at least 12 figures dressed in black, wearing black turbans, standing at varying intervals along the shoddy brown rectangular walls of the compound. After Hamad uttered the password, "Al Andalus," the guards at the door opened the gate and let them enter, since their arrival had been anticipated for days.

No light came from the one-storey farmhouse. Old shutters and black-out curtains on the interior of the windows prevented any light from showing through the windows. Once inside, candle light revealed three men, clad in local grey robes and white turbans, seated on cushions in the dining area of the farmhouse.

The man seated in the middle of the threesome was the leader. A sturdily-built 45 year old 5' 10" Saudi, the Al Qaeda Chief of Operations and ranked number three in the chain of command, Rahman bin Azara was an imposing figure. His chiseled features, the heavily accented crow's feet near his eyes and his stern brown eyes gave an aura of a man of vast outdoor experience; his face reflected the stress of many close encounters and battles. Osama bin Laden had elevated him to this position after the death of the last successor to his well-known former Chief of Operations, Khalid Sheikh Mohammed, who was captured in a police raid in Peshawar, Pakistan in 2003. Bin Laden regarded Rahman as a trusted brother, with an endearing friendship steeled in the numerous operations they had conducted together, first against the Russians after their invasion of Afghanistan, later against the Afghan Communist government in the early 1990s, and still later against the Americans after the September 11, 2001 attack and continuing after their retreat from Tora Bora.

The Chief rose from his cushion, greeted his two guests with kisses in the Afghan style and then invited them to sit down:

"Muhammed, it is a great honor for me to meet with you tonight. I know of the many ways your family and your tribe has helped us in the past. You have given us weapons, food, a place to sleep and protection. You have showed us true Muslim hospitality, and we express our thanks as your invited guests."

"May it please Allah, we welcome your presence here," replied Muhammed softly. "You have helped us to keep our Islamic way of life and helped steel us against intrusion from the hated Americans as well as President Musharraf's army and intelligence service."

"It is true, my brother, we have aided you," replied the Chief. "Also remember we still have friends in the Pakistani Inter-Service Intelligence unit. During the 1980s, both the hated CIA and ISI trained the mujahideen in Pakistan in military tactics and weapons and gave them plenty of ammunition and weapons. The ISI also provided logistical help, trucks, and mules, whatever it took. They even worked with the mujahideen in Afghanistan, going on missions with them against the Russians. While some of the President's appointees in the ISI want to get rid of us now, there are many whom we still regard as comrades."

"I agree with you," answered Muhammed, nodding his head. Turning to Hamad, the Chief smiled warmly:

"Hamad, I welcome you to our base here. My colleagues on my right and left, Sheik Zaifel Turallah from Jordan, and Deputy Chief of Operations, Ahmed bin Aziz from Saudi Arabia, also are honored by your presence."

The Sheik and Deputy Chief echoed that sentiment.

"I, too, am delighted to be here, in your presence," replied Hamad warmly. "I have heard that you want me to lead the next great mission on your agenda."

"Hamad, we have developed enormous respect for you over the years. You have been an outstanding Al Qaeda warrior. The capture of the infidel's tanker and the sale of the oil and payment of ransom were executed with great precision and success. Allah Abkar! The Great One has been with you and your crew throughout that mission."

"I am deeply honored by your words," Hamad replied proudly.

The Chief invited his guests to sit down and join them for dinner. They ate a meal of rice cakes, vegetables and sweet cakes, and downed it with some local tea. During the meal, the Chief and his two deputies proudly told them of some recent successes in southern Afghanistan and in Kabul.

Pausing for a moment to gather his thoughts, the Chief continued: "Hamad, your successful mission gave us the springboard to launch our next major attack on the world. You may wonder why we needed so many millions. Well, the sum of U.S. $185 million can open many doors for our operations throughout the world. With that booty, we can pay our followers, pay for their travels, their training, their spread of propaganda, and their creation of new websites. I could go on, of course. Most importantly, we now have the chance to acquire a nuclear weapon, an errant warhead or several of them. Acquiring such a weapon is obviously extremely difficult. But now we have sufficient funds to do so."

"Do you have some ideas on where we could find them?" asked Hamad, somewhat surprised by the scope of the mission.

"First of all, let's start with which places are off limits: Libya and Iran. Libya decided to take a different path and surrendered its capability in return for recognition and economic development from the infidels. Iran probably does not have such weapons yet and would not, even if it had such a weapon, allow it to leave the country. Why you may ask? It would face strong retaliatory measures, such as a Zionist or American air strike on its nuclear-related facilities, a risk we think Iran would not want to take. Also, we don't believe we could get one from North Korea. The Kim regime needs them for its own purposes now. And it is too closely watched by the United States and their allies."

"Okay. Where then?" said Hamad quizzically.

"We also put the former Soviet republics off limits. We know from published reports in the West and by the U.S. Congress that the republics, such as Ukraine, have returned the nuclear arsenals they formerly held to Russia.

"Is Russia a possible target then?" continued Hamad probing further.

"We initially thought so," replied the Chief authoritatively. "We heard that Russia's former nuclear arsenal has not yet been adequately secured against theft or loss. While the infidels have spent millions on such a project, it is far behind schedule. President Bush is now trying to accelerate the process with Mr. Putin, but it is reported that it will take about five to eight more years to do so. We thought we might be able to recruit a disgruntled high-ranking officer or nuclear scientist to our cause."

Pausing to pour another glass of water, the Chief continued: "Upon further reflection, we decided to abandon trying to acquire a weapon there. We learned that the use of the weapons required at least three separate persons to give clearance, including Putin himself. This made our plan unworkable."

"If Russia is out, who is left?" asked Hamad now puzzled.

"We spoke with some of our Pakistani brothers who have contacts with some former members of Dr. Khan's network in this country. You may recall that Dr. Khan helped transfer some nuclear technology, we heard, to North Korea, Libya and probably Iran. Now, after the exposure of his involvement and his subsequent house arrest by the Pakistani authorities, it is virtually impossible to try to buy one here. President Musharraf keeps any nuclear activity under his direct supervision. He has, we think, several trusted army commanders whose sole duty it is to secure all of the country's nuclear weapons. The nuclear arsenal and the related infrastructure are probably also now closely monitored by the Americans. The President knows this, but he has to allow it if he wants to keep his current alliance with the Americans.

"So Pakistan is clearly off limits?" interjected Hamad.

"Not entirely. We think there still may be a weak link we can exploit."

"Why do you believe that?" asked Hamad.

"We believe that we'll be able to buy a nuclear weapon or two for about U.S.$125 million to U.S.$135 million from a site in Pakistan or transported elsewhere by a disgruntled scientist or several of them. That's our first major step."

"Assuming we accomplish that, what are the next steps?" asked Hamad.

"Here is the remaining plan. Second, once we have the weapon, we will transport it by freighter from Karachi to its destination in the Grand Cayman Islands or Kingston, Jamaica. Third, we'll buy or rent a motorized yacht registered in the Grand Caymans, which would then go from there into Fort Lauderdale or Boca Raton, Florida or would leave from Jamaica if the freighter shipping the weapon was slated to stop in Kingston. We now believe it may be safer to leave from Jamaica rather than from Grand Cayman. It also may be safer to dock in Boca Raton at some fancy hotel since the security is far more lax there than at Fort Lauderdale where many cruise ships depart and return. We have to study these issues further.

Lastly, the yacht could proceed northward to a yacht club in Greenwich, Connecticut or Oyster Bay or Port Washington, New York, or City Island, New York and from there to the East River in New York or further south to Philadelphia. Now we favor New York. The weapon's or weapons' explosion in the East River near 42nd Street would have a greater impact in New York because of the number of people in Manhattan and because it is the Great Satan's financial heart. But the target could ultimately change depending on the time of the year the attack is undertaken.

You and the brothers you choose for this mission will work out the details for steps two, three and four. My two brethren at my side will give you the information you need concerning step one."

Hamad rose and walked toward one of the covered windows, reflecting on the magnitude of his task. He returned to the sitting area and said, "I'm overwhelmed by what you plan. We'll have much planning and training to do. This will take months, maybe years. The risks are tremendous. You know that."

"Yes, we do, Hamad. That's precisely why we picked you. We believe that, with Allah's help, you will carry out this mission and succeed, despite the many risks, including death or capture, you face."

"With Allah's help, I'll succeed. May the Great One guide me and us on this mission. Another blow from us on New York City would cause hundreds of thousands of casualties and trigger an economic collapse there. We'll then have struck another major victory for our Muslim brothers."

"Exactly, Hamad, you clearly see the beauty of it. Such a strike would show the infidels they have no true security in their country. The stock markets would collapse. People would become fearful of making new investments in that country. The people will then realize that their government can't be trusted to protect them. They were promised true security against us after September 11. This will show it never happened. The attack should trigger economic crisis elsewhere, population flight, dislocations. The rest of the non-Muslim world may then panic like a bunch of dominoes. Our star will rise to new heights from the ashes of the infidels."

For the next two hours, the Chief's two colleagues discussed the plan to get a nuclear weapon or two in detail. They gave Hamad a list of sites in Pakistan, the names of disgruntled personnel and the numerous routes that could be taken to get the weapon out of the country and onto a freighter for a Caribbean destination. With his excellent memory, Hamad was able to absorb the information given to him readily. The deputies then gave him a list of the names of several web sites they might use to communicate with him and the secret codes and code words to use on them.

The meeting lasted until about 1:00 a.m. Finally, the five men rose and moved to the other side of the room where blankets and several rugs had been placed. After a brief prayer, the plotters went to sleep, excited that they were about to embark on a mission of the highest consequence.

CHAPTER 12

STIRRINGS IN THE WEST

August 28, 2006

Every Monday, the MI6/CIA counterterrorist center in London bustled with activity when the scheduled weekly meetings took place between the top six members of the center.

Anne had worked into the wee hours on three successive nights to pull together the assessments allocated to the CIA contingent. She had spoken with some of her senior analyst colleagues at Langley by secure phone and received their written analysis by encrypted email. After reviewing each of them in detail, she incorporated the London's unit's own evaluation of the items in question. She had also contacted, and had the center's MI6 colleagues contact, analysts at MI6 in London for their assessment. These were provided to the center by either courier or encrypted email. Initially, the British staff at the downtown location had resisted releasing top-secret data directly to a CIA member of the center, but they gave in at the direction of the center's chief, one of their own countrymen.

After she prepared her written assessments, Anne passed them out to her other five colleagues so that they each could read them in advance of the meeting.

Anne was proud of her finished work product. She had reviewed and analyzed the assessments and added her own summary conclusion. The result, she thought, was succinct, no more than six pages in length. At the end of her report, there were several questions she thought the center should try to answer.

Anne thrived on working with potential leads or analyzing vast databanks with the aim of discovering some insights or overlooked events. She did not shrink from reviewing hundreds of pages of data that others might find unduly burdensome.

Roger spent the weekend lifting weights, practicing his martial arts and riding his bicycle around the outskirts of London. But the therapeutic effects of these activities quickly evaporated after he studied Anne's reports Sunday evening.

The meeting was to start at 1:00 p.m. Arriving five minutes early, each attendee selected a sandwich, pastry and drink from the side table located at one end of the conference room. The conference room on the second floor where they met was secure. No communication could be heard outside the room. Even a listening device placed outside the room's windows would be ineffective. The room was a marvel of engineering, albeit at a great cost.

Nigel Thornton chaired the meeting. He first reviewed the agenda and asked if the sequence listed should be followed or changed. Roger suggested that the group might want to review the Mideast, African and Indian Ocean issues first because of the great turmoil in Iraq and its possible ripple effects. Iranian ties to the Shiite-dominated south of Iraq had increased and their presence felt more in that country. Jihad had become the rallying cry and more Muslims, including Al Qaeda, were pouring in as part of the insurgency against the West. Nigel polled the members, who agreed to the change.

Then the group turned to Anne's report.

"That Mideast report reflects an extremely negative trend from our collective point of view," said Nigel first. "We are highly concerned about what has happened in Iraq. The sectarian conflict between the Sunnis and the Shiites, which had been smoldering, has erupted dramatically, with potentially devastating effect on the future unity of the country."

"And what about Hamas in Palestine?" Roger asked.

"I think the rise to power of Hamas is not only unexpected, but also ominous in terms of destabilizing the region," replied Nigel. "Reports coming from our own boys in Beirut state that Al Qaeda might try to create a bridge or beachhead in the Gaza Strip and the West Bank to use at sites for attacking Israel."

"In both of these places, we also see creeping Iranian influence," Clifford added. "Take the Hamas situation. The West threatened to cut off funding (except on a non-governmental local basis) and who decided to help? Iran. Then look at Iraq. The Iranians have increased their ties with the Shiites in the Basra area and have also smuggled more deadly and sophisticated improvised explosive devices into the country."

"In addition, the current Al Qaeda head in Iraq may help target other countries as well," said Gregory, looking at the report in his hands. "Look at the shelling that took place in Jordan at the Red Sea port of Aqaba in August 2005. Then there was the massacre at the wedding in Amman and the shoot-outs at several other hotels in November, 2005."

"Your report states that there has been no recent progress in tracking him down," said Nigel looking at Anne. "The United States has committed special forces on the ground to capture or kill him."

"The CIA thinks he was in Tal Afar in northwestern Iraq, but was forced to leave because of the coalition's attack and the retaking of control over that city," Anne replied quickly. "We think he may be within a 10 mile radius of the Syrian border, in case he's forced to flee Iraq. We're working with Iraqi informants to get precise information as to his whereabouts. We have a special CIA unit operating with U.S. Special Forces trying to track him down. But, despite all these efforts, we don't have a real time fix on him."

"And let's not overlook Syria," Nigel added. "They still haven't stopped the flow of insurgents, money and weapons into Iraq. The Syrians make a pretense of trying to reduce this traffic - by beefing up their border guards or by putting up more barbed wire - but such token acts don't stop the infiltration. Also, President Assad is promoting ties with the Iranians, which could further stir up the volatility in the region." He took a sip of coffee.

"Let's hear your report, Roger."

"O.K. this is what we have in mind as a near-term action plan:

First, Iraq, we're beefing up our resources to get Zarqawi's successor. If we get him out of the way, I think Al Qaeda will be weakened. True, they'll come up with another leader, but he'll may not be as effective as Zarqawi.

Second, we have developed a special plan to target the flow of personnel and weapons from Iran at or near such border. Our satellites are tracking truck and maritime traffic regularly to help us stop the flow. The CIA thinks this data is a very high priority item. This is it for the moment," said Roger, looking at his colleagues around the room.

"Gregory, what's the plan concerning Hamas?" asked Roger.

"Right. Our group's counterterrorist financial activities unit is now working with Israeli intelligence to try to cut off outside funding to Hamas, a group our governments definitely oppose. This coordination program is highly confidential and must never make it to the radar screen. We also have developed, with Israeli aid, a small network of informers, Palestinians who will give us data concerning Al Qaeda's presence there. These folks don't want to see Al Qaeda in their territory as an outside uncontrollable force because it potentially would screw up their hard-fought self-determination and put the destiny of Palestine in foreign hands. We'll see what will come of this coordination shortly."

"Let's pass over Lebanon and Hezbollah at this juncture. We can return to these topics later," Nigel said. "I want to hear Anne's report on the Indian Ocean issues."

"There are several important developments on this front," replied Anne, looking down at her notes. "First, 23 terrorists that were in jail near Yemen's capital escaped, including the guy who masterminded the *USS Cole* bombing and another who participated in the attack on the French tanker off Aden. As a response, we have put up several more drones near the capital and along the routes to the mountainous area. We are following any movements that may identify these escapees on a real-time basis. If we find them, we'll terminate them with Hellfire missiles from the drones.

Second, we're trying to increase our cooperation again with the ISI in Pakistan. We need its help in trying to identify vessels that leave from ports in the south with cargo that will be sold to aid the Taliban and Al Qaeda, especially heroin coming out of Afghanistan. This information can be passed onto the U.S. Navy, so that it can intercept those vessels. The Navy has already captured some ships on its own initiative, including one headed for Yemen or eastern Africa with a cargo of about $3 million in marijuana. I have further details on the cooperation measures we're taking, but won't recite them now."

"Any further thoughts, Anne?" Roger asked.

"Yes. Third, we have recently added three extra personnel on the ground in Indonesia, who are outwardly members of our embassy in Jakarta. We put them there to focus on the piracy issue and get an accurate assessment of the threat from that source post-tsunami. It has been hard to get a real fix on the severity of the threat in part because the tsunami caused such devastation in Banda Aceh, and killed so many pirates there and close by. So we cannot report on any real progress on that front yet. We consider this a work in progress."

The group broke for coffee before discussing the Lebanese situation and the continued threat posed by the Hezbollah. Then they turned to the European agenda, which they proceeded to discuss for several hours.

"The Danish cartoon fiasco may be used as a recruiting tool by Al Qaeda," said Tim, referring to the protests ongoing in Muslim communities across Europe over crass images of the Prophet Mohammed recently circulated by the Danish press. Our colleagues in Danish intelligence have downplayed any grave threats, but they might be overly optimistic. I suggest that we try to develop some leads on increased threats there. Al Qaeda is trying to develop contacts with certain Muslims in Copenhagen, to little effect, thus far."

Nodding in agreement, Nigel looked at his watch and remembered he had an outside engagement within minutes. Raising his left hand, he interrupted the discussion:

"I think we ought to conclude at this point," he said, clearing his throat. "At next Monday's meeting we can continue our European analysis. As usual, this meeting has been very helpful in terms of coordinating our views. Now, we must work on developing a response to the threat in question. Thanks for your help," he rose nodding to everyone collectively.

CHAPTER 13

INITIAL WESTERN RESPONSE

August 29, 2006

One day after the counterterrorist meeting at AIVD headquarters, Amrit Friesen took his young, longhaired dachshund, Willy, for a walk along the Herrengracht Canal. This was an early morning ritual. Few people were out around 6:15 a.m. and the silence of the city was only broken by the lapping of the Amstel River against the canal walls and sounds of nearby houseboats. Alone, with a salty breeze of air and water in his face, he could think clearly and freely.

Amrit had served with Dutch intelligence for more than 20 years. Although his work focused on domestic threats to Dutch security within the Netherlands, he had spent years abroad in different capacities: first as a junior officer with the Dutch consulate in Jakarta, and then with the Dutch consulate in Amman, Jordan. He had enjoyed initiating many assignments in the field, and then, given his supervisor's approval, carrying them out effectively. He relished one instance in particular, when he tracked down a local terrorist group in Jakarta, who were planning to arrange the illegal entry of some of their members into the Netherlands. That assignment required him to visit several sleazy bordellos in Jakarta, get drunk with some of the patrons and use the acquired information against the group. He had had a fight at 5:00 a.m. with a young Indonesian over a beautiful Filipino prostitute that ended up with the two men becoming fast friends once they agreed who would go first. Thereafter the young Indonesian became a source of invaluable information.

Those colorful field days, he mused, were now long gone. His beautiful, young wife, Ingrid, fully satisfied his longings for love and a family, while maintaining a job as a newspaper correspondent for one of the local dailies. He loved his two little girls, Anna and Maria, aged seven and five.

But he brushed those thoughts away. He thought of his Indonesian fieldwork in connection with the *Argus* piracy, which, he believed, had occurred in the Strait of Malacca. After yesterday's meeting, he had spent hours poring through the AIVD's database with the help of two of his aides. There was some general information, most of which came from newspaper articles reporting the status of piracy in and around Indonesia, that proved helpful. But there was virtually no substantial analysis of the severity of piracy in Indonesia, or details concerning its organization, except for some facts concerning the Banda Aceh pirates, most of whom had died in the recent tsunami.

Suddenly, Willy's bark broke his train of thought. As Willy raced after a ball about 30 meters away, he looked up and saw a bus pass nearby with a big "Fly to London" ad on its side. Yes, he thought, perhaps our colleagues in the West, either in England, or, more importantly, at the CIA, could provide some of the answers. He was not sure where such an approach might lead, but it was worth the effort. Turning on his heel, he quickly returned to his four-storey canal house, with a bewildered dachshund in tow.

He was eager to get to his office. As soon as he arrived at the AIVD offices, he switched on his computer searching for the codes used to contact his counterparts in London and at Langley. He found them easily and sent them each the following encrypted emails:

"Top Secret
August 29, 2006

TO: MI6 Headquarters, London, United Kingdom
       CIA, Langley, Virginia

Re: Immediate Request for Cross-Border Assistance

"Gentlemen:
A Dutch-operated supertanker carrying 2 million barrels of oil was hijacked off the Indonesian coast during the night of August 11, 2006 or August 12, 2006 between the hours of 7:00 p.m. and 7:00 a.m. Our preliminary data suggests the piracy occurred in the Strait of Malacca or in the Indian Ocean, most probably the former. The oil was apparently sold to an unknown buyer, and the Dutch agents paid U.S.$ 75 million as ransom to recover the vessel. The total piracy haul was over U.S.$150 million.

We are going to check our database further for any additional information we may have.

We need your help immediately. We need your input on piracy groups or individuals who may be involved. We may need your satellite data to trace any maritime movements in the area on those two nights.

We await your immediate reply and will be available to talk by secure telephone or by videoconference or meet in person.
                                   Sincerely,

                                   Amrit Friesen
                                   Chief, Counterterrorism Unit, AIVD"

Amrit informed the members of the unit who had attended yesterday's meeting that he had decided to seek help from MI6 and the CIA.

On a daily basis, MI6 in London received hundreds of encrypted emails and many secure telephone calls from its far-flung staff throughout the world. The administrative staff forwarded them to the intended group or groups or directed them to a particular unit if one was not specified.

This morning was no different. An efficient young female secretary forwarded the email from AIVD to the Chief of International Liaison. Once he received it, he forwarded the email to Nigel Thornton, head of the secret joint counterterrorist center.

When Nigel arrived at his office that morning, he invited Roger over for coffee and a discussion about the highlights of Monday's meeting. After Roger left, he checked his emails, first reviewing the correspondence and memoranda given to him by his middle-aged secretary, Agnes, who had worked with him for years. The email from the Netherlands promptly caught his attention. After opening it and reading it, he immediately went into Roger's office.

"Roger, I apologize for this interruption," he said, handing it over. "Please read this email. I think it's important."

"This looks serious," said Roger, scanning it quickly. "Regardless of whether the piracy was committed by criminals or another group, it certainly was a big haul. Still, I'm not sure there is any immediate tie-in with our activities."

"Maybe, but we may want to probe into this further. Please send them a reply suggesting a secure telephone conference call today at about 1:00 p.m. London time."

Roger sent the reply to Amrit Friesen at the AIVD headquarters in Amsterdam. Twenty minutes later, he received an affirmative answer and returned to Nigel's office.

"We're on for 1:00 p.m. I think we should have one member of each team sit in. What do you say?"

"Fine, I'll get Tim, my number two. Who will you bring?"

"I'll get Anne, if she's available."

"Okay, Roger, see you then."

Awaiting the conference call, Roger began to feel the flow of adrenaline, similar to when he went on a significant Special Forces mission before the Gulf War in 1991. He remembered that his group of 10 had infiltrated Iraqi territory at night before the coalition invasion and traveled for about 12 miles under the protective cover of a moonless sky. Their mission was to locate any nearby Iraqi Army oil storage tanks and chemical capacity near the frontlines. While on reconnaissance, they had encountered a heavily armed contingent of the Republican Guard protecting a behind-the-lines storage facility for a nearby tank regiment. As they engaged in a brief, hot and heavy firefight, Roger and some of the members of his unit were nearly killed by Iraqi machine-gun fire. After killing at least five Iraqi soldiers, they retreated across the border and rejoined their Special Forces unit. Intuitively Roger felt he might soon be engaged in another reconnaissance mission in the field. He sensed he would soon find out.

At 1:00 p.m., the foursome gathered in the conference room on the second floor. The call came in from Amsterdam timely on a secure line:

"Good afternoon. I'm Amrit Friesen and my assistant, Hans Kramer, is on the line."

"Good day," Nigel replied. "I am Nigel Thornton, and I'm on with my assistant from MI6, Timothy Wentwood, and two of my CIA team members, Roger Dunleavy, and his assistant, Anne Brix."

"O.K. We'll start from what we learned in the Netherlands," said Amrit getting down to business.

Relating the details of his interview with the representative of the Dutch agent of the *Argus*, Luks Brinhoff, Amrit's report took about 15 minutes. The group in London listened closely.

"Well, folks, any thoughts?" Amrit asked, after he concluded

"Clearly the pirates are a highly trained group," Nigel replied. "We discussed the piracy threat in that area a few days ago. It was a subject we planned to pursue further. You can't tell whether this hijacking was done by a highly efficient criminal gang or some other group. Based on the facts, I think we may be dealing with a group other than a bunch of criminals. Roger, what's your take here?"

"The Dutch agent said the tanker was in Karachi and that an Egyptian and a young Pakistani were in on collecting the ransom money," Roger said, sifting the information. "We know from recent public and private reports that Pakistan is a hotbed for Islamic militancy, including the port of Karachi. The Egyptian's connection to this hijacking may be very significant. My sense is that we could be dealing with an Al Qaeda operation."

"We know that Al Qaeda was behind the *USS Cole* bombing in 2000 and we also think it was behind the attack on the French tanker off Aden in 2002," Tim added. "The Egyptian Muslim Brotherhood may have carried out terrorist attacks in Luxor and other places, but not abroad. Other terrorist groups in Southeast Asia have attacked people at Bali and elsewhere, but never at sea, at least not as far as we know. So I tend to agree with Roger. Obviously we'll have to study this matter much more closely."

Anne had been listening intently.

"We know that since September 11th the United States has put a lot of pressure on tying up the movement of funds to Al Qaeda and other terrorist groups," she said, concentrating on the ransom aspect of the operation. "We have adopted stiff financial regulations and obtained the cooperation of the members of the Organization of Economic Cooperation and Development as well as other banks and other financial institutions in many parts of the world. We think our strategy may have helped dry up some of the group's funding. But of course, some funds still get through. In any event, Al Qaeda may have been forced to undertake a dramatic theft to get a large amount for its operations. Or, they may need big money for some other purpose that we don't know about."

"Amrit," Nigel interrupted. "I think this gives you a sense of our collective point of view which is just a preliminary reaction."

"It has been very helpful," said Amrit. "We know that Indonesia has been the source of a lot of piracy activity. Before the tsunami hit, some 8,000 people made their living operating out of, or near, Banda Aceh. But most of the piracy in our database points to small stuff, such as yachts, small trawlers, fishing boats, that kind of thing. So I don't think we're looking at traditional pirate activity. I think we have a new group here, something much more professional. In addition, we know that the pirates involved found refuge in Pakistan, where Islamic militants are often welcomed. So we may be dealing with some Islamic militant group, and, I daresay, the scale and dramatic scope of the operation - hijacking an oil supertanker - suggests the presence of Al Qaeda."

"I think we should try to get our hands on the satellite data from the National Security Agency," said Nigel, looking at his hastily scribbled notes. "Let's reconnect by videoconference this Friday at about 4:00 p.m. That will give you more time to gather further information, Amrit, especially from the Dutch agent."

"That's fine," said Amrit.

"Sounds like a plan," quipped Roger. "Look forward to speaking to you then."

Amrit hung up. In London, the four agents began comparing notes, searching the clues as they talked. They sensed a major operation might be unfolding at this very moment. But they could not grasp its full significance.

CHAPTER 14

FURTHER PLOTTING IN PAKISTAN

August 29, 2006

At about 7:00 a.m. the following morning, five Al Qaeda militants were awakened by the sound of distant gunfire. Several guards rushed in excitedly from the courtyard of the compound reporting they heard explosions, like artillery shells, about 12 kilometers to the east. The Chief of Operations, Rahman, climbed up to the second floor of the farmhouse. Through a small opening in the blanket covering the inside of a window, he peered in the direction of the explosions with his long-distance night vision binoculars. Smoke was billowing from a village, some 10 kilometers away. He felt he was in imminent danger, and ran down to the ground floor.

"There is a battle going on in that village," Rahman said to the assembled group. "We know that Musharraf has stepped up attacks against foreign elements in Waziristan. He did this to please and impress the evil Bush in order to get more aid from the Great Satan. Over a year ago, there were some big battles that took place with local tribesmen and some foreigners they were protecting. But then things quieted down. From the reports we've received from our local friends and the Taliban in the region, we know that the Pakistani Army has definitely increased its attacks in this area after a long period of relative inactivity. I think it best we all leave the area quietly and unseen."

"Where will you go?" Hamad asked.

"My two deputies and I'll go higher into the mountains," replied Rahman. "But for your safety, it's better that you don't know our exact whereabouts. If the Pakistanis or CIA catch you, they may torture you to get information. Look what they did to one of my predecessors, Khalid Sheikh Mohammed. After the Pakistanis captured him, they handed him over to the CIA, who took him to some secret base. There they grilled him repeatedly, especially over the September 11 attack and the contents of his captured computer. They tortured him to tell them all he knew."

"I understand fully" Hamad nodded. "I plan to return with Muhammed to his village at Miran Shah. I think we'll be safe there since the Pakistani Army already attacked the area and left."

"Don't worry. You will be safe with me, Commander," said Muhammed, placing an arm on Hamad's shoulder. "My tribe in the village and nearby area will do everything to protect you."

Hamad embraced Rahman, kissing him on both cheeks. "Salaam Aleikum," he said.

"Take care, Hamad," said Rahman, disengaging himself. "We have entrusted you with a major mission, second in importance only to the September 11 attack. We know you will do it and do it well. May Allah be with you and protect you."

Rahman, his two deputies and 10 black turbaned guards immediately left the compound through a small, almost invisible, door in the rear. Lying flat on the ground, they crawled to the tree line in a nearby wooded area about 40 meters away. Upon entering the woods, they split up into two groups of four men and one of five men, ensuring a modicum of safety. A large group traveling together might indicate a presence of an important figure. Their destination was a known mountain retreat where Rahman usually stayed with his contingent. This retreat was about 20 kilometers away from the one maintained by bin Laden and al Zawahiri.

Hidden in the woods and the natural camouflage it provided, Rahman watched the ongoing battle in the village some 10 kilometers away. Brown Army helicopters gunships raked the village with cannon fire and rockets. The dull thud of continuous artillery could be heard kilometers away, followed by sporadic bursts of return gunfire. The Taliban, Chechen and Arab militants, together with local fighters, were probably taking heavy casualties. But there were always replacements - new recruits eager to take up the Al Qaeda cause, some because they were poor and needed money to survive, others because of their hatred for the West and still others who believed in jihad on religious grounds.

The three groups continued winding their way through the woods separately, keeping three kilometers between them. Rahman and his four young guards proceeded northwest for over 10 kilometers. Once out of the woods, they climbed up winding paths of mountainous area, through perilous ridges and cliffs, until they came to their destination - a small village of about 100 inhabitants nestled about 2,000 meters up in the mountains. Rahman's destination was a small one-storey farmhouse heavily reinforced from the inside with concrete. Although it provided good protection from small arms fire and rocket-propelled grenades and even from air-to-ground rockets, it could easily be destroyed by well-aimed artillery or a laser-guided bomb dropped from an airplane.

Despite these risks, Rahman felt safe. He had organized an early warning system to alert him against unwanted outsiders who might want to capture or kill him. Many of the nearby tribes had agreed to provide a sentry to watch the roads or the woods from high elevations nearby or down along the valley. If any of the sentries saw an intruder or group approach, they would warn the next posted guard by radio, who in turn would relay that information to a local family living near the Chief of Operations. Rahman also knew that an American group crossing the Afghan border, some 15 kilometers away, would make enough noise with their Humvees or other vehicles to alert the sentries. He also believed that an approaching Pakistani Army contingent could be easily recognized far in advance.

Although confident and a tested battle veteran, Rahman knew he faced constant danger. He knew he was hunted; a U.S. $25 million reward had been posted for his capture. He was sure the local tribesman would protect him as an honored guest, especially one so important to bin Laden. The threat he feared most was a special commando raid from across the border by the United States counterterrorist unit created to capture bin Laden and his key henchmen. For this reason, he also had constructed two sets of long tunnels, at least two and a half meters high and two meters wide that led from his house and that of his neighbors to a cave about 500 meters above in the mountains. In this way, men and weapons could be moved rapidly, without being seen.

Before long, his two deputies arrived with their respective guards. The three Al Qaeda leaders shared a meal at Rahman's house and discussed the day's events. Their 10 guards returned to their homes no more than 100 meters away, readily available if needed.

Meanwhile, Hamad and Muhammed retraced the path they had followed the night before. The battle they could see and hear was to their northeast. They headed south and then southwest with their two guards toward Miran Shah. After traveling without incident for about 12 kilometers, they came to an abrupt halt and hid along the wooded trail. Two Pakistani Army trucks passed by on a road about 100 meters away heading westward toward the Afghan border. The foursome hoped they had not been seen. Suddenly, two soldiers from one of the trucks fired several rounds randomly into the woods, some of which whizzed by overhead. Hamad hoped these were only haphazard shots. He knew his group was no match for the perhaps 40 Pakistani soldiers. They listened closely. No patrol entered the woods. The trucks continued moving further to the west.

Although Hamad thought his group was safe, ever cautious, he motioned for them to remain silent in their concealed position underneath several huge uprooted trees. Footsteps from an approaching group could be heard only about 30 meters away to the north. A few minutes later, 35 Pakistani Army troops in brown camouflage uniforms, passed by in two columns. Several of the troops peered in their direction but did not see them; the militants' brown, beige and black clothing provided sufficient camouflage. Beads of sweat formed on Hamad's neck. Time seemed to stand still. Suddenly, two soldiers left the main trail and stood within 15 meters of their hiding place. Hamad heard then speaking in Pashtu; one said, "nobody is here." They turned back to join the column and Hamad finally began to relax.

As soon as the Army left, Hamad and his group continued their trek southward. Twenty minutes later, they found the truck they had used the day before, parked underneath a tree outside a small village. As added protection, Hamad and Muhammed asked the two guards to join them for the trip to Miran Shah.

Fearful of surprise road blocks or other unexpected encounters with Pakistani soldiers, they drove back to Miran Shah cautiously, along back roads, through areas where, Muhammed knew, they were well protected. They arrived at his home two and a half hours later, in mid-afternoon, just in time for a late lunch. His sons welcomed him, rejoicing that he and Hamad had returned safely from their important meeting.

After a filling meal, Hamad rested for several hours. He planned to return to Karachi as soon as possible to link up with his Al Qaeda group and begin implementing the secret plan. He asked Muhammed to join him on the return to Quetta. Muhammed's first-hand knowledge of the Waziristan landscape and tribes could be vital, especially on the ride south to Wana and from there by bus to Quetta, where they would part.

While he rested, Hamad thought of the importance of the strategic mission given him, one that was sacred; one he would have to succeed in fulfilling. At afternoon prayers, he called on Allah's help once again. He prayed for a successful mission that would prove to be a giant step in helping Al Qaeda attain its goal: a caliphate from Southeast Area through North Africa and into Spain where Sharia law prevailed under a theocracy ruled by all seeing and pious mullahs well-versed in the literal meaning of the Koran.

CHAPTER 15

FURTHER CIA/AIVD INTERFACE

August 29, 2006

Within several hours of the conference call with AIVD, the members of the counterterrorist center had marshaled their individual resources. Since the CIA contingent was five hours ahead of Langley, the work done by the London crew would be extremely useful for those in Virginia. The London group also had direct access to CIA servers in the States, enabling them to pore over potentially useful databases.

Anne immediately requested any available satellite data that dealt with NSA imagery and communications. Although she had no idea whether a United States satellite had traveled over the Strait of Malacca on the nights of August 10-11, 2006, and was uncertain what data the imagery might yield, she recalled how her analysis of tire tracks taken by satellite photographs had led to the capture of a Serbian general responsible for murdering many innocent Bosnian civilians. Perhaps, with a little luck, satellite data might reveal a helpful clue now.

At Roger's direction, Gregory emailed one of his buddies at the Indonesian desk at Langley asking for recent information on piracy activities in Indonesia and the Indian Ocean. Following that, he sent an encrypted email to the CIA staff at the U.S. Embassy in Jakarta.

Searching through the main CIA database, he noted 34 incidents of piracy reported in the Indian Ocean, the Arabian Sea and the Strait of Malacca over the past two years. These included 15 in the Strait of Malacca, all of which involved small pleasure yachts, except for a 75 foot fishing trawler and a an old 2,600 metric ton freighter. The Indonesian authorities had apprehended five of the perpetrators, but 10 more remained at large. In the Indian Ocean, mostly off the coast of Africa, he saw there had been 17 incidents of piracy also involving the takeover of small yachts and fishing boats. The African nations nearest the incidents had only apprehended the pirates in three of the attacks. Because of the small size of the vessels hijacked, the U.S. Navy had not intervened. No supertanker had ever been seized.

All but one of the piracy attacks near Indonesia had taken place in the Strait of Malacca, the majority within 30 miles of Banda Aceh, then a hotbed of piracy activity. Two attacks took place on the western side of Banda Aceh, but the rest occurred further east of Banda Aceh in a wide stretch of the Strait, an area conveniently close to home, so that the pirates avoided capture.

Both Anne and Gregory had labeled their requests "urgent" and hoped to receive responses from Virginia and Indonesia within a day. It had been a long, gritty day.

"I'm bushed," said Gregory folding himself into a chair in Anne's office. "I'm going to grab something at Black Swan. They have excellent Shepherd's pie. Want to join me?"

Anne looked at him over her computer screen. "A beer or two would definitely lift my spirits," she said.

"Okay. I'll wait for you downstairs."

The pub was bustling and the bar was three deep in regulars, talking animatedly. Managing to find a corner table, Anne and Gregory ordered two Heinekens.

"I absolutely needed a place like this," said Anne, looking at the boisterous crowd at the bar.

"Me too."

"I decided to skip my usual routine."

"What's that?" asked Gregory.

"I usually work out at a gym about five blocks from here before going out to eat or having something at home. But tonight, I decided to cool out a bit," Anne paused, and then added, "This piracy report spooked me. I think it's big time."

"I think so too," Gregory nodded. "This group is professional. What scares me is what they plan to do with all that money."

"I don't get it," said Anne, leaning forward and holding her forehead in her hand. "Those pirates were able to hijack a supertanker, steer it to a safe port, and then dispose of the oil and the ship before anybody found out. How did they do it? Think about it, Greg. How could they have avoided our Navy patrols in the Arabian Sea?"

"I don't know," said Gregory shaking his head. "The Navy probably was not patrolling their shipping lanes. The Indians don't seem to patrol aggressively or go way out in the Arabian Sea."

"What about our Navy? Do you think they could have fooled us?"

Gregory signed. "It's possible. We just don't know yet."

"What kind of feedback do you expect from Jakarta?"

Gregory took a swallow of beer before answering. "I don't know," he said slowly, as if thinking aloud, "I've heard that the embassy has an experienced crew and recently beefed up its CIA staff. But the Indonesian police and intelligence units don't like having the CIA messing around in their country. They tolerate them, but aren't too happy about it."

"Well," said Anne, looking down at the lines in the oak table. "I've asked for satellite data, but don't know what to expect on that front. It's a long shot. I was lucky in the past. Let's hope I'll be lucky now."

Their meal finally arrived. Greg devoured his Shepherd's pie, while Anne hungrily attacked her fish and chips. Over another round of Heinekens, they compared notes on the operation of the center and agreed it was functioning well. But they also agreed it had yet to be fully tested:

"Greg, I think this piracy project might be a major test for the center - a chance to pool all our available resources."

Gregory nodded. "Could be. The MI6 group is doing its own digging. Nigel told Roger that MI6 would have its data sorted by Thursday afternoon."

"That gives us about a full day to integrate our findings with theirs.

"Exactly."

"Then, on Friday, we can expect further input from Dutch intelligence?"

"Yes."

Anne pushed her plate away. "You know this collective effort just might work."

"Let's hope so. It's still early," said Gregory skeptically. "We may get very little helpful information from the requests each of us made."

They left the pub and went their separate ways. Anne returned to her one-bedroom flat on Ovington Square on the second floor of a recently restored Victorian townhouse. The flat was sparsely furnished. Her sitting room took up most of the space: a long rectangular room with red brick walls and a fireplace. The parquet floor was covered by a six by nine foot Persian carpet. A traditional sofa and two armchairs with matching ticking surrounded a low coffee table. Her flat was convenient to the office, only a 15 minute brisk walk away.

Anne had become used to living alone. A divorcee of 10 years, she had married her husband, Wayne Chatswood, when she was 22. They had raised two sons in Arlington and, once they had graduated from college, she left her husband. Although they had spent many happy years together, traveling extensively, skiing, sailing and enjoying the companionship of several close friends, over time marriage had proven too confining for her. She wanted to fulfill her potential at the Agency, unimpeded by family obligations. Since their divorce, she had concentrated almost entirely on her job, taking time out for random pleasure, including an exercise regime of aerobics, weight lifting and Pilates. By the age of 47, she was a superb analyst, an accomplished marksman and in top physical shape. She was a "natural" selected for the counterterrorist center in London.

By the time Greg returned to his flat in north London, he was in an extremely pensive mood. Pouring out two fingers of single malt, he sat down on his extremely comfortable Swedish couch, thinking about the day's events and the ramifications of the piracy incident. The hijacking of a mammoth oil tanker was no small exploit. It was, as Anne remarked, big time. Nothing like this had ever happened before. Not for a moment did he consider this a simple act of piracy. There was more, much more, to it. He smelled danger and sensed he was about to embark on a mission that could pose a grave threat to him and his colleagues as they tried to unravel this sinister incident that had occurred - where? In the Indian Ocean? In the Arabian Sea? In the Strait of Malacca? - So far away from the familiar confines of his flat with its Scandinavian furniture, his library filled with spy novels, his queen-sized bed, where he spent many a restless night thinking of his beautiful wife, Jane, and their 10 year old son, Jim.

As a child, he adored reading stories about Blackbeard and other pirates who preyed on English and Spanish ships in the Caribbean. Glamorized by Hollywood, they were heroes. Or the English and Spanish were not exactly without blame. Somehow, they deserved to be attacked by a swashbuckling Errol Flynn, who would rescue a beautiful maiden while stealing their cargo. But those were innocent and very different times.

He had been born and raised in Ithaca, New York, a small, serene community, home to Cornell University and the site of a former movie-making center in the 1920' s and '30s. His childhood was unremarkable, but for the fact that he had always loved the outdoors. Joining the Boy Scouts, going on treks and overnight camping in the hills surrounding Lake Cayuga, hiking, canoeing, and snow-shoeing, he had become an outdoorsman and learned to be self-reliant. As he grew up, he acquired many friends both from his neighborhood and at school. Although gregarious by nature, he was also calm and considerate. His teachers adored him and he attracted people like a magnet - including some of the more mature beauties at high school who had become his girlfriends.

Thinking about the past, he got up and poured himself another drink. He thought about Jane and Jim whom he had last seen in Falls Church, Virginia. He missed them deeply. He felt he had known Jane forever. They had met on an Outward Bound hiking and camping expedition when they were both 19. After graduating from the University of Virginia, they decided to live together. Jane had a brilliant mind, a bubbly personality and beautiful green eyes. Living in London, apart from her for over a year, Greg missed her company and passion for lovemaking. As he finished his drink, he decided he would go to sleep.

Anne and Greg were pleased to receive responses from Langley and Jakarta in the late afternoon of the next day. Anne's contact at Langley told her the NSA had the satellite imagery she wanted, but could not get it to her in London until a day or two later. The CIA staffer in Jakarta informed Gregory he hoped to give him an updated report the next day that would include data from Langley. In the interim, Anne and Greg continued to analyze the *Argus* piracy from the information on hand.

Two days later, at about 4:00 p.m., Anne received the satellite data from Langley: 26 high resolution photos blown up into different sizes covering the nights of August 11 and 12, 2006, from 10:00 p.m. to 4:00 a.m.. She studied each photo closely. One photo, taken on August 11, 2006 at 4:15 a.m., revealed a vessel in the Strait, which was far larger than any other ship in the area. She measured the vessel's dimensions in the photo and then multiplied that size by the size of each pixel. Analyzing this photo against her extensive database of maritime vessels, photographs and diagrams, she realized that this vessel was an oil supertanker of the Malacca max class, identical to that of the *Argus*. From other data, she learned that no other supertanker had gone through the Strait for four days following the *Argus*.

Something was missing here. Where was the intercepting vessel? Why can't I see another, smaller craft nearby? She decided to call her colleague at Langley, Bud Hansen, and ask him to enlarge the photo by maximizing the number of pixels surrounding the ships for a distance of five miles. She knew Langley had the equipment to do so - or the Agency could get the NSA to do so. In any event, she would get the data.

Four hours later, she received a response by email. Poring over the six higher resolution photos, she still could not see any craft near the *Argus*. She rose from her office chair in frustration, walked down the corridor, poured herself a cup of Earl Grey decaffeinated tea from the kitchen and drank it slowly. After 10 minutes, she felt calmer and decided to look at the higher resolution photos one last time before leaving the office.

After lining the six photos up side-by-side and studying each one in sequence, she still could not find any other small vessel near the *Argus*.

CHAPTER 16

RETURN TO KARACHI

August 29, 2006

Dressed in clothes worn by Waziristan tribesmen, Hamad and Muhammed traveled to Wana on an early evening bus. Then they continued on to Quetta. The trip went without incident.

When they arrived at the main terminal in Quetta early next morning, the station was bustling and chaotic with travelers forming long lines to purchase tickets. About to part company, Hamad and Muhammed embraced each other.

"Muhammed, you have been a most trusted guide and dear friend," said Hamad, looking at him with something resembling affection. "I thank you for sharing your home and protecting me. I'm eternally grateful to you."

"I acted in no special way towards you, Commander. I just showed you our brotherly Muslim hospitality."

"May Allah continue to shine on you and your family. Thank them for me."

"I will, Commander. And I know you will succeed with the plan."

"Yes, Muhammed. With Allah's help, I will."

Walking out of the station, Hamad spotted an outdoor café. He ordered coffee and a pastry as he waited for the next bus to Karachi - another eight and a half hour ride if there were no unwanted surprises. From his vantage point on the square, he had a full panoramic view of the scene before him and was mildly disconcerted by the mixture of nationalities, mainly Chinese: Chinese businessmen going into office buildings, Chinese construction workers squatting near their trucks, and Pakistanis of all ages engaged in buying goods and window gawking. As he sipped his strong coffee and nibbled on his oven-fresh pastry, Hamad mused that he had no quarrel with these people. The Chinese posed no threat to Al Qaeda. He liked the Pakistanis in general, but he hated the Pakistani Army, the country's president and most elements of the ISI with a passion. They were assassins who had combined to kill or capture many members of Al Qaeda and the Islamic militants who supported them. Checking his watch, he realized that he had to go.

The bus to Karachi was filled to the point of overcrowding, but did not run into any roadblocks en route and arrived finally at the final bus terminal about 30 minutes late because of heavy traffic on the main highway. Hamad was one of the first off the bus, impatient to move his legs after the long journey. He was also terribly thirsty and stopped at a nearby café for some water. Once seated, he checked the scene to make sure he was not being followed, and took note of the seven army soldiers guarding the terminal, a potential terrorist target.

Confident he was not being followed, Hamad went to a taxi stand at the end of the street, stood on line for a few minutes and finally got into a cab. Twenty-five minutes later, he got out about seven blocks from his destination. He took his time walking, making sure no one was following him, or saw him entering the secret headquarters of Al Qaeda on the northern outskirts of Karachi. Zafir, Hajib and Mahmoud were still there.

"Commander, welcome back," said Zafir warmly. "We're glad to see you. We expected you this morning."

"I'm glad to be here in one piece," said Hamad quietly.

"I'm sure you have lots to tell us," Zafir said.

"I do," Hamad replied.

"Please give us an account of your trip with Muhammed. We need to know all the details to update our planning in the future, when we send other friends to the north. We want to hear about the latest news about Musharraf's activities against us in that region."

"Here's what happened," said Hamad sitting down on a cushion against the wall.

He told the group about the roadblock outside Quetta, about the Pakistani Army attack near his meeting place in North Waziristan and about the numerous army patrols in and around Miran Shah. In his opinion, he said, the Pakistani Army was geared up, at least for the moment, to inflict major damage and casualties on militants in that area. While the local tribesmen could still be counted on for protection, there was a serious risk that a sizeable number of Al Qaeda members and their supporters could be captured or killed.

"Did you find Muhammed and his tribesmen trustworthy?" asked Hajib.

"Muhammed and his family would fight to the death to protect us," Hamad replied quickly, looking directly at Hajib. "His four sons took great risks to protect us when I was there. Muhammed also told me that, since he was one of the most prominent village elders, the other villagers would follow his lead, as would neighboring tribesmen."

"Even in the face of a major threat? An attack by the army which might completely destroy their village and their homes?" probed Hajib.

"Yes, I believe so," answered Hamad firmly. "Muhammed said his tribe hated all Westerners because they believed the West wanted to destroy Islam and its way of life. They believe Musharraf is a mere puppet dancing to the tune of the Great Satan."

"So they would fight the army to protect us," Hajib concluded.

"Yes."

"Hamad, it's crucial we judge Muhammed's loyalty. He knows where our number three person, our Chief of Operations, is.

"He is completely trustworthy," Hamad said firmly.

"Good." Hajib relaxed noticeably. "I'm satisfied."

Hamad then proceeded to discuss some aspects of his new mission with the group. Bearing in mind that the Chief of Operations had instructed him to compartmentalize, he was careful not to reveal all the details. He told them another major attack was being planned against the West, this time with a nuclear weapon, acquired in either the Ukraine or elsewhere. Hamad watched his companions as he spoke. The

Egyptian's mouth opened and Hajib's jaw dropped. They both realized that the Al Qaeda leadership was raising the stakes dramatically in its confrontation with the United States and the Western powers. Mahmoud squirmed in his seat.

"Obviously, as a loyal member, I don't question your orders," he said. "But won't the U.S. President reply in kind with a nuclear weapon that would kill many of our Muslim brothers?"

"Our leaders considered such a risk, but discounted it. The Chief of Operations said it isn't in the American character to kill thousands, or maybe, hundreds of thousands, of innocent civilians with a nuclear response."

"How can we be sure of that?" Mahmoud asked.

"We can't," snapped Hamad. "Our leadership believes Americans won't play this card. Bush is in too much trouble at home over Iraq and Afghanistan. Many U.S. religious leaders he listens to will not want him to respond this way. The Europeans are too weak-kneed to go down that road alone. Since most of them were against the invasion of Iraq, they certainly won't support this kind of a response or do it themselves."

Mahmoud digested this and nodded.

"There is one additional point," Hamad went on, moving closer to Mahmoud. "The leadership believes that a Western nuclear response against a Mideast country could permanently damage or disrupt the supply of oil for an extended period of time. The U.S. wouldn't want that."

"That's a good point," said Mahmoud. "If, say, an all Saudi unit carried out this attack, it would be highly unlikely for the U.S. to bomb Saudi Arabia and risk damaging the flow of almost 8,500,000 millions of barrels of oil a day."

"Exactly."

"World oil prices would go sky-high and hit the greedy Americans and Europeans hardest," Mahmoud said, excitedly.

"Yes."

"The Chinese would probably try to stop such an American response, since China is Saudi Arabia's second largest oil customer," Mahmoud went on.

"Also, the Iranians might stop selling oil to the West and, if they have a bomb, use it against Israel, America's biggest ally in the Mideast," Hamad smiled. "The Americans certainly don't want that to happen!"

He paused for a moment.

"Of course, if Tel Aviv or Jerusalem were hit, we would lose many Palestinian brothers. But, you see, any American response in kind is fraught with great risk."

"I can see the beauty of this plan," Hajib exclaimed. "We win and the infidels lose."

In high spirits, they broke for a hearty lunch. Sitting on cushions, they spoke freely, laughing as they ate, drinking a strong Indian tea.

An hour later, after Zafir and Hajib excused themselves, Hamad began speaking to Mahmoud about the movement of money.

"What I will tell you is for your ears alone, my brother, and for one or two of your closest financial experts. Do you understand?"

"Yes, Commander, I do."

"We have U.S. $110 million at the Mideast Islamic Bank in Dubai in the name of a Dubai corporation, Trading Ventures Ltd.," said Hamad. "The registered owner of all of the shares of trading is a Cypriot corporation which is outwardly run by an Egyptian businessman, Rish el-Amad, its president and managing director. The Cypriot outfit is a bearer share corporation; the shares are held by the owner but his or its name is not listed on the share certificates in the public records. The owner is known only to our top leaders and the lawyer who created it."

"I understand," said Mahmoud listening attentively. "Go on."

"O.K. Now you know that we also have another U.S. $75 million from the ship's ransom money that you brought here. The Chief of Operations thinks we may have to use about U.S. $30 million from this source for our mission, in other words, a total of U.S. $140 million.

"I follow," said Mahmoud.

"With this U.S. $140 million, we plan to buy one or two nuclear weapons," continued Hamad. "Your job will be to move the money from the Mideast Islamic Bank to the seller or sellers of the weapon."

"The movement of funds could be very dangerous," gushed Mahmoud, shifting his position on the floor. "Any person who actually carries millions in cash is an inviting target. It is imperative that only you, my two closest financial experts and I know about this - and, naturally, our Chief of Operations in North Waziristan."

"I agree," Hamad nodded.

"If we try to convert the Dubai funds into cash, the amount involved would arouse suspicion both in the bank and the U.S. Treasury, which keeps track of all U.S. dollar movements around the world," continued Mahmoud soberly. "Moreover, I doubt the bank could get its hands on that amount of cash readily, if at all."

"So what do you have in mind?" asked Hamad softly.

"It may make sense to buy euros, since use of such funds would not be subject to the same strict scrutiny by the Americans or the European regulators," replied Mahmoud.

"That may be a wise alternative," said Hamad. "But aren't there other ways to make the payment?"

"Yes. We could arrange for several banks to issue a letter of credit in favor of the seller – – a promise by the issuing bank to make a payment upon the satisfaction of a certain condition or conditions. In such case, typically the seller would be not be paid by the bank until the buyer certifies in writing that it has the goods and until the bank receives the signed original of the buyer's certification."

"Explain to me further about bank promises, Mahmoud. I know about them generally, but I've never used one before."

"I've used letters of credit many times in my import-export business in Cairo. I ask my local bank to issue one when I receive, say, a shipment of vegetable oil from Indonesia. The seller is paid when the issuing bank receives confirmation that my company, the buyer, received the goods and I deliver my company's original of the signed certificate to such effect to my bank. The issuing bank then sends the payment for the imported goods by wire electronically to the buyer's account in, say, Jakarta, and the buyer gets his money. That's generally the way it works."

Listening closely to Mahmoud's shrewd analysis, Hamad realized that the movement of funds was going to be difficult. The seller was not going to part with the weapon before making sure he or they received payment. Moreover, any seller might want to be paid first, or at least receive a substantial part of the money, upfront, before the weapon was sold. The seller might also insist on proof of the buyer's financial capability to make the entire payment.

After reflecting for several moments, Hamad asked:

"If our seller wants us to prove that the buyer has the money to make the purchase, how can we assure him of that in a way that keeps certain of information confidential?"

"We can do it," Mahmoud answered. "We can have our bank as the buyer's bank confirm to the seller's bank through direct bank-to-bank communication, followed by a written confirmation to the seller's bank, that the buyer has the requisite funds on hand and there is no lien or other claim on them."

"But, Mahmoud, if the price exceeds U.S. $110 million, our bank won't be able to give the full confirmation."

"True, Commander. Of course, we can always add the other U.S. $30 million to the account before then."

"But won't bringing in such amount of cash arouse suspicion at the bank?"

"Yes, Commander, it might. But some banks turn their eyes away. They want the deposit and don't ask certain troublesome questions."

"This part could be tricky," Hamad mused. "We may have to put the balance in a friendly bank, maybe even in Pakistan, or else move it to another safe bank outside the country. After all the training we undertook to carry out the hijacking, we're not going to risk losing any of these funds. Understood?"

"Yes, Commander."

"We will talk further on this subject, Mahmoud. Please give it some thought. I'm sure that your financial acumen and many years of business experience will be of great help to me. I'm going to rest now and consider some other aspects of the plan."

"I'm staying here," said Mahmoud, spreading his arms in a circle. "So take your time. I'll be available when you need me, Hamad."

"Great. I think you'll be a great help to me, Mahmoud," Hamad repeated. "I trust you."

"The feeling is mutual. See you later, Commander."

The Egyptian went to his room upstairs. It was furnished in a Chinese style with goods imported from China. A large desk with an inlaid pattern of lighter wood was placed near the front window. A small tan sofa lay across from it. The low queen bed had carved China figures on the headboard. Certainly, the room would satisfy a visiting businessman from China, a façade assigned to fool any spying eyes.

Mahmoud was pleased with his role as a key financial expert for the bin Laden-led group. He had known Osama's second in command, Dr. Ayman al Zawahiri, for over 15 years. Dr. Zawahiri had been impressed by the zeal, resourcefulness and financial acumen of the younger man. They had spent numerous days together in coffee houses, private homes and at universities often at night, cajoling, prodding and inciting young Egyptians to join the Muslim Brotherhood in Cairo - an Islamic group banned for many years in Egypt. Dr. Zawahiri was one of the intellectual leaders of the movement.

Mahmoud could still recall a secret night time meeting held with Dr. Zawahiri in the basement of a Cairo University professor's small apartment building. The windows to the basement had been painted black several years before. During the two-hour session that was attended by at least 30 interested students, arguments went back and forth. Some students were excited by opposing the regime; others held back. The room was hot and stifling; there was a strong smell of sweat.

During the height of the discussion, Mahmoud noticed one student departing. Alarmed, he promptly warned Dr. Zawahiri that the student could be a spy for the regime. The Doctor immediately told the students to leave and disperse while he and Mahmoud waited. Once the group left, the two men followed. When they were 50 meters away from the building, 20 Egyptian intelligence agents raided it. Finding the basement deserted, they fanned out in the neighborhood. Fortunately, Dr. Zawahiri and Mahmoud were able to duck into a friend's house close by where they spent the next day. When they left, they found out that the intelligence agents captured five students and killed two others. The Doctor and Mahmoud had been lucky. As organizers of the event, they knew the intelligence agents would have tortured or killed them both.

This narrow escape prompted Mahmoud to protect himself. He became a martial arts expert. Deciding to go further underground, he made use of his university degree and business courses and became a businessman. After forming a corporation, he began dabbling in the resale of local goods. Over several years, he amassed substantial profits. He expanded his business by importing goods from other Arab countries and reselling them, and, in turn, began to sell Egyptian-made goods abroad.

Then, one day in 1998, he received a telephone call from an unexpected source. Doctor Zawahiri said he needed him for a different Islamic cause, for Al Qaeda, and explained the role he could play for them in the financial arena. Mahmoud was receptive. Over the years, he had become increasingly upset over the lack of increase in the standard of living in Egypt and in most of the Muslim world. He felt deeply that this was due to the role played by the West, which consistently backed strong rulers who ignored the needs of their people. Realizing he might be of aid to an appealing Muslim cause, he accepted. For years, he worked undercover for Al Qaeda, without arousing the suspicion of the Egyptian authorities.

CHAPTER 17

FURTHER ANALYSIS BY THE CENTER

August 30, 2006

Early Wednesday evening Gregory received the following email from the CIA in Jakarta:

TOP SECRET

"Gregory:

Here is our update on piracy activities in and around Indonesia:

1.   Piracy activities have ceased in the Banda Aceh area. The tsunami killed over 7,000 pirates there. The settlement reached between the separatists and the Indonesian Government has provided enough good will at present to reduce any unwarranted activities that could embarrass the central government.

2.   The number of piracy attacks in the Strait of Malacca dropped from 38 reported incidents in 2004 to 12 in 2005. We think this may be due to the increased joint patrolling undertaken by the Malaysian, Indonesian, Singaporean and Thai naval units.

3.   The more remote eastern parts of Indonesia may become more troublesome in the future, but we have no evidence that a group so far away had the capability to undertake an attack in the Strait.

4.   There are gaps in the joint patrols undertaken by the patrolling parties. There is no 24-hour full-time patrolling undertaken throughout the Strait. Thus, a group that studied the patrols might be able to detect certain windows of opportunity.

5.   We find no evidence of any recent piracy attacks off the northwestern coast of Indonesia in the Indian Ocean.

6.   There are stretches of the coast of Sumatra between Kualalangsa and Bagansiapippi that are sparsely populated and are not routinely patrolled on land by the Indonesian Army. Our detailed maps show there are many coves along that vicinity that could potentially serve as staging area for private groups. Many people who live there at or below the poverty level strongly embrace Islam. These factors make this area a potential sanctuary for a piracy group. We found nothing to date that reveals that Al Qaeda or any other radical group may be operating from there. But there is a distinct possibility they could be. For that reason, we intend to explore that region more closely within the next 10 days.

7.   In short, we believe that the attack on the *Argus* probably took place in the Strait, but we have no hard evidence to support that conclusion.

8.   We will give you a written update within the next 10 days."

Gregory pondered the import of these conclusions. He added some of the Jakarta findings to his analytical database, planning to share the report with his colleagues.

When Anne arrived at her office on Thursday, fresh from a well-earned good night's sleep, she resolved to unlock the clues contained in the Langley photos. Armed with a double Illy espresso, she looked at the photos again and began to compare the six of them one by one. Her initial review disclosed no key to the puzzle at first. But when she looked at the enlarged photo with the highest resolution in the morning light for the second time, she saw four white dots on the railing of the stern of the supertanker. Puzzled by their presence, she immediately called Bud at Langley, whom she knew was working the late night shift.

"Bud, I'm so glad I got hold of you now. The enlarged photos you sent me may prove helpful, but I'm not sure. Take a look at number six and see if you can get a higher pixel count on it for me."

"O.K., I'll try," replied Bud with his Southern drawl. "What you are looking for Anne?"

"I see some strange white marks on the stern's railing. It may only be the gaps in the pixels themselves. But since they don't occur throughout the stern's railing, it may be significant. Of course, it may turn out to be rusted areas on that part of the railing and nothing more."

"I get it," Bud said. "You're also lucky. I can have four higher resolution photos of number six for you within two hours. How's that for service?"

"I owe you, Bud," Anne replied sweetly. "Speak to you soon."

Nigel had scheduled a meeting for the top six in the group at 3:00 p.m. that afternoon to review their tentative findings to date. This meeting would also help them prepare for the conference call with the AIVD a day later. Anne hoped she could report some breakthrough to her colleagues by then.

Anne checked her email about noon. Good old Bud. She now had the four additional photos she wanted. As she studied them closely, she could see that the four white spots on the railing were not from the pixels themselves; these spots did not appear anywhere else. What would make such marks? She had it: grappling hooks or wire rope marks. Her mind raced to the images from The Longest Day, the movie about the Allied invasion of Europe on June 6, 1944. There the soldiers climbed up rocky beach cliffs using grappling hooks. Yes, that could be it. How else could the pirates have climbed over the rear of a vessel measuring 30 feet? She had it. This was what she was looking for.

She raced into Roger's office.

"Roger," she said excitedly. "I think I know what happened to the *Argus*."

"You're kidding, Anne," Roger laughed. He looked at her. "No, I know you too well. You work like a demon. Tell me more."

"I reviewed the satellite photos. When I analyzed them initially, I saw nothing. I asked for additional ones with the highest pixel resolution available. In those, I saw four white marks on the vessel's stern railing. I think they're grappling hook marks. That explains how the pirates boarded the vessel."

"Couldn't they have boarded by any other way, such as by helicopter?" asked Roger. "In that case, those marks may only be rust marks."

"I doubt a helicopter could have been used," Anne replied quickly. "First, an aircraft out at that hour of the night would have attracted too much attention. The air controllers from either Indonesia or Malaysia would have picked up its presence, triggering an alarm. Second, a copter would have been easily heard by the crew of the *Argus* and would have eliminated the element of surprise. Besides, it may have been too difficult to land a copter on the vessel at night if the ship was rolling."

"You may be right. As a matter of fact, I think you are."

"Exactly," said Anne breathlessly.

"Tell the rest of the group about this at our afternoon meeting," said Roger.

When they met, Nigel went around the room asking each person to report on his assigned task of the investigation to date. Timothy started first by reporting on the assessment made by MI6's main headquarters on piracy activity in the Strait. It concluded that joint and individual patrolling by the littoral nations was far from foolproof. After that, Gregory delivered a similar assessment that he received from his Jakarta counterparts.

Anne was next:

"I think the attack took place on August 11, 2006 between 1:00 and 4:15 a.m.," she said. "The satellite photos I received from Langley show four white marks on the vessel's stern railing that, I believe, came from grappling hooks. While I can't be 100% sure about this, there's no other explanation that makes sense."

"Do the photos show any pirate craft nearby?" Roger asked:

"No, they don't," Anne replied. "That remains a mystery and I would like to have your input on that issue."

"When I was in the British armed forces, we used terrific camouflage during some of our operations, but we were never invisible," Clifford exclaimed. "Similarly, none of our naval vessels or planes is invisible."

"Our Stealth bombers are invisible to radar. But they can be seen in a photograph," Roger added.

"Maybe the pirates got hold of that technology used in the Stealth or something similar and applied it to a small fast boat, like one of our torpedo boats," said Tim. "Then what?"

"It's possible," Nigel said. "At a press conference earlier this year Putin announced that the Russians had developed new stealth technology that made their planes impervious to missiles shot at them. If that's true, and we think it may be, then maybe someone applied the same technology to other types of craft as well."

"You think the Russians would have shared their new state secrets with anyone?" Roger asked. "I don't think so."

"I agree with you," said Nigel. "The answer lies elsewhere. Take Pakistan for example. It developed and shared its nuclear technology with Libya, North Korea and probably Iran. We also know their scientists were working on other cutting edge military technologies to offset some of the advantages that India had."

"While Musharraf's fighting the Taliban and other foreign insurgents in the country, some in the ISI still maintain their old connections to the militants and are interested in helping them," said Roger. "They might be helping Al Qaeda."

Nigel turned to Tim and Clifford:

"I want you two to investigate this angle further," he said. "I suggest you contact our chaps in India to see what they can pry out of their military buddies."

"We'll do that immediately," said Tim, glancing at Clifford, who nodded in reply.

"I'll check with Langley," added Roger. "I think we may have a meaningful discussion with our AIVD friends tomorrow."

CHAPTER 18

AIVD'S INDONESIAN INQUIRY

August 31, 2006

Prior to Friday's scheduled videoconference with the CIA/British counterterrorist center in London, the AIVD conducted an additional investigation.

Several days after their meeting in Rotterdam, Hans Kramer of the AIVD telephoned Luks to find out if he had obtained any additional information concerning the *Argus*.

"Luks, this is Hans," he said. "I'm following up on our meeting in Rotterdam. Have you any more information?"

"Yes, I do. We sent an inspection team on board the *Argus*. They inspected the ship from top to bottom and found it in good working order, except for some minor deck damage caused by the typhoon. They also said there were no bombs on the vessel."

"Did any one check the ship's computer or radio to see if any recorded communications were made by the ship's crew after it left Singapore?" asked Hans.

"Yes, we did," replied Luks. "We found that the captain of the ship had sent an email to the port operator in Rotterdam on August 19, 2006 at 3:00 p.m. advising that the vessel had suffered extensive engine damage during a typhoon and was headed toward the nearest port for repairs."

"Did the captain mention the port where the ship was headed?" asked Hans.

"No."

"Since the captain knew where the vessel was located when he sent his email to Rotterdam, he presumably would have known which port he was heading to for repairs." Hans remarked. "Don't you agree?"

"I do," replied Luks.

"So it would appear that he did not want to relate that information to the port operator for one or two reasons – – either he didn't know, which is highly unlikely, or he was not permitted to tell the operator, which, I think, is the case here," Hans continued excitedly.

"I agree with you. The captain was very experienced and knew the routes well. I'm sure he knew what port in the area could repair his vessel. It's clear that the pirates stopped him from doing so."

"Anything else, Luks?"

"We checked with some of the other port operators and shipping agents, but no one knows what happened to the crew of the *Argus*. We simply don't know whether any of them are being held hostage or are dead. But there is one additional point."

"Yes?"

"When my colleague, Theo von Ringen, examined the *Argus* before we handed over the ransom money, he noticed that the bunk areas for the ship's seamen (except the captain's and the mate's quarters) had been scrubbed clean. He also said there were areas of the floors that were lighter in color than others because they seemed to be so heavily scrubbed. Most importantly, he saw bullet holes in the walls of the bunk areas. The inspection team we sent in made the same observations."

"The stains may not be significant," replied Hans. "It could be that the crew decided to do a thorough cleaning of their area. Or possibly someone tried extra hard to remove blood stains from the floor. But the bullet holes are another story. Their presence strongly suggests that a slaughter occurred there."

There was silence on the other end.

"Have you filed your insurance claim yet?" Hans asked.

"No, we're still waiting. We have another 20 days to do that. We want to get the latest update from you before filing because your information may affect the claim."

"Sure. We'll give you an update for your firm's information only," said Hans. "Obviously you can't quote our findings in your claim - other than to say that the facts are based on your information and belief."

"We understand," Luks replied deferentially.

While Hans worked with the ship's agent, Amrit Friesen spoke to Christian Roeter, the chief Dutch intelligence agent in the Dutch Embassy in Jakarta. Since Indonesia was a Dutch colony before it became independent in 1949, the Dutch maintained many old trusted friends and reliable contacts there. Having been Christian's boss in Jakarta for several years, Amrit thought that the embassy might be particularly helpful. He also recalled he had aided the AIVD in Amsterdam when he was in Jakarta. He was sure Christian would help him with his inquiry since it fell within the scope of AIVD's jurisdiction covering international crime or international terrorism and because they were good friends.

At Amrit's urging, Christian dispatched two of his staff to Pangkalansusu and Tanjungbalai, two small towns on the northeastern coast of Sumatra, to meet with two trusted colleagues who lived there. Toon Huyens, a heavy-set, old-timer with many years of experience in Indonesia and other parts of Asia, and Henrika van Dunn, a 35 year old, vivacious and worldly woman recently added to the staff from the Amsterdam headquarters, met with a local businessman, Victor Suriban. A resident of Pangkalansusu (located west of the port city of Belawan) for over 30 years, Suriban was the owner and manager of the largest supplier of nautical and maritime equipment in the area. Bald and sporting a white goatee, Suriban was a hands-on owner, having worked up through the ranks of the business; his heavily calloused hands reflected his years of rigorous work. He had firsthand knowledge of the local yachting and shipping scene in the region, since many ship owners and seamen regularly came into his store for supplies.

The meeting took place in Suriban's second floor office at his store in Kualalangsa to make it appear merely business in nature. After the agents introduced themselves, they took seats at the spare round conference table. Suriban's secretary brought in coffee and biscuits.

"We're here on official business," said Huyens, looking at Suriban directly. "And we were told that since you aided the Dutch Embassy in the past, perhaps you could be of help to us now."

"What is it you want to know?" asked Suriban.

"We have a few questions that might concern several of your customers about equipment you sold or about activities in the area," Huyens responded, leaning forward in his chair.

"Go ahead," asked Suriban. "I'll try to answer them as best as I can."

"Have you any idea what each ship owner or customer does for a living?" asked Huyens.

"Generally, I do. There may be a few new faces that come in from time to time that I know nothing about."

"Regarding your regular customers, those that buy from you and have been buying from your periodically for years, do all of them use their ships for legitimate business purposes?" asked Huyens.

"Yes. Most of my customers are fishermen who work regularly around here. I've been down to the docks and often seen the catch they bagged that day. A few take out tourists or other visitors on full or half day fishing trips. I've eaten with many of these people and count some good friends among them. Occasionally I take a few guys out for a meal, as a way of promoting my business."

"And are these regular customers … local folk?" Huyens probed further.

"Yes, they are."

"Now, how many new customers can you recall doing business with recently?"

"Maybe five or six, sir," Suriban replied easily.

"Are these customers Indonesians or do they come from other countries?" asked van Dunn.

"Sometimes it's hard to tell. I would say most of these new customers are people who moved here from another part of Indonesia," Suriban answered. Pausing for a moment, he added. "Now that I think of it there are two fellows who look like they come from the Middle East. I can't be sure of that."

"What makes you say they might have come from the Middle East?" Huyens asked, sipping his coffee.

"When they were in my store buying a stock of supplies a couple of weeks ago, I overheard them speaking Arabic before they approached the counter. I know it was Arabic because my mother was Egyptian and taught me to speak Arabic when I was a child. Once they were at the counter, they placed the order in the local dialect."

"What supplies did those two order?" Huyens added, sensing an opening.

"It is hard to recall exactly. The usual sorts of things – – several nautical ropes, air mattresses, a few lanterns and some duffel bags."

"Do you know what kind of boat they had?" asked van Dunn.

"No, I don't remember," said Suriban. "It didn't come up in our conversation."

"Do you know where they lived?" continued van Dunn.

"No, they didn't give me a local address," answered Suriban. "They bought their goods and drove off in a car."

"Do you remember what their car looked like?" van Dunn added.

"No, I never saw it."

"Have you heard any gossip about an act of piracy in the Strait that may have been done by someone in this town or this area," Huyens interjected.

"Occasionally I see an article on piracy in one of the Indonesian dailies or pick up news about one on the internet. When that happens, there's generally idle gossip in the bars or cafes about who may have done it. But I never listen too closely. I consider it idle chatter."

"No names, no particular individuals, no groups?" Huyens pursued.

"Some names may have been mentioned, but I don't remember any of them," replied Suriban.

"Do you remember when you last heard conversation on this subject?" asked Huyens.

"Yes, I do. It was sometime in the middle of October, 2005. I recall it was my birthday. I was celebrating with a friend when I overheard the people at the table next to mine speaking about the recent hijacking of a yacht."

"Do you remember any of the details about what was said?"

"No I don't. I dismissed it as the work of criminals."

"Is there anything more you can think of that may be of interest to us?" asked van Dunn.

"No, not at the moment," replied Suriban rubbing his chin.

At that point Huyens and van Dunn looked at each other, finished their coffee and rose.

"Thank you for agreeing to see us and for your hospitality," said Huyens. "We may return to discuss a few more items in the future. If so, we'll let you know in time to arrange another meeting."

"That's fine," Suriban replied softly. "I'm glad to help. My father was proud of his service in the Ministry of Interior for the Government. He told me he had enjoyed working with the Dutch Embassy and instructed me to help when I could."

"Thanks again and goodbye," Huyens and van Dunn said in unison.

Upon their return to Jakarta by air, the two Dutch intelligence agents met with their chief at the embassy to report on what they learned from Mr. Suriban. Roeter asked for a written report within the next four hours because the information was urgently needed in the Netherlands. Huyens and van Dunn wasted no time. Three hours later a four page memorandum was ready. Pleased with their work, Roeter immediately sent the report by encrypted email to Friesen in Amsterdam, who received it a day before the scheduled videoconference.

Friesen called Kramer into his office on Friday morning to prepare for their afternoon videoconference. The Dutchmen were delighted that they had developed some specific additional clues to the piracy of the *Argus*, which they would share with the center in London within seven hours.

CHAPTER 19

THE TARGETED INDIVIDUAL

September 1, 2006

Commander Hamad left the Al Qaeda headquarters residence in Karachi at 7:00 a.m. the following day to meet with Awad and Mirza at the safehouses. Standing at the compound's front gate, he surveyed the area before deciding to leave. The street was deserted, except for two teenage boys, dressed in jeans and laden with filled backpacks, obviously en route to their local school. Hamad sensed he was safe. Quickly he walked to his parked car located some 150 meters from the headquarters' gate.

Since traffic was light at this hour, it took no more than 20 minutes to arrive at safehouse # 3, where Captain Johannsen was being held hostage. As a matter of precaution, he parked his Toyota about 100 meters from the entrance. Rapping on the entrance doors twice – – two knocks in tandem – –he uttered the password, "Al Andalus" to the armed guard standing watch near the front door. The password had profound meaning for all of his crew: Al Andalus was the Arab term for Spain when the country was under Moorish control over 900 years ago.

Once inside, the Commander met with Awad. After they hugged each other, Hamad said:

"My brother, I am fortunate to be here. I managed to get through an army roadblock. Then I came within 15 meters of being discovered by a Pakistani Army patrol and witnessed an army attack on a village nearby. I took these risks in order to get briefed for our next mission."

"Commander, you have lucky stars," Awad replied. "Time and time again you come face to face with extreme danger, and walk away safely. I saw this before when I was at your side in Afghanistan."

"It is true, Awad. I must have well-honed survival instincts. Besides, it's not yet my time to seek paradise."

"We all have a lot to do for our cause first," Awad said.

"Exactly," Hamad nodded. "We have a new mission of great importance, which I'll discuss with you when I'm ready. I ask you to serve once again as my faithful lieutenant. I'll need to rely on you in many different ways."

"I'm honored to be at your side, as always," said Awad. "I sense the rest of the crew needs some action. After our adventures on the *Argus*, it is very low key here."

"You will all have your chance soon," Hamad said. "But we must be patient."

"Of course, we're all trained to be patient," Awad lowered his eyes deferentially.

"Tell me, how is our hostage?" Hamad asked.

"He's fine. His spirit is low; I think he senses he soon will be killed. If you look at him, you can see a resigned expression on his face. He now has a beard because he has not shaved since we captured him."

"We shall see what we do with our Norwegian friend," said Hamad slowly as he thought quickly about his options. "He might still be useful to us. Continue to hold him here."

"We'll do so, Commander."

After a thoughtful pause, Hamad continued:

"Is everything under control at safehouse # 4?"

"Yes. Mirza joined me here two days ago. He gave me a report. The first mate, Henriks, is also depressed; he figures he will be killed shortly."

"Have you noticed any one snooping around here?" Hamad asked suddenly.

"No, Commander. I have at least one guard. He constantly keeps watch on all outside activities near the house. He's concealed near the second floor curtained front window. We have seen no one observing us. We have also checked the windows and walls for bugs, and found none."

"Has Mirza told you whether his safehouse has come under any surveillance?" asked Hamad, as he continued his line of questioning.

"Yes, Commander. Mirza confirmed that the crew found no signs of any one taking any special interest in that house."

"Good. We must make sure we're all safe at present. I also don't think it would be prudent to visit the other safehouses now. It would be unwise to see more than one - just in case someone in following me." Awad nodded mutely.

"Come," said Hamad. "Let's get the others."

Hamad then shared some tea and sweet cakes with four of his pirate crew on the floor of the sparsely furnished kitchen on the rear of the first floor. About 30 minutes later, he left the safehouse, returned to his car and drove off to the Al Qaeda headquarters in the northern part of the city.

Inside the headquarters compound later than morning, he went to his room on the second floor to ponder his next move. He knew Mahmoud was working on the financial issues, moving their booty without arousing suspicion and protecting the funds until they had the weapon in their hands. But Hamad was faced with another daunting task: to find a disgruntled Pakistani nuclear scientist whom he could woo with the prospect of undreamed riches.

He remembered the list of names of several scientists that had been given to him by bin Azara's deputies: Mamood Ishan, Rashid Assamalam and Mohamed Shah. Turning on his computer, he did a Google search of each of them. He was curious to see what was posted about the three. Also, he wanted to check on whether there was information that confirmed what he had been told about each of them in his secret meeting with the Chief of Operations' deputies.

He focused on Rashid Assamalam first. He learned that he was a Professor of Nuclear Physics at Qasid-i-Azam University in Islamabad, and had been there for over 20 years. Rashid was educated at Heidelberg University and had received his PhD from the Massachusetts Institute of Technology in 1982. His excellent Western education was instrumental in getting him a departmental appointment at one of Pakistan's best educational centers. After four years, he joined Qasid-i-Azam University. Reading further, Hamad noted that Rashid worked as a consultant to the Pakistani nuclear center at the Wah Cantonment Ordinance Complex, located about 50 kilometers northwest of Islamabad, the same complex where Abdul Qadeer Khan first oversaw the development of Pakistan's embryonic nuclear weapons programs. Now aged 47, Rashid lived with his wife and 15 year old daughter in a private residence in the eastern part of Islamabad.

Al Qaeda's secret briefing, based on first hand contact reports, revealed that Professor Assamalam felt he was substantially underpaid for his consulting work at the nuclear center on current nuclear projects. Thus, the professor appeared to be a potential target. He was both hungry for money and had access to the nuclear center where fissionable materials were used.

Mamood Ishan was Hamad's next focus. Public sources confirmed he was one of five key scientists working at developing an extremely powerful atomic bomb for the Pakistani military, a bomb more dangerous and destructive than any other in the country's arsenal, whether detonated in the air or on the ground. The location of this project was not revealed. However, it was rumored that a secret military project existed in a heavily guarded, isolated compound about a mile away from the main building at the nuclear research center at the Wah Cantonment Ordinance Complex. Mamood had earned his engineering degree in Pakistan and then received a master's degree in advanced nuclear physics in France. Following his return from France, he worked as a nuclear scientist in Pakistan for almost 17 years. He was not married. Several articles reported that he was fond of young, beautiful women and had almost married an attractive French university student, Nicole Renard. He, too, lived in a private residence in the western part of Islamabad.

The secret briefing on Mamood disclosed, again from those close to him, that he was angry at not having been appointed the Chief Scientist on the key atomic bomb project. The position had gone to one of the other five scientists, who was a close friend of the general in charge of President Musharraf's personal security. The briefing went on to reveal that Mamood craved special recognition, some public acknowledgment relating to his superior skills that would ensure the success of these most important nuclear projects. Mamood's lifestyle also required lots of extra money, far greater than the salary he received from Pakistani government for his services. Thus, to the Al Qaeda chiefs, he was an ideal target – – he had access to the most secret military programs of the government, he was both frustrated and angry and he needed lots of money. In addition, Al Qaeda learned that he had been recently appointed as the third staff member of the official Pakistani delegation to the International Atomic Energy Agency ("IAEA") to compensate for his lack of promotion. Since the IAEA was located in Vienna, he often traveled there for meetings. The briefing concluded that he could be contacted abroad, far from the close observation by the Pakistani security staff.

The third potential target was Mohamed Shah. Pakistani published reports revealed that he was one of the generals appointed to oversee the development of Pakistan's atomic weapons program. A long-time friend of former President Mohammed Zia ul-Hag, he rose in the military ranks over a period of 30 years. In the late 1980s, he became actively involved in the country's nuclear weapons programs and was responsible for overseeing the country's uranium enrichment plants - first at Sihala and later at Kahata. After 1984, he oversaw the work at the Ras Koh test site in the Chagai Hills area. This led to his selection as one of the key military figures in charge of the atomic weapons program development undertaken at the Wah Cantonment Ordinance Complex. The general was married, had a son and a daughter, and the family lived near the military barracks at the Ordinance Complex.

During a secret briefing Hamad learned that General Shah was avidly anti-Western and felt great sympathy for Al Qaeda. He felt that the United States had humiliated the Pakistani military by failing to deliver the F-16 Phantom jets long promised to the country. He also believed, as many of his fellow officers did, that Pakistan was being short-changed by President Bush once again - when he agreed to deliver nuclear technology to India, Pakistan's archrival, in March, 2006, without offering anything of equivalent value to Pakistan at the same time. In addition, several of the General's fellow officers also revealed that the General felt a promotion to a higher rank was in order but his request had been left pending for over two years.

Based on this background, Al Qaeda senior deputies believed the General was a good potential target. He had access to key nuclear sites and deeply-seated grievances. He thus might be tempted to help, given the right price.

Hamad now pondered over the choice he now had to make. His thoughts brought him back to 1988, when he was fighting with the mujahideen against the Russians in Zahir Province in eastern Afghanistan. At the time, the Pakistani ISI personnel were aiding the Islamic freedom fighters with weapons, food and training. He and his group, together with one of several ISI group commanders, had to go on a reconnaissance mission against a Russian fortified position. Rumors abounded that some ISI commanders were playing a double-game: aiding the mujahideen on one hand, while secretly helping the Russians for money on the other. Hamad worried that he and his group might be killed in a possible ambush if he selected the wrong ISI group commander to join his unit as an advisor.

Faced with three choices, he opted for the youngest of the three ISI officers. Fortunately, he chose wisely. His group successfully reconnoitered the Russian position and then, with additional men, was able to overrun the position successfully and killed many Russians stationed there. By contrast, another mujahideen outfit chose the oldest of three ISI group commanders and was massacred in an ambush about 50 kilometers to the north. He later learned that the oldest ISI group commander had been recruited by the Russians.

Reflecting on this, Hamad knew he risked a death sentence. If he was arrested by the ISI, he knew would face days of endless torture followed by certain death. If the CIA nabbed him with the ISI, he would, no doubt, be transported to a secret CIA site, in a country where the police commonly used torture to break their prey. He could not make a mistake now.

This ominous threat made his choice clearer. He sensed that recruiting Mamood Ishan made the most sense. Since the man was a bachelor, he could come and go more readily without arousing suspicion from a family member. Moreover, Mamood worked on a day-to-day basis with fissionable materials, while the professor and the general did not. Also, a preliminary meeting with him could be set up outside of Pakistan, away from those charged with security under the Pakistani nuclear weapons project, most likely in Vienna, where Mamood would have much greater freedom of movement.

Hamad knew he had to reflect further on his choice but, at the moment, he felt comfortable with his decision.

Now he began thinking about a likely venue for his first meeting with Mamood. After he learned the list of activities posted on the IAEA site, he saw that a Scientific Forum was to be held at its headquarters in Vienna on September 19 and 20, 2006. The Forum was open to any participant of the 139 member states of the IAEA who wished to attend at its own expense. Following that, the next meeting was slated for October 16 to 20, 2006 in Vienna – – an International Safeguards Symposium on Addressing Verification Changes – – and was open to any participant of a member state. That meeting would also take place at the IAEA headquarters. While Hamad favored an early rendezvous, either of those session dates was acceptable to him. In any case, he reasoned that he needed at least two meetings with Mamood to assess him, and then engage him. The Commander assumed that he personally could get to Vienna from Karachi easily.

The only problem was whether Mamood would be attending either or both of the IAEA events. To find this out, he considered pretending to be a possible attendee of the participants from the IAEA and use a fictitious name to get a list from another country. He would use an internet café in downtown Karachi for this purpose. If that failed, he then would review some of the published materials, including some international nuclear activities trade journals or websites, to obtain a list of the scheduled attendees.

But there might be an easier way, he thought. Perhaps a Pakistani newspaper might yield the information. Searching through an Islamabad daily and a Karachi newspaper that dealt with Pakistan's security needs in general, he was unable to find the data he sought. Suddenly he saw what he needed. An Islamabad newspaper dated September 2, 2006 carried a piece about a prominent scientist scheduled to receive an award from the Khan research center. The article revealed that he would be attending the IAEA Scientific Forum in September, and further, yielded a list of the other names of Pakistani scientists attending. Mamood's name was listed among the scheduled attendees.

Hamad smiled. It was ironical that the computer, a product of the infidel's culture, proved so helpful to him! Now he did not run any risks of uncovering the names of the attendees.

If was now time for the late afternoon prayer. Hamad knelt facing Mecca on the prayer rug in his office. Eyes closed, he lay prostrate as he recited the daily prayer dutifully. He knew he would soon be embarking on a new stage of his mission. He knew that his preparations had to be precise and carefully thought out. He prayed for Allah to guide him.

CHAPTER 20

VIDEOCONFERENCE – LONDON/AMSTERDAM

September 1, 2006

The videoconference room was on the third floor of the center's office in London. It was about six meters wide by eight meters long and featured a brown inlaid rectangular conference table surrounded by 12 burgundy high-backed ergonomic leather chairs. Nigel, Tim and Cliff sat on the long side of the table near the door, while Roger, Gregory and Anne sat opposite them. A Japanese videoconference monitor, measuring 38" X 20", faced them in front of the wall to the rear of the building. The shades were at their usual mid height. The windows were made of one-way glass, so that no one could see into the room.

At 4:00 p.m., the screen came to life. The London group peered at the Dutch intelligence agents, Amrit and Hans, and the Dutch could see the center's six people present.

"Amrit and Hans, it's good to see you chaps," said Nigel.

"Same here," replied Amrit. "This is Hans on my left and I'm Amrit."

"I am Nigel Thornton. Clifford McCarthy and Tim Wentwood are on my immediate right and left. Sitting across from me, from left to right, are Anne Brix, Gregory Markel and Roger Dunleavy."

Amrit nodded.

"Since we last spoke a week ago," he said, "we have developed several leads that I want to share with you. First of all, the Dutch agent for the *Argus*, a Mr. Luks Brinhoff, told us that the captain of the ship had informed the port operator in Rotterdam that a typhoon had severely damaged some of his engines and that he was headed to a port for repairs. Significantly, in his email, he didn't reveal the name of the port, which any captain with over 35 years' experience, would have known. We think he was prevented from revealing his destination by someone on board. This report occurred at 3:00 p.m. on August 19, 2006. Should I go on?"

"Go on, please. Let's have the whole report first," answered Nigel.

"O.K.," Amrit said easily. "Second, you may remember that Mr. Brinhoff went to Karachi to pay the ransom with a colleague - an engineer from the ship's company. The engineer inspected the ship from top to bottom alone at night. During the inspection, he saw many bullet holes on the walls of the crew's quarters – not the captain's and first mate's quarters - and noticed that certain parts of the crew's floor were lighter than the rest of the floor due to heavy scrubbing."

Amrit cleared his throat.

"Third, we learned that two men speaking Arabic, who were relative newcomers to the area of Pangkalansusu, purchased ship supplies from a local trusted businessman in that town in early August, 2006. This data came from our Dutch intelligence staff in

Jakarta who interviewed the businessman, who, by the way, helped our embassy staff in the past."

Amrit moistened his thumb and turned over a sheet of paper:

"Fourth," he said, looking at the camera, "as we told you at our last meeting, one of the persons who helped the pirates collect the ransom money was Egyptian. He is the same man who came on board the jet carrying the Dutch agents at the Cairo airport.

Fifth, regarding the crew, we think that most or all of the ordinary seamen were killed. We don't know what happened to the captain or the first mate of the ship. It's possible they are still alive. The captain's name is Christian Johannsen, a Norwegian, and his first mate is Feliks Henriks, a Dutchman.

That concludes our brief report." Amrit put his papers on the table.

"Now let's hear what you folks have to say."

"Your report is very helpful," Nigel said politely. "If you don't mind we'll discuss it further after we give you our overview." He picked up a sheath of papers from the table.

"First, satellite data given to us by the CIA shows some evidence that the *Argus* may have been boarded from the rear of the ship on the night of August 11, 2006 between 1:00 a.m. and 4:15 a.m. When Anne studied the blown-up high resolution photos closely, she saw two sets of parallel white marks spaced about two meters apart. In her view, these were grappling hook marks on the railing of the stern, the likely entry point. But there is a very puzzling feature here."

"What's that?" asked Hans.

"The satellite photos don't reveal any boat or craft in the immediate vicinity of the *Argus*. And we believe it highly unlikely that they would have used a helicopter for several reasons: (a) the noise would have attracted too much attention, and thereby would have alerted the *Argus*'s crew, and (b) a night-time landing on a rolling tanker would have been very difficult to accomplish."

"We agree with you," said Amrit.

"So we think that the pirates had some way to make their attack boat invisible, using some new technology or a new application of a proven technology," continued Nigel. "Maybe their group gained access to a new application of the technology used on the Stealth bomber, which makes it able to avoid detection by radar, but, in addition, makes the boat invisible both to the human eye and cameras."

"Highly unusual, for sure," quipped Amrit, "but new applications are always coming on line."

"Yes. As I was saying," continued Nigel, "second, we learned from a Jakarta source that piracy attacks in the Strait dropped significantly to 12 incidents in 2005 from 38 reported incidents in 2004. This was due mostly to the tsunami that killed many pirates at Banda Aceh and the increased patrolling by the littoral countries. The catch here is that there are gaps in the patrolling. They don't take place around the clock, or in all of the areas. In short, there is a gap in coverage."

"O.K.," said Amrit, "so where does that lead?"

"Assume that the pirates studied the patrol patterns over a period of months or even a year," Nigel went on smoothly. "Assume further that the group had observers in the ports where the patrolling vessels left. It is certainly possible that, under these circumstances, a group could have detected an unguarded opening, a gap when joint patrols or individual patrols did not occur. If they had a fast boat that left from a protected area on the Malaysian or Indonesian side of the Strait, they could have intercepted a targeted ship. Remember the Strait is narrow, at some points only 20 miles across."

Amrit grunted: "That's possible."

"A dramatic attack at sea such as this shows, in our view, the footprint of Al Qaeda," Nigel said. "As examples we have the attack on the *USS Cole* in 2000, the attack on the French tanker off Aden in 2002, and the aborted attack on a British ship off Morocco in 2004. All of these major naval or attempted naval attacks were carried out by Al Qaeda. We think they're probably behind it. And that concludes our short report."

He poured out another cup of coffee.

"Now that you have supplied a Middle East connection - the Egyptian I refer to - as part of the ransom scheme, and additionally the fact that two Arabs bought ship supplies in that town in northeastern Sumatra, our conclusion seems probable."

"I would like your group to evaluate our findings and give us some feedback now," Amrit replied.

Roger was the first to speak up.

"Your third point, Amrit, may be the weakest finding. It could be potentially significant, I agree. But, on the other hand, there may be quite a number of Arabic-speaking Middle Eastern folks who live throughout that northeastern coast of Sumatra and who are honest people. We may be jumping to a conclusion here."

"That may be so," replied Amrit. "But I think their presence requires either you or us to make further inquiry."

"The CIA staff at our Jakarta Embassy plans to investigate the northeastern coast of Sumatra between Kualalangsa and Bagansiapippi in the near future," interrupted Gregory. "On the pretext of exploring tourist development and bringing some foreign investment into the country, they may initiate a mission with an Indonesian business development group. By necessity our staff would then have to look at a variety of beachfront and fishing opportunities, beaches, inlets and the like."

"That sounds like a good first step," said Hans. "We can also do something similar with the local businessman in Pangkalansusu or use some other ruse to see what we can learn."

"Amrit, you said there was a possibility that the captain and the first mate of the *Argus* may be alive," Anne said. "At the very least it appears they were not killed in their quarters. But we don't know that they weren't killed with the rest of the crew."

"We agree with you," said Amrit. "We don't really know what happened to them."

"O.K.," Anne continued. "Let us suppose they're alive. If they are and we can find them, we can then talk to them and get some hard information on the pirate group."

"True," said Nigel.

Anne then continued: "If they're alive, they may be held as hostages," Anne looked at the camera. "But where? We think the *Argus* unloaded its oil in Karachi. They may be held hostage in Karachi or elsewhere in Pakistan. We should try to get some of our friends in the Pakistan intelligence service that we consider trustworthy to help us here, either acting jointly with us or by themselves."

"Roger, why don't you have your group follow up with the ISI on that front?" Nigel suggested.

"We'll do that," said Roger, nodding.

"Let's discuss your satellite data," Amrit said. "How accurate are those night-time shots?"

"Very accurate," said Anne confidently. "For years, our satellites have used infrared technology for night-time photography. The photographs have superb high resolution and are reliable. We can usually interpret what we see very clearly."

"What bothers us is the absence of a pirate craft," said Amrit. "What if there was a mutiny on board? What is part of the crew of the *Argus* hijacked the vessel and killed the other crewmembers? Have you explored that possibility?"

"No, we haven't," replied Nigel. "Has AIVD looked into the issue?"

"Yes, we did. Mr. Brinhoff had a copy of the ship's manifest sent to the Singapore port authority. Mr. Brinhoff received a copy of the manifest from the engineering team his office sent to inspect the *Argus*. When we ran it through our database, we found that no crewmember was on any watch list or had engaged in any terrorist activity."

"Please send us a copy of that manifest and our unit will check it as well," said Roger.

"O.K.," said Amrit. "We'll send it to you before we leave the office today."

"That concludes today's session," said Nigel rising. "I think this was very useful. I suggest that we confer by videoconference next Friday. At that point, we can give each other an update on our respective investigations."

"That makes sense," replied Amrit. "Of course, if you need us earlier, just let us know."

"O.K.," said Nigel. "We'll be in touch next Friday or sooner, if necessary."

After the videoconference ended, the group lingered trying to piece together the little information they had. Although they had some good leads, they realized they had no fix on the location of the terrorists or any knowledge regarding the crew: were they being held as hostages? Where? Their somber faces reflected a desperate need for positive information. Moreover, they were completely in the dark regarding motive. How did the terrorists plan to use the ransom and the oil money? But they all agreed on one point: the money spelled trouble. They left knowing that they had to go into action quickly.

CHAPTER 21

INDONESIA

September 6, 2006

Arriving in Jakarta after a long flight from London, Gregory Markel and Tim Wentworth went directly to the Gran Mahakam Jakarta, a four-star hotel in the center of the city. After freshening up, they took a taxi to the Dutch Embassy, eager to start their mission. The embassy was a sturdily built modern four-storey building with an abundant number of windows that provided excellent views of the nearby area. Because of rising Islamic fundamentalism and attacks on Western targets, security was tight. High brick walls provided a partial shield, while armed sentries watched all visitors closely. Once inside the building, they walked over to the receptionist's desk and asked to be announced. An attractive Indonesia secretary, wearing a white blouse and a dark blue skirt, led them into a conference room on the third floor. There they awaited the arrival of their host, Christian Roeter.

Energetic as usual, Roeter entered the room with a smile and greeted his guests warmly. To the Americans, he seemed an unlikely candidate for an intelligence agent. He was pudgy, somewhat disheveled and clearly not in shape. His cheeks were flushed and he needed a haircut. But this initial impression was undercut by the alertness and vitality of his clear, deep blue eyes. And, as they learned later, the Dutchman had been a former wrestling champion at his university in Amsterdam.

After an exchange of pleasantries, Roeter and the two agents helped themselves to the rijstaffel buffet at a side table against the rear wall of the room. Over lunch, Roeter confirmed that a six-day beach and resort development excursion had been set up as part of the Netherland's development cooperation with the Indonesian Government. The aim of the excursion, he explained, was to select one or more coastal sites for hotel and beach development to draw more tourists to the country. The group was to consist of representatives from three Western countries: the United States, England and the Netherlands, joined by three prominent businessmen from Jakarta and two officials from the Department of Industry and Trade. In fact, this outside "development group" was a front for five highly capable intelligence agents, including himself and two of his assistants, Toon Huyens and Henrika van Dunn. The excursion was to start the following day, with a flight to Maden, the country's second largest city and major port.

Pleased with the plan, Gregory and Timothy spent a few hours at the embassy digesting the materials Roeter provided to them about tourist spots in Indonesia and the current economic affairs of the country. Using Roeter as their sounding board and critic, they presented their respective developmental ideas to him. After reviewing the potential viability of the proposals, Roeter was delighted with his guests' knowledge. It was evident that they had done their homework before coming to Jakarta. Satisfied that their knowledge and interest would provide an excellent cover, Gregory and Timothy proceeded with the true purpose of their mission: to locate a base the pirates may have used when they hijacked the *Argus*.

Early the next morning, the group of 10 traveled to Maden on a Bombardier jet chartered for the occasion. They landed on a cloudy day in the port city. On the tarmac, a waiting van took the group to the port of Belawan about 25 kilometers away, where a 35 meter gleaming white yacht owned by one of the Indonesian businessmen in the group awaited them. The yacht's six rooms provided ample space for the group. A crew of four was available to cater to all their needs. A small pontoon boat that could sit eight people was at their disposal to ferry members of the group to various on-shore sites for closer inspection.

In his capacity as leader of the Western development group, Roeter, dressed entirely in white, suggested that they travel up the coast of Sumatra in a northwesterly direction first to Langsa, about 150 kilometers northwest of Medan, and then down the coast as far as Bagansiapiapi on the Strait of Malacca. After debating the merits of the route, the group approved Roeter's proposal. The locals did not realize that this route had been chosen by the London counterterrorist center in conjunction with AIVD as the most comprehensive for uncovering the site of a pirates' base, given speculation as to the possible point of interception of the *Argus*.

Given his orders, the captain steered the yacht up the Sumatra coast towards Langsa, at a leisurely pace, which he figured would take about five to six hours. As they started out in the late afternoon, the group was unable to observe much of the coast in detail. Instead, the focus was on a gourmet seafood dinner provided by the Malaysian chef, who prepared a sumptuous seafood medley blending the local catch of the day with shrimp and octopus. Everybody gathered at the long dining room table and wore colorful patterned shirts and light slacks. Heinekens flowed liberally. There was a general air of bonhomie aboard.

The officials from the Department of Industry and Trade were at home in this environment, having been previously entertained lavishly by many businessmen. The Western development group waxed enthusiastic over the outing, as they engaged in light repartee, displaying detailed knowledge of recent developmental activities on the island. Four hours later, after several rounds of mixed tropical drinks and a satisfying meal, the group disbanded jovially as they returned to their designated rooms to await the following morning activities.

The new day brought abundant sunshine and a cloudless blue sky. Swells of two to three feet from the Strait gently rocked the vessel. At 8:00 a.m., a lavish breakfast was served. Everyone carried their plates deck side to observe the nearby shore from at sea.

Shortly thereafter, the Western group and two Indonesian businessmen took the pontoon boat to get a closer view along the shoreline outside of Kualalangsa, a small village. Roeter directed the first mate to steer the boat from northwest to southeast about 50 meters off the coast so that they could see the various coves and inlets that lined the area. As they did so, Tim and Gregory, apparently looking for a first rate hotel and beach site, used their high powered binoculars to observe the shoreline closely. This exercise continued for five hours, as the boat meandered in and out of many places along the jagged coastline. On at least three occasions, various members of the Western group landed on shore ostensibly to check the condition of the soil, the nature of the terrain, the thickness of the surrounding vegetation or the forested areas and access to a nearby village or city. Huyens went with Van Dunn once; Roeter joined Gregory and Tim twice. Planning to follow this agenda twice a day, the group assumed they could cover the entire area targeted in their initial plan.

The yacht shadowed the small runabout at a distance of about two kilometers in a parallel path. Once the morning's foray was over, the group returned to the nearby yacht for a welcome lunch break. In the afternoon, the same group of seven resumed their search. By the end of the first day, they had covered an area of over 85 kilometers.

They found no telltale signs of a pirates' lair that first day. On a cove near Pangkalansusu, Gregory and Tim saw what appeared to be a path of tire tracks in a wooded area near a sandy beach, but found no pier or dock. They assumed that the area was probably just used by some local fishermen. Had they traveled another 50 meters further up the shoreline they might have discovered several huge clumps of bushes atop a mound over an inlet that camouflaged two metal gates hidden beneath them. These gates concealed the cave opening where the pirates' all black patrol boat was hidden. But the lair remained undiscovered.

Lively discussion ensued over dinner that night. The group decided to attempt to rank the top three potential development sites from the scenarios they had witnessed firsthand during the day. Gregory and Tim agreed to act as the excursion's scribes, faithfully recording the group's ultimate views on the day's prospects and the varied reasons for site-selection. Once the get-together dissolved, the agents continued their own private discussion, comparing mental notes from the day's reconnaissance.

Blessed with excellent balmy weather, the group wound their way along the coastline down to the outskirts of Belawan the following day. Keeping to the same routine, the pontoon boat with its group of seven, including a governmental official, two businessmen and four from the Western group, meandered in and out of inlets and coves. The group walked along several possible beachfronts and observed miles of shoreline. Over the dinner that night, they again led a lengthy discussion over which sites presented the most promising tourist attractions. Satisfied with their choices, the dinner meeting concluded. Once more, the agents held their own caucus, concluding that they had developed no leads that day.

Awakening to a heavy thunderstorm the following morning, the participants faced a dismal day. Owing to the rain, some decided to forgo their on-shore reconnaissance and fish or relax instead. As a result, only five took the runabout: the same four from the Western group and one businessman. To the agents, this leg of the excursion was most opportune, since they guessed it was the second closest point of the interception of the *Argus*. Once on shore, they took painstaking care in observing the coves and inlets, searching for a hidden cave or camouflaged dock. In some cases, Huyens and van Dunn traveled about 300 meters up two inlets on different parts of the shoreline, but again found no sign of any hidden boat slip. The businessman with the group took note of the great curiosity displayed by the two Dutch representatives, but dismissed it as mere enthusiasm for the task.

The next two days produced similar results, as the yacht traversed the area between Tanjungbalai and its final destination: the small town of Bagansiapiapi, located in the delta of the Rokan River, some 300 kilometers from their starting point of Belawan. While the shoreline differed from place to place, there were a few outstanding beach resort prospects and the onshore reconnaissance again failed to reveal any pirates' boat site.

On their return trip to Belawan, the development group reduced some 15 top tourist prospects to eight. While the rest of the group relaxed, and smoked excellent local cigars, Gregory and Tim went off to compile a written summary of the advantages and disadvantages of the top prospects. They gave a copy of their memorandum to each member of the group.

Once aboard the chartered jet at Medan, the governmental officials invited everyone to attend a conference dinner they would host three days after returning to Jakarta. All enthusiastically agreed to attend.

Outwardly, the excursion was a success. The officials from the Department of Industry and Trade were ebullient about possible development projects, envisioning an increased flow of tourists and needed revenues for the country's economy and, perhaps, a little gift or two. The three local businessmen were delighted by the opportunity of becoming partners with Western developers. The Westerners, although outwardly pleased with the profitable opportunities potentially available to them, were inwardly upset since they were unable to find the location of the pirates' secret base.

The morning following their return to Jakarta, Gregory and Tim went to the Dutch Embassy where they attended a joint videoconference with their center in London and the AIVD office in Amsterdam. Nigel, Anne, Roger and Clifford participated from London, while Amrit and Hans were on hand from Amsterdam.

"Hello to all of you," said Nigel, opening the discussion. "I think most of us know each other, except for you chaps in Jakarta."

"Nice to meet you," said Roeter amiably. "I'm Christian Roeter. This is Toon Huyens on my right and Henrika van Dunn is on my left. As you know, we got to know two of your group already."

"Hello, Toon and Henrika. It's good to have you helping us," replied Nigel breezily. "Let me introduce Anne Brix and Clifford Roberts on my right and left, respectively."

Everyone smiled and nodded.

"Well," Nigel resumed. "What did you find on your excursion? Anything useful?"

"We searched well over 300 kilometers of the Sumatra coastline from Langsa down to Bagansiapiapi and found no pirates' base or boat," Roeter replied, taking the lead. "We obviously couldn't do an in-depth 10-meter-by-10-meter-search without blowing our cover."

"There are a few additional areas we may want to revisit," added Gregory, rising from his seat to go to a map on the wall behind him.

"From what I heard to date," he continued, "we really don't know the exact point where the hijacking took place."

"That's true, Greg," said Anne. "The satellite photos taken at 4:00 a.m. on August 10, 2006 revealed that the boarding had taken place by that time, which was when we first saw those telltale white marks on the rear railing of the supertanker."

"We estimate that the tanker was probably moving at about 20 knots an hour and left its Singapore naval escort about 125 kilometers from Singapore," continued Gregory. "It's about 600 kilometers from Singapore to a point about 60 to 80 kilometers from Belawan, the port north of the major city of Medan. Depending on the speed of the boat used by the pirates, they could have left from any place within at least 100 to 150 kilometers of that possible interception point."

"The satellite photos gave us the exact coordinates of the tanker's location when the shot was taken," Anne interrupted. "It was 99.52 degrees latitude and 4.5 degrees longitude."

"But that doesn't tell us the exact time the hijacking occurred and *where* it occurred," Gregory continued. "And we still don't know whether they came from the Thai, Malaysian or Indonesian coast. We all assume -maybe rightly or wrongly - that they probably came from the Indonesian side because that coast has more remote areas and may have been less vigorously patrolled."

"We're definitely going to have some private discussions with our Malaysian and Thai Embassy personnel to see what they might be able to develop," said Nigel.

"That makes sense," said Tim. "It's also clear that we have lots more digging to do here in Indonesia as well."

"Any hunches you have, Christian, that you have not shared with us?" asked Amrit hopefully.

"I've been in Indonesia for many years so I have a feel for the landscape here," Christian answered. "Typically the Indonesian Navy patrolled more heavily between Banda Aceh and Lhokseumawe up on the far northern coast of Sumatra - because of the heavy pirate presence in and around Banda Aceh before the tsunami hit. It also patrolled more regularly near the narrow points of the Strait between Meskum and Tanjungbalai. I recall that they patrolled less vigorously where the Strait broadened, figuring that most pirates didn't have a craft capable of hijacking a vessel some 60 to 70 kilometers offshore."

"Go on," said Amrit.

"If that's true, and the pirates knew of those patrol patterns, which I assume they did, they may have picked their target destination at a wider point of the Strait, far north of Medan and northeast of Langsa. I may have had different thoughts earlier, but, upon reflection, that scenario seems to make the most sense logically."

After pausing to take a sip of water, Christian continued:

"Also, the pirates may have assumed they were less likely to run into a naval patrol from a neighboring country that far offshore."

"Good observation," said Amrit.

"Given the information developed to date, I think we ought to speak to our friends in the Indonesian, Malaysian and Thai navies to find out if any patrol ran into the tanker and to learn what they know of piracy activities in the possible jump-off points from their respective countries," said Roger, all-business.

"I second that," Nigel nodded in agreement.

"Christian, I want you and your colleagues to continue your investigation on that northeastern coast of Sumatra," Amrit said decisively.

"O.K.," Roeter replied.

Nigel raised his hand:

"I want you, Gregory and Tim, to stay in Indonesia while the investigation continues," he said. "The rest of our team will continue working on the probe from here and through our personnel on the staff of our embassies in Malaysia, Thailand and Singapore."

After the videoconference ended, everyone went separate ways, eager to unearth a tangible lead. The agents realized that time was not on their side: they did not know where the pirates were at present or what their plans were. Facing this worrisome threat, the agents were fully aware that they had to make some progress very soon. In some quarters, an unspoken skepticism lay beneath the surface.

As the investigation unfolded along separate paths over the ensuing months of October, November and December, little emerged of a helpful nature. According to British sources, a Thai naval patrol checked on the status of the *Argus* on August 10, 2006, and the Captain of the tanker advised that all was fine on board. The Indonesian Navy reported that there were no piracy activities in the area from Langsa down to Bagansiapiapi. The on-the-ground investigation led by the intelligence contingent operating out of Jakarta produced no further leads. Although they conducted a comprehensive investigation of the shoreline from Langsa to the area around Tanjungbalai, they found no pirate base or dock. By the end of 2006, much to their consternation, the London counterterrorist center and the AIVD were still in the dark regarding the pirates' whereabouts and their intentions.

CHAPTER 22

STALKING OF THE PREY BUDAPEST/VIENNA

September 18, 2006

As the non-stop flight to Budapest took off from the Karachi International Airport, Commander Hamad relaxed in his coach seat. He looked like some of the other Pakistani businessmen on board. He wore a light gray business suit and a blue Oxford shirt. He had put his highly patterned tie in his small black carryon bag. As he settled back in his seat for the eight hour flight, he pulled out several Eastern Europe business magazines and began to read them. He felt safe in his businessman's cover; no one knew he was en route to Vienna to recruit a Pakistani scientist. When he requested a bottle of water from one of the Hungarian stewardesses, a 5'6" dark-haired beauty with penetrating blue eyes, she eagerly responded to his request and gently brushed her hip against his arm when she returned with his order and smiled warmly.

Her look reminded him of a young French woman he had loved in Beirut in a bygone era, in his days as a "fauve," a wild beast.

After Hamad had finished his university studies and obtained a degree in electrical engineering from a Lebanese university, he tried for over a year to land a job with one of the major Western engineering firms doing business in Lebanon. Repeatedly he dutifully showed up for an interview. Each time he was told there were no openings. He felt his talent, for which, he worked so arduously, was being wasted. During this period, he grew increasingly depressed and restless. Often, he could be found seated outside a small pizzeria shop talking to his friends.

Unemployed and with bleak prospects, he turned to the capital's nightclubs on Beirut's boulevards and in its backstreets, wandering from one to another. He was also a favorite of some of the local prostitutes. His life was clearly in a downward spiral.

Then, one night, at one of his favorite nightclub waterholes, the El Alcala, he saw a 20ish, dark-haired curvaceous beauty dancing with abandon with a group of her girlfriends and one Lebanese fellow. Hamad immediately crossed the smoke-filled dancing area to where she was dancing and joined in, although he certainly did not know the Western dance beat or her dance steps. It did not matter to him that he might appear a bit clumsy dancing. It was more important, he felt, to show that he had an interest in joining them, and, in particular, her.

This beautiful woman, with enchanting green eyes was Nathalie Ferrer, who came to work in the main headquarters of a Lebanese bank, as part of a French university exchange program. A daughter of a well-to-do French lawyer, Nathalie was both smart and adventuresome. She had been pursing governmental studies at the Sorbonne, but wanted to experience a more exotic environment. She decided to become an exchange student during the last semester of her senior year – – and landed a job in the foreign exchange department of the bank in Beirut. She thrived in Lebanon's exotic cosmopolitan ways and decided to stay there after her exchange status ended. She continued to work for the bank.

She enjoyed Hamad's company immensely. She was the first woman who was both a soul mate and a passionate lover. Often they would lie on the queen-size bed in her apartment near the beach and look at the moon's reflection on the Mediterranean – – and talk of their dreams. Their relationship lasted for almost a year and a half.

Then, unexpectedly, she learned that she was being transferred to the bank's branch in Paris for at least a two-year period, an opportunity, she felt, she could not pass by. Hamad took the news badly and felt that she betrayed their love. She tried to reason with him that such was not the case, but her words were ignored. He left abruptly and did not speak with her for the next two weeks. She finally reached him on the day of her departure to Paris. She asked him to forgive her, but he was unwilling to do so and continued to feel slighted. She said she would return to Beirut once again, but he told her he doubted that.

He immediately began to drift into a depressed state. He again sought work, but could not get a job of interest to him because of an economic downturn in the country. He began to drink again.

Then, as Hamad gazed at the beautiful sunset through the plane's window, his thoughts drifted to the time he was recruited in Lebanon for "jihad."

He had been downcast from being jilted by his lover and unable to find acceptable work. One day a Syrian imam came into a café on a street adjacent to one of Beirut's principal promenades and sat at a table next to where Hamad was eating. The imam started a conversation and soon the two were engaged in a serious discussion of Syria's role in Lebanon and the need to spread the Islamic religion. The imam sensed that Hamad was seeking an outlet for his frustrations and casually asked whether he might have an interest in fighting against those who threatened Islam. They spoke intensely that day and agreed to meet again for lunch the next day. After they spoke further, the imam invited Hamad to join him that evening for dinner with a warrior who returned from fighting the Russians in Afghanistan. That night Hamad heard detailed accounts of the heroic fight the mujahideen were waging against the Russians, the godless infidels who had destroyed an Islamic nation. Hamad was receptive to their stories. He became enthralled by the vision that his talents might now be recognized – – and, without much reflection, he gladly agreed to go to Pakistan for training before going into battle in Afghanistan. Hamad believed that, in a way, he might be able to purify himself after his years of debauchery and drifting. Doing jihad provided a potential rebirth, a new beginning for him.

Hamad's thoughts now returned to the present. The smooth flight relaxed him. He now began to focus on his current recruitment mission.

He decided it was best to travel first to Budapest by air and then by an hour-and-a-half train ride to Vienna. He had received first hand reports that the airport security in

Vienna was far tighter than that in Budapest, in part because of the presence of several major international organizations in Vienna – – the IAEA, the European headquarters of the Organization of Petroleum Exporting Countries ("OPEC"), the headquarters of the Organization of Security and Cooperation in Europe ("OSCE") and certain agencies of the United Nations. He felt he would face less potential scrutiny by traveling via Budapest.

After the plane landed on time, Hamad cleared customs easily without any questioning and boarded the train for Vienna at Nyugati Station in Budapest. When the train crossed the Austrian border, the Austrian border guards came on board and checked Hamad's passport and stamped it, and did the same for the other passengers. He arrived at the main railroad station in Vienna, Wein Westbahnbof, at about midnight, a bit weary in body but buoyant in spirit.

He had previously booked a room at a four- star hotel, the Hotel-Pension Arenberg, located on Stubening near the city center. As an important Pakistani businessman, he had to stay at a first-class establishment. When he arrived by taxi, he went to the front desk to check in and then went to his room. Again, his false Pakistani passport, showing his name as Hamad el Abim, passed the test. The hotel registration clerk raised no questions about it when he showed it to her.

Hamad realized the Scientific Forum sponsored by the IAEA started tomorrow. He reviewed his plan of action for the next three days and felt optimistic that his recruitment effort would succeed. Yet he still harbored some nagging doubts that the scientist might not cooperate.

He slept well and woke up at about 6:00 a.m. Today he hoped would be rendezvous day. He had photographs of the IAEA headquarters provided to him by his cohorts and had studied the IAEA website. He had also studied the photographs of Mamood Ishan closely. He was about Hamad's age, 40. He was about 5'8," had curly dark brown hair and dark brown eyes with very bushy eyebrows, was a bit overweight, and typically dressed in conservative dark blue business suits when he attended important meetings or conferences. He also had a small scar above his left eye. He also knew that Mamood spoke Pashtu, Arabic and English. Since his mother was English, he learned the language from her before she died when Mamood was 10 years old. He also knew that Mamood was one of three Pakistani delegates to attend the Scientific Forum. He realized the presence of the other Pakistanis could prevent his talking to Mamood alone, but he hoped he could overcome that potential obstacle.

Since the Forum was slated to start at 9:00 a.m., he reconnoitered the area around the IAEA headquarters at Wagrammer Strasse 5 beforehand. He then had to station himself nearby so that he would be in a position to identify Mamood as he entered the grounds. As he drove towards the IAEA building, he passed many stolid and solid historic structures set back from the tree-lined streets, a testament to the lingering grandeur of the bygone Hapsburg dynasty.

The attendees soon began to arrive. Some came by hotel shuttle bus or limousine. Others arrived by taxi. Still others came in their own or rental cars. Hamad initially walked by the main entrance as if he were on his morning constitutional. This pretense enabled him to go to the end of the long block and return on the other side of the street in the same direction he first started. On the return, he stopped behind a large oak tree, took out his pair of small Japanese binoculars and carefully observed the attendees as they arrived. Finally, after 75 attendees had passed through the main entrance gate, he found his prey: Mamood entered the compound, together with two other men who, Hamad presumed, were the other two Pakistani delegates.

From his earlier reconnaissance of the headquarters compound, Hamad knew that there was only one entrance. Thus, he could watch the attendees as they left. He also had learned that the Forum would end the day's session at 5:30 p.m. and that there would be an evening cocktail reception sponsored by the IAEA for the participants from 5:45 p.m. to 7:15 p.m. He decided to leave the area and return around 4:30 p.m., an hour before the Forum's first day session ended.

When he returned at 4:30 p.m. precisely, he parked about 200 meters from the entrance, around the corner from Wagrammer Strasse. Traffic in the area was light. He pretended that his car had overheated, and he raised the hood and added some water to the radiator. This gave him an excuse to remain there for a several hour period without attracting too much attention. He kept his binoculars by his side and waited. The time passed slowly. A beautiful sunset, with the sun as a bright orange orb, appeared at about 7:20 p.m. But there still was enough light for observation.

The vigil soon bore fruit. Mamood and the two other men with him emerged from the entrance at about 7:40 p.m. and immediately went into a radio-dispatched taxi. As the taxi pulled away, Hamad slammed the hood of his car closed, hopped into the idling car and began to follow the taxi at a distance of about 200 meters. Hamad soon realized he had to keep much closer so as not to lose his prey.

Slowly, the gap closed. As the taxi turned on Parkring, Hamad was about 40 meters behind the taxi, although there was a car between the taxi and him. As the taxi passed the OPEC headquarters building, the car in front of Hamad turned off and Hamad closed to within 30 meters.

The drive to the Donauzentrum Hotel where the Pakistanis were staying took about 15 minutes. Hamad left his car with the hotel valet and followed the three Pakistanis at a distance of about 20 meters. He hoped they would head to the hotel's main dining room - and they did. The 12 foot ceiling, copies of old master original paintings adoring the walls and the thick Persian rugs covering the floor gave the room a nineteenth century old world feel. He dined across the room from where Mamood and the Pakistanis were and planned to finish before they did. Since he had not eaten much during the day, his chicken paprikash with steamed vegetables and rice tasted scrumptious. The two strong Illy espressos he then imbibed helped to heighten his senses.

When he finished, he left the dining room and waited, a bit impatiently, in an easy chair in the hotel lobby, which gave him a clear view of anybody leaving that room.

Shortly thereafter, the three Pakistanis left the dining room. Hamad immediately approached the group and accidentally bumped into Mamood and knocked his papers down.

"I am so sorry I ran into you," said Hamad in English. "That was very clumsy of me. May I make it up to you? I invite you all for a coffee or tea in the bar or at a nearby interesting café I know."

Mamood looked at his two fellow delegates and said: "That sounds like a good idea. I will accept. What about you two?"

"No, Mamood," said one of the older attendees, Ismael Raeed. "We'll go upstairs. It has been a long day. We have had enough activity for one day. But we thank you, sir, for your invitation.

"I'm sorry you won't join us. By the way, I'm Hamad el Abim," said Hamad.

"Nice to have met you, Mr. el Abim," said Ismael.

When the two other attendees left, Hamad said to Mamood:

"What shall it be, the hotel bar or a nearby café or watering hole?"

Hamad sensed what the answer would be. Mamood quickly replied:

"A local watering hole sounds more exciting to me. Let's go there."

"All right, but remember you are my guest."

"O.K.," said Mamood. "I didn't yet introduce myself. I'm Mamood Ishan and I come from near Islamabad. Where are you from?"

"I'm from Karachi," replied Hamad. "And I know how to have some fun."

The two left the hotel in a taxi and arrived 10 minutes later at an attractive dimly-lit café that catered to foreigners, the Steubenmeister. About half of the café's 30 tables were filled. A violinist played a Hungarian gypsy song. The waitress stood nearby ready to serve their customers from the dessert carts overflowing with mouth-watering strudels, chocolate cakes and fruit tarts. Mamood and Hamad each ordered a cappuccino with a piece of apple strudel.

Mamood spoke first.

"Why are you in town, Hamad?"

"I'm here to market our spice products to the Austrian market," Hamad said in a relaxed tone. I have a list of key potential customers. Of course, if I can land an order with Julius Meinl am Graben, that renowned Vienna six-storey gourmet food store, I'll be absolutely delighted. And how about you? What brings you all the way to Vienna?"

"I certainly am not in your field. I'm attending the Scientific Forum sponsored by the IAEA on behalf of our country," said Mamood.

"It sounds like a nuclear energy roundtable discussion," replied Hamad.

"Yes, that's the subject, of course. There are about 80 participants from about 30 countries. We have three from our country, including myself."

"How long will you stay in Vienna?" asked Hamad.

"I'm planning to leave on September 22nd, the second day after the Forum ends," replied Mamood.

"I'm not sure how long I'll stay," said Hamad. "It depends how my marketing works out. If I make a few sales, which I expect to do, I will probably stay a few extra days. I'm not married so that I don't have to rush home to my family."

"The same with me," replied Mamood. "I like to chase women, and love them, but I don't wish to get married at present. Maybe, someday, I'll change my mind."

"Why do you think that may happen," asked Hamad.

"For years, I worked extremely hard and long hours to rise to the top of my department. Then, after all my big efforts, my center promoted another of my fellow scientists to the top job of Chief Scientist of Nuclear Projects."

"When did this happen?" asked Hamad.

"About one month ago," replied Mamood. "The center has tried to keep me happy. They raised my salary. They asked me to represent the nuclear center at this Forum now and at the International Safeguards Symposium scheduled in Vienna toward mid-October."

"Did those steps satisfy you, Mamood?"

"No," said Mamood in an angry tone. "I feel like I was stabbed in the back. I have been working as a nuclear scientist for over 17 years – – and, I might add, on some very important but hush-hush projects. I have great credentials and technical knowledge. I feel like leaving, but I don't know where I would go at present. And that explains why I may be willing to settle down."

"I'm not interested in settling down yet. I think I will try to build up my business, and then once I reach a certain goal I have in mind, I may be able to relax a little more."

Hamad then excused himself and went to the bathroom. He had felt Mamood's honest anger and thought he could test it further.

When he returned, he said to Mamood: "You mentioned you are a nuclear scientist. Do you mind if I ask you a question or two in that area? I won't be offended if you say no."

"It's okay," replied Mamood. "Go ahead."

"I imagine you have a strong opinion on President Bush's agreeing to provide advanced nuclear technology to India while not giving us any similar help."

Mamood replied heatedly: "I do. I thought his helping our arch enemy under these circumstances was a grave mistake. I surely hate what he did. Do you agree, Hamad?"

Hamad echoed Mamood's annoyance. "Yes, I do. I think the United States made a terrible mistake. Its action humiliates and makes us appear in the eyes of the world as untrustworthy and not reliable."

"What you say, Hamad, is true. We spent a lot of time at the nuclear center analyzing the apparent terms of the United States-Indian nuclear agreement. We surely see a major increased threat to our national security from this action. This development will cause us, I think, to speed up the timetable for our development of certain weapons we're now working on."

"I agree with you about the increased threat India will pose to us," Hamad replied. "There is probably no way to prevent some of the transferred technology from being used by India for military purposes in a secret way."

Mamood replied: "We could have a long discussion on this issue, but not tonight. I have to be at the Forum tomorrow again at 9:00 a.m. and have to get up early. If you are free tomorrow night, would you like to get together?

Hamad then said: "I'm available and would be delighted to join you again tomorrow night. Let's meet at your hotel after dinner, say, at 9:30 p.m."

"We're on," replied Mamood. "I'll meet you in the lobby then."

They then left the café and hailed a taxi. The taxi stopped first at Mamood's hotel and Mamood got out. "See you tomorrow night at 9:30 p.m. Thanks again for tonight."

"I'm glad we met," said Hamad. "I'll see you then."

Hamad then returned to his hotel. He was delighted with his initial encounter with Mamood. He was still far from sure whether he could persuade Mamood to agree to the Al Qaeda plan. Be patient, he thought. Today was the first step, tomorrow the next step and then we shall see.

CHAPTER 23

SECOND MEETING – VIENNA

September 20, 2006

While Mamood attended the Scientific Forum session on its second and last day, Hamad spent the day reconnoitering several nightclub bars for that night with Mamood. Dressed in jeans and a gray sweatshirt, he wandered through several of the seedier parts of Vienna. These areas seemed relatively tame during the noon hour. He knew, from his prior experience in Beirut, that the same areas would come alive at night, a beacon for the wayward and those seeking the company of accessible women, some for having and others for mere flirtations.

When night came, Hamad dressed for the evening. His tan and beige hounds tooth sports jacket showed well against his light brown tan slacks. He arrived promptly at Mamood's hotel at 9:30 p.m. and was glad to see that his guest was already waiting for him in the hotel's lobby, possibly eager for a change of scene.

Hamad spoke first: "How was your session today?"

Mamood replied: "Very interesting. We discussed several nuclear topics in depth. I could tell that many of my foreign colleagues were extremely well informed and knowledgeable.

Hamad looked at Mamood's face closely and sensed an openness to a change of pace from his day's activities. Hamad initially concealed his plan for the evening, as a resting jackal with one eye open surveys a gazelle drinking water in a carefree manner nearby. He then asked Mamood: "Where would you like to go tonight?"

"I'm new to this city," replied Mamood. "What do you have in mind?"

"I assume you have already eaten. Am I right?" said Hamad.

"Yes, I again ate with my two fellow scientists," replied Mamood.

Seizing the opportunity he hoped to have, Hamad then replied: "Let's have some fun. I know several of the nightclubs in town where we would be most welcome."

"That sounds fine to me," said Mamood excitedly.

They then took a taxi and drove to what the natives considered a more sinful part of their town. The taxi driver knew the route to this area well, as if he had made this trip many times before with many out-of-town arrivals.

Hamad barely recognized some of the same streets he had sauntered through only hours ago. Tame during the day, the area projected a more sinister feel at night. The overhead lights, now about 25 years old, provided dim lighting for the streets, and comfort for those who did not want to be highly visible. From what Hamad remembered, there were quiet back alleys that provided a discreet alternative exit from some of the entertainment spots. The flashing neon signs, which came to life at night, proudly announced the names of the various establishments. The Bieremeister and Der Schwartze

Katze, each beckoned men to come in for a good time. The well-dressed burly bouncers out front served as a warning for the unruly.

Hamad suggested to Mamood that they go to Der Schwartze Katze, because he had heard it had many attractive young women, and Mamood promptly agreed. Hamad sensed this would be the case, based on the intelligence he had been given about Mamood's playboy bent. When they entered the nightclub, a vivacious well-endowed tall blonde led them to a table along the left side of the smoke-filled room where they would have a good view of the stage, 10 meters in length. There three beautiful, curvaceous dancers undulated to the throbbing beat of American rhythm and blues music and then wrapped their legs around three meter high dancing poles in provocative poses.

Mamood spoke first in an excited tone: "I've not been to one of these clubs in over a year. You certainly won't find them in our country."

"I've been to several of them in the past, too" replied Hamad. At that point, his thoughts flashed to a much earlier time and place, to some of the seedy smoke-filled clubs of Beirut when he was restless, depressed and searching for an outlet for his pent-up energies.

"While I observe our Islamic ban against drinking almost always," continued Mamood, "I like to have a drink or two when I'm in this type of club abroad."

"I'm like you," stated Hamad. "I'm strict at home, but looser when I am out of the country."

At that point, a leggy 5'8" dark-haired waitress dressed in short shorts and a low-cut red bra approached the men: "Welkommen, what are you drinking?"

Mamood instantly replied: "A Grey goose martini." Hamad took note quietly of his companion's sophisticated taste.

"An excellent choice, mein Herr. And you?" said the waitress now turning to Hamad.

"I'll have a vodka tonic with Stolichnaya," Hamad replied nonchalantly.

"Excellent." And the waitress left.

Mamood's eyes wandered over the action in the club and glistened. He exclaimed to Hamad. "Look at all of these beautiful women."

At that point, a sturdily built 5'6" green-eyed blond, wearing a black tank top and matching bikini bottom, confidently approached their table.

"Mein Herren, I'll be glad to dance for you, O.K.?"

Both men smiled broadly and said, "Yes, go do it."

The music had now switched to the Rolling Stones' "Jumping Jack Flash." Inge began to move in rhythm with the music, extending her arms up and down. She first sidled up next to Hamad, approached him with her well-exercised rear, and gyrated up and down in front of him. She made sure to brush his legs and gently sat in his lap for a second or two while turning her face toward him over her shoulder and giving him a wide smile. Inge knew she was a good dancer and could turn on most of the men she danced for, and with good reason. She had a gorgeous face, a young athletic body, strong legs and beckoning curves all over, and, in addition, although often concealed, she was smart. She could feel Hamad's right hand lightly graze her right buttock as she moved upwards and then felt him put several euro notes in the top of her bikini bottom.

When that song ended, she looked at them and said: "Another dance?"

Mamood said: "Absolutely."

Another Rolling Stones' hit, "Satisfaction", began to pulse throughout the club. Inge now approached Mamood frontally. As she swayed to the throbbing beat, she leaned over him with her ample, firm chest and placed her breasts about a few centimeters from his nose. Her Guerlain fragrance, L' Instant, wafted into Mamood's nostrils, and he began to sweat slightly. She then straddled his right leg, moved downward and upward in a rhythm to the beat, and made gentle but steady contact with Mamood's leg. She continued doing this move for almost 30 seconds. She knew when she made this move, her muscular legs excited all the men – and usually led to larger tips, if not an invitation to meet later, for only a drink, or, perhaps more. She knew that if her legs felt good next to his, how easy it was to imagine those strong legs fully wrapped around a watcher's body. As the song was about to end, Mamood slipped many more notes into her bikini bottom and touched her inviting hip at the same time.

They then invited Inge to join them for a drink, and she ordered a glass of champagne, knowing that she would earn even more money from the club's owner as a percentage of drinks her customers ordered while she sat with them. Both men were delighted to have this beautiful woman next to them. The conversation ranged from the women who worked at the club to a comparison of other nightclubs in town. Inge told them pointedly that she had worked as a lap dancer at several other Viennese clubs, but felt that Der Schwartze Katze was the best. The girls, she believed, were best protected here from unruly guys and the owner paid them on time honestly, and did not attempt to cheat them. She also believed that this club attracted a higher class of customers, not just some drunken university students out for a good time or young soldiers from some of the neighboring countries, including from some of their Eastern European neighbors. After another champagne, Inge left and said she had to work some of the other tables as well, but hinted that she might return later.

Mamood was clearly excited by the night's events so far. He certainly did not hide his enthusiasm either. He then turned toward Hamad and said: "I love these bigger Western women. They seem so at ease with their sexiness, which drives me wild."

"I can see you have not done this for a while," replied Hamad. "You are almost like a young kid who came into a candy shop."

"A little like that," said Mamood. "I love their looks, the way they feel, and their scent."

"You clearly like women very much. Don't you?" replied Hamad.

"Yes, I do. But not just one. That's why I don't think I can settle down."

"Is it because you think the next one you may meet could be better than the last one you spent time with?" continued Hamad.

"That's close to the truth," answered Mamood. "I seem to need the high that comes from the freshness of a new scene, a new encounter."

"I think I understand," said Hamad. He was delighted with Mamood's openness to him. He paused and realized that he had to share some insights about himself as well, without showing whether they were truthful or made up for a desired effect. "I'm a little different. If I were serious about settling down, I'd need a soul mate, someone in tune with my innermost self. At the moment, I'm just out for some good fun."

They then ordered another round of drinks. Several other lap dancers displayed their wares eagerly and gyrated for these out-of-towners. One was a Swedish strawberry blonde, a leggy 5'11" beauty, but with an icy look. Another hailed from Frankfurt, Germany, a curvy, green-eyed brunette with killer thighs. A third came from France, a 5'4" tall, brown-haired, brown-eyed 25-year old who was a gymnast. But none of them had the fire of Inge or aroused them as she had.

Before they left, they looked for Inge and saw her finish a dance at a table with four American businessmen. They could not help notice that her bikini was now overflowing with euros, part of her haul for the night. They waited until she came over to them. They said their goodbyes.

Eager to make a good lasting impression, Mamood spoke first: "I hope I can see you again."

Inge replied coyly. "Peut-etre." Then she smiled broadly. "Auf wiedersein, mein Herren."

Their eyes followed her as she moved in a straight line away from them. Inge smiled at her mother's advice: "Always try to make a good last impression on the people you are with." She knew that those two men, especially Mamood, would not forget her sense of style and beauty.

The two men then left the club, immediately found a taxi waiting nearby and returned to Mamood's hotel. Each was initially lost in his thoughts about the evening's activities. Then, after a brief silence, as the taxi barreled along the now quiet streets, Mamood said:

"Hamad, I'll be coming back to Vienna in less than a month. My next meeting starts on October 16th. I think I will be able to fly in a day or two early. Can you meet me again?"

Hamad paused before he replied. It was important, he knew, to conceal his eagerness to meet again. He then added in a matter-of-fact manner:

"I'll arrange my schedule to be able to be here when you are," replied Hamad. "As I told you before, I have scheduled meetings in Frankfurt, Rome and several other cities. I can then come back to Vienna when you are here."

"Excellent. Let's make this firm. I'll see you on October 14th at 7:30 p.m. for dinner. Let's meet in my hotel lobby."

"Sounds great, Mamood. I'll be there."

The two men then shook hands, and Mamood left. Hamad then had the taxi driver take him to his hotel.

When Hamad returned to his room, he felt very pleased with himself. He had met his target. He had befriended his target. He felt that he had hooked his fish. The question remained whether he could haul him in for his plan. He now had several means at his disposal. Time would soon tell.

CHAPTER 24

THE RETURN TO VIENNA

October 14, 2006

The Commander began to set his trap on the night of October 13th, the day before Mamood was to arrive in Vienna for the IAEA sponsored International Safeguards Symposium. After a quiet dinner in his own hotel where he ate a grilled monkfish over a juicy risotto with porcini mushrooms, he hastened to Der Schwartze Katze. Another attractive door attendee showed him promptly to a table on the right side of the club. As soon as he sat down, he looked from right to left searching for Inge. At first, he did not see her. Hopefully, he thought, she was just on a break and had not quit working at the club. He felt a bit impatient and drummed his finger on the table. A young brunette then approached him for his drink order, and this time he ordered, for a change, a Bloody Mary. While he sat sipping his drinks, several dancers approached him, but he suggested that he was waiting for someone and politely asked them to return later. After stirring his drink and then slowly sipping it over the next 15 minutes, she appeared on stage. Her pole act was one of the most provocative he had seen. And her slow dropping of her diaphanous blouse roused those looking. Her well-rounded and firm breasts were luscious and were well suited to her heavenly body.

When she finished her stage dance to a loud applause and a few bravos, she put on her top and came off the stage. At first, she went to the bar for a glass of water, and cooled out for a few minutes. While doing so, she looked around the room and recognized Hamad. She decided to go up to him.

"Guden tag, mein Herr," said Inge. "Good to see you again."

"The pleasure is mine, Inge," replied Hamad warmly.

"Are you waiting for your friend?" she continued.

"No, not tonight. But, he'll be around for the next few days."

"Would you like me to dance for you?" asked Inge.

"Of course, you are great!" replied Hamad. He knew he had to continue to show that he was at ease and enjoyed himself at this type of club. Inwardly, he felt awkward; his years of fighting, training and commitment to Allah clearly had changed him from his days in Beirut.

Inge then proceeded to sway to the beat of the American song, "Celebration," moving up and down, first facing Hamad and then turning her bum to him. Then she moved very close to him and sat in his lap for several seconds. He touched both of her hips gently and she let them linger there. What a shape this girl has, Hamad thought. She then faced him frontally and moved her breasts right in front of his mouth while she swayed right and left. Then she brushed his legs, first his left and then his right. Hamad could feel his temperature rise.

When the song ended, he stuffed several large euro notes in her green bikini bottom and asked her to join him for a bottle of champagne. She accepted his invitation with an easy smile and then sat next to him, crossed her luscious legs and eyed him closely. The bottle of Moet Chandon arrived immediately.

"Inge," Hamad started. "I'm delighted that you are still here. I was not sure I would find you again."

"Don't worry, Hamad. I'm not going to leave this place any time soon. I told you why, in part, before. Also, the money is pretty good."

"That's good to know," said Hamad. He felt relieved that she would be continually available.

"I'm glad you and your friend, what's his name, ah yes, Mamood, will be here for a while. You are some of my nicest customers," she said.

"Well, we love what you do – – and we have fun being here," continued Hamad. "I'll tell you a little secret, but you have to first promise me to keep it between us."

"O.K. I will. What's up?" asked Inge.

"I know Mamood likes you a lot. I think he would love to spend more time with you, both here and outside of the club."

"You know, the management here does not like us to go out with the customers outside of the club. But they don't truly enforce this rule. So I make up my own mind."

"So you might then be willing to see Mamood when you finish up at the club or at another time?" asked Hamad.

"Sure, if he wants to get together with me, I'd be glad to meet him," she answered. He detected eagerness in her voice.

"That would be great," continued Hamad. Then he paused for a moment, looked directly into her eyes and added: "If you need help in your apartment rent or want some item you've been unable to buy, just ask me. I'll be glad to help you out."

"I get your drift, Hamad," she said, a bit unruffled. She had similar offers in the past and realized it came from the territory she played in. "Mamood is some lucky guy to have a friend like you."

Hamad said: "I think you are right. But, as I said, let's keep this quiet."

"As I told you before, I'll keep my word," she said.

"By the way, Inge, what is your last name and where do you live," asked Hamad.

"My full name is Inge Seegan and I live in a nearby apartment, which is only about a 20 minute walk from here. I'm from Vienna." Hamad made sure to remember these details.

They continued to drain the champagne and chatted amicably for about the next 30 minutes. After they finished, Hamad then told her they hoped to see her tomorrow and she said she would be here.

When he woke up the next morning, Hamad had mixed feelings about Inge. In truth, he felt drawn to her; he could not remember when he last made love to a woman.

But he knew she could serve a much better purpose. His duty to a higher cause demanded he sublimate his feelings. Still, it hurt.

The night of October 14[th,] he met Mamood in the lobby of the Donauzentrun. Hamad suggested they go to a quiet restaurant, der Stuebenhaus, a few blocks away, and Mamood promptly agreed. Hamad knew he needed a place where their conversation was not apt to be overheard. He had scouted the vicinity before and knew that the restaurant had an excellent menu and provided privacy. He had earlier noticed that there were several private corner tables that were separate from the two long banquettes where most of the diners ate.

Upon their arrival, Hamad asked for a corner table, and they were seated there immediately. Once seated, they ordered some mineral water. Hamad looked around and saw that the closest diners were out of hearing range so that they would be able to converse without being overheard. Then Mamood spoke first:

"It's great to be back here again, my friend. I have had a tough month."

"Why, what happened," asked Hamad.

"They asked me to work a couple of weekends a month for increased pay," answered Mamood.

"What is wrong with that?" asked Hamad.

"I work hard enough as it is, almost 10 hours a day for five days," answered Mamood. "I like to relax and have my own time on the weekends."

"I can understand that," replied Hamad. "Doesn't the increase in pay ease your pain?"

"The increase is piddling," said Mamood angrily. "It really doesn't make a big difference in how I live." At that remark, Hamad noticed that Mamood's facial expression tightened, a sign of his inner rage bubbling to the surface.

Hamad sipped his drink, looked around the restaurant for a moment and then asked: "Why the big push on your time?" asked Hamad, as he tried to penetrate deeper into his companion's angst.

"That Indian agreement with the United States," replied Mamood as he hit their table with his right fist. "Our government had decided to speed up the timetable on several of the projects I'm working on. I certainly didn't need this to happen, especially after being passed over for the top job."

"At least you're getting a change of pace here in Vienna," said Hamad in a light-hearted tone in a show of empathy.

"That's certainly true," replied Mamood. "The symposium on safeguards in nuclear programs and the verification of them is especially interesting to me because, in my duties, I'm the scientist in charge of safeguarding our nuclear weapons programs."

"And we know the nightlife here is excellent," continued Hamad.

"No question about that," answered Mamood. He then looked at a nearby table where several middle aged Italian businessmen were heatedly talking.

They both ordered a scrumptious wiener schnitzel with nockerel followed by an excellent tossed green salad stuffed with Italian mushrooms. When their meal was over, they left the restaurant and walked several blocks before finding a taxi. They had agreed, at Mamood's urging, to return to Der Schwartze Katze.

When they arrived at the club, they again were promptly seated, but this time at a table on the right side. The place was bustling again tonight. The stage was active with two young beauties dancing around the poles they used as props while displaying their ample bosoms and exquisite legs to the excited crowd that ringed the stage. A large Japanese contingent was present tonight. There were at least six tables they occupied – – and the lap dancers made sure that they gave liberally from their wallets. Hamad could see Mamood look around the room searching for Inge, and then he saw her. She had just finished a dance and went to the bar for water. Mamood asked their waitress to get Inge's attention, which she did. Inge then slowly approached the table smiling and said warmly:

"How are you Herren doing tonight? I've not seen you for a while."

"The pleasure is ours," answered Mamood. "We're delighted to see you again. Please dance for us."

The "Two of Us," an American hit, blared through the speakers. Inge stood in the middle of both of them, clad in a leopard blouse that bared her coveted chest and a matching leopard bikini bottom. She slowly moved her sturdy frame, then pumped her arms, and then began to sway side to side. In doing so, she first brushed against Hamad's left leg and against Mamood's right leg and then repeated that move. She then turned around and moved her solid butt first toward Hamad and then toward Mamood. She then moved ever so slowly backward toward Mamood until she was about three inches from his lap. Then she closed that distance and sat briefly on him, first for a couple of seconds and then for slightly longer and then moved upwards. Then she turned around, looked Mamood in the eye and leaned over him while keeping time to the music. As its paced quickened, so did Mamood's heart race. The music ended – – and she laughed.

"Brava, brava," shouted Hamad. "Let's have another." Both men then put euro notes in her bikini bottom. Inge pushed her blond curls off her face and waited for a moment.

Then a new British disco sound hit the airwaves and Inge immediately caught its staccato rhythm. She shimmied in front of both of them and then teased Hamad with some wicked hip sways. To their surprise, she then jumped onto their table and danced facing Mamood. When she swayed to the beat now, her strong, curvy legs were now above Mamood's eye level and, from his vantage point looking up at her; she appeared to be an amazon, a very luscious one. She then turned around and lowered her rear up and down. Mamood could not help but notice how agile she was and how good she looked from the rear. She then dropped to the table and spread her legs at the dance's end. Inge could see that Mamood was sweating; she knew she had aroused him.

Hamad was delighted. He suggested that they share several bottles of champagne, a Piper Heidsieck, and Inge eagerly joined them.

After several glasses of champagne each, they all began to laugh easily. Inge told a few funny jokes, which they both enjoyed. Mamood then turned to her expectantly and asked:

"Inge, are you free after work tonight?"

"Yes, for you, I am," she replied emphatically. "I get out of here in about an hour. I suggest we meet two blocks away, on the southwest corner. I'll stop by here before I leave."

"That's great," replied Mamood. "I'll see you soon."

As soon as she left, Hamad turned to Mamood and said: "I think you may be in luck. I think you may have a new friend."

"I hope you are right," Mamood said. "She's very exciting to me. I can't wait until she's done with her shift." Hamad could see the excitement in Mamood's eyes. Mamood's smile revealed that he now felt at ease.

The two then finished the champagne. They both turned to look at the din coming from the Japanese businessmen who were now joyfully getting the attention of at least 10 dancers. Mamood turned to Hamad and said:

"I hope you're not angry that I asked her out. I think she likes you, too." Mamood waited anxiously for Hamad's response.

"It's fine with me, Mamood. Go to it. I'm not hurt in the least."

Mamood felt relieved and comforted by Hamad's response.

A little before 1:00 a.m., Inge came, said her shift ended and told Mamood she would meet him up the street within 10 minutes after she changed. Hamad and Mamood then left the club and walked up the street, which was still active because of the nightclubs on the corner. They agreed to meet at the nightclub tomorrow night about 9:30 p.m. Within 10 minutes, Inge showed up and she and Mamood walked away in the direction of her apartment. Hamad then found a taxi and returned to his hotel, pleased that his plan had just entered a new phase.

When Mamood arrived at Inge's apartment, a neatly and modernly furnished one bedroom apartment in a 25 year old apartment building, she opened some more champagne and then said she would be right back. He looked around. The woman had a large collection of CDs, mostly pop stuff, but also many of the classics, Mozart, Beethoven, Liszt and Schubert. When she returned, she was wearing a diaphanous black cover-up over a black bra and bikini outfit – – and looked ravishing. Before long, she kissed Mamood, hugged him tightly and led him to her bedroom. There, before her queen-sized bed, in dim light, she faced away from him, slowly disrobed, first her cover-up and then her bra and turned toward him. He was awestruck by her beauty and embraced her eagerly. They fell on her bed. They kissed passionately, and then Mamood began to kiss her all over going down her luscious body to her knees. And then he entered her. They both felt the excitement that new lovers experience, the taste and feel of another person in the most intimate of ways. She then mounted him frontally and slowly swayed up and down, as if she were continuing a very private lap dance, and, at the same time, dangled her breasts near his mouth. They moved together effortlessly. Mamood began to moan as she continued her rhythmic up and down movements, and then he gasped as he came deep within her. She, in turn, moved for a few more turns and then cried out with delight – – and then lay quietly on top of him. Shortly thereafter, she rolled off him and they slept blissfully next to each other for the next six hours, she against his back.

When they woke up, Mamood eagerly turned her on her side and sought her pleasure again. They moved in this spoon position, first slowly exploring each other. Then, as their passion increased, they each moved faster, against each other. Mamood warmly held her left shoulder with his left arm and her tight abdomen with his right hand. He then ran his right hand slowly down her upper right leg and then touched her taut thighs. Soon he was lost in her, and she in him, and they felt the fountain of love and warm juice flow simultaneously. Mamood felt very happy. He was overwhelmed by Inge's lovemaking and tenderness.

They parted company about noon after a leisurely breakfast. He told her he would love to see here again tonight – – and she eagerly agreed. Mamood then returned to his hotel to review some materials that he would discuss at the first session. She in turn, relaxed for several hours, and then went out shopping for some new dresses in the afternoon, sensing that she soon might need them.

Hamad met Mamood at Der Schwartze Katze at 9:30 p.m. sharp. The bouncer recognized them and let them right in, while others, not so fortunate, continued to mill about. After they were seated at a table, Inge came over, did a dance for them and then left to work some of the other tables. Hamad suggested to Mamood that they leave for a while and go to a nearby café, der Muller, for some good coffee and a pastry and Mamood, a bit reluctantly, agreed.

After they each ate a delicious apple strudel, Hamad asked Mamood:

"How did last night go, my friend?"

"Excellent," answered Mamood. "I'm sure lucky to know this woman. While I have chased many beautiful women before, I've never met one as exciting as Inge." This was a surprising statement for a worldly man who pursued many skirts in the past.

"I'm delighted for you," replied Hamad. And he was, for several good reasons.

"And what about you? Are you not interested in any of these curvaceous creatures at the club?" asked Mamood, who hoped now to draw Hamad out.

"I am," answered Hamad. "And I'll pursue one of them I have my eye on. But I want to discuss a very private matter with you first."

"Go ahead. You know I'll listen closely and hold what you say in complete confidence," replied Mamood, who was not sure what to expect next.

Hamad then briefly closed his eyes, and remained pensive for several moments as if remembering many terrible scenes he had witnessed. He then said:

"Many years ago I was a lost soul in Beirut, where I grew up. While I was skilled in engineering, no one wanted my services, and I felt down, an outcast in my own country. An imam I casually met opened my eyes. Before I knew it, I traveled to Pakistan to train with other mujahideen there for the holy war to rid Afghanistan of those infidels Russians then defiling that country. This then became my own personal jihad, and thousands like me shared that vision."

Hamad stopped and looked at Mamood, who was listening to him closely. Hamad continued:

"I crossed into Afghanistan in early 1987 and what I saw there changed me forever. As we moved into eastern Afghanistan toward Kandahar, I saw the ghastly killing and destruction that the Russians brought to that country. I witnessed firsthand a group of six Russian helicopters destroy a small village at the entrance to a valley in retaliation for an attack at their base. They machine gunned all the villagers, women, children, old men; it made no difference. They slaughtered their animals, sheep and cattle as well. Every building was destroyed by the rockets the helicopters shot; nothing was left standing. The whole village was reduced to rubble. Blood literally flowed in the streets. The stench of the bloated dead was so strong I had to pull my cape over my nose."

Hamad paused and saw that Mamood was now squirming in his seat. They both took a sip of water. Mamood motioned for Hamad to continue and he did:

"Then, one day, near Khost in eastern Afghanistan, a group of my fellow mujahideen and I led a night-time raid to overrun a small Russian outpost. The gunfight was furious. The Russians were well armed. But, by virtue of our surprise attack at 3:00 a.m., we caught most of them sleeping and killed all 30 of them. We freed two villagers held as captives who had been tortured for several days, hung by their roped hands to a meat hook and brutally beaten by the Russian soldiers with clubs. They were lucky, they told us. I asked why. They said a group of 10 elders had been invited for dinner as a reconciliation measure. But this turned out to be a terrible trick. After they all drank teas at the outpost's headquarters, the Russians seized eight of them and skinned them alive. We cried with the two villagers who, by then, were overwrought from their experience."

Mamood, who was listening with rapt attention to this tale, then said:

"Continue, Hamad. Tell me more. I have heard some bad things the Russians did there, but nothing as you described."

Hamad paused for a moment, aware that he now had the full attention of Mamood and then continued:

"Over a two-year period, I participated in many raids and attacks on the infidel Russians throughout Paktia Province, around Khost, and in and around Kandahar. I escaped death at least five times. Once a Russian chopper appeared over a ridge by surprise, machine-gunned my fellow warriors and me. Luckily, I was able to throw myself into a cave inside a rock overhang just as the bullets whizzed by me. Eventually, though, we won. The Stingers we got – – those shoulder-fired ground to air missiles – – destroyed so many of their helicopters that they had to curtail their air combat missions in support of their spread-out troops."

"When the Russians finally withdrew in 1989, we were overjoyed. We, the mujahideen, had pushed out the godless Russians who had soiled an Islamic state. We had freed our Muslim brothers from their yokes. I felt the power we then commanded. I felt I had made a difference in this cause and my passion for it continued unabated. I lived in Afghanistan for years thereafter and fought against the Communist government and then the Northern Alliance and then with the Taliban when they took over almost 90% of the country. I had become a 100% holy warrior."

"I then became a trusted lieutenant under Osama bin laden and Dr. Zawahiri in Afghanistan. I helped to organize and run their training camps. Under their influence, I came to believe in the creation of a new caliphate that would spread from the Middle East through North Africa and be governed by a pure interpretation of the Prophet's words in the Koran. I came to see clearly how the Western culture and nation were rightly viewed as alien to our dreams and to be opposed and shunned as godless infidels."

Hamad then looked away for a moment and continued:

"I, like you, am very upset with the United States and its world domination," said Hamad. "I'm sick and tired of our Muslim brothers in Pakistan being insulted by that President Bush. I'm upset by the treatment of our Muslim brothers in Palestine and in Iraq, to name a few places. The Zionist occupiers of our holy land in Palestine fill our daily lives with insult and treat our brothers there as dogs. The crusaders soil our holy places in Saudi Arabia because of their greedy need for oil. Can you imagine that the United States consumes almost a quarter of the world's daily supply for oil, and yet, has only about 5% of the world's population?"

"I don't see how this involves me," asked Mamood, who was unnerved by the direction of their conversation.

"I want to strike a blow against them, one they'll never forget. You can help me," said Hamad.

"How?" asked Mamood in a surprised tone.

"You can help me get one or two small nuclear bombs and train us to detonate them," said Hamad.

"Are you serious?" asked Mamood in almost an incredulous tone.

"Yes, I am," replied Hamad. He paused, and, with a stern expression that came from deep within him, added: "I'm willing to give my life to see this happen. And I can make you an extremely wealthy man – – and you then can have Inge or any of the other attractive women you want."

Mamood drew silent, thought for a moment and said:

"You really think I could smuggle the weapons out from the plant in which I work, don't you?"

"I do," replied Hamad. "And I'm prepared to pay you $110 million to do so and get them to me."

"You have that amount of money available?" asked Mamood incredulously. "And you're not kidding?"

"Yes, I have the money available," said Hamad. "You could then lead whatever fabulous life you seek in some place you choose and with any maiden or maidens of your choice. Think of it, this is a rare opportunity."

Mamood hesitated for a moment, took his eyes off Hamad and quietly reflected before he spoke. He took another bite of his pastry. He then looked up and said: "You are asking me to risk my life for this, a tall order."

Hamad then replied in a tone of absolute conviction: "I know that. We both are."

"Hamad, I sincerely believe you have become my friend. I feel that in several ways, especially the way you backed off from Inge. But I have to consider whether I want to do this and, then, whether your plan is feasible."

"Ask yourself, Mamood, are you happy where you are, underpaid, angry, asked to work harder. For what? Assume you stay where you are, will you be satisfied. I don't think so."

"Hamad, you may be right. What you say is true. I know, in my heart of hearts, I'm also drawn to Western women."

"Think about what I say overnight, Mamood. You don't have to decide right now."

"I will, Hamad. I promise I will."

"There's another point here, too," continued Hamad. "We can be heroes in the eyes of almost 1.2 billion Muslims. We can strike a blow for all of them."

"I know that," said Mamood, as he continued to reflect on the importance of that issue to him.

"If you agree to help, we can then start discussing all the details entailed in what we will then do," said Hamad.

"I follow that," answered Mamood.

"Let's meet at this cafe tomorrow night, October 16th, at about 8:30 p.m." said Hamad.

"I'll be there," said Mamood.

The two left the cafe and returned to the nightclub. Several of the attractive dancers performed for them, including the German, green-eyed brunette who came to their table on the first night they were at the club. As 1:00 a.m. approached, Hamad left with Mamood and then walked up the street several blocks and awaited Inge's arrival. She showed up about 10 minutes later, greeted Hamad warmly and then she and Mamood walked to her apartment. Hamad found a taxi in front of der Muller and took it to his hotel.

As he was about to fall asleep, he focused on what decision Mamood would make. He reviewed what he had told Mamood and thought his approach was fine. He felt uneasy that he could not completely control the outcome, but he was confident he dealt too many good cards to be ignored -- an unthinkable sum of money and an exciting young woman to spend time with.

Mamood brooded for hours before falling asleep that night. He was torn by cross currents. On the one hand, he recognized that he crossed the moral barrier against causing harm to mankind when he decided to work on Pakistan's nuclear program and its developments of its own atomic weapons. Clearly, as a Pakistani patriot, he had no moral qualms about using the weapons in the country's arsenal against India, its foremost enemy. So, he asked himself, why he should have any hesitation now. The tug he felt now was that the use of such weapons against India would be an act of self-defense, a righteous action in his eyes, while the action to be taken by Al Qaeda was an aggressive act of initiation. Somehow, this seemed to make a difference to him.

As he wrestled with this dilemma, other thoughts flooded his mind. Islam to him primarily meant peace, harmony and community. But the Prophet and his followers also engaged in aggressive acts of war or otherwise to subdue their enemies. And then there was the question of women and money, dangled before him for his taking. He could envision an exciting lifetime with Inge, spent together passionately and in fabulous luxury in any way they chose to live it. Besides, he would never have any financial concerns again.

Added to this cocktail of angst were the risks that Mamood was asked to take. Clearly, he knew that he could be killed by the Pakistanis for committing such a heinous act. Also, he realized that he could become the target of revenge by those who suffered from his conspiratorial act or by others who many have learned of his new-found wealth or even by his Al Qaeda co-conspirators. He finally went to sleep as the sun was coming up over the horizon.

Hamad arrived at der Muller 15 minutes early the next night, found a quiet table along the rear wall and waited for Mamood to arrive. The cafe was crowded with both local neighborhood folks in jeans or other casual after-work clothes and by some foreign business types still dressed in their good European suits. When the appointed time came and went, Hamad continued to sit calmly. After a while, his calmness disappeared. When the bells of a nearby church chimed nine times, he became concerned that all his efforts to recruit Mamood might be wasted. He ordered a second cappuccino and continued to wait for his companion. Finally, at 9:30 p.m., an hour late, Mamood came into the café. He apologized to Hamad profusely and explained that the end of the day reception for the attendees went much longer than he had anticipated.

"I thought, for a moment, that perhaps you might not come tonight," said Hamad, relieved by the arrival of his targeted coconspirator.

"That would have been unthinkable, Hamad. Remember I owe you," answered Mamood.

"True, but I may have overestimated you and your interest in my project," replied Hamad, a comment designed to test Mamood.

"No, you didn't. I made my decision. I'll help you," said Mamood firmly. Hamad looked closely at Mamood and detected no signs of nervousness or deception in his calm look. "Fantastic!" Hamad said gleefully.

"You made me realize I've been thinking in more provincial terms – – Pakistan vs. India," added Mamood. "You opened my vision. I see I can do a lot more for our fellow Muslims than I thought possible before. I remembered, too, how proud I felt when my mother read me those heroic tales of the Prophet nightly when I was young. I also felt then a great sense of peace and being connected to an historic larger community of kinsmen. Your heartfelt tales made a deep impression on me."

Hamad now knew he could begin the next phase of the plan – – obtain and pay for the weapons and then move them out of Pakistan.

After they each ate a grilled chicken breast sandwich on a Viennese round roll with French fries, Hamad continued his discussion of the steps he wanted to take. He suggested, out of caution, that these issues would best be aired in a private place.

Mamood then interjected: "Let's go to talk at Inge's apartment. I told her this morning that I would meet her at her apartment because of my session and meeting with you. When she heard that, she gave me an extra key to her apartment so that I could let myself in this evening."

"Perfect," replied Hamad, who smiled broadly at this good fortune.

They then left the café and walked about 20 minutes to Inge's apartment. Once inside, Mamood sat down on the sofa and Hamad sat near him in the chair near the end of the couch. Mamood then asked Hamad to describe his proposed procedure. In response, Hamad said:

"The funds for the payment are in two places. We are now in the process of arranging for their movement out of our accounts when needed."

"Hamad, I trust you, but I have to be assured that payment will be made at a mutually agreed time," said Mamood.

"We'll work this out together," replied Hamad confidently.

"There's also a first step I need," said Mamood. "You have to satisfy me that you actually have the money you say you have."

"I think that you have to open one or two bank accounts in a country or countries you select, where such matters will be handled discreetly," replied Hamad.

"Obviously, I'll have to think about my choice further." "Off the top, I'd probably select Switzerland or one of the Emirates, perhaps, Dubai or Abu Dhabi," said Mamood.

Hamad then said: "Once you select your bank or banks, we or you will tell them to make what we call a soft probe to verify that we have the funds in question. This can be done on a bank-to-bank basis. Then your bank can confirm it to you directly, preferably in person."

"I follow what you say. I think that, when this IAEA symposium ends, I may take a three-day vacation in the Emirates and open an account there" said Mamood. He then hesitated and added:

"I also think I'll need an upfront payment for taking the initial risk since I'll clearly be the active party in the procurement plot," continued Mamood, who shifted restlessly on the couch.

"How much do you want?" asked Hamad, who had expected such a response from his colleague.

"Ten percent, U.S. $11 million, at the outset," replied Mamood.

"I'll see what we can do," replied Hamad. "I think that may be doable, but, if so, it comes with a major condition."

"And what is that?" asked Mamood.

"If you try to cross our group, there will be serious consequences for you," said Hamad sternly. "We'll be able to follow your movements. I tell you this so that you can appreciate the seriousness of your agreement to help us."

"Hamad, I don't intend to run off with the initial money and try to disappear," replied Mamood. "I think your payment binds us both together more firmly. In this way, you'll want to continue with me rather than with another scientist."

"Okay. Then we understand each other," said Hamad, who looked at Mamood with a serious expression on his face. "I will let you know our decision on the initial payment tomorrow night, when I suggest we meet again."

"That's soon enough for me," said Mamood.

Hamad then returned to his hotel, excited by the realization that he had started down the road to fulfilling the nightmarish Al Qaeda plan. He mulled over the potential different ways to handle the money movement. He then called Mahmoud, who had previously returned to Cairo from Karachi. While it was 1:30 a.m. in Cairo, Mahmoud had been fully awake and alert.

"Mahmoud, I need your help now," said Hamad.

"Go ahead, Commander."

"I think the fish is hooked," Hamad continued.

"Excellent," replied Mahmoud.

"Our friend wants to open a new account to receive an initial payment now before he ships the goods later," Hamad said. "He's not sure whether it should be in Switzerland, Luxembourg or Dubai."

"I don't think he should open one in Europe, including Switzerland or Luxembourg," replied Mahmoud. "Since 9/11, the European banks have scrutinized money transfers to them much more heavily than ever. I've even heard that the opening of a new account by an established business outside of the entity's country at a bank not used previously could take weeks."

"Why," said Hamad. He knew he could rely on his Egyptian colleague for a straight forward and experienced answer.

"They need the usual personal, banking and legal references, but, most importantly, they want to know the source of the money, how it was earned and over what period of time," replied Mahmoud.

"Okay. I understand. So where do you think he should do it?" continued Hamad.

"I'd say Dubai," said Mahmoud. "Perhaps he could open up an account at the bank where we have our big account. If he wanted to have an account elsewhere in Dubai, a second account, he could do that as well."

"Good thinking, Mahmoud," said Hamad. "If he used our bank, it would be very easy for us to give him the proof he wants of our financial capability."

"Exactly," replied Mahmoud. "I could arrange for the senior vice president in charge of our account to meet with him. I'll tell him it is one of my new trading customers. He'll love the idea of my sending more business his way. I can then also instruct him to confirm, in their face-to-face meeting, and in a confidential letter to him, that my trading company has the funds for the orders."

"I like your thinking, Mahmoud," replied Hamad, satisfied by what he had heard. "I may add one condition – – that our friend cannot move the money from his account at our bank for at least 60 days, a testing period to confirm that he won't disappear with the money."

"You can do that if you want, Hamad," replied Mahmoud. "That should work." He then paused and added thoughtfully: "Over the years I have developed a very close relationship with the senior vice president. Sometimes I have received some information that shouldn't have been passed to me, such as some private information about my customer's adverse financial condition that had not been disclosed to me before."

"O.K.," said Hamad. "Advise the banker that our customer wants to meet with him in about four to five days. I think our friend can travel then because his business in town ends."

"I'll take care of it," replied Mahmoud. "I'll send you his coordinates by our usual form of email within a few minutes."

"Excellent," replied Hamad.

Hamad immediately received the encrypted email on his own computer, copied the data and then destroyed the email. He then went to sleep easily after that.

While he slept, his soon-to-be-accomplice, Mamood, enjoyed another night of passionate love-making with Inge. Aroused by their intimate conversation, they reveled in their warm embraces and then their exploring each other. Each was a consummate and experienced lover – – and their shared squeals of joy left them both smiling.

The next day was bright and sunny, with a cool breeze, a harbinger of another satisfying day for each of the coconspirators. By pre-arrangement, Mamood and Hamad dined at a small restaurant, der Staube, a few blocks from the nightclub. Hamad ate an excellent sautéed grouper over spinach with nockerel, while Mamood dined on a succulent wiener schnitzel with red cabbage. They spoke quietly because the restaurant was crowded, with diners seated all around them. Mamood told Hamad that the IAEA conference session had been both enlightening and stimulating and that he had spoken for about 20 minutes on a nuclear verification issue. Hamad shared with Mamood that he had been working out some of the financial details.

"Mamood, I've discussed the situation with our financial expert. He thinks that you should have your account or accounts in Dubai, not in Europe. The banks here will ask too many questions, especially uncomfortable ones about the source of the money."

"I hear what you say," replied Mamood, who seemed to expect such an answer. "I'm no expert in these matters. But even I have heard that it is difficult for people from the Middle East and other parts of the Muslim world to open bank accounts in Switzerland and elsewhere in Western Europe, especially if they receive a large transfer of funds."

"So you do understand," said Hamad, in a gentle tone.

"Yes, I do," continued Mamood. "I may open up a small personal account at the bank Inge uses or another bank here in Vienna. Then I can deposit a few thousand euros here and have some spending money."

"I think that would be fine," said Hamad. "Do you think you could fly to Dubai when the conference is over?"

"Yes, it ends on the evening of October 20th. I can go on the 21st and then return here for a few days with Inge," replied Mamood without hesitation.

"Excellent," said Hamad.

"As for Dubai, I'll obviously need the bank and the bank officer I should meet," said Mamood. "Do you have that information now?"

"Yes," replied Hamad. "Here is the information you will need."

"I assume this officer handles your account," said Mamood.

"Yes, he does," replied Hamad.

"I also assume that he may be the one who can confirm your outfit's financial capacity," continued Mamood.

"Yes, he can," replied Hamad. "He had also been instructed to make the U.S. $11 million transfer into your account the same day, if you are satisfied with our proof."

"Superb," said Mamood. "I just have to show up with my passport, present myself to him, ask him the necessary question and that's it." Mamood then waited expectantly for the answer, his eyes riveted on Inge's library.

"Yes, that's all you have to do, except there is one condition we want to add," replied Hamad. Mamood then leaned closer to Hamad and asked:

"What is that?"

"We want you to keep the money there for 60 days untouched. That period will give my group time to judge that you are in fact working for us – – and make sure you don't vanish, a small but necessary precaution."

"My friend, you clearly have the makings of a shrewd businessman," replied Mamood. "I understand – – and I accept your condition."

"Good, then we have a deal," said Hamad.

"Yes, we do," replied Mamood, smiling warmly as he reached across the table to shake Hamad's hand.

CHAPTER 25

DUBAI ROUNDTRIP

October 21, 2006

The gleaming new British Airways Airbus 321 jet took off from Vienna International airport in Vienna at 7:30 a.m. bound for London, about a three and a half hour trip. Mamood sat contentedly in his coach seat and gazed at the fluffy cumulus clouds below the plane as it cruised at an altitude of about 10,000 meters. It was an auspicious day for him. The clear blue sky above him matched the clarity of his mindset. He was proceeding down a path from which there was no return. But the rewards that lay ahead of him were too inviting.

After a three and a half hour layover at London Heathrow Airport, he then boarded a Boeing 777 for the next non-stop leg to Dubai.

Almost seven hours later, at about 10:30 p.m., Mamood was over the sparkling blue waters of the Persian Gulf for the first time. The calmness of the waters contrasted with the volcanic conflicts raging off its borders. This area with its vast wealth of oil resources and reserves had become an area of increased conflict in recent years with the rise of a possible nuclear-powered Iran viewed as an incendiary threat throughout the region.

As the jet banked to the right and approached the Dubai International Airport, Mamood could see the vivid and stark contrast between the desert sands of ancient days and the ultra-modern glass high-rise office buildings and hotels, lit up at night set apart with brilliant green golf courses. On the route from the airport exit road to the central part of Dubai, he could see the modern buildings grown in size. Finally, when he entered one of the main boulevards, he marveled at how the oil wealth of the country and its innovative real estate practices had transformed the area. In recent years, Dubai had become a new Arab mecca for both tourists and commerce, fueled by its growth in commerce and by the perceived increase in disdain felt by many Middle Easterners towards the United States and many parts of Europe.

Mamood reflected on the modernity surrounding him, a sea of change from so many areas of his native Pakistan. For years on a personal level, he had experienced daily a road to modernity, as he used his extensive knowledge of nuclear physics and engineering to help his homeland to increase its nuclear arsenal since the early 1990s. Still, it was clear to him that his country was still mired in the many problems of the past – – its unsolved conflict with India, the vast poverty found throughout many rural areas and the conflict between the conservative religious parties and Musharraf.

After a restful night at the Gulf Hill Hotel, a quiet hotel overlooking the peaceful waters of the Persian Gulf, Mamood felt excited about the day's prospects. He dressed in a dark suit and white shirt, since he wanted to present a serious side to the banker he was soon to meet. He then checked out of the hotel sensing it was best to find a second hotel for Sunday night.

Within a half hour, he arrived at the tall headquarters edifice of the Mideast Islamic Bank, a Dubai registered bank located on one of the main boulevards of Dubai, Mankhool Road. As was true through much of the Middle East, the bank and businesses were open on Sunday. As soon as he walked through the main entrance doors, he felt surrounded by an aura of great wealth. Polished desert-toned marble floors contrasted vividly with Austrian crystal chandeliers that adorned the main floor ceiling. He immediately asked a male clerk to advise his contact, Abdul al-Hassan, that he was here. The clerk gave him a pass to the third floor, where the bank's Global Wealth Management Section was located. The officer's secretary, a Dubai native dressed in a long black skirt below her knees, stockings and a beige blouse, ushered Mamood into a 4½ by 5 meter conference room. The shades were pulled about half way down to deflect some of the sunshine and to create, he thought, an element of privacy. The highly polished marble inlaid table was the centerpiece of the room, while the swirl-design wine and beige Persian carpet, which covered most of the floor, helped to muffle sounds from the room. Clearly, this was a room designed to convey a sense of privacy and confidentiality, where secrets could be uttered which would not leave the bank's province.

Mr. al Hassan, dressed in a well-tailored Canali suit, a hand-made shirt and attractive red Chervet tie, entered the room. Five feet eight inches in height and with a substantial girth, al Hassan conveyed the solidity a 50-year-old banker was meant to project. The officer's secretary then brought in cups of mint tea for both of them. Mamood felt at ease in these comforting surroundings. Mr. al Hassan gazed at his new soon-to-be rich client and sensed Mamood's seriousness of purpose immediately.

After several niceties, Mamood then addressed the banker directly:

"I'm here to open an account for my Cypriot trading corporation, East/West Trading Ventures S.p.a., of which I am the sole registered owner." He then pulled out a certified copy of the corporation's certification of incorporation as well as a copy of the corporate stock register, certified by the corporation's Cypriot's lawyer, showing Mamood as the only shareholder. Mamood smiled politely as he did so. He knew he had to act through an intermediary and, yet, at the same time, show that he was the ultimate beneficiary of the corporation's operations.

Mr. al Hassan reviewed the documents presented to him and was satisfied. He then asked Mamood for a letter of reference from his lawyer, a bank reference letter and his passport. Mamood then gave him the signed original of his attorney's letter as well as a letter from the officer of Creditanstalt in Vienna; the first attested to Mamood's good character and the second to his good status as a client of such bank. Mr. al Hassan called his secretary in to make a copy of the passport.

Mr. al Hassan took a sip of tea and smiled as he drank it slowly, savoring it. He paused and, with an air of deliberation, then said:

"Here are the papers for you to sign. As you can see, there are two signature cards and a corporate resolution. Please sign all of these and then place a check on the box where it shows you will be signing any check or other withdrawal singly, if that's the case."

"Yes," said Mamood. "I will be the sole signatory on the account." He then read the forms closely, signed where necessary and returned them to the banker.

Mr. al Hassan then typed this information in the computer in front of him and, within 10 minutes, he gave the account number for the new account to Mamood.

"That was easy," said Mamood in a pleased tone.

"Yes, we can act very fast in the case of our trusted new customers. In this case, you came strongly recommended by one of our well-known customers, who were prepared to vouch for your character as well as your integrity. That made this easy."

"I brought 800 euros with me for my initial deposit," said Mamood in reply, almost casually. He then added: "I hope that's enough for you initially."

"Yes, it is," said the banker without hesitation.

"I'm also here for another reason," said Mamood as he began to shift the conversation to another sensitive area.

"Yes, I have been briefed by my client," said Mr. al Hassan in a matter-of-fact tone. "I've also been instructed by my client to take certain other actions with you on its behalf."

"Go ahead, please," responded Mamood quickly.

"First, I confirm to you that my client has the financial capability to satisfy your trading invoice, which I understand will be in the range of U.S. $110 million," said the banker. He then removed a letter to such effect on the bank's letterhead stationary from the white folder in front of him, and handed it to Mamood.

Mamood looked at the official letter closely and his face lit up, confirming what he had hoped would be the case. "Excellent," he then added.

"Second, I have been instructed to transfer U.S. $11 million in euros to your new account here today," said the banker. He then showed Mamood a withdrawal slip for such sum drawn on the "buyer's" account and a deposit slip for such sum in the name of his corporation.

"I'm now going to effectuate this transfer now," continued al Hassan. "I will bring you back a Xerox copy of the withdrawal slip with our banking reference numbers on it, together with a stamped original of your deposit ticket. Please give me a few minutes."

With that, Mr. al Hassan left the room. Mamood quietly sipped the last of his mint tea, as he waited patiently for the banker to return. He did not have to wait long. Within 10 minutes, al Hassan returned and gave Mamood his documents.

"I believe this completes our business, Mr. Ishan," said al Hassan. He then smiled warmly at Mamood and continued: "Here are several of my cards, which also includes my cellphone number on the back. I only give that out to my important clients."

"I appreciate that," replied Mamood politely. "I also will remember your treatment of me as an honored guest. I thank you for all your help."

Mr. al Hassan then followed Mamood out of the conference room and escorted him to an executive dining room on the 20th floor of the building. The six tables, discreetly set apart from each other, in the 20-meter-by-20-meter room, afforded a breathtaking view of the Persian Gulf to the north and west. Mamood could clearly see the bustle at the port piers, where many container-laden vessels were being unloaded by heavy cranes.

After a leisurely hour and a half lunch, Mamood felt stuffed. The hummus they shared was very fresh; his grilled fish over a bed of couscous and grilled eggplant strips was very satisfying. Mamood mused to himself. Perhaps my full feeling comes not only from the meal, but also from the money I now control.

Mamood then thanked al Hassan for his courtesies and he left the bank. He took a leisurely walk about six blocks to the west of the bank, then hailed a taxi and proceeded to his second destination, unannounced and unknown to anybody – – a branch of the International Development Bank of Dubai. As in the case of the Mideast Islamic Bank, this bank also had a magnificent modern glass structure of 25 stories with special tinted windows that glowed with the bright rays of the afternoon sun. This bank also displayed a sense of wealth, with its black-and-white marble floors accented by many varied multi-colored Persian and Afghan rugs.

There he met with one of the bank's vice presidents, Mohammed al Shala, in charge of opening up of accounts for non-residents. Mr. al Shala was a younger version of Mr. al Hassan, he thought, although the banker now before him had an athletic build. Well-prepared, Mamood presented a duplicate set of the papers he had given to al Hassan earlier, as well as his passport, and gave the officer 700 euros as the initial deposit. The banker asked Mamood to describe his corporate activity, to which Mamood replied:

"We're in the import-export business and buy and sell mostly electronic products and various commodities, such as steel, copper and other items. Sometimes we also take advantage of other opportunities with our resources."

"How long have you been in business," asked the banker, as he continued his interrogation, a routine he followed many times before.

"For over 15 years," replied Mamood. "Since we expanded our business in Europe and in the Middle East, we decided only recently to use an offshore Cypriot entity for most of our new business in those areas."

"I see," said the banker. "You wanted to have an established presence closer to your customer base."

"Yes, exactly," continued Mamood, who was glad he had learned how to present himself to the banker.

The banker then returned in about 15 minutes and gave Mamood his new account information and a stamped receipted initial deposit slip. The two then shook hands and parted, and Mamood left the bank. He looked at his watch; it was now about 6:00 p.m. He felt the cool breezes from the Gulf wafting through the boulevards.

He then walked slowly to a taxi stand about two blocks from the bank and went to the Grand Hotel, where he had booked a superior room for one night. The hotel was beautifully appointed and combined Western efficiency with Middle Eastern graciousness. The lobby had several large beautiful Persian rugs. The hotel had an excellent spa and health club, a large business center and, of course, various conference rooms, large enough to accommodate a group as small as 20 and as large as 300. The hotel also had a revolving restaurant on the top floor, with an outdoor terrace that served as a favorite meeting place for many young and not so young business people.

Mamood decided to unwind in his room and keep to himself. Ordinarily, he would have dined in the rooftop dining room and at least surveyed or partaken of the social scene there. But this time was different. He wanted to keep a low profile in the country and avoid being noticed to the extent possible. Also, he had a fantastic woman waiting for him, which curbed any interest he might have in meeting a woman here. Besides, he had little spare time to spend, since he knew he would be on the 9:30 a.m. British Airways flight in the morning back to Vienna via London. Most importantly, he felt satisfied by the day's events, as if waking to a peaceful and happy dream. In a space of 12 hours, he had opened two bank accounts and now had U.S.$11 million in euros in his account, a fantastic sum far beyond any sum he had ever dreamed of having.

He ordered room service several hours later and ate a grilled fish on pita with tomatoes on the side. He then took a luxurious bath in the marble-covered modern bathroom, settled in his comfortable bed and slept peacefully.

The return flight to London and then to Vienna took over 11 hours and passed easily, despite an hour and a half layover in London. Mamood thought of the dangers that lay ahead of him at home, a monumental task that almost defied any rational solution. Somehow, he would hatch a plan that would work, he reasoned, although he knew the odds were greatly against him. He felt, as he had for several years now, that he had to continue to lead his life to the fullest. Now, however, he faced a major threat to his accomplishing that goal – – he might be caught stealing, or conspiring to steal, some of his country's nuclear weapons. He tried to push that thought out of his mind, like the hum of the jet's engine. He had to learn to live with it, and, as a disciplined person, he believed he could do so. Again, he reasoned, this was a case of mind over matter, so he would try to banish that worry to the dark recesses of his mind.

Then his thoughts turned to Inge. What a lucky find. He had learned that she was a university graduate but wanted to pursue an adventuresome life where she could act out her fantasies freely. She had told Mamood that, when she had matured as a teenager, she sensed she held a special attraction for men. Yet she held herself in check for many years until she first made love to a classmate when she was 20. After her graduation, she had worked in the marketing department of a pharmaceutical firm and had earned a decent salary plus substantial commissions. But she had tired of the job, finding it too confining and straight-laced for her. Again, she had been constantly aware of the way she aroused the male doctors and male personnel in the hospital and clinics to whom she promoted her firm's products. She then decided to try dancing at a nightclub and learn where that nighttime work led.

Within an hour of arriving at the Vienna airport, he went to Inge's apartment. He immediately found a note for him on the coffee table in front of the couch: "I should be back here by around midnight. Tonight is one of my short shifts. I'll see you then, sweetheart."

Mamood waited in the apartment until her return. At first, he began reading one of her Balzac novels, Pere Goriot, since he had never read any of them. But he became impatient and began pacing around the apartment. He realized that he had very strong feelings for Inge, the first time in years that he had any such feelings. But his feelings ran deeper this time; this woman made a greater and deeper impact on him. She was both very intelligent, independent and feminine, a heady brew. He then thought of Hamad and thanked him quietly for his leading him to this woman.

While he was lost in these thoughts, Inge returned. When he heard her key in the door, he rushed to open it, embraced her tightly, and kissed her warmly.

"How can you look so fresh after so much dancing, Inge?" asked Mamood curiously, as he took a step back to look her over.

"It's sometimes easy," she replied. "I pace myself. I know when to take breaks."

"There has to be more to it than that," he continued.

"There is." She then looked at him eagerly and said. "I go to the gym to work out strenuously twice a week and do an hour of Pilates twice a week. I have been following that routine for almost five years now. So that keeps me in great shape and makes me fit aerobically."

"There is no question that you are in great shape," he said with a light laugh. "Now I know why you are an indoor athlete too." She laughed loudly and said:

"You do rather well too, you know."

After a vodka shot each and some quiet intimate conversation, they went into her bedroom. Again, they made passionate love. He especially enjoyed it when she mounted him. He could then freely feel her all over, her luscious, strong legs, her rounded rear and her beautifully shaped full bosom, and watch her fantastic body move more freely. Somehow, he sensed, her dancing at the club aroused her as well, because she felt like a tigress when she finally came home to make love to him.

They both slept blissfully in each other's arms when they finally became exhausted.

As they had discussed before his trip to Dubai, Mamood told her when they first woke in the morning that he had to return to his job in Pakistan that afternoon, but that he planned to return in mid-November and mid-December, 2006 to attend the next two IAEA conferences scheduled for those dates. As before, she was delighted with the news, and gave him an especially warm send-off when he left.

"I'll miss you, mein lieben. But I will eagerly await your return," she said as she continued to hug him tightly.

"Inge, my dream of dreams. I'll hurry back," Mamood said quietly, almost tearfully.

He then hailed a taxi, with mixed feelings, and boarded the early afternoon Air Pakistan flight bound for Islamabad. He knew that he would meet Hamad there, within a day or two after returning. He also knew that he would receive a coded letter or email that gave him the time and place for the rendezvous.

CHAPTER 26

WAH CANTT, PAKISTAN

October 25, 2006

After his momentous trip to Vienna, Mamood returned to his home on the outskirts of Wah Cantt with mixed feelings. While he yearned to be with Inge again, he knew that he had a mission to carry out, one that could change his life, and perhaps, the world, forever.

He had lived in the northwestern part of Islamabad for years. Several years ago, he decided to move to Wah Cantt in order to avoid the tedious and ever increasing longer commute to work. He had bought a two-storey brown wooden-framed house with a small backyard, where he could sit outdoors. Mamood relished that he now had a 15 minute commute to the nuclear facility in a special restricted zone, the Pakistan Ordinance Factories. The appeal of the house lay in its apparent privacy, since it was situated about 40 meters from the nearest dwelling, another house occupied by a young Pakistani businessman, his wife and three children. Mamood had hired an older man, a Pakistani widower about 55, to cook his meals, shop and clean the house.

His drive to work that morning in his four-door Toyota Camry felt different. He became aware that he was focusing on the turns in the road and the location of individual shops and businesses in a way he had not experienced before. This was a more heightened focus, caused, he believed, by his need to be extra vigilant of all the details of his life, especially of his work. One mistake, one minor inattention to detail, he now knew, might cost him his reputation, his job and, most importantly, his life.

The Pakistan Ordinance Factories, a military complex of at least 14 factories, located about 50 kilometers northwest of Islamabad, had been founded in 1951under the auspices of Pakistan's then Prime Minister, Khawaja Nazam-u-Din. During the past 55 years, the facility expanded, as did the security surrounding it. It was common knowledge that the Factories produced a whole line of many major products for the Army, Navy and Air Force, including light and heavy machine guns, automatic rifles, ammunition, tanks and other vehicles. It was also well known that the facility had expanded over time to accommodate the growing needs of the Pakistani armed forces. Trucks moved in and out of the complex on a daily basis hauling needed supplies and components to the base and leaving with finished weaponry destined elsewhere within the country.

Security, in general, was tight at the complex. Armed military guards served as sentries at the various entry points into the complex. A high steel mesh fence surrounded the entry complex. Persons employed there brandished their identification cards to gain admittance. Vehicles were regularly subject to inspection. Low-strung concrete barriers were moved into place, if needed. Security personnel were also present in the various factory buildings throughout the complex. A large wooded area, northwest of the complex, served in part as a buffer zone. In short, the area was an armed camp.

Within this broad complex, there were a number of special security areas that contained several large rectangular buildings, each almost a football field in length. These structures housed special weaponization programs, although the exact nature of these programs had not been publicly revealed. Mamood knew what went on in them because he worked there. These buildings were the workplaces where Pakistan's atomic bombs and other atomic weapons had been manufactured and assembled in the past under tight military control.

Security in and out of the structures was especially tight. Only personnel with top-secret clearance were permitted into these restricted facilities. Armed guards checked each person's identification cards closely. Video cameras served as roving eyes throughout each building; they were in hallways, at the entrances, inside the laboratories, the supply rooms to the labs and in the weapons storage facility. Occasionally the guards would use trained dogs randomly to sniff personnel and their bags upon entering or leaving the area.

The security units serving this area had a central control unit. There several persons monitored the video cameras on a 24-hour basis. They were under orders to examine any suspicious activity and to report their findings to the office of an Army brigadier general in charge of overall security at the complex. The camera coverage was designed to cover 100% of these high-security buildings. In fact, there were several gaps in coverage, but these would not be noticed unless someone examined each angle of coverage very precisely.

Mamood worked in the most sensitive building, building # 3, in this high security zone, where the actual manufacture of several of the atomic weapons took place. As the second most senior scientist on the Defense Production staff, he had unlimited access throughout the high-security zone. This meant he could go anywhere within the facility and he had the access codes to all the various sensitive rooms and buildings. Since he had worked at the facility for about 20 years, he knew the guards securing the sensitive area well and had been to their homes on many social occasions. Yes, Mamood was well known and trusted by his fellow workers and guards. The guards did not mind that he had on occasion bought a small suitcase into his workplace so that he could conveniently change into another outfit before leaving for an important function or meeting.

When Mamood entered building # 3 that first morning on his return, he went to the men's locker room to change. He took off the jacket of his suit and put on a long white coverall with many pockets. When certain operations were in progress, he also had to wear a protective visor that covered his entire head and contained a coated eye shield that allowed him to see through the visor. But he did not need the visor for today's scheduled work.

From the men's locker room located on the north end of the building, he leisurely walked down the western hallway to gain access to the manufacturing room, a 170-meter by 80-meter area. He slowly passed the weapons storage area, a 50-meter by 40-meter all concrete bunker with one-meter thick walls, which was virtually impregnable. There were two entry doors, separated by a meter and a half, each having their own special access codes. While he had walked the hallway almost daily for many years, he noticed for the first time that two new cameras, located high up on the wall, had been installed to provide better surveillance over the entryway to the storage room. The storage room had three levels; the floor of the upper level was even with the floor of the entire building. The two lower levels were built underground, one to a depth of 30 meters and the other to a depth of 10 meters. He also noted that an armed soldier was stationed between the two entry doors to verify the credentials of any entering person and to obtain a superior officer's approval for the removal of any weapon from the bunker by any person.

As he proceeded to the main manufacturing area, Mamood was struck by the ingenuity that would be needed to get any weapon out of the bunker undetected. He began to feel tension in his neck as the difficulty of his mission, its virtual impossibility, seeped in. But he let this thought pass quickly. He knew that he had overcome many struggles in his lifetime; first the agony of his mother's death when he was young, only 10 years old, and then his becoming an orphan upon his father's death when he was 16. He had worked extremely hard as an engineering student and succeeded in eventually becoming one of the most highly regarded scientists in Wah. He knew the challenge he faced now was his most difficult, but, like the others, he believed he would succeed in overcoming it. At this point, he did not have the solution, but he felt strongly that he would develop a successful one.

He worked that morning on overseeing the final manufacture of the cone of a new nuclear-carrying missile that had been under development for several years. As he learned during the luncheon break, the staff had received new orders to accelerate further the development time for a launch to April 30, 2007, only six months away. The scientists understood that this accelerated pace had been triggered in response to the United States-Indian nuclear technology transfer agreement in February, 2006.

The day passed exceedingly slowly for Mamood. He was anxious for the workday to end at 8:00 p.m. so that he could rush home to check his computer for an encrypted message from Hamad. After making the 15-minute trip by car home, he immediately went to his computer room. He scanned his emails, but much to his disappointment, there was no message from Hamad. Perhaps, tomorrow would be the day, thought Mamood.

When he returned home the next night, he again immediately scanned his emails. Then he saw one from afriend@pak.net. At first, the message would not open. Ah yes, he thought, I must type in the password "Cordoba." Then he typed the password in and read the terse email:

"Meet me for fishing trip in Karachi tomorrow at 9:00 p.m. at the nautical supply outlet across from pier 7." He then inserted the code to decipher the email, and the message then read: "We'll meet inside the door of the mosque two blocks north of the main government center in Islamabad tomorrow at 9:00 p.m. Do not reply unless you cannot be there."

Mamood could not wait for the next night to arrive. Again, his next day at work passed slowly. While he still enjoyed the work he was doing at the plant, he was becoming increasingly focused on his new higher goal. This split vision, he sensed, might distract him from the immediate job task at hand from time to time. When that happened, he tried quickly to overcome it.

He left the plant a half hour early that night, at about 7:30 p.m. He rapidly drove to Islamabad and made good time since the traffic was lighter at this time of night. Most of the commuters from Wah to Islamabad had already completed their return trip. As he wound his way through the still busy streets, past the bustle on the still-teeming sidewalks and the filled outdoor cafes and small markets, toward his destination, he was pleased that he was 15 minutes early. He went into the designated mosque, removed his shoes and socks and washed his hands. He then went into the main prayer area, dropped to his knees on an attractive but well-worn red prayer rug and prayed for several minutes. Raised as a Muslim, he remembered the many hours his mother spent reading passages from the Koran and explaining them to him. Over time, these lessons helped instill vivid images of the Prophet in his mind and gave him a sense of belonging to a large intertwined community. After he finished his prayer, he got up and waited for Hamad near the inside door of the mosque.

At 9:00 p.m. sharp, Hamad entered the mosque wearing a topi, a white cap, and the traditional long white outfit, the ghutra, worn by many Pakistani men. He nodded to Mamood, took off his sandals, washed his hands and went to pray for a few minutes. When Hamad had finished, he then approached Mamood:

"Mamood, may peace be with you."

"And the same for you."

"Let us go to a nearby café up the block I know," said Hamad softly, but with a conspiratorial smile. "We can talk quietly and be alone there."

Mamood and Hamad then left the mosque and went into the Azam Bakery Café, when most of its patrons were sitting at the outdoor tables. They sat at a corner table, inside the café where they felt would not be overheard, and each ordered a chicken kebab with rice dinner. After they chatted amicably for a while, Hamad steered the conversation to a more serious vein:

"My friend, I hear that you traveled to the new Muslim mecca of Dubai."

"Yes, I did," replied Mamood. He then paused, looked around and added: "As you know, it was strictly business. I opened the account at the Mideast Islamic Bank and have the money you transferred."

"Excellent," answered Hamad. "I knew you would have no difficultly in opening the account."

"It went like clockwork," said Mamood. "The banker was very cordial to me. I thank you for arranging that set-up for me."

"Our pleasure," replied Hamad, satisfied that this phase of the plan was now in place.

He then looked around to make sure no one was listening or even looking in their direction. Satisfied that he was unobserved, Hamad continued:

"Our needs, as you recall, are very specific. As I told you before, we need a potent weapon, ideally two of them, that can easily be transported. The weapons have to be able to destroy a three to four square mile area."

Mamood became pensive for several moments. He reflected on the Pakistani arsenal he was aware of and then replied: "Clearly, we have to eliminate almost all of the weapons we have. They can be delivered only by aircraft or missiles."

"Of course, I understand," said Hamad. "We certainly were not going to try to steal a missile. A large bomb is also out of the question. And I'd imagine that the mechanism to explode it is too complicated to work out."

"That certainly narrows the options," said Mamood, whose face now looked more drawn than usual. "We conceivably might be able to use a nuclear-laden cone from one of our missiles. However, getting one out of the plant would be virtually impossible."

"What else is there?" asked Hamad, who clearly sensed the difficulty of his group's requirements.

"We do have some nuclear artillery shells," replied Mamood. "But developing a mechanism to explode a shell that is not shot out of an artillery piece would require an enormous amount of engineering work."

"Can it be done?" asked Hamad in a hopeful tone.

"Probably," replied Mamood. "But developing it may take too long – – and there is no project I am aware of which calls for such work to be done."

"In that case, it probably couldn't be done or might expose you," said Hamad. He now shifted slightly in his chair, feeling a bit uncomfortable but not showing it outwardly.

"That's true," continued Mamood feeling somewhat perplexed. "We may have to think of something else."

"Ideally, we'd love to get our hands on a small bomb, one that actually fits into a suitcase and can be easily detonated by a trained person," said Hamad.

"Again, that could take months or even longer to develop," said Mamood. "It sounds easy as a concept, but perfecting such a device is difficult. Again, I don't recall any project that calls for that kind of device."

"Since you said you don't 'recall,' maybe you could check on that further," said Hamad in a hopeful tone.

"Yes, I think I can do that," replied Mamood. He then sipped his mint tea and relaxed for a moment.

"Good," said Hamad.

"I'll need a least a week, if not longer, to consider what to do," replied Mamood.

"We'll wait," answered Hamad. "Do what you have to do. Then let us meet at the mosque at 9:30 p.m. a week from now. If you are not ready, just send me an encrypted email and let me know when you can meet."

"I think that will work, my friend," responded Mamood.

The two then stood up, embraced each other and left the café in separate directions. Mamood returned to his car and drove off. Once en route to Wah by highway, Mamood reflected on the evening's talk. He knew he had to figure out a solution, a practical one that would work, a task he knew would be exceedingly difficult to accomplish.

Hamad was pleased by the meeting. He trusted Mamood and respected Mamood's intelligence. He knew that the scientist had enough incentives to satisfy the Al Qaeda needs and sensed that Mamood would work day and night to accomplish that end.

CHAPTER 27

RENDEVOUS IN ISLAMABAD

November 2006

After his meeting with Hamad, Mamood spent the next week diligently pursuing his work at the plant. He decided to take advantage of his lengthened work schedule mandated by the Government. He even volunteered to put in several hours of overtime three times that week. His colleagues admired his work ethic and came to recognize that he should have been elevated to the position of Chief Scientist. Clearly, in their eyes, he had earned it. Mamood knew, however, that his perceived enjoyment of his increased workload had little to do with his love for his work. He needed the extra time at the facility to engage in his own clandestine research, for his own selfish ends.

He had previously reviewed the orders to accelerate certain weaponization programs given to the Production Division at the plant by the Pakistani military. Most of his staff had focused on that part of the order that mandated the acceleration of several parallel missile development programs, including the deployment of a more accurate multi-headed warhead missile, and the development of a more mobile medium range missile, to name a few. But the orders also called for the accelerated maintenance and upgrades of the existing weapons in the arsenal to extend their useful lives. This important part of the Pakistani deterrent could not be overlooked. Some of the weaponry was over 12 years old. It was crucial that all available armaments be brought to battlefield readiness within the next 12 months, by October 31, 2007.

Mamood paid special attention to the maintenance/upgrade program. This gave him complete access to the weaponry in the storage area and, as the most senior scientist under the Chief Scientist, he was authorized to direct the bringing of weapons from the storage area to the maintenance portion of the plant, with the approval of the military officer in charge of the storage area. The maintenance/upgrade order also gave Mamood the right to review the list of all atomic weapons on hand so that he and his staff could organize an orderly program and timeline for completing the tasks.

As he worked late on the evening of November 7, 2006, Mamood sat pensively in his Spartan-like office at the plant, and stared at the computer monitor in front of him. He took a mental break, checked his calendar and closed his eyes for a moment. November 7th, he thought, what does this day mean to me or to others? Then he mulled over his proposition for a moment. Of course, the Communist revolution took place on November 7, 1917 and the Russians celebrated that day each year with parades, parties and a day off, a far cry from what he was now experiencing. His thoughts lingered on the Russian connection for another moment. My goodness, that is where my solution may lay.

Many years ago, he recalled that he and his fellow scientists had attended a scientific forum in Karachi, participated by representatives of many countries, including

Russia. There he and his colleagues had met some Russian nuclear physicists, a few old-timers. After one of the Russians had several vodkas at the post-forum reception, he joked about how he had helped to develop a low kiloton atomic weapon for the KGB that they were able to install in a suitcase and could potentially kill up to 100,000 people. The others who overheard the story thought it was just a drunkard's silly boasting. Then Mamood remembered that General Aleksandr Lebed, former secretary of the Russian Security Council, who ran for the presidency of Russian in 1996, also claimed that some of the suitcase bombs developed for the KGB in the early 1970's were unaccounted for and might fall into the hands of terrorists. The Russian Government, in turn, dismissed these claims as nonsense and stated that such a weapon never existed.

And now Mamood remembered that he had heard several unconfirmed reports that Pakistan had developed a similar bomb as a potential additional deterrent in case its main nuclear arsenal were destroyed. If he could substantiate their existence, and if they were in the plant's storage facility, then he might have a chance to succeed with his mission.

He checked the secure computer's list of inventory in the storage facility. It listed several short-range missiles, a number of artillery shells and about four nuclear bombs, but there was no mention of any small atomic weapon. He then reviewed some of the older historical files. As he scrolled down through that old inventory list, he noted that there were four items identified as "miscellaneous." When he tried to check further, he found no additional data that revealed the identity of those pieces. Frustrated with that result, he decided he would requisition two of the four "miscellaneous" items for a maintenance/upgrade treatment. Only then could he determine what the items were.

The following afternoon Mamood requested the two "miscellaneous" items identified by the letters "P-S1" and "P-S2" be brought to the maintenance area at 8:30 p.m. that same night. After taking an early break for dinner in the complex's nearby cafeteria, he returned to the maintenance area. Two guards arrived promptly at 8:30 p.m. – – and each carried a suitcase. Mamood examined each of the suitcases carefully and then stored them in a locker in a secure room off to the left of the maintenance area. Mamood could hardly conceal his delight.

Before leaving for the evening, he decided to do a computer search on another secure site for a schematic of the suitcase bomb. One hour later, he found one in a rarely used file. It showed a detailed diagram of the bomb, including each of its components. A linked site had the instructions for detonating it. He now understood that these suitcase bombs could be the weapons he might try to steal.

But he knew he faced many obstacles before trying to do so.

When he arrived home late that night, he knew he was not yet prepared to meet with Hamad tomorrow night, the scheduled meeting night. He sent Hamad an encrypted email at midnight which, when deciphered, read as follows:

"Can't do our fishing expedition when you planned – – but will be available three days later." He received a reply that, when deciphered, read: "Agreed."

For the next three days, Mamood spent half his time working on the missile cone project and the other half on his maintenance projects. One of the maintenance projects entailed upgrading some of cone's components on a short-range missile. After spending one hour on that project with several other members of the Production Division, he then turned to analyzing the weaponry in the suitcase bomb to determine whether it was still in good working order and usable and whether the facility had replacement parts, if needed.

Over the next three days, he spent more than 30 hours assiduously studying and testing all the components of the suitcase bomb. This fission bomb is triggered by use of a gun device that shoots one subcritical mass into another subcritical mass to produce a super critical mass, which can, in turn, furnish a sufficient number of neutrons to initiate fission upon detonation. He tested the electrical circuitry and found it, albeit crude, in sound operating condition. He also determined that the bomb's fissile ingredients had a substantial remaining useful life. He noted that the triggering mechanism of the gun device had deteriorated and might not be stable, but he hoped he could stabilize it, rather than replace it. He also discovered that some of the rivets on the cover of the suitcase had become loose and several had rusted severely, but he felt he could readily fix that minor problem. On the other hand, there was no test data that showed this bomb had actually worked. Nevertheless, he believed he had a device that potentially could be detonated, but he recognized that there was a risk, as with other nuclear weapons, that inexplicably it might not explode.

Mamood was now ready for his rendezvous with Hamad. On that night, shortly before 9:30 p.m., he again entered the mosque and proceeded to pray after washing his hands and feet. He then waited inside the mosque near the front door for Hamad to arrive. At the appointed hour, Hamad, clad in an all-white outfit and topi, appeared, went inside and began to pray. When he finished, he joined Mamood and the two agreed to go to another nearby café and seek a quiet corner table. This small café, they both agreed, was older than the first one and dirtier, but their dinner, grilled lamb cubes on a skewer, was worth the wait and they ate heartily. After a while, their conversation turned to the key subject, and Mamood spoke first, and in a confident tone:

"I think I may soon have what you want."

"Tell me more."

"To my surprise, I located two suitcase bombs," replied Mamood. "They each have about a 10 kiloton force. Each can kill thousands of people. The number depends on where you explode it."

"Is there a major difference if it is exploded on land or at sea near a shore line," asked Hamad.

"Yes there's a big difference," replied Mamood. He then took another bite of his kebab, chewed it thoroughly and then explained: "If exploded at sea, much of the explosion would be diluted by the water and lose a lot of its killing power. But if the device were set off on land or at dock side, you'd get a much more effective killing effect."

"You will help guide our planning as to what is best," said Hamad, knowing that he needed Mamood for many different tasks. "What problems do you have now?" asked Hamad.

"I still have to run a few more tests on them and make sure the triggering mechanism will work."

"How long will it take?" asked Hamad, hoping for a near-term solution.

"About another two to three weeks," replied Mamood.

"Do you need all that time," asked Hamad impatiently.

"Yes, I do," replied Mamood with conviction. "This device may have never been tested in practice. We want to make sure that they're not duds."

"I understand," replied Hamad in a resigned tone. "Do you feel confident that it will work?"

"If my tests go as planned, I'd stand behind them," said Mamood. "They should then work, but remember that there is always a risk that the bomb may not go off. This sometimes happens."

"Take whatever time you need to assure me that they will work," said Hamad. "That's crucial."

"That's fine with me," replied Mamood, who then added:

"Also, keep in mind that I'm leaving tomorrow, November 12th, for another IAEA sponsored conference in Vienna." It starts on the 13th and lasts through the 15th. You know, of course, that I also want to spend a few extra days with Inge. I won't return until the 18th or the 19th."

"I'll be patient, my brother," said Hamad. "I'm delighted that you are having a great time with Inge. Take good care of her."

"I will," replied Mamood enthusiastically.

"Let's schedule our next meeting at 8:45 p.m. on December 3rd," said Hamad. "If you are not ready then, send me an email and pick a new time."

"Agreed," replied Mamood.

The two conspirators left the café, hugged each other and again went their separate paths. Mamood hurriedly drove home, since he planned to take the morning flight to Vienna in about eight hours and had to pack long before then. He knew he would have little sleep that night. His companion, Hamad, walked for a while, lost in thought about the problems he still faced, before returning to the safehouse in the capital where he was staying.

CHAPTER 28

RETURN TO VIENNA

November 12, 2006

The Pakistani nuclear scientific team of three, including Mamood, flew on British Airways from Islamabad/Rawalpindi Airport to Vienna, via a connection in London, an approximate 14 hour and 45 minute flight. They each chose an aisle seat, one behind the other. After weeks of his herculean efforts, Mamood enjoyed the relative quiet on the flight. Finally, he thought, I have a day off; a day out of the office, in his mind, qualified as such. When they arrived at night, they returned to the same hotel he had stayed at before, the Donauzendrum. Mamood went to bed by midnight, knowing that he wanted to be fresh for the next day's events. He left a message for Inge, and told her he would see her at Der Schwartze Katze tomorrow night, the 13th.

Mamood attended the IAEA conference on "Quality Assurance and New Techniques in Radiation Medicine." While the second part of the subject matter did not interest him, the first did. He hoped to gain some new insights on quality assurance techniques and standards in the medical area that he might then be able to apply to his field of use. One paper presented by a Norwegian scientist in fact attracted his interest. He thought he might be able to test an additional feature of his pet project more accurately.

At the post-session reception held at the agency's headquarters, he dutifully made his required appearance and rounds. He chatted amicably with some of his European counterparts from the Netherlands, Germany and France. On the surface, he was animated, engaging and interesting. He wore this mask well. His thoughts, in fact, were elsewhere – – he was anxious for the reception and the accompanying dinner to end.

After returning to the hotel with his fellow Pakistanis, Mamood returned to his room, as if he were retiring for the evening. Shortly thereafter, he changed into a black turtleneck and a pair of black slacks, put on his leather jacket and left, excitedly, for the club.

Upon his arrival, the now familiar tall blond hostess seated him at his favorite table along the left wall, which also held a good view of the stage. As he settled in his seat, he looked around the room hoping to spot Inge. Then he saw an attractive leggy blond, with her back to him, dancing before three older Japanese men who were seated at one booth. She then began to shimmy and move up and down. Mamood immediately recognized the woman's shape, her legs and the dance – – it was Inge. His eyes now began to follow her every move and he felt his hunger for her rise. He knew, before long, she would come over to him.

After Mamood finished half of his vodka tonic, Inge then joined him. She was thrilled to see him; her eyes danced with pleasure. To the people at the club, she did not appear to be outwardly affectionate towards him. But after she ordered champagne, she squeezed his right thigh gently under the table and placed her left leg right next to his leg. They agreed quietly to meet at their usual spot, two blocks away from the club, shortly after 1:00 a.m. When that time arrived, they then took a taxi to her apartment.

After settling in on the sofa next to her, Mamood asked her:

"How did this past month go for you?"

"Well, my love," she answered, "I was at the club for my usual stint of five nights a week, sometimes six if one of the girls was out. Some of my girlfriends and I lunched several times and once we went to see a German expressionist show at the Kuntshalle. That was great, especially some of the Beckmanns and Kirchners."

"I didn't know you found time to go to museums," he interjected.

"Why not," she quipped smiling broadly. She then went to get some water for each of them and returned. "I love art museums. I've gone to them throughout my life. There is a lot you don't know about me."

"I agree," replied Mamood. "But I'm very interested in learning much more about you."

"I think, peut-être, you'll have that chance," said Inge with a mischievous tone.

"Excellent," he continued. "I've not been to many museums. I'm familiar with some of the Islamic art shown in Islamabad, but I haven't been to the art museums in the West."

"Maybe you'll have your own personal guide then," she said eagerly.

"Why not," he interjected.

"Yes, by the way, I also took the train to Budapest for a two-day break," she continued. "That city always charms me. There are so many interesting and intimate spots for romance as well. Perhaps we'll do a short trip together."

"I love the idea," replied Mamood, with an eagerness designed to please her. "Perhaps after my conference ends on the 15th."

She then kissed him warmly and longingly and hugged him tightly. After a few minutes, he took her hand and led her to the bedroom. Inge enjoyed removing her own clothes. As she turned her back to him, she slowly let her skirt drop and then her blouse. Then, as she smiled coyly over her shoulder at him, she slowly removed her black underpants and wiggled her rear slightly as she did so. At that point, Mamood began to disrobe. He then began to kiss her at her knees and work his kisses up to her tight abdomen and then to her inviting breasts. And then he lost himself in her innermost private beauty. She, in turn, reveled in his warmth towards her. As she felt his hunger for her rise, she too became more excited and squeezed him more tightly with her sturdy thighs. Then they both, sated with love, relaxed and fell asleep in each other's arms.

Scientist by day and lover by night, Mamood somehow found the energy to do both and well. While he needed more sleep, he knew he would have ample time to do so at some point in the not too distant future. He felt he was on one moving continuum, where the night turned into day, and the next day soon became night. In this way, the conference seemed to end faster than he originally expected.

Mamood then took Inge to Budapest for a two-night holiday. He followed her suggestion that they take a leisurely boat ride down the Danube and then return to Vienna by train. As they made their way down the river, they passed charming and highly manicured old Austrian and Hungarian towns, witnesses to many historic events that occurred along or by use of the river. They also enjoyed the changing landscape, from the lush green found in Austria to the mixed green and brown landscape found in Hungary. As they approached their destination, they marveled at the magnificent palace and citadel overlooking the Danube on the Buda side of the river.

They stayed at the Hilton Hotel in Pest, which was adjacent to Utca Vaci, a more than half-mile long stretch of cafes, restaurants, and upscale shopping, including vendors of world-class crystal. Their room faced the Houses of Parliament, stately and study pre-war structures adorned by steeples and ornate designs near the top of them.

During their stay, they explored both sides of the Danube. They took leisurely strolls near the Palace and along the charming neighborhoods within several miles of the Chain Bridge crossing. They ate a romantic dinner at the Kaltenberg, near Utca Ulloi, where strolling violinists played heart throbbing gypsy folksongs, while they dined on veal paprikash, dumplings and red cabbage and sipped an excellent full-bodied Hungarian wine.

They both loved their romantic holiday and felt the trip ended too soon. Certainly, it whet Mamood's appetite for further travels with Inge, and she felt the same. After they returned to her apartment, they sat quietly on the sofa for a while. He then spoke to her of the days ahead and his schedule:

"I'm working almost day and night on some very exciting projects now that I have to complete soon. Obviously I can't say what they are, except that they're important."

"I know you can't speak about your work much," Inge replied. She knew that his business side remained thoroughly shrouded. "You have to keep your country's secrets to yourself."

"Someday soon I suspect I may have more free time, and I eagerly await that day," he continued. She could tell by his tone that he sincerely meant it.

"I do, too," she replied excitedly.

"I'll do all I can to return here as soon as I can. You know that, Inge, don't you?" he said.

"Yes, yes, I know and feel that," she said.

"I'm glad you feel it. I'm overjoyed that we have met," he continued. He leaned over and nuzzled her neck playfully.

"Me too, Mamood," she said warmly.

"It's possible I may have to do a highly secret mission which may take some time," he added. "If it goes well, I may decide to spend much more time in Europe or elsewhere."

"That sounds a bit cryptic to me," she replied.

"It's supposed to be," he continued. "The mission may help me to change my life, but I can't go into that now."

"You don't have to, mein lieben. I trust you and I'll be waiting for you."

"I love those words, Inge," he replied. "You make my heart leap with joy."

"It's the same with me, Mamood."

They then embraced tenderly and, shortly thereafter, made passionate love and fell asleep. When he departed the next morning, Mamood gave her a long goodbye kiss and told her he would return late on the night of December 10 for the next IAEA conference, unless an emergency prevented him from going. From her window, she watched him get into a taxi and leave.

The 12 and a half hour flight back to Islamabad via Doha, Qatar on Qatar Airways seemed exceedingly long. Mamood was lost in his thoughts about Inge, her mind, her love of fun, her scent and her body. He had never felt so strongly attracted to any one woman as he did now. Yet he held back from telling Inge directly some of his innermost strong feelings for her. Maybe this was his way of protecting himself from being hurt, he thought. While in the past, he was the one who usually ended a relationship with a woman he had dated, occasionally, the reverse had happened and he had been hurt. Typically, he did not dwell on such a wound for more than a month or two. But this woman had penetrated deeper. And he wanted to have her in his life for a long time.

CHAPTER 29

PROGRESS AT WAH

November 20, 2006

Mamood returned to his workplace the next day eager to make further progress on the entire project for which he had a major responsibility. In the eyes of his fellow scientists and production team, he appeared most interested in completing the multiple warhead missile upgrade, the top item on the Pakistani Government's agenda. The engineering staff and computer experts worked tirelessly on upgrading the tracking mechanism on the missile in an attempt to meet the April 30, 2007 test launch deadline.

That project faced two difficult issues. The first was adding at least two additional warheads to the existing Shaheen-II missile that had undergone extensive testing. The second was to develop a secure and reliable central tracking center at the overall brain center for the multi-warhead missile. Each warhead had its own guidance system, which had to be coordinated with and ultimately controlled by the missile launch center. Each warhead also had its own jamming system as part of its defense. While each warhead operated independently, a maneuver one might make in self-defense could potentially conflict with a maneuver or the trajectory of a sister warhead launched at the same time from the same missile. The production team worked with batteries of computers manned by knowledgeable scientists to solve these issues.

Typically, at about 3:00 p.m. on most afternoons, Mamood would then begin to focus on his maintenance projects. He again worked in part on the short-range missile cone component upgrade project. Then, after a while, he turned to trying to upgrade the triggering mechanism on the suitcase bomb, a problem that did not lend itself to an easy solution. Without an effective and reliable triggering mechanism, there was no assurance the bomb would detonate. The problem had to be fixed.

When he returned to his home that night, he was unusually tense, almost overwhelmed by the pressure to succeed and a short timetable to produce an excellent result. He had adequately handled pressure from development timetables or approaching launch dates in the past. But this pressure was different. He knew that his life depended on the outcome he achieved, a risk factor he never had to confront before.

For years, Mamood had worked on various scientific aspects for the further development of Pakistani's atomic bombs. He had assisted in the creation of a more advanced gun method mechanism that fired a uranium bullet into a uranium target that, in turn, formed a supercritical mass and created the fission that acted as a catalyst for the nuclear explosion. Armed with that experience, he felt confident that he could stabilize the triggering mechanism for the suitcase bomb.

He then spent most of eight workdays testing the triggering mechanisms developed at the plant for other atomic weapons. He ran simulated tests at the plant with such devices and found that, of the 10 he tested, all were working properly. He then closely reviewed the sequence of the movements in the triggering devices before the final one. He and his fellow scientists jointly monitored these tests and analysis.

Mamood also had previously arranged for two gun method triggering devices to be assembled as replacements for those in the two suitcase bombs. This process took about two weeks, but the new devices were now ready. While he had not yet decided whether to make the substitution, he knew at a minimum that he had to use the new ones for testing purposes.

He then ran simulated tests for three days with non-fissionable materials with these two new devices to confirm their operational readiness. Each time he ran the test the new device worked flawlessly.

Satisfied with these results, he then decided, with some trepidation, to have the new triggering devices installed in the two suitcase bombs as replacements for the old unstable ones, a delicate procedure that took a day to complete. He also arranged for new rivets to be inserted on the outsides of the suitcases whenever necessary.

When Mamood returned to his home that same evening, he felt excited and a sense of accomplishment. Now that he was about ready to pursue the next stage – – stealing the weapons – – he sent Hamad an encrypted email setting up the next meeting which, when deciphered, read:

"Meet me at the mosque on December 6, 2006, at 8:45 p.m. to pray together." They had previously decided that such rendezvous point was the safest place to meet, since men could congregate there at almost any time without being questioned.

Two days later, Mamood arrived at the mosque 15 minutes early after his 40-minute drive from Wah. Hamad was punctual, as usual. Each prayed alone at a different spot in the mosque for about 15 minutes. Then, after they put on their shoes, they left the mosque and walked separately to the nearby Azam Bakery and Cafe. Hamad entered first and selected a corner table; Mamood joined him several minutes later.

Hamad looked at Mamood, saw the dark circles under his eyes, and immediately said:

"You look tired, my friend."

"I am," Mamood replied in a weary tone. "I have worked day and night to fix what you want." As they ate a delicious chicken kebab with onions and peppers, Mamood then spoke animatedly about his technological success:

"These suitcases have sat in storage for over 10 years. As far as I could check from the plant's records, no one had moved them since they were placed there."

"Until you decided to play with them," Hamad interjected quickly.

"Yes, that seems to be the case," replied Mamood.

"What did you have to do with them," continued Hamad.

"As I told you before, I had to run some tests on their electronic circuits and the triggering mechanism and evaluate the fissionable element."

"And now you are finished?" asked Hamad in a hopeful tone.

"Yes, I am," Mamood replied excitedly. "I put a new gun method triggering mechanism in them. I think they're now ready for use."

Hamad then leaned over to Mamood and slapped him on the back with his right hand:

"That's great news," said Hamad with a big smile.

"Yes, but now I have to figure out how I'll get them out of the plant and without arousing suspicion," continued Mamood.

"How heavy are they?"

"About 40 kilos each," replied Mamood.

"Clearly, they're too heavy for one person like you to carry."

"Probably," answered Mamood. "Inside the plant, we move it around on a small trolley with wheels which looks a lot like an airport baggage cart. It's possible I can move it near the entrance or side loading door on the trolley and then carry it a short distance to my car."

Hamad sat back in his seat and rubbed his chin. He then looked at Mamood skeptically and said:

"I hope your idea is workable. Otherwise, you have to come up with a different solution. What about the guards at the plant's entrances? Won't they pose a major problem?"

"There are two guards at each of the two entrances," replied Mamood. "Occasionally one takes a break for about 10 to 15 minutes, which leaves only one guard on duty at that point."

"O.K. Then what do you plan to do?" asked Hamad.

"The guards know me very well," replied Mamood with a sense of satisfaction. "I've been at the plant for over 15 years. They have occasionally seen me come into the plant with, and leave, with a small bag or a suitcase."

"What happened when you did?" asked Hamad.

Mamood paused before answering. He felt he was being cross-examined and his judgment was being questioned. But he kept his cool demeanor and replied:

"Initially, during my first two years there, the guards questioned me and asked me to open my suitcase. When it happened, I explained I had to leave the plant after work and go directly to the airport to catch a plane. When they then checked my bag, they saw I had several changes of outfits, a few shirts and other personal items."

"Did they check on you again," continued Hamad, anxious to know the answer.

"No, after that they just permitted me to come and go without asking me to open my bag," replied Mamood. "In fact, once my bag was very heavy and I asked the guard to help me carry it to my car and he did."

"I'm not convinced that your plan will work," replied Hamad in a somewhat impatient tone. "If it doesn't, I and my group will be very unhappy."

"Obviously, I'll have to consider my proposed exit plan a lot more," continued Mamood. "Somehow I know I'll be able to do it." As Mamood's voice trailed off, Hamad sensed that Mamood's self-assured tone was more of a disguise to mask his own self-doubt.

"I understand that you will too, Mamood. I have great faith in you and you know that."

"Yes, I do," replied Mamood proudly.

After ordering another round of mint tea, Hamad then discussed his detailed plan for the transfer of the weapons to him. Mamood questioned him on some aspects of the plan, but eventually he felt satisfied by Hamad's answers. The group of four Pakistanis at the table nearest to them then left. Hamad, aware that they would not be overheard, then proceeded to the payment issue:

"We now have moved the necessary funds to pay you to the Mideast Islamic Bank in Dubai, so the additional U.S. $99 million is now there," said Hamad. "But we converted our dollars there to euros because we think it is less likely it will be looked at by any European regulators. Our friends there tell us that it is highly unlikely that any movement of that amount will be questioned by the Dubai banking authorities."

"Why is that?" asked Mamood.

"Dubai has become a prime tourist destination for the Muslim community and a trading hub for the Arab and Muslim world," replied Hamad, based on the information given to him by his Egyptian financier. There are many routine large trading transactions involving several foreign entities, with the seller and the buyer each based in a Muslim country or another country.

"Is that all your relying on?" asked Mamood in a questioning tone.

"No, there's more. Mr. al Hassan, whom you met, is a trusted friend of ours and the officer at the bank charged with supervising foreign trading transactions. We know he won't raise any questions here. We moved money around with him before."

"The bank, I assume, has a compliance department," said Mamood. "It could probe further."

"I've been told that will not be the case where the supervising bank officer personally approves the transfer in question," replied Hamad. "In that case, he'll advise the compliance department in advance and get its blessing first. Since Mr. al Hassan has been there for years, the back office will give him the necessary green light in any event."

They then ordered another round of mint tea and asked for some sweet cakes as well. Noise in the café died down as other customers left. After that, they began to discuss the timing of the payment. Hamad was mindful that Mamood had to be entirely satisfied on that front. Hamad then asked Mamood to consider several alternatives that he had been instructed to use.

"Mamood, our group thinks we should do a so-called table top closing. We will have our representative at the bank. Once I call him to let him know I received the weapons and use a code word to identify the transaction, he will deliver to Mr. al Hassan a signed copy of the bill of lading for a fictitious set of goods – – heavy industrial machines in this case – – acknowledging we received them."

"Then you transfer the money," said Mamood.

"Exactly," replied Hamad. "Once the banker receives the signed document, he will transfer the funds to your account at the bank and tell you he has done so in the presence of our representative."

"That may work, Hamad," replied Mamood. After a brief pause, he looked directly at Hamad and said: "But I think I'd prefer that he wire the money to me at another bank in Dubai, the International Development Bank of Dubai, where I set up a second account, and then receive a confirmation from the second bank of its receipt of the money."

"Why is that?" asked Hamad in a surprised tone.

"I'd just prefer it that way," replied Mamood coyly. "I trust you to the grave, Hamad, but your group knows this Mr. al Hassan too well. I need someone more independent to watch out for me."

"I understand now," replied Hamad. Aware that the Pakistani had a good business instinct, Hamad then decided to steer the discussion to the timing of the weapon's transfer:

"This means that you'll want to delay my leaving with the weapons until you know the money is in your bank. Am I right?"

"Yes, that's what I want. You understand my thinking perfectly, Hamad."

"I'll go along with that," continued Hamad. "It just means that we'll have to spend some additional time together when we have our special rendezvous."

Then they left the table, hugged each other and went out of the cafe. While they went their separate ways, they were actually moving along on a common path toward a common goal and each knew such was the case.

When Mamood returned to the plant the next day, he followed his usual routine – – the MIVR project in the morning and the upgrade projects in the early afternoon. During a 15-minute morning break, none of his fellow production workers and scientists even noticed that Mamood took a stroll around the plant for exercise. Certainly, they would not have believed that he was reconnoitering the entrance and exits of the buildings and the routines of the guards again, a practice he started about 10 days ago. Similarly, no one would have considered it strange that Mamood chatted with the guards at the main entrance for several minutes or that, two days later, during his exercise break, he would spend some time with the guards stationed at the loading station exit. Again, there seemed nothing out of the ordinary when two additional empty suitcases, held in the weapons storage area, were brought to the ground floor of the plant for a maintenance check.

Mamood waited for what he considered the most opportune moment to act. Throughout his many years at the plant, he noticed that the guards seemed most lax on Thursday nights, right before the start of their weekend. For that reason, Mamood drove to the factory that day with a large black suitcase he had purchased from a new department store in Islamabad on sale a week before. As he carried it into the plant that particular Thursday morning, January 4, 2007, he felt very tense, but did not show it. He walked through the security gate, kidded with the two guards about their weekend plans, entered the plant unquestioned and proceeded nonchalantly to the scientist's changing area. There he stored his weekend suitcase in his changing alcove. That afternoon he did a final maintenance check on the suitcase bombs, and made a memorandum to such effect in his daily log.

He kept to his usual overtime routine. This time the wait until about 9:30 p.m. seemed interminable. All the personnel who worked in building # 3 had left hours ago. He was now alone, except for the armed guard at the entrance to the weapons storage facility, who could not see the loading dock area from where he was. Finally, when the hour arrived, Mamood left the building through the loading dock exit on the west side of the plant and took a leisurely stroll toward the rear of the building. As he hoped, the two sentries were no longer guarding that exit; they had left. The next shift was not due to arrive for a half hour.

Mamood hurriedly returned to the storage room on the main floor, placed a suitcase bomb on a trolley and went rapidly down the loading dock ramp to his waiting car parked in the lot on the west side of the building, about 40 meters from the loading ramp exit. While the outside area was dimly lit, Mamood saw nobody. He felt his heart race as he pushed the weapon-laden trolley towards his car. In the quiet of the night, he could hear the voices of the sentries guarding the front gate. He prayed that no one would take a break and amble toward the parking lot. He listened attentively, and fortunately, he did not hear any approaching footsteps. Finally, he arrived at his car. He then strained to lift the first suitcase bomb and, with some effort, managed to place it in the trunk.

He then immediately returned to the storage room for the second suitcase bomb. Again, he quickly loaded it on the trolley, retrieved his own suitcase from the empty changing room and then went down the exit ramp to his car undetected. Before he left the loading dock, he looked up and down and saw no one. He then wheeled the trolley quickly to his car. After he barely managed to lift and then place the second suitcase bomb in the rear seat of his car, he wheeled the trolley quickly up the ramp and to a side wall in the manufacturing area and then again left the building, this time with his own suitcase filled with his change of clothes. He looked at his watch. Only 13 minutes had passed. He breathed a sigh of relief that the next shift of sentries for the side exit ramp had not arrived early.

He could not believe his good fortune. His observations had proved correct. His hoped-for lax security coverage gave him the opening he needed and he seized it.

He drove very cautiously on his 15-minute drive home. When he was about to pull into the driveway of his garage, an Army truck with 12 armed soldiers lumbered by, but did not stop. He again exhaled softly, a narrow escape, and then drove his car into his garage and closed the door behind him. So far so good, he thought. The rendezvous with Hamad for the weapons transfer was now only 30 hours away, on Saturday about noon.

CHAPTER 30

WEAPONS TRANSFER FROM WAH

January 5, 2007

Mamood stayed indoors during his 30-hour vigil, awaiting the arrival of his Al Qaeda brother. He slept fitfully that first night, Thursday. Since he had avoided going to the local mosque for the Friday prayer sessions, he prayed quietly at home in a room off his study on the second floor. To his surprise, the multiple prayer sessions spent in quiet contemplation calmed him for a while, and, at the same time steeled him for his next encounter. However, his inner calm was shattered after dinner on Friday night when he heard a loud bang go off on the street nearby his house. At first, he thought it was a shot, perhaps, by a police officer or Army soldier. When he peeked through the shutter of the front window in the main room, he saw a car belching smoke from its exhaust and then heard the car backfire for a second time. Finally, he realized that he would have no peace of mind for an extended period and that he had to learn to adapt to that reality. Whether he could turn his intellectual understanding into a livable reality was yet to be tested. That Friday night, besieged by worries, he again slept about four and a half hours restlessly.

His vigil ended about noon on Saturday. As expected, a three year old, gray Honda four-door van with some three inch rusted dents on the two right doors, pulled up into his driveway. The name "Fine Spices Trading Corp." was emblazoned on the left side of the vehicle above the words "Rawalpindi/Karachi." The van could carry a sizeable amount of goods given its one and two thirds meter high interior space and three and a third meter length of storage room. In fact, the vehicle was almost fully packed with bags and cases of assorted aromatic spices, among them, cinnamon, cumin and cilantro. Through the slightly parted curtain slat, Mamood watched Hamad in his white ghutra and topi and a dark-skinned, young Pakistani he had not met before, similarly dressed, approach his front door. After the pair of double knocks, Mamood opened it and Hamad and his young accomplice quietly entered.

Mamood and Hamad embraced each other as brothers. Aware of Mamood's suspicious glance towards the newcomer, Hamad then introduced his companion, Atiq Barooqi. Mamood and the youngster then hugged each other. Hamad then tried to put Mamood at ease:

"My brother, we're all among friends here. My ally, Atiq, is 100% loyal. He's a black belt in Taekwondo, an expert marksman and a proven fighter. He is here to protect me and my cargo."

"A friend of yours, Hamad, is my friend too," Mamood replied in an accepting tone.

"I didn't want Atiq to wait in the van," continued Hamad softly. "That could look suspicious, especially if he waited there for any extended length of time."

Assuaged, Mamood replied: "That makes sense, Hamad. Your friend can stay in the front room here while we conduct our business in my study upstairs. But first, I'll take you into my garage. Follow me."

A sturdily-built five foot seven inch tall muscular man, Atiq then sat on the brown couch, which sat on top of a geometrically-patterned brown and gold hand-made Pakistani rug, three and two-thirds meters by two and a half meters, which covered about three quarters of the floor of the room. Opposite the couch were two brown leather chairs that served as companion pieces for the couch. Atiq clearly looked the imposing guard he was; his steely eyes showed his grim determination to do whatever he had to do on this mission.

Mamood led Hamad to his car and opened the trunk first. Proud of his accomplishment, he said to Hamad:

"I knew I could do it. It was incredibly lucky to find these two black beauties. But here they are."

Hamad now saw firsthand what he and his leaders had longed to possess. All the prior talk about having a nuclear weapon seemed so abstract and remote, as if present only in some distant dream that is merely glimpsed but not fully remembered or held. Now he was both awed and overjoyed:

"That much power is in that suitcase. It's hard to believe."

"Yes, I know," replied Mamood excitedly: "The destructive power that can be unleashed by it is unbelievable."

"Allah, May the Great One be praised," cried Hamad, and he dropped on the ground facing toward Mecca, a show of respect for this deliverance from above.

After Hamad stood up, Mamood then asked him to step back slightly. He then opened the suitcase in the trunk and showed Hamad the device inside. Hamad's mouth opened and his jaw dropped. Hamad then exclaimed:

"It is Allah's wish that we have this. Otherwise, it would not be here. Do you understand, my brother?"

"Yes, yes, I do," answered Mamood. He then moved to the right side of his car. "And the second identical bomb is in the backseat of the car."

Hamad then opened the door and began to reach out with his right hand to touch the suitcase, but immediately stopped. Mamood noticed his hesitation:

"It's okay. You can touch it, Hamad. Neither of them is armed. There are safety guards on each of them that are in place so they don't go off accidentally."

Hamad then turned to Mamood and asked: "Where are the instructions on how to detonate the weapon?"

"I will give you some written instructions and diagrams separately and tell you more about them at another time," replied Mamood.

"No," said Hamad. "I need a set now. You can give us instruction and a demonstration in the future."

"Okay. If you insist, I'll give you an encrypted set of instructions and diagrams now," replied Mamood coyly. "Once the additional money is transferred to me, I'll then give you the code to decipher them. Is that okay?"

Hamad was acutely aware that Mamood had some reservations on this point and did not want to question him further. He replied: "That will work for me."

Mamood then led Hamad to his study. Whey then arrived, Hamad first glanced around the room. He took in the floor-to-ceiling library on three walls filled with scientific journals, books and articles that Mamood had amassed over the years. He also saw a number of Pakistani, Indian and Western novels that lined several shelves on the right side of the library. There were two computers on top of a hand-carved rectangular wooden desk, with three pull-out drawers on the lower right. He knew Mamood spent hours working there.

Mamood felt that he was in an extremely vulnerable position at this point. He realized the Al Qaeda twosome could easily overpower him, kill him, and simply take the weapons without paying for them. Then he began to dismiss the thought. He trusted Hamad and felt a tight connection to him, like two distant cousins who meet for the first time and shortly thereafter bond closely. Also, Mamood believed that they needed him to show them how to transport the weapons safely and surreptitiously and detonate them. Moreover, he felt that he demonstrated that he was trustworthy. He had not touched any of the U.S. $11 million transferred to him by Hamad and carried out the requested theft of two nuclear weapons from his plant. After exorcising his concealed angst, he came to believe that, on balance, he would be safe.

Once settled into Mamood's study, Hamad turned to the money transfer:

"My brother, the bank has been open for several hours. I'll call Mr. al Hassan now to start the transfer."

"That's fine," replied Mamood. "I'll call my banker at the other Dubai bank to alert him to the transfer as well."

Hamad dialed the Mideast Islamic Bank and immediately reached Mr. al Hassan:

"Good morning, my trusted friend. How are you today?'

"I'm fine," replied Mr. al Hassan. "You colleague from Egypt, Mr. Mahmoud el-Abadi, is sitting here. Do you want me to put him on?"

"Yes, I do," replied Hamad in a serious tone.

At that point, Hamad heard Mahmoud's voice. He now brought the phone closer to his ear.

"My friend, I'm here per your instructions. We have the money needed to complete the purchase. I hope that all is in order on your end."

"Yes, it is, Mahmoud," said Hamad, who was comforted by the Egyptian's presence and reliability. "Do you have the original bill of lading showing our receipt of the goods?"

"Yes, I do," answered the Egyptian in his serious business tone.

"Then give it to Mr. al Hassan now," continued Hamad.

There was a pause, and he heard Mahmoud speak to the banker. "Okay, it's done. I just delivered it to him," replied Mahmoud. "I'll put Mr. al Hassan back on now."

Hamad then heard Mr. al Hassan's voice:

"I now have the original bill of lading stating that you received the goods. Per your colleague's instructions to me, I am ready to initiate the wire transfer of the U.S. $99 million now. I just need to type in the beneficiary's name and banking coordinates."

Hamad then waited a few seconds and said: "I will put the beneficiary on with you now." He then handed his cell phone to Mamood, who immediately said:

"This is Mamood Ishan. I appreciate your help here. Please confirm that you have all the documents you need to make the U.S. $99 million transfer to my designated account."

"Everything is in order," replied al Hassan in an authoritative tone. "I have all the funds in euros and the original of the bill of lading with the acknowledgement of receipt. As you know, we'll be making the transfer in euros at today's exchange rate of U.S. $1.275 for one euro."

"Excellent," answered Mamood, who tried to conceal his excitement. "Here are my wiring instructions.

Payee: East/West Trading Ventures

Bank: International Development Bank of Dubai

Account: 347896001

Swift Code: IDBDSSCC

Attention: Mr. Mohammed al Shala, Vice President."

"Fine, I have then," said al Hassan. "Send me a fax now to confirm them. Here is my personal fax number, 00171767828. I'll stay on this line."

Mamood then put the phone down on his computer desk chair, took a piece of Xerox paper from his desk, put the instructions on it and faxed it to Mr. al Hassan immediately. A minute later, Mr. al Hassan came back on the phone:

"I have your fax, Mr. Ishan. I'll now send the wire and call you with our wire reference number within 15 minutes. Is that satisfactory with you?"

"Yes, it is," replied Mamood. "My friend here will stay on the phone with his colleague until you return." He then handed the cell phone to Hamad.

Satisfied with the money transfer so far, Mamood then telephoned Mr. al Shala, whom he had alerted earlier that morning. After exchanging some niceties, Mamood advised the banker about the pending wire:

"As I told you before, I'm about to receive a wire transfer from the Mideast Islamic Bank for U.S. $99 million in euros. I should have the wire reference number for you within about 15 minutes. Okay?"

"Yes," replied al Shala. "Make sure you put the wire to my attention here."

"We did that already."

"That's fine," replied al Shala. "I'll stand by here and await your call."

Twenty minutes later Mamood received Mr. al Hassan's call on his telephone:

"I sent the wire. The wire reference number is 20061217006113272. If you want me to confirm it in writing to your banker, I will do so."

Mamood, delighted with the news, then replied:

"Yes, send it by fax to Mohammed al Shala."

"I'll do so immediately," responded al Hassan crisply.

"Thanks," said Mamood happily. "I appreciate all your help."

About 30 minutes later, Mamood received a call from his banker at the International Development Bank of Dubai:

"Mr. Ishan. I was able to trace the wire. We are now crediting your account with the funds, a total of U.S. $99 million in euros, less a $20 wire transfer fee. If you want to check the balance in your account, you can use our website which I gave you earlier."

"Excellent," said Mamood. "You have helped me tremendously. I'll be in touch with you soon."

"I look forward to hearing from you, Mr. Ishan. We are at your service." With that, Mr. al Shala ended the call.

The money transfer, a big worry to Mamood, was now complete; he now had U.S. $110 million, a vast fortune far beyond any of his wildest dreams. With his leg of the transaction behind him, Mamood addressed Hamad in a more relaxed tone.

"Hamad, you can now transfer the weapons to your van."

"We'll begin to do that now," replied Hamad eagerly. He then added: "You'll now give me the code so that I can decipher the instructions and diagram."

"Yes," replied Mamood. He then handed Hamad an index card with the code on it. Hamad, in turn, placed it in a small hidden pocket on the inside of his pants.

Hamad and Mamood then returned to the first floor. Hamad immediately asked Atiq to help him load the bombs onto the Honda van. Atiq first backed the van out of the driveway, turned it around and then backed it partway into Mamood's garage. Hamad and Atiq then placed each suitcase bomb in a separate wooden box that was one and a half meters wide and about two meters long that Hamad had manufactured in Rawalpindi at an Al Qaeda-owned mechanic shop, based on the information that Mamood had given him. The boxes were fully lined with lead panels so that the contents of the suitcase would avoid detection from any x-ray inspection.

The loading of the van took about 15 minutes. Hamad then embraced Mamood warmly and said:

"We'll be headed south now. I expect to contact you within several weeks' time. Again, I'll do so by encrypted email. Don't disappear on us."

"I await your word, my brother," replied Mamood.

"You are very resourceful and clever, my friend," continued Hamad. "We still need you to guide us. But we will pick the time and place."

"I understand," said Mamood. "I'll be available. I owe you a lot. Remember I also joined your group. I want you to succeed."

"May Allah protect you," said Hamad. "You'll have to take whatever steps you need to protect yourself as well. At some point, your plant will notice that the items are missing."

"I know that," replied Mamood softly. "I have every reason to protect myself fully."

"Goodbye, my friend," said Hamad.

The Al Qaeda twosome then drove off. As was his habit, Hamad did not reveal his destination to Mamood: Karachi. He did this once again to compartmentalize the knowledge about the operation. The fewer the people who knew his full plan the greater the likelihood it would be kept secret. He looked at Atiq for a moment, mindful of the burden he now carried – – getting the weapons to his next destination and then out of the country.

CHAPTER 31

DRIVE TO KARACHI

January 6, 2007

While Mamood, his co-conspirator, had been working to steal the weapons, Hamad had been deeply immersed in this plan to get the weapons out of Pakistan. An expert planner, Hamad thought of various alternatives and then played them out visually.

Secure in the confines of an Al Qaeda safehouse in a three-storey apartment building in Rawalpindi located on the western outskirts of this bustling city, he weighed the pros and cons of each route over several days, dissecting all of the myriad details with great precision.

He had rejected the air route, a flight from Islamabad to Karachi, immediately. He knew that trying to check the suitcases through gate security was unthinkable. While the screening procedures at Islamabad International Airport were far from perfect, they were efficient enough, in Hamad's mind, to discover what the suitcases contained.

He had dwelled for a longer time on taking the suitcases with him via the train from Rawalpindi to Karachi. It was the easiest way to travel between the cities (other than by air). He had heard some stories of some Pakistani Army soldiers boarding trains to ferret out some terrorists or fugitives, but the intelligence report he received from his brethren said such actions took place very infrequently. At first blush, the train had some appeal. The trip would take about 28 hours, assuming that there were no unusual delays. Moreover, he and Atiq could sit in separate but adjoining first class compartments, so that each could provide immediate assistance to the other, if needed, or avoid detection if the other were detained. The drawback that concerned Hamad most was the high visibility of the large suitcases. Clearly, they had to remain with their carriers and could not be stacked at the end of a car along with the baggage of other riders. Hamad knew that the suitcases always had to be within his sight or that of an accomplice. In his mind, that significant drawback led him to reject the train route.

He had also considered renting a small boat and taking the bombs down the Indian River from its most northern navigable port to Karachi, where the river flowed into the Arabian Sea. He felt that a small craft would retain its anonymity easily in the presence of many other similarly sized vessels, a major advantage. However, Hamad knew that the Pakistani naval units and the police patrolled the river and might make a spot check on his vessel. In such case, he believed that he had less room to escape from such a scenario. For this reason, he dropped this alternative.

That left him the route he chose to follow – – taking a van directly to the docks of Karachi. This plan, of course, required far more than that. Hamad knew that the biggest threat on this route was a surprise Army or police roadblock that led to a search of all vehicles and their cargo. Hamad decided to counter this potential threat by deploying three lead vehicles spaced about two kilometers in front of the other. Each of the vehicles in front of Hamad's van could warn him if the Army or police suddenly set up a roadblock in the direction they were all headed. Certainly, it was not a foolproof plan. The roadblock could occur behind the three lead vehicles and in front of Hamad's van. Even if he had a warning, he might not be near an exit on the road he could take to avoid the blockade or might be unable to turn around and head north. Also, depending on the number of troops or police at a chance roadblock, the Al Qaeda operatives in the lead cars might be able to shoot their way out of a roadblock, since they all carried an Uzi and a rifle-propelled grenade launcher.

Although Hamad predicted that no alternative he pursued was risk-free, he believed that he had the greatest freedom to maneuver in a vehicle.

Before leaving Mamood's home, he had sent a coded email to the three drivers who were part of the convoy and told them to meet him at the first service station on the M2 Motorway, the main national highway between Rawalpindi and Lahore, a distance of about 280 kilometers, at 6:00 p.m. that same day. Since the members of the convoy team were on a standby alert, they were ready to go immediately when called.

Hamad waited until about 3:30 p.m. before he left Mamood's garage. This left him two and a half hours to get his destination about five to seven kilometers northeast of Rawalpindi. He assumed the roads would be crowded with the weekend approaching its end. The traffic to the east of Wah was heavy, but he managed to arrive on time at the designated service station, which also had a convenience store.

Hamad had selected Awad and Mirza, the pirates' two squad leaders, to command the second and third convoy cars, and to be spaced four and two kilometers in front of him. The Commander selected one of Mirza's squad to lead the convoy, and stay six kilometers in front of Hamad's van. The other passenger in the lead convoy cars came from three different Al Qaeda cells in Rawalpindi, who were considered highly loyal and fierce fighters. Five of the group of eight ordered a hot mint tea at the stop, while the other three ordered a cold drink. Once they finished their beverages, they returned to their respective vehicles. Before doing so, everybody synchronized his watch with the time on Hamad's watch, 6:20 p.m. Each person knew his mission – – to protect Hamad's cargo until it was on board a freighter in Karachi – – and was prepared to die to carry it out.

The lead vehicle left first headed in the direction of Lahore. Three minutes later, the second vehicle commanded by Mirza left. After another three minutes passed, the third vehicle commanded by Awad followed in the same direction. Hamad then looked at his watch, and three minutes later, he drove his van onto the highway initially headed to Lahore, before swinging south toward Bahawalpur, a further distance of about 425 kilometers, and thereafter another approximate 1050 kilometers to Karachi.

All the men carried two cell phones, one with a walkie-talkie capability that enabled each to hear any conversation, and the other a conventional one without such a hook-up. Thus, if any vehicle gave a warning to Hamad, the others in the convoy were also sure to hear it and react to any developing crisis.

Fortunately, for the convoy's members, the vehicles traveled the entire length of the dual three-lane highway to Lahore quickly and without incident. Clearly, Hamad, Atiq and other convoy numbers felt highly tense. They each knew that, without warning, a dreaded roadblock could be put up, and then they would have to respond. As Hamad drove, this image haunted him. They made this 280 kilometers stage in about three and three-quarter hours, caused in part by the many toll plazas on the highway. Hamad selected this route because he knew that the Rawalpindi-Lahore road was well-built highway constructed by Daewoo under a special agreement with the Pakistani government. He could not help but notice that the commercial giant's name was evident throughout this stage, on hillsides and at service stations. During the trip, Hamad also felt some comfort in knowing that the concrete barriers in the reserve area between both directions provided added protection in the event a vehicle headed toward Rawalpindi crashed into the divider, a highly remote but still potentially dangerous threat to the van's cargo. He felt more comfort from the absence of lights along the highway, since he believed it made his vehicle more anonymous.

Hamad had planned for the group to stop at the second service station on the main highway south of Lahore, which they did. The group milled around outside the convenience store sipping a tea or soft drink for about 10 minutes before trekking south. Hamad could sense the excitement in the voices of his fellow travelers. He studied the faces of all of his compatriots slowly, first that of Awad, then Mirza, Atiq and the others. Most of them had a wired serious look, an elevated alertness, exactly the trait he wanted in his protectors.

Before leaving the area, Hamad and Atiq made sure that the blankets that surrounded the two suitcases, used to cushion them against any severe bumps on the highway, were solidly in place and were will well secured. After they were satisfied on this item, Hamad motioned for Atiq to drive the next stage toward Bahawalpur, about five and a half hours away.

So far, so good, thought Hamad as he strapped himself into the passenger seat. He kept his walkie-talkie on in case he received any warning from a convoy member. As a precaution, each convoy member had been instructed to maintain telephone silence, except in the case of an emergency.

As they continued southward, Hamad saw many trucks, minibuses and vans headed in both directions transporting their goods or passengers to their respective directions. He noticed that the traffic had become lighter in both directions in the last half hour. He checked his watch, and it was now 10:50 p.m. He looked at the speedometer; the lit marker showed that they were now moving at about 80 kilometers an hour. As the van barreled down the highway, Hamad kept looking to the shoulder of the highway and at the approaching exits in case the van had to make a quick maneuver. The rear lights of the vehicles in front of them appeared as buzzing fireflies at night, bobbing up and down.

Hour after hour passed, as did the cities they rapidly skirted or passed through. The names reverberated in his mind: Harappe, Multan and finally Bahawalpur. Again, he checked his watch, and saw that it was now almost 4:00 a.m. on Sunday morning. He then motioned for Atiq to pull into the approaching service station, the second one on the main highway between Bahawalpur and Sukkar, the next designated meeting spot for the convoy.

Hamad led Atiq into the station's convenience store and joined five of the other six members of the convoy, who had arrived shortly before. The other member, Awad, remained outside the store watching Hamad's vehicle. They each ordered a well-deserved beverage or two, a sweet cake and a sandwich and sat down at several of the tables on one side of the store. Other travelers, mostly dressed in white ghutras and a topi or a different headpiece, who had stopped here for late night refreshment lounged in the rear of the shop. Hamad also placed an order for Awad and brought it out to him outside.

Hamad looked around the area, took a well-earned stretch, putting his arms behind his back and then arching backwards. He then slowly turned to Awad, who was seated on a bench, and said:

"My brother, we made good progress so far. I hope the rest of the trip goes as smoothly as this part."

"Let Allah be with us the rest of our journey to Karachi," replied Awad. He then continued to eat his sandwich rapidly.

"I'm confident he will be," continued the Commander in a reassuring tone. Then the Commander added a note of caution:

"I've heard some reports, Awad, that the Government is now closely monitoring movements from the area around Quetta through and around Sukkar, which I believe is about 150 kilometers from where we are. I think they're troubled by the increase in rebel activity in Baluchistan as well as the presence of Taliban and Al Qaeda operatives in and around Quetta, who then go into Afghanistan to rouse anti-Kabul sentiment and attack governmental outposts."

"As we approach Sukkar, we have to be extra careful and vigilant. Am I correct, Commander?" asked Awad, although he knew he had already anticipated the correct answer.

"Yes, you are."

Hamad then left Awad so that he could finish his early breakfast. He then motioned for the other six operatives to join him outside. He gave the group a quick update about the perils around Sukkar. He then went to Awad's van, took out one of the detailed maps of the Sukkar area and showed them the side roads they might have to use as they neared the area. Each convoy member closely studied the map and made mental notes of these escape routes.

The convoy then continued its southward journey, which each vehicle spaced about two kilometers apart. Hamad was delighted that all of the walkie-talkie cell phones remained quiet for well over an hour and a half.

As the lead vehicle driven by Kamal, a member of Mirza's squad, rounded a turn several kilometers to the south of Sukkar, Kamal saw the nightmare they dreaded.

As Kamal surveyed the scene ahead of him, he saw five Army trucks lined up across the road headed south, each with a heavy machine gun and two operators in the rear of each truck. There were at least 50 armed soldiers who took up various positions at both the barricades and along the side the trucks. He could also see that four soldiers were poised to inspect each vehicle. He then quickly spoke loudly into his two-way phone:

"There are five Army trucks up ahead about 800 meters from where I am and about 50 soldiers from them just set a barricade on the main road. Do what we discussed. I plan to be stopped."

Mirza, who was driving the second car in the convoy, immediately looked for an exit off the highway and saw one 300 meters in front of him and over 3000 meters from the road block. He knew he could not be seen by the soldiers manning the roadblock because he was at least 1,000 meters from the left turn in the road that then went in a straight line down into the valley where the troops were now stationed. The hilly terrain before that left turn shielded his vehicle from the soldiers' sight. As he left the National Highway rapidly, he could see that dawn was breaking in the east.

Forewarned, both Hamad and Awad accelerated their vehicles and moved at about 120 kilometers an hour and raced to the next exit up ahead, the one that Mirza saw and then took in the direction of the smaller city of Phariaro, less than 40 kilometers to the southeast of their present location south of Sukkar. They all hoped that exit would provide a sanctuary for them, like seeking shelter in a mosque before a dangerous thunderstorm strikes. They hoped they would hear no alarming news from Mirza, who went down the exit and was now the lead car. The walkie-talkies stayed silent. Once Hamad's van made it through the exit, Hamad spoke to Mirza and Awad on his two-way cell phone calmly and said:

"I think we'll be fine, my brothers, but we have to keep on the lookout for other similar surprises. Until further notice, let us now continue to go west/southwest and then take the Indian Highway all the way to Hyderabad, a distance of about 475 kilometers. We'll stop briefly there and then consider whether to continue on that highway into Karachi or to pick up the National Highway then and proceed to Karachi."

As expected, Mirza replied first: "I'll lead the way."

Awad then said: "I'll follow as before."

The now three-car convoy continued again, with the same two kilometer spacing as before. Hamad breathed a sigh of relief. He knew that his brush with the road block could have proved fatal one way or another. He envisioned that that the lead cars of his convoy may have had to crash through the barriers at high speed and then engage the soldiers in a quick, but heavy, gun battle, and probably his brothers would be killed in the ensuing fight. If he had been unable to escape in a nearby exit or cross the road and proceed northward, he knew he and Atiq too might have been killed.

The next 475 kilometer stage fortunately for them provided uneventful. The traffic on the Indian Highway now moved more slowly than that on the National

Highway, perhaps due to the beginning of a new day with its early new truck traffic transporting needed commodities for Hyderabad and Karachi. Hamad could see that there were Pakistani, Chinese and Afghan trucks on the road, a testament to the change of times and the increase in trade with both neighboring countries. The slow pace did not bother the convoy members; they were simply delighted that they encountered no further roadblocks. This stage of the journey took about six hours.

On the southern outskirts of Hyderabad, the convoy stopped at a small crowded cafe with many outdoor tables. The early afternoon sun made them all sweat profusely once they were seated outside. They rested their weary limbs before ordering a pita sandwich with grilled chicken and rice and tea for lunch. They eagerly gulped the bottles of water brought to the table. After lounging for about a half hour, Hamad decided that the group should take the National Highway from Hyderabad to Karachi, which he estimated was about 200 kilometers away and about an estimated three and a half hour drive.

As the sun continued to bake the convoy cars, the group wound its way to the southwest. Finally, after a grueling almost four-hour stretch, they saw Karachi and the blue Arabian Sea that lay along its shores, their long-awaited destination. Once inside the city, Hamad told Atiq that he would drive the van to the port. The traffic was extremely heavy, causing massive tie-ups at many intersections. But Hamad knew the side streets well and soon, after weaving in and out of several streets near the port, he parked the van in the port's main parking lot, near the other two cars driven by his accomplices. He and Atiq then waited until the night superintendent of the port, an Al Qaeda member, showed up. As was his habit, he arrived promptly at 6:00 p.m. and went into his office. At that point, Hamad drove his van to the port facility main gate, where the superintendent's appointed guards immediately lifted the gate and let Hamad's van enter, together with the other two convoy cars.

Hamad immediately drove his van, followed by the other two cars driven by Mirza and Awad, about 50 meters from the berth where the SS Barooqi, a Pakistani freighter bound for Dubai, was then loading. The superintendent, dressed in a short-sleeved tan shirt and khakis, ambled over to Hamad's car. He had been briefed by Zafir el-Amin that some spice goods had to be loaded onto a freighter immediately and securely. Aware that he had an important task ahead of him, he joined Hamad where he had parked and then said:

"The freighter at this berth is scheduled to leave for Dubai tomorrow morning at 6:00 a.m. I can arrange for a container for your spice cargo to be loaded on the ship immediately, if that's what you want."

Hamad, who knew that the superintendent was an Al Qaeda member and had been briefed, replied immediately: "Yes, let's do it as soon as possible."

The superintendent then swung into action. He approached the seaman in charge of loading the freighter and announced, in an authoritative tone, that a late arriving cargo had to be loaded on board now and gave him a superseding manifest reflecting the additional container and its contents. The superintendent then arranged for a white container on top of a nearby truck with the name All Asian Transport on it to be brought near Hamad's van. Several of Hamad's group then loaded the spice cargo, including the two specially made wooden boxes with the suitcase weapons hidden inside, into the container. Then a loading crane hoisted the container onto the vessel and placed it alongside the other containers on deck.

The superintendent then examined the manifest of the crew on the vessel with great interest and showed it to Hamad. He, in turn, went down each name and smiled when he saw the names of two of the pirates' men, who had taken part in the hijacking of the *Argus*, as seamen who were part of the *SS Barooqi's* crew. He smiled knowingly because each of those crewmembers had been instructed to safeguard that special container, although they did not know its true contents. Pleased with that step, Hamad handed the manifest back to the superintendent and said happily:

"You've done a great job for us. Your loyalty has been shown again and again, my brother. May Allah continue to guide you and your family."

"I accept your kind words," answered the superintendent. He was proud that he was able to help this important leader. He then left Hamad and returned to his office.

Once the superintendent left, Hamad motioned for Awad and Mirza to join him:

"My brothers, we have some work to do now at the safehouses. After that's done, we'll leave the country immediately for the Middle East."

"I follow whatever you say, Commander," replied Awad. Mirza's nod of his head showed he agreed as well.

Hamad and Awad once again drove to safehouse # 3 through the busy Karachi streets, a 25-minute drive. Hamad and Awad each parked their vehicle about 50 meters up the street from the entrance to safehouse # 3 and surveyed the area from their cars to see if the house was under surveillance. After they concluded they were safe, they left their cars and entered the house. Immediately thereafter, Hamad ordered Awad to kill Captain Johannsen since he was no longer needed as a hostage that could have served as a bargaining chip if the house were under attack. Hamad first visited with Captain Johannsen, whom he noticed had lost a considerable amount of weight:

"Captain, I'm here to let you know I must leave now. I see you have suffered in our hands in this house."

"You know I have, Commander," he replied.

"We don't always treat our guests well," replied the Commander in a stern tone. "But soon you will not suffer any more."

"Look, Commander," said the Captain. "I helped you and saved the life of you and your crew during the typhoon. Doesn't that count for anything?"

"Yes, it does," replied the Commander. "But only up to a point."

"Commander, for God's sake, spare me. I have a wife and two children. I'll never mention anything about your piracy of the *Argus*. I promise, with all my heart, that I will not reveal your name or that of any of your crew. I promise. You have to believe me."

"I wish I could," answered the Commander in a cold tone. "We know that there are serums that can be used to make you talk, whether you resist or not. You can't guard against that."

"Please, Commander," the Captain pleaded. "Spare my life so that I can see my children again."

Suddenly the Captain sank slowly to the floor. Blood oozed from a small hole in the center of his forehead. Awad, ruthlessly loyal to the Commander and the cause, shot him with a silenced pistol.

Hamad then instructed Awad to have his remaining squad wrap the Captain in a white sheet and drop his body with heavy stones in the Arabian Sea from a section of the beach road at night.

The Commander then instructed Mirza by cell phone, using their prearranged code words known only to them, to kill Henriks at safehouse # 4 and dispose of his body in the same way.

Unmoved by the Captain's death in front of his very eyes, Hamad then ordered his two squad leaders to meet him at the Jinnah International Airport at 7:00 a.m. the next morning so that they could board the 9:00 a.m. flight from Karachi to Dubai.

CHAPTER 32

DUBAI

January 8, 2007

Dawn was breaking as Captain Krueger and the 18-man crew of the *SS Barooqi* let go the lines dockside, raised anchor, and set out on the azure waters of the calm Arabian Sea alight with the rays of the rising sun. It was 6:00 a.m.

The freighter was loaded with cargo bound for Dubai, Kingston, Jamaica and, ultimately, Jacksonville, Florida. Containers of all size, shape and color stamped with the names of international shipping companies were securely fastened on deck. The trip to Dubai would take two and a half to three days, depending on weather conditions. ETA was approximately 2:00 p.m. in the afternoon of January 10, 2007.

Ashan Mamooqi and Hassan bin Nedel, two members of Mirza's squad, were assigned on deck. Typically, they spent most of their time checking and rechecking the containers to make sure they were secure. Nobody noticed that either one or the other was on the deck at any single time. Everybody assumed they were both extremely responsible seamen.

Ashan Mamooqi, a sturdily built Pakistani of medium height with dark brown hair, a neatly trimmed beard and penetrating brown eyes offset by a wreath of crow's feet. His muscular chest bulged beneath his light brown tee shirt. Born to a poor family in Quetta, he was educated at a local madrassa, where he was taught the Koran by rote, eschewing courses in science, mathematics and social studies. About 30 years old, he was not married and had been an Al Qaeda member for at least eight years. He had weathered many firefights in Afghanistan, including the terrible B-52 bombings by the hated Americans. He had also undergone extensive maritime training, and was an extremely loyal follower of Commander Hamad.

Hassan was from Tangier, Morocco. A veteran seaman with over 20 year's experience, he was familiar with all aspects of running a ship. He was tall and lanky with light brown hair, cold hazel eyes and a scar on his right cheek, which highlighted his hawkish features. Raised by a poor, religious family, he had been steeped in the Koran from an early age. His educational background was broader than that of Ashan, since he had attended and completed high school in his port city. He was married to a Moroccan woman and they had one son, who was now 10 years old. During a long layover in Karachi, he was recruited for Al Qaeda by a local fundamentalist group.

The voyage was uneventful. While U.S. Navy destroyers and other vessels patrolled the Arabian Sea, they took no interest in this 100,000 metric ton freighter, an ordinary commercial vessel that typically plied these waters.

A day before arriving at Dubai, the vessel's captain sent the port's maritime authorities a manifest listing the names and nationalities of the members of the crew, together with a manifest of the ship's cargo, most of which consisted of cotton goods, shirts and textiles and other sundry cargo, including some cotton goods and spices bound for Jamaica. In the eyes of the Dubai port operators, neither manifest aroused any suspicion. Most crews frequenting that port were of an international blend, ranging from Morocco, Egypt, Bahrain and Pakistan to India. The Captain, Otto Krueger, came from Hamburg, and had over 20 years' experience. The cargo was also commonplace; the United States was Pakistan's largest export market and the country's largest export consisted of cotton goods and textiles bound for the United States. Several containers of cotton goods were also designated to be unloaded at Dubai, a process expected to take about two days. The port had become increasingly busy, due to the large increase in trade which passed through Dubai for home consumption and for re-export to other countries throughout the world.

As the freighter approached Dubai through the calm waters of the Persian Gulf, many crewmembers came up on deck to view the stupendous office towers, hotels and other buildings that sprang up from the desert kingdom, a testament to Dubai's increased prosperity and the worldwide commercial role it now played. Ashan and Hassan had not seen Dubai for several years and were impressed by the tremendous changes in the city's silhouette.

At the direction of the port operator, the *SS Barooqi* dropped anchor about one mile out in the Gulf awaiting an available berth for unloading. At about 8:00 the next morning, a berth for the vessel became available. A tug guided the ship to dockside at the terminal at the Jebel Ali Port. Captain Krueger's first mate came offshore and gave the harbormaster a copy of the ship's manifest showing the cargo that was to be unloaded. The harbormaster asked him for a copy of the crew manifest. Since the vessel was ultimately headed to the United States, all passports belonging to the crew had to be presented. The first mate handed them over. The representative then scanned each passport against his computer and was satisfied when no negative referral appeared. No one in the crew had been identified on the watch list as a possible criminal or terrorist. The port's computerized facilities were up-to-date and operational and the watch list was updated periodically as a matter of routine. The composition of the crew might have been considered problematic from an American point of view because of the presence of crewmen from Pakistan, Morocco, Egypt and Bahrain. But in Dubai, such make-up posed no issue. To the port operators, they were their Muslim brothers.

Once this formality was accomplished, the unloading of the vessel began. A large crane began lifting the containers bound for Dubai off the vessel and onto a waiting line of trucks. Since there were 15 containers that had to be unloaded, the process took several hours and was only completed at 11:30 a.m. Once the containers were loaded onto the trucks, a port operator representative checked off the containers' serial numbers to confirm that the correct cargos had been offloaded.

Noteworthy to Ashan and Hassan, there was no inspection of the contents of any of the containers offloaded – – and no one came on board to inspect the rest of the vessel's unloaded cargo. Apparently, the port operator had not received from the United

States any notice of suspicious cargo bound for the States. Hassan, who was more experienced than Ashan, knew that many foreign ports, including Dubai, had agreed to buy scanning equipment to conduct inspections of any suspicious cargo bound for the United States (as required by the Bush administration under the Container Security Initiative) by a screening center in Virginia. Identification of suspicious cargo was obtained by scanning an electronic manifest sent at least 24 hours before cargo was loaded onto an ocean carrier destined to arrive in the United States. He had heard, however, that this equipment was not adequate to inspect all containers and that only a small fraction of them were actually inspected. He also knew that the U.S. congressional uproar over Dubai's planned purchase of the Peninsular & Oriental Steam Navigation Company – – a British company that oversaw the running of the port operation at six important American ports – – had an ironic twist. If the purchase had gone through, Dubai Ports would have agreed, as part of the deal, to subject cargo in Dubai to the most modern and complete inspection beyond even that sought by the Bush administration, including the expensive modernization of the port. He smiled inwardly. Such a rigid and thorough inspection would have to wait. However, he remained unconcerned. His cargo was not bound for the United States and, thus, was outside rigid inspection guidelines.

By 2:00 p.m. that same day, the *SS Barooqi* pulled away from the terminal heading into the Persian Gulf, bound for the Suez Canal and the Mediterranean Sea. Since it was a sunny, clear day, visibility was excellent. The air was balmy; a cool breeze came from the southeast, a welcome relief to those on dock. The freighter soon passed through the quiet waters of the Strait of Hormuz. Members of the crew could see several U.S. naval vessels, two destroyers and a cruiser, patrolling the waters. Their primary mission was to make sure that this vital shipping lane, that accommodated tankers carrying Saudi, Kuwaiti and Iraqi oil to foreign markets, remained open, without threat from any neighboring country.

Shortly thereafter, the vessel passed through the Gulf of Oman. Once out of sight of the U.S. patrols, the Captain set his course more than 200 miles from the coast of Somalia. Increasing acts of piracy along the Somali coast posed a threat to any vessel venturing too close to those shores. The Captain knew from a United Nations report that there had been 45 attempted hijackings, 19 of which were successful, off the Somali coast during a 15-month period ended March 31, 2006. The ship's registry did not matter to these pirates; they had overtaken a South Korean fishing vessel, a Georgian cargo ship and a Panamanian oil tanker. Ashan and Hassan quipped to each other that it would be a terrible stroke of luck for themselves as pirates to be taken hostage by Somali pirates.

However, no piracy threat materialized as the vessel headed south and then southeast through the Arabian Sea. The Captain was delighted when he saw several additional U.S. naval destroyers and a U.S. aircraft carrier pass several miles to the east of them when they were 250 miles off the coast of the Somali/Yemen border. He realized that their presence might have prevented any preying by Somali pirates on his vessel.

The freighter headed into the Gulf of Aden, a protected and quiet passage that led past the new U.S. naval base at Djibouti into the Red Sea. The ship was making excellent time, averaging about 22 knots an hour. At that rate, they would arrive at the Suez Canal in about three full days.

A day and a half later, they passed the port of Jeddah on the western coast of Saudi Arabia, the most important port in the area. The passage through the Red Sea was the most peaceful of the entire voyage. Clear sunny weather continued to provide excellent visibility. The waters were the calmest of the journey. However, the area was also the busiest since many ships sought to cut their transportation time by going through the Suez Canal. The crew on deck saw a steady trail of ships headed both north and south either approaching or leaving the Canal.

The *SS Barooqi* soon came to the Canal; the Captain had advised the Canal's operator of the ship's scheduled arrival. The lock system slowly moved the freighter forward as the water level rose in each succeeding lock. Finally, the ship cleared the Canal and passed into the Mediterranean bound for the United States, via Jamaica, an approximate 12 to 14 day trip.

The freighter began its westward journey through the Mediterranean at sunset. Pink clouds drifted by slowly and a few seagulls flew rapidly over the ship's bow before heading back to the Egyptian coast. Several miles to the west an oil tanker, which had also left the Canal, was visible.

Captain Krueger knew from experience the Mediterranean passage was the easiest and safest part of the ship's voyage. There was no piracy threat. Various ships belonging to the United States Sixth Fleet regularly patrolled these waters. In addition, the ship could steer well over 50 miles from any island or country as part of its route. Similarly, the Captain was aware that he would not run into any major storms on this part of the route that could imperil his vessel.

The ship journeyed slowly past Crete to the north and the coast of Libya to the south, past Malta and Sicily. The crew could easily make out the Tunisian coast and the lights from the northern Tunisian city of Bizerte twinkling in the distance. Plying further westward, the freighter passed by the coast of Algeria and then Morocco. Shortly thereafter, the *SS Barooqi* approached the Strait of Gibraltar and then passed into the Atlantic Ocean.

Heading due west, south of the Azores, the ship altered course to the southwest in the direction of the Caribbean and its next destination, Kingston, Jamaica. The Atlantic was turbulent at this time of year, with swells of 10 to 15 feet and occasional rain showers. Thereafter the Captain steered the ship to the south of Puerto Rico and the Dominican Republic.

Almost 13 days after passing through the Suez Canal, Kingston harbor came into view. The port's commercial activities were minor compared to that of Dubai. The unloading facilities at the Kingston Trans-Shipment Terminal had recently been upgraded and modernized, but were much smaller than those at the Jebel Ali Port. Since Captain had alerted the harbormaster of the ship's anticipated arrival time, a berth for unloading was made available within three hours of its arrival in the harbor.

As Jamaica was also a party to the Container Security Initiative of the Bush administration, the Captain had sent a manifest of its cargo as well as that of the crew to the port authority at least two days in advance of its arrival. The port authority and its U.S. Customs representative paid little attention to the cargo of cotton goods headed to the States and did not choose to inspect the containers of cotton goods and spices that were offloaded in Kingston. The freighter docked on a weekend and the employees of the port facility were in a hurry to finish their appointed tasks as soon as possible and not look for extra work. From the port, one could hear the loud Reggae beat of a local festival nearby. The sounds of singing voices, laughter and the shuffling feet of dancers carried throughout the unloading facility.

The unloading process began at noon on the arrival date. A new crane lifted 15 containers from the ship's deck. Ashan and Hassan watched closely as the white container marked All Asian Transport they had safeguarded so carefully was hoisted overhead and then lowered onto a waiting truck to be taken to the container storage area at the port, pending pickup by its customer or designated freight forwarder.

CHAPTER 33

WAH, PAKISTAN

January 10, 2007

Several days after Mamood left the Wah Containment Ordinance Complex for another IAEA meeting in Vienna, the Brigadier General in charge of security, Omar Kareem, ordered an inventory of all weapons at the facility. Beefy and bespectacled in his early fifties, with watery hazel eyes, the General was a familiar face in Pakistani governmental circles. Often seen at officer receptions and banquets, he mingled easily with his military cohorts, including President Musharraf himself. He made friends easily and managed to climb up the military ladder securing plum appointments along the way. One of these was overseeing Pakistan's atomic arsenal at the Wah facility where he strove to prove that he was the right person for the task.

The order for an inventory inspection came as no surprise to those in the complex. It was a necessary precaution, part of the routine maintained to keep the country's arsenal safe. One morning, Colonel Ibrahim Ashani, a member of General Kareem's staff, went to the weapons storage unit to check the missiles and warheads on site against the computer weapon record. Colonel Ashani, an army veteran, with 15 years of experience in security matters, was a trusted aide. The arsenal's completed computer list was a highly secret document and only he, the General, Mamood and the Chief Scientist at the facility had access to it without further clearance.

Displaying a solemn demeanor, the Colonel entered the weapons storage area. He immediately counted the missiles, one by one, and checked their serial numbers against his computer list. As he ran his hands on one of the Shaheen II missiles that lay on a heavy steel removable rack, he smiled slightly, reveling in the unbridled power it contained. An enemy could clearly be brought to its knees if a number of these missiles were unleashed. An avid equestrian, the Colonel considered these missiles modern racehorses of doom and destruction. Shaking his head, he went on to the next missile.

Half an hour later, he descended to the second level to check off the warhead cones. An overhead lamp illuminated the gray cones and cast eerie shadows behind the multilevel storage racks. Continuing his underground inspection, the Colonel paused to look around the room and marveled at its construction. Protected by thick concrete walls on all sides, with a six-inch lead shield on the inside of the walls, the storage facility was virtually impregnable. As he raised his right arm to check the cones on the highest level of the rack, he shuddered slightly.

After two and a half hours of hard work – – reviewing three levels of arsenal firepower – – the Colonel decided to take a break. He went down the loading dock exit ramp and walked slowly toward the rear of the building, enjoying the fresh air. Stopping for a few moments, he breathed deeply and ran moist palms through his thick dark brown hair as he gazed up at the sky.

The sunshine made him squint. He definitely needed to unwind. An accurate accounting was an enormous responsibility and weighed heavily on him. Soon he would be done, he thought, and then he could go back to his normal routine of administrative duties - a far less demanding task.

Feeling refreshed, he walked back up the exit ramp to the manufacturing and testing area that was adjacent to the weapons facility. Holding his list tightly, he began to examine each weapon and those readied for testing. All of the components in the Shaheed II missile upgrade project were on hand, and he happily checked those off. Moving to the north part of the floor, he examined all the sensitive components for the maintenance of each project in progress and noted they were all present.

Then he walked to a section of the west wall and opened the door to the scientists' special projects room. There he saw two slightly worn, black suitcases resting in the corner. Earlier, he had identified items PS-3 and PS-4, which were located on the third level of the storage area. He assumed that these two in the corner must be PS-1 and PS-2 because they had been brought to this area for maintenance. Satisfied by what he saw, he was about to leave the special projects room when he turned to look at the suitcases again and noticed that they bore similar scratch marks on their exteriors - as if each had been subjected to the same wear and tear. He decided to take a closer look.

Opening one of the suitcases, the Colonel saw a gun device. The rest of the bomb appeared to be missing. He immediately checked the other suitcase and found the same set up - a gun device minus the deadly ingredients of a bomb. Sweat broke out on his forehead. This cannot be, he thought. Was this a discarded gun device? Automatically he began rubbing his neck. Had someone taken the fissile material and the rest of the bomb's contents? Or worse still, had someone taken the suitcase bombs PS-1 and PS-2 and left these discarded parts on purpose?

Hiding his anxiety, he left the manufacturing plant and strode back to the Ordinance Factories security command center to have a quiet, confidential conversation with the General. He knocked twice on the General's office and entered without waiting to be invited inside. Seated behind his desk, the General eyed the Colonel closely. His chief assistant's military bearing and his muscular, six foot frame were comforting. The Colonel's bushy eyebrows were raised and he ran a nervous hand through his thick hair. Something was amiss, the General thought.

"What's up, Colonel? Have you completed the inventory?" The General's voice was gruff.

"I did, sir. All the items are accounted for, but I think we may have a big problem," replied the Colonel unhappily, shifting from one foot to the other.

"A problem? What kind? You've got to be kidding. We've had great security here for years," the General said, raising a fist in his excitement. He rose from his chair, walked over to the Colonel, and took him by the hand to a worn brown leather sofa against the opposite wall. They both sat down.

"Now tell me what this is all about," the General continued, putting his hand on the Colonel's shoulder.

"Sir," the Colonel's voice faltered, "here's what I know. We have four suitcase bombs in the arsenal numbered PS-1, PS-2, PS-3 and PS-4. I saw PS-3 and PS-4 on the third level in the weapons storage facility. When I went to the scientists' special projects area, I saw two additional suitcase bombs there."

"So, what's the problem?"

"When I opened them up, they each contained only old discarded gun devices – nothing more."

"Go on," the General's lips tightened.

"Each suitcase bomb weighs about 45 kilos, but these weighed only about seven kilos a piece."

"So what's your read of the situation?" asked the General, rising. He began pacing the room slowly, rhythmically.

"I think that two suitcase bombs are missing and that the old gun devices have been replaced by new ones," the Colonel said softly.

"And you think those two suitcases you saw were planted there to give the appearance that all four suitcase bombs were on the premises," the General continued, following Colonel Ashani's line of reasoning.

"Exactly, sir. I think they were left there to create the appearance that the suitcase bombs were still being worked on, when in fact, they were no longer here."

"Did you check the scientists' logs to see if PS-1 and PS-2 were being maintained or upgraded."

"Not yet, sir. I wanted to get your approval first."

"You have it now." The General's face was flushed with anger.

"I would advise you, Colonel, to keep our conversation to yourself. We must not raise any alarms. But get to work immediately and report back within half an hour."

"Yes, sir," replied the Colonel, turning on his heel and walking out smartly.

Left alone, the General slumped back on his sofa, shaken by what he had just heard.

Colonel Ashani walked back purposefully through the main floor to the manufacturing facility where 20 or so engineers and scientists were working on their respective projects. Once again, he entered the special projects room, sat down at the main computer station, put in his authorization code and tapped into the facility's menu. Immediately he scanned the scientists' daily log reports, looking for any mention of work done on PS-1 and PS-2. Flipping through voluminous reports, he finally came upon an entry in Mamood's log dated December 27, 2006 stating that he began upgrade/maintenance work on certain miscellaneous weapons referred to as PS-1 and PS-2. Reading further, he saw that Mamood had upgraded the gun device in each of the two suitcase bombs and had removed the existing ones because of their apparent unreliability. As he continued to read, Colonel Ashani noted that Mamood had not reported anything further about the upgrade project or whether it had been completed, leaving the impression that more work was needed. Finally, the Colonel noted that the logs failed to mention any suitcase bombs were missing.

By now convinced that the two suitcase bombs were indeed missing, the Colonel made his way back to the General's office, bearing the ill-fated news.

"General, I checked the logs," he said. His face was ashen.

"And?"

"The two suitcase bombs were upgraded; a new more reliable gun device was installed in each of them."

"Okay."

"But there is no mention that they're missing," the Colonel continued.

"Of course not," snapped the General, glancing angrily at his aide as he paced up and down. "No one would put that entry into the logs."

"Of course, sir," agreed the Colonel looking down at the floor.

"And your conclusion, Colonel?"

"I believe they are missing," he replied softly, approaching the General's desk. "I think someone took them and tried to conceal the theft."

"We have a very big problem here, Colonel," said the General solemnly, turning to face the Colonel. Anger and anxiety twisted his features. He looked disheveled. "It's my job to keep our arsenal secure – – and I didn't do it."

"It's not your fault, General. How could you have prevented it? Our overall security plan is excellent."

"You are very kind, Colonel. I know how loyal you are. But this happened on my watch. I'll be blamed, and rightly so."

"What should we do, sir?"

"The President must be informed immediately. No doubt, he'll want to undertake a major investigation. Hopefully he'll keep it under wraps as long as possible," the General replied stoically.

He sat down at his desk and called the President's Chief of Staff, Mohammed Doha, an old high school buddy. Quickly he explained that two suitcases, each containing an atomic bomb, were missing from the Wah facility and, in his opinion, were stolen. Stunned by the news, Doha replied he would contact him immediately after speaking to the President.

As the General waited anxiously for the incoming call, all sorts of dire scenarios flitted through his mind. He knew that the consequences of an atomic theft were disastrous. It would be the end of his military career. The secure phone rang in his office. Quickly he picked it up.

"General Kareem, this is Vice President Dolani."

"Good evening, Mr. Vice President." The General's voice was strained. It was no small thing to be speaking to the second most important political figure in Pakistan.

"I have just been told about the missing weapons which you reported to the President's Chief of Staff. We're going to start an immediate investigation to try to locate them. I will be working with the President's own security staff, with the help of our ISI, for approximately three days. If we don't solve the theft and recover the weapons by then, we will subsequently need your complete cooperation in helping with our investigation - and I know I can count on you."

"Of course, Mr. Vice President," the General replied deferentially.

"By the way, have you any clues as to who may be responsible for this terrible crime?" the Vice President asked.

"Not at this point, Mr. Vice President. But we do know that one of our scientists recently worked on those bombs and we're trying to get in touch with him now."

"The Chief of Staff will keep you informed. Make sure to report any of your findings directly to him. I suggest you let him know as soon as possible, whether you contacted the scientist and what information you learned from him. That's all for now. Of course, this is strictly confidential. Is that understood, General?"

"Yes, Mr. Vice President," replied the General solemnly.

"Good. Good night, General."

"Good night, Mr. Vice President."

The General replaced the receiver and sat back in his desk chair. He felt like a shattered piece of glass, broken beyond recognition. Whatever the outcome, whether or not the weapons were recovered, his tenure at the factory was over. Moreover, he might be dismissed from the Army and imprisoned for years for gross dereliction of duty. All his adult life he had been a loyal soldier and an amiable comrade to his military and governmental colleagues. He had worked assiduously to gain the rank of Brigadier General. Now, his reputation, his career, everything he had worked for, was gone in a fleeting instant.

After brooding about his bad luck for some time, he broke out of his gloomy mood. Perhaps he could save himself from the horrors he envisioned if he recovered the weapons. Following the Vice President's dictates, he tried to find Mamood immediately. He had the Colonel call Mamood's secretary at about 10:30 p.m. Mamood's secretary told the Colonel he was out of the country for a week's vacation before heading to the IAEA conference in Vienna, scheduled to be held the third week of January. She then gave the Colonel Mamood's cell number and the phone number and address of his hotel in Vienna. Thankful for her help, the Colonel hung up.

He telephoned Mamood on his cell but was unable to reach him. He left a message saying that it was urgent that he call back to discuss a matter of grave importance. He also left a message for Mamood at his hotel in Vienna.

Downcast, the Colonel returned to the General's office to inform him that he had been unable to reach Mamood, but that he would continue trying. Looking gaunt and battered, the General again sat down next to the Colonel on the office sofa.

"Colonel, we have to do our own quiet investigation starting at 6:00 a.m. tomorrow. I want you to examine the arsenal's records to check when the suitcase bombs were delivered to the manufacturing facility. Then look at the scientists' log books and the chronology for the work done on those devices and by whom. Let's see who else may have been involved."

"Yes, sir," the Colonel answered obediently. "I'll be finished by noon tomorrow."

"That's good enough," replied the General, looking sadly at the floor.

By noon the next day, the Colonel reported to the General that the storage room officer delivered the suitcases to the manufacturing floor on November 8, 2006 at 11:00 a.m., and that Mamood and two engineers had worked to maintain and upgrade those two weapons over the ensuing three-week period. He saw that Mamood had arranged for a simulated test firing of the weapons by using a new gun device for this purpose and that, because of its success, Mamood had installed the new gun device in each weapon.

The General digested this report sitting erectly at his desk. "We now have a grasp on what initially happened to those two bombs," he said. "But we still don't know who took them and where are they now. That's the mystery."

"If I may, sir," replied the Colonel eagerly, coming closer to the General's desk.

"Yes, you may. Go ahead."

"Mamood may have the answers. As I see it, anybody working on the manufacturing floor could have taken the weapons. That makes for almost 50 suspects right there. Given the security surrounding that plant, I doubt an outsider would have been able to get inside the plant or leave with the weapons."

"I agree with you," said the General soberly. "This was an inside job."

"What do we do now?" asked the Colonel politely.

"I think we'll get some help on this investigation immediately," said the General as he rose from his desk. "I want you to be fully available at a moment's notice."

He ushered the Colonel out of his office. Once alone, he lingered in the center of the room, pondering his next step. While he did so, his secretary informed him on the intercom that three men were there to see him. He asked to have them shown in and consulted the mirror near the door to check that his uniform looked fresh and that his many medals for valorous service were properly arranged on his left chest.

His secretary ushered in three men he had not met previously. One was a general from the President's security section, and the other two, a Colonel and a Major, were from ISI, the Pakistani intelligence service. Noor Ahmed, a sturdily built 47 year old Major General, was a trusted national security advisor to the President, having worked with him for many years. His hair was prematurely gray and his dark brown eyes were set off by extensive crow's feet, signs of stress, or outdoor life, or a combination of both. His dark brown uniform, adorned with rows of medals, looked fresh and newly pressed. Colonel Abdul Hasim and Major Ali Kassem were two elite members of the ISI charged with investigating grave national security breaches. Colonel Hasim, a tall, wiry dark-haired officer, who sported a mustache, had risen rapidly in the ranks of the ISI, due in part to his relationship with General Ahmed, his long-time friend from high school. Major Kassem, a barrel chested figure with piercing hazel eyes, had gained the confidence of Colonel Hasim over the years due to his well-regarded investigative talents.

General Kareem led the awe-inspiring threesome to his leather sofa, while he sat facing them as if under a spotlight. Seconds later, his secretary arrived with a tray of steaming tea and sweet cakes. Without preamble, General Kareem turned directly to General Ahmed:

"I know why you are here," he said. "How can I be of service?"

General Ahmed edged forward on the couch.

"The President put me in charge of the investigation of the missing bombs. I brought in our friends from ISI." He paused as if searching for the right words.

"As you know," he went on, "this security lapse is of the gravest national importance. These missing bombs not only pose a threat to our government, but also to others, especially in the West. After several botched assassination attempts against the President, he's determined to find these weapons at all costs."

"I understand fully. We'll help you in any way we can," General Kareem said with determination.

"I know we can count on you. Here's what we have in mind. First, we're going to impose a lock-down at the manufacturing facility for at least three days. No one is to leave. This isolation will put a lot of pressure on those in the plant. We'll soon be able to see who sweats and who doesn't."

"That's a good start," replied General Kareem.

"Second, my ISI colleagues will interview everybody who is at the plant now or who has worked there during the last three months. My staff will then further interview those who are culled by the ISI," continued General Ahmed.

Pausing to sip his tea, he cleared his throat and continued:

"Third, over the next 24 hours, I want you and Colonel Ashani to review all the computer records at the plant and all of the laboratory notes. After you do that, give me a short report on your conclusions and make sure to give our ISI colleagues complete access to the same files. I have instructed them to come up with their own findings within 24 hours of receiving your report."

"That will demand a lot of work, General, but Colonel Ashani and I will definitely be able to do it," General Kareem said confidently, knowing that his Colonel had done almost all of this work already.

General Ahmed then rose and eyed each man sternly:

"Lastly, we'll meet here at 9:00 a.m. on day four, to review our collective findings. That day, either we will locate those weapons or we won't. I hope, for all our sakes, that we find them."

The threat did not go unnoticed. General Kareem squirmed in his chair and looked away from the Major General's piercing eyes.

"Is this plan fully understood by everyone present?" asked the Major General, rhetorically.

General Kareem and the two ISI investigators nodded in agreement.

"Excellent," continued the Major General. "Let's start immediately. Our ISI friends brought along five additional, most trustworthy, colleagues. My security staff has already posted 10 of the President's security guards, each armed with a Kalashnikov, to isolate the manufacturing plant. We've also restricted access to the complex as a whole."

Colonel Hasim reached for his cellphone and ordered the five other members of his team to meet him on the floor of the manufacturing plant immediately.

With General Kareem and Colonel Ashani leading the way, the group of five headed to the plant. The special security guards, dressed in black uniforms with white trimming, had already surrounded the plant and were posted at the front gate of the complex. When they arrived inside the manufacturing facility, General Kareem ordered the 45 engineers and scientists to stop their work. Surprised by the General's order, the workers obeyed immediately. Then he ordered them to line up in groups of six, which they did promptly. He explained to them that an investigation had started at the plant and that no one would be permitted to leave for the next four days, unless he himself approved the departure.

The ISI personnel, seven strong, decided to use the scientist's rooms and laboratory space on the west side of the plant to conduct their interviews. Colonel Hasim and Major Kassem had given each of the other five on their staff a list of questions for the engineers and scientists as well as other areas to explore. The Colonel and the Major ordered each individual at the head of the line of the two groups of employees to come with them for an interview. The other five ISI investigators similarly chose to interview an engineer or scientist in the front of each grouping.

This laborious process continued for 15 hours on the first day ending by 10:00 p.m. There was a noticeable stench of sweat in the interviewing facility, caused by the anxiety of those examined and the proximity of people in close quarters. As each interview took about three hours, the investigators were able to interview 35 of the 45 employees on hand. The ISI staff took lengthy notes during their interviews for study by other reviewers, if necessary. General Kareem arranged simple sandwich luncheons and spicy chicken and rice dinners for all on hand. He also ordered in army cots, bedding, towels and soap for both employees and investigators during their overnight stays at the plant.

The following day, the ISI staff pursued the same lengthy investigations until they had interviewed all of the 45 employees present as well as an additional five who, while away from the plant, had been rounded up.

While the ISI focused on their interview sessions, Colonel Ashani completed his identification of the relevant computer records and project laboratory notes prepared by those working on the various projects at the plant, including Mamood's notes. When he finished that task, he wrote a report listing the personnel who had worked on the upgrade of the suitcase bombs, their function, and the work they did on the project and the date or dates of service. His report revealed that three engineers and Mamood had worked on the project, each having had full access to the suitcase bombs during the time they were upgraded at the plant. He concluded that these four were his primary suspects, but that Mamood was the most likely culprit. Mamood had returned his urgent call late at night when he was asleep, and left a message on the Colonel's cell phone that he would contact him the next day. Despite this apparent attempt at cooperation, the Colonel suspected that Mamood's extensive foreign travel to attend various IAEA conferences over the last several months might have led him to criminals who desperately wanted to steal the bombs.

Colonel Ashani presented his report to General Kareem at the close of the second day of the investigation. Reviewing it closely with the Colonel, the General personally examined some key lab notes that Mamood had personally prepared, as well as the notes of the engineers who had worked to upgrade and make the two new gun devices. It was clear to the General that the work had been done in an orderly way in accordance with the presidential directive to modernize and upgrade certain weapons, and maintain the country's existing arsenal. The lab notes revealed Mamood had last worked on the project on the night of January 4, 2007, a Thursday. Discovery of the missing suitcases was made on the following Wednesday, January 10, 2007.

The General began to pace around his room nervously, recognizing that a full week had elapsed since the weapons were last reported present at the plant. He directed the Colonel to make several changes to his report and to give him four copies of the report within the next four hours. As Colonel Ashani was about to leave, General Kareem patted him on the shoulder and praised him for crafting an excellent report, one that the Major General and his two key ISI investigators would find succinct and informative.

The ISI investigative team spent half of the third day finishing their investigation at the plant. Colonel Hasim and Major Kassem identified the fingerprints found on the two black suitcases left in the scientist's rooms as those of Mamood, one of the engineers, Ahmed Shah, and Colonel Ashani. In their view, these made Mamood and Shah the two most likely suspects. After reviewing all of the interview reports prepared by the other members of the staff, they decided jointly to question the three engineers who had worked with Mamood on the suitcase bomb project.

They questioned Ahmed Shah first. An engineer in his fifties, he had worked at the Ordinance Complex for over 10 years. He and his family – – a wife and two teenage girls – – lived a quiet life in Wah. Chubby, of medium height, Shah had toiled dutifully at the plant without adverse incident for years. He was considered a good worker and most trustworthy by his colleagues at the plant. Shah's interview revealed no new information or leads, other than to give a picture of Mamood as a diligent, hardworking, highly talented, smart scientist, a nationalist who was extremely proud to help develop the country's nuclear arsenal. Similarly, the joint interview of the other two engineers did not disclose any new leads. As in the case of Shah, these two engineers testified to Mamood's hard work, unquestioned loyalty and scientific talent. They noted that, over the past month, he had worked the most at the plant, working late on many evenings, even alone. In short, none of the three engineers raised any suspicions as to Mamood's activities.

On the third day of the investigation, the rest of the ISI staff at the plant, together with five additional ISI members now assigned to the investigation, checked out the background and daily living habits of the employees at the plant. They interviewed the imams at several mosques in Wah, searched the employees' homes, and in certain instances, confirmed the employees' recent travel plans.

That night Colonel Hasim gathered his investigative staff to go over each member's material findings and to prepare a joint written report. After a four-hour session, Major Kassem wrote the final version of the report, which Colonel Hasim found satisfactory, but inconclusive. In his group's eyes, Mamood remained the primary suspect, although his motive or motives were far from clear.

The next morning Colonel Hasim and Major Kassem met General Kareem and Colonel Ashani at the General's office. Fatigue showed on all their faces. Each studied the other's report closely. Sitting around the General's sofa, they had an open, free-wheeling discussion. Their conclusion was not surprising: the culprit was Mamood. They could not figure out why he might have stolen the bombs. Based on the interviews conducted, they learned that he had occasionally vented anger and disappointment at being passed over for the Chief Scientist's spot at the plant. Was this a sufficient motive? The investigative team certainly did not know for sure, but it might have been the root cause of a long-standing resentment, a possible catalyst for the theft. The team dismissed Mamood's habit of cavorting with several beautiful women as insignificant. They surmised that this social life was a necessary outlet for his hard work.

Although satisfied that Mamood was their prime suspect, the group was mystified as to the whereabouts of the missing weapons. Colonel Hasim rose from his chair, paced around the room anxiously, closing his eyes for a moment. Then, he looked at General Kareem.

"General, it is time for us to call Major General Ahmed on the secure line you have here," he said solemnly.

"Go ahead, Colonel," the General said with resignation. "Dial him now. I'm sure he's waiting to hear from us."

Colonel Hasim walked over to the red phone on a small table next to the General's desk, and dialed the Major General's special security hot line number. It rang several times before he heard the Major General's deep voice on the other end of the line.

"Who is calling?"

"Major General, this is Colonel Hasim. I'm here with General Kareem, his chief assistant, Colonel Ashani, and my chief aide in the investigation, Major Kassem."

"Are you ready to give me your joint report?"

"Yes, we are. I'm turning the phone over to General Kareem now."

"O.K."

"Major General, this is the bottom line," said General Kareem. "We think Mamood Ishan, the second most senior scientist at the plant, is the prime suspect in the theft of the weapons. One of the engineers at the plant may be involved too, but we don't think so. However, we have been unable to locate the missing weapons and don't know where they are at present."

"Where is the scientist now?" replied the Major General indignantly.

"We don't know. He was supposed to attend an IAEA conference in Vienna, but he never checked into his hotel. He did return one call we made to him, but only left a message on my aide's cell phone late at night. We have not heard from him since."

"This is bad news, General. The missing weapons could be anywhere. Have you considered where they might be?"

"Yes, we have. Your ISI staff searched his home and found no clues or leads. His home looked as if everything was in order and as if he planned to return."

"Did the ISI find his personal computer at home, General?"

"No, they searched for it. Apparently, he takes it with him when he travels abroad. He can't take any of the computers at the plant that contain our sensitive data. They're permanently attached to the work stations in the scientists' laboratory rooms at the plant."

"So you don't know where the missing items are, General?"

"That's correct," replied the General meekly.

"In this case I'll inform the President that, unfortunately, we must report this incident to the United States and seek its help immediately," the Major General said, his voice shaking with anger. "This is too grave a matter. We must jointly try to recover the bombs at all costs."

"What do you want us to do at the plant?" asked General Kareem.

"Continue the investigation at the plant," he shouted. "Keep the lockdown in place, for another week. Then report to me on January 20th. Is that clear?"

"Yes, Major General, very clear."

CHAPTER 34

WASHINGTON, DC

January 15, 2007

The White House Chief of Staff, Frank Ralston, was enjoying a quiet moment at 5:30 a.m. Sipping a cappuccino slowly in his dark, wood-paneled den, he reviewed the upcoming events of the day. Another typical Monday, he mused reflecting on his two grueling years of service: a meeting with the President at 8:00 a.m., a staff meeting at 9:00 a.m., a visit with the Secretary of State at 11:00 a.m., a working lunch at 12:30 p.m.; and so on. His train of thought was broken by the persistent ringing of the secure phone next to him. He picked up the phone immediately.

"Hello, who's calling?"

"Mr. Ralston, this is President Musharraf's Chief of Staff, Mohammed Doha."

"Good morning. How are you?"

"I'm fine, but I have some bad news to share with you."

Alarmed, Ralston moved the phone away from his ear. His fingers inched along the desk searching for pen and paper.

"What's the problem?" he asked.

"Two of our small nuclear weapons, two suitcase bombs of 10-kiloton strength, are missing. We think one of our top scientists at our main nuclear facility, Mamood Ishan, is responsible for the loss."

"When did this happen?"

"We found out on January 10th that they were missing. We're not sure when they were taken, but we think it may have been as early as January 4th.

"Do you know where the weapons are now, Mr. Doha?" asked Ralston, deliberately pacing his words.

"Unfortunately, we don't. That is why we decided to call you now. We want you to help us find them as soon as possible."

Knowing that an immediate crisis was at hand, Ralston leaned forward, taking charge.

"I'll inform the President and the Director of National Intelligence immediately. I'll call you later today, about eight hours from now."

"Thank you, Mr. Ralston. I'll await your call."

Without finishing his cappuccino, Ralston picked up his briefcase and quickly left his Tudor-style home in Falls Church, Virginia to go to the White House. Although in his mid-fifties, he still had plenty of energy and spirit and, at moments like this, he was glad he kept his six-foot frame in good shape. Fifteen years spent in Washington as a Congressional staff member and later as a political consultant had been occasionally tedious, but he was far from spent. His training at Harvard, where he majored in government, and at the Woodrow Wilson International Center for Scholars at Princeton, had helped prepared him for crisis management, where his colleagues gave him high marks. Even then, his friends knew his ample intelligence and his amiability would take him far in any career he pursued. At Ralston's urging, his driver made great time, arriving at the White House at about 6:30 a.m. Automatically he began to review his papers for his staff meeting later than morning, but soon realized that he could not concentrate on them. His heart raced, as he pondered the risks that came with the tragic news from Pakistan. Cleaning his clear-rimmed glasses, he looked at his watch as he thought of the steps to be taken. It was time to meet with the President, an intimate friend for almost eight years.

He went into the small dining room located near the Oval Office and greeted the President warmly.

"Mr. President, you look well rested. I don't know how you do it, given all the problems we face."

"It's easy, Frank. I go to bed early so I can be fresh for the next day. I've been doing it for years and it works fine for me. How was your Sunday?"

"Sunday was great, Mr. President. But today is a different story."

The President looked at his advisor quizzically, motioning him to sit down at the table. A bit shaken, Ralston continued:

"I just received a call from Pakistan's Chief of Staff, Mohammed Doha. He told me that two of their atomic weapons, suitcase bombs with a 10-kiloton strength, are missing and that one of their top scientists, Mamood Ishan, may have taken them. Worst of all, he added, that they did not know where the weapons are now and requested us to help them."

"My God, this is the last thing we need," said the President as his face began to redden. "Iraq is still a hotbed. Lebanon is still a minefield – – they're in full swing over there. Afghanistan has become a mess. And now we have to deal with this problem."

Ralston nodded, sharing the President's exasperation.

"After that Khan mess," the President went on, "with those nuclear weapons designs ending up all over the globe, I made it clear to President Musharraf that he had to put a lid on any nuclear item moving from his country and tighten the security over his nuclear arsenal. In our face-to-face meeting, he assured me he would personally oversee both issues. But obviously he didn't." Getting angrier, the President banged his right fist on the table.

"O.K., Frank. Let's get John Punt at National Intelligence on the line right now."

"I'll do it immediately, Mr. President," said Ralston going over to the secure phone on the sideboard and dialing the number.

"John," he said, "this is Frank Ralston. I'm sitting with the President and," he added with emphasis, "he wants to speak to you now."

He handed the phone to the President, who spoke heatedly:

"John, I have received some terrible news and you have to get to the bottom of it immediately. The Pakistani Chief of Staff told Frank this morning that two of their atomic weapons are missing – – two suitcase bombs of 10-kiloton strength. They think a Pakistani scientist, Mamood Ishan, took them or is involved in the theft."

"Mr. President, is this news public information?"

"No, John, it's not and I want it kept under wraps while we carry out our own intensive investigation. We don't want to tip off the thief or thieves."

"I understand, Mr. President," Punt said solemnly.

"I'm not finished, John. I want the CIA to run this with you and, of course, get MI6 in on the chase on a hush-hush basis. Do you understand?"

"Yes, I do, Mr. President, loud and clear," replied Punt decisively.

"That's it for now, John. And I want your preliminary report on status by 5:00 p.m. tonight."

"I'll do that, Mr. President. You can rely on me."

"I know I can, John. Thanks. I urgently need your help on this one."

"You'll get it, Mr. President," said Punt eagerly.

Putting down the receiver, the President rose from the table. His ruddy complexion had turned ashen.

"Frank," he said, pointing his finger at his Chief of Staff, "You have to keep on top of this one personally. The last item I need on my watch is another 9/11. We have to find those weapons."

Punt sensed the suppressed anger in the President's voice. Embattled on many fronts, he knew the last thing the President need was another security crisis at home. After a year and a half on the job, Punt knew that, as Director of National Intelligence, he would involve all of the resources of the country's newly-connected counterterrorist arms, including the top-notch joint CIA-MI6 counterterrorist center operation based in London.

He immediately called the head of MI6 in London, Geoffrey Felix, informing him of the Pakistani atomic weapons theft. He urged his counterpart to instruct the joint counterterrorist center to give the matter the highest priority. He added that he would be sending him a picture of the prime suspect by encrypted email within the hour.

After the call ended, Felix telephoned Nigel Thornton.

"Nigel, good afternoon."

"Good afternoon, Geoffrey. To what do I owe the pleasure?" Home alone, eating lunch, Nigel placed his sandwich on the kitchen counter.

"I have bad news and need your help immediately."

"What's up?"

"Pakistan just informed the United States that two of its atomic weapons, two suitcase bombs of 10-kiloton strength, each weighing about 45 kilos, are missing and that they believe a disgruntled Pakistani scientist, Mamood Ishan, took them or is involved in the theft."

"Oh my God, this is a real nightmare," said Nigel greatly agitated. His eyes rested briefly on the unwavering green of the trees outside the windows of his sitting room as he paced the floor. "There are terrorists all over the world clamoring for weapons like this. We have to find out who has them and where they are as fast as we can."

"Exactly, Nigel. Get on it now and keep me posted. By the way, this is to be done quietly. No press. You understand?"

"Of course." Once more, Nigel looked out his Andersen windows, beyond the trees, at the cumulus clouds moving slowly in the blue sky.

The enormity of this task did not overwhelm Nigel - and with good reason. Over the years, he had developed great ease in cutting through the bureaucratic ways of MI6. On intimate terms with his colleague, the head of MI6, Nigel rose through the ranks and took on plum assignments, often with excellent results, a product of his fine investigative work. Loyal to the core, he was one of MI6's finest.

He immediately sent his top MI6 and CIA groups a confidential email marked "urgent" informing them of the atomic weapons theft in Pakistan and calling a meeting at 3:30 p.m. that afternoon. During the remaining hour and a half, he desperately tried to think of all the possible groups that might want these weapons.

Everyone arrived on time and proceeded to the conference room on the second floor of the center. Before sitting at the table, they helped themselves to soft drinks. Nigel's colleagues noticed the drawn look on his face; the wrinkles in his forehead seemed more pronounced than ever.

"We have a hot item here – – and we have to nail it before it hits us," said Nigel, speaking slowly. "As I told you, Pakistan informed the United States this morning two of its atomic weapons, suitcase bombs of 10-kiloton strength and weighing about 45 kilos each, were reported missing on January 10th and a Pakistani scientist, Mamood Ishan, was involved in the theft. The Pakistanis also reported that they conducted a several day investigation but didn't find the weapons and don't know where they are."

He paused to take a sip of tea: "Our job is to find the weapons and who has them," he continued, setting his cup down firmly, "and then recover the weapons as soon as possible - at any price."

"Do we have more information to go on in addition to what you just told us," asked Roger, clearly rattled.

"Unfortunately, I don't," said Nigel.

Roger walked rapidly to a large map of the world on the wall behind one end of the conference room table and pick up a pointer that lay on a nearby table.

"Let me give you my immediate reaction, if I may," he said, slapping an area on the map.

"Go ahead," replied Nigel.

"Pakistan is bordered on the west by Afghanistan, on the north by China and to the east and southeast by India. I very much doubt that any one in Pakistan would have tried to take the weapons into China. The border is tightly patrolled; travel into that western region is highly restricted and any outsider in that area would be too visible."

"I agree," said Nigel and Gregory moving their eyes from the pointer to Roger.

"I think we can eliminate India as an exit route as well," Roger continued, raising his voice slightly, a reflection of his heightened excitement, as he moved the pointer to a newly designated area. "Given the stormy relations between the two countries, the border between India and Pakistan is probably more tightly controlled than the Chinese-Pakistan border."

"What about Afghanistan as an exit route?" asked Nigel.

"Highly unlikely. I doubt that anyone stealing weapons would risk running the gauntlet of patrolling American or NATO forces in the east and southeast right up to the border, or the local warlords or drug barons and their cohorts within the country."

"So what's your hypothesis?" asked Clifford impatiently.

"I think he probably left the country by sea," replied Roger, moving the pointer to the Arabian Sea.

"That's a good working assumption," Anne interjected. "It is highly unlikely that the thief would have tried to move the weapons by air, either on a commercial or private flight. We know all baggage is supposedly checked - whether carryon or cargo. That's too high a risk. Even trying to get the bombs onto a private aircraft would have run the same high risks, although the security requirements may have been different from those of the public carriers. Of course, cargo inspection or security at the boarding gate might have been lax. Still, I don't think anyone would take that kind of risk."

"O.K.," said Clifford. "Let's say that the nut who took the bombs would not have driven out of the country with them or left with them by air. Then what?"

"I think the weapons left the country by sea or are still there." Tim said.

"Wait!" said Anne excitedly. "I just had a brainstorm. Remember the hijacking of the *Argus* and the sale of the oil? We know the vessel turned up in a port of Karachi and the tanker, we think, was unloaded there. What if there's a link between the money the pirates received from the sale of the oil and the ransom of the ship and theft of the weapons?"

"You mean those pirates may have used their booty to buy the weapons?" asked Roger sitting back in his chair and rubbing his chin.

"Exactly."

"Tell us again, Anne, how much money was involved?" Gregory asked, leaning forward at the table.

"If I recall, it was well over U.S. $100 million," Anne replied quickly. "Of course, I can check our files and confirm that."

"Do that," Nigel said.

"O.K."

"You may have come up with something, Anne," said Nigel slowly, as if thinking aloud. "It's possible that the pirates may be linked to the theft of the bombs. Obviously, there's a lot we don't know because we never learned who those pirates were." He rose to pour himself a glass of water and began pacing up and down:

"Let's start with the assumption that the weapons were moved from Pakistan by sea. If pirates were involved, that would make sense since they would be most comfortable at sea. But this is only a guess. We have no hard evidence to support this line of thinking."

Gregory, who had listened quietly to what had just been said, interrupted Nigel:

"Excuse me, mates," asked Gregory, who had been listening quietly all along. "Aren't we going too fast here?"

Nigel looked up at him.

"Tell us what you think," he said, regaining his seat at the table.

"Look," Gregory said. "It's only 10 days since the weapons were last seen at the Ordinance Complex. It may well be that they're still in Pakistan. From what we understand, the Pakistani ISI is continuing its in depth investigation of the theft and President Musharraf is personally getting reports and updates from the ISI every 10 hours. Given the intensity of the investigation, it could be that the thief is lying low and waiting for the hunt to die down."

Gregory paused to take a sip of his iced tea and went on:

"We know that the Pakistani Government has used surprise Army roadblocks, random searches at checkpoints, searches on trains and buses and broad neighborhood searches by ISI personnel to catch Al Qaeda or other terrorists," he went on, "I think we should get a read from our ISI pals on the status of their in-country investigation and what steps they're taking to recover the weapons."

"I believe Gregory has a good point here," Nigel agreed. "Our investigation must be multifaceted."

The others nodded in approval.

"Let's break up into two teams," Nigel continued. "I want Clifford, Tim and Anne to pursue the pirate angle and the escape by sea scenario. Roger and Gregory will interface with our ISI colleagues to see what we can learn from them. I'll try to develop some other leads and possibilities. Is everybody on board?"

Everyone agreed with this division of labor.

"Good," said Nigel. "In this case, let's meet two days from now at 1:00 p.m. to see what we have learned. "We must make some progress soon; the stakes are too high."

He rose, patted Tim on the shoulder and left the room. Roger and Tim went to Roger's office to discuss contacting ISI. Gregory, Anne and Clifford remained to consider their next steps.

CHAPTER 35

ISLAMABAD/NORTHWEST TERRITORIES

January 15, 2007

The early Monday morning meeting between President Musharraf, Major General Ahmed, Colonel Hasim and Major Kassem was very stormy. It took place in a well-appointed conference room several doors away from the President's office. Dressed in his crisp military uniform, the enraged President, who was normally calm and orderly when dealing with his subordinates, banged his right fist repeatedly on the table.

"I want answers, not questions," he barked. "Do you understand me? This breach of security is far worse that the Khan quagmire. Those weapons must be located!"

"We're working on all levels to accomplish this, Mr. President," replied Colonel Hasim. "I have ordered 250 men under my direct control engaged in a dragnet of all the known key terrorist outfits operating in our country, rounding up operatives and interrogating them as we know best."

"Where are they searching now?" asked the President, staring at the Colonel.

"This morning at 6:00 a.m., I ordered them to sweep Karachi and Quetta, then to proceed to Lahore and, finally Islamabad/Rawalpindi. Recently we located some of the safehouses used by Al Qaeda, Jamaat al-Dawat and the now banned Lashkar-e-Taiba."

"That could well take days, even weeks, and we may not find what we want," replied the President impatiently. He looked at the group assembled with a steely gaze. "It may be necessary to take some uniquely decisive steps now."

"What do you have in mind?" asked General Ahmed.

"I want to mount a big commando raid with some of our elite units right around Taal - about 10 to 15 kilometers from the border - and north of Miran Shah. They should be backed by about 2,500 Army troops now operating in the Northwest Territories."

"What is the specific aim of this mission, Mr. President?" asked General Ahmed, fidgeting in his chair, feeling uncomfortable.

"Based on our Army and intelligence reports, I know that significant remnants of Al Qaeda operatives and the Taliban fled from Afghanistan and are operating there under the protection of local tribesmen in the area. With this type of lighting strike, we should be able to capture some important Al Qaeda operatives or Taliban commanders, and, if so, pry information from them concerning the theft, without, of course, disclosing the nature of the theft."

"I see," said General Ahmed, rubbing his left hand along the many Army metals that hung on left side of his chest. "May I also suggest that we invite some of our American friends at the CIA to ride with the commandos as observers?"

"Why do you think that will be helpful?" asked Major Kassem, who had said nothing up to then.

"It will show them that we are doing everything possible to rid the country of foreign terrorist elements and to recover the missing weapons," observed General Ahmed.

"I'll go along with that, General, but I want you to inform Langley directly *now* so that they can have their observers ready in two days' time."

"I'll take care of that right away, Mr. President," the General replied.

"I expect you three to be here tomorrow morning at 8:00 a.m. with an update," said the President emphatically. "That's all for now."

As soon as the President left the meeting, General Ahmed called John Punt on the secure phone next to the small couch in the office, requesting that two CIA agents located outside of Pakistan come to meet him at his headquarters within the next 36 hours. He explained that they were needed as observers for a clandestine assignment so secret that the Pakistanis wished to avoid alerting the CIA contingent at the U.S. Embassy in Islamabad for fear of leaks.

Within an hour, Punt contacted the CIA Director at Langley, who, in turn, called Roger Dunleavy at the joint counterterrorist center in London, demanding that two agents go to Islamabad immediately.

Roger was amazed at the timing of the call. He told Nigel that the Director of the CIA had ordered Gregory and him to go to Islamabad on a clandestine assignment for several days. This, he added, would provide his unit with excellent entrée for meeting some of the key ISI personnel on the bomb case. Lastly, he told Nigel that he and Gregory would give him an update three days later, on January 18th.

Given the importance of their clandestine mission, Roger had arranged transportation for himself and Gregory aboard a Hercules C-130J departing from Fairford Air Force Base in Gloucestershire bound for Bagram Air Force Base north of Kabul. Both men wore long-sleeved blue shirts over heavy turtlenecks underneath warm parkas and khaki pants that tucked into hiking boots. Each carried a small bag containing the barest of essentials, plus a 9mm-Glock pistol and a satellite phone. They knew they would get little sleep during the coming week.

They were airborne three hours later. The new C-130J, with its vastly improved extended range of about 2,075 miles when normally loaded, headed first to Ramstein Air Force in Germany, where it was to pick up some additional armored personnel carriers, machine guns, night vision goggles and ammunition for the American troops on duty in and about Kabul. From there the plane was to proceed directly to Islamabad.

The flight proceeded without incident. The huge jet came in over the snow-covered Hindu Kush Mountains, with their massive peaks of over 4,700 meters, to the north of the Afghan base. As it landed on a clear frosty night about 7:00 p.m., huge drifts of snow were evident around the base and up in the nearby mountains. After routing the Taliban in 2001, the Americans had substantially improved the airfield so that it was capable of handling most types of aircraft. Unloading was quick and efficient. Within four hours, the plane took off again bound for Islamabad.

Highly skilled and well-trained United States Air Force pilots made frequent flights over the 4,000-meter peaks into eastern Afghanistan. The plane landed at Islamabad International Airport on time, about 1:00 a.m. on Wednesday morning and taxied to a remote hanger far from the main terminal. At that hour, there was little activity at the airport. Two Pakistani Army officers, a Colonel and a Captain, met them at the hangar and arranged for their transportation to the nearby Army base.

Located some 15 kilometers outside of Islamabad, the Army base was teeming with activity. Although hardly visible against the night sky, Roger and Gregory counted at least 30 helicopters, all foreign-made, including some U.S. AH-64D Apache helicopters, all lined up 75 to 100 meters away. Within 40 minutes of their arrival, about 300 men from an elite Pakistani commando unit left their barracks and assembled near the rows of helicopters. Clad in camouflage outfits and lightweight parkas, the troops wore black camouflage on their faces. Most of them carried Kalashnikovs; a few carried light and heavy machine guns and some sniper rifles.

The troops were on a specific mission to attack foreign elements and their tribesmen protectors near Saada, a small Pakistani village close to the Afghan border in Paktia province. President Musharraf's orders were to capture as many Taliban and Al Qaeda members as possible for interrogation and imprisonment and to kill as many of the groups as possible. The Pakistani Army high command had already alerted members of the U.S. Tenth Mountain Division operating in the Paktia border area of the impending attack to get their help along the Paktia border area in cutting off escape routes into Afghanistan. This maneuver - a variation of the so-called hammer and anvil approach - was one previously employed by American forces in conjunction with the Pakistani Army on raids at the Afghan side of the border.

The helicopters lifted off at 3:00 a.m., heading for the surrounding mountain area outside the targeted village to set up a blocking position near the border, thus preventing any retreat from the groups under attack. About 2,500 Pakistani troops, backed by artillery, planned to lead the main U-shaped attack on the Taliban and Al Qaeda personnel believed to be in the area.

At about 3:30 a.m. the main body of Pakistani soldiers moved out of their existing positions some 10 kilometers from the targeted area. A crescent shaped moon provided a sliver of light for the continuous stream of trucks that ferried the troops to a point four kilometers from the attack zone. There, the troops dismounted and assembled at three separate starting points. Moving slowly behind a mountain ridge with lights blacked out, the trucks could not be seen or heard by the enemy. Two troop units, numbering 750 men each, began advancing to the left and right, flanking the main unit of 1,000 men that advanced in center position. Each attacking group moved in two columns of troops about 10 meters apart. To maintain the element of surprise, the commanders instructed all troops to maintain radio silence and not talk until the attack was to begin. Many of the men had night goggles that permitted them to see well into the distance.

Their breath was vaporous in the cold night air and their movements cast eerie shadows across the terrain as they edged forward.

Very few sounds emanated from the targeted village and the surrounding area. The troops assumed that the village locals posted sentries outside some of their buildings at night where key elders lived, whose function it was to alert the tribesmen in the event of an attack by the Army or by occasional marauding bandits.

As the three Army groups moved slowly and cautiously through the farmland on the outskirts of the village, two snipers assigned to the center group expertly picked off two sentries. The crack of the rifles alerted the other sentries who radioed the elders that an attack was underway. Immediately, several Taliban commanders with their bands and the 25 Al Qaeda operatives – – all treated as important guests by their tribesmen hosts – – swung into action, joined by able-bodied males of the tribe.

By 4:30 a.m., the night sky was lit up with moving flicks of red and yellow from the rounds fired by the soldiers and their adversaries. Fire from the Pakistani troops poured in from three sides, to the north, east and south of the village. A heavy barrage of continuous mortar fire hit the village center as well as some of the cultivated farmland nearby. Shortly thereafter, artillery began to pound the village, destroying building after building.

Supported by this heavy fire, the Pakistani soldiers moved steadily over the surrounding farmland towards the entrance to the village. From that range, heavily armed Taliban and Al Qaeda contingents kept up a steady machine gun fire that raked the Pakistani position, killing over 50 soldiers and wounding another 60. The tribesmen also picked off a number of advancing soldiers with their excellent marksmanship. As the battle progressed and continued to intensify, the artillery, mortar and small arms and machine gun fire from the Army began to take a heavy toll on the villagers and their guests.

With the village males serving as a rear guard, the surviving Al Qaeda and Taliban personnel escaped via tunnels built under the senior elders' houses, exiting on a mountain ridge to the west of the village. Their escape plan was simple enough – – cover the few kilometers that led to the porous Pakistani-Afghan border in neighboring Paktia province and pass into Afghanistan unmolested.

Almost a kilometer above the village, 40 members of an Al Qaeda and Taliban band moved in two columns westward, a route apparently left open by the attacking Pakistani Army. Climbing quietly and quickly up the treacherous rocky mountain ridge, they calculated that they were only about three to four kilometers from the border and potential safety. But they had no such luck. Approaching the top of the ridge, they were shocked to see many Pakistani troops spread out about 100 meters from their position, barely visible in the early morning sky. They were unaware that they faced an elite unit that had been airlifted in by helicopter to the northwest of the village to prevent detection. All at once, the elite troopers laid down a heavy fusillade of machine gun and rifle fire, killing 10 members of the escaping militants instantly and severely wounding five others. The foreign operatives sought shelter along the ridge line while returning heavy fire.

The battle raged for another 15 minutes. Finally realizing that they were no match for the opposing overwhelming force estimated at close to 300, the Taliban commanders and their men, together with the Al Qaeda operatives, reluctantly decided to surrender. Roger and Gregory, who had been embedded with the elite unit, watched the engagement unfold from the relative safety of their position to the rear of the elite unit.

As dawn broke over the ridge, the elite troopers tied up their captives' hands with ropes, took their weapons and marched them about three kilometers north northwest. There, 30 helicopters, spread out over a one-kilometer area, awaited the return of the troops. Out of the original 40 escapees, only 25 survived, including five wounded.

After the elite troops placed two captives each on 12 of the helicopters and one on the thirteenth, the choppers took off, heading towards the Army base where the mission had started, a flight of about one and a half hours. Impressed by the battle-hardened methods of the elite unit, Roger and Gregory were delighted with the success of the battle and the ensuing capture.

Once the helicopters had landed safely at the base, the Colonel, who led the elite troopers, proudly touted his success to the Major General Omar Mohammed, who was in charge of the elite unit, The Major General, in turn, conveyed the good news to General Ahmed, who was waiting anxiously for the outcome of the mission. Over breakfast with the President at 7:00 a.m. that morning, General Ahmed informed President Musharraf of the raid's success and advised him that all of the 25 captured insurgents were now in the hands of the ISI, awaiting dreaded interrogation. The President remarked tersely that he hoped the interrogation would finally lead to a breakthrough in the hunt for the missing weapons.

After breakfast, General Ahmed invited Roger and Gregory to meet with him in his office at the Presidential headquarters. Arriving at 9:30 a.m., they were ushered into the General's well-appointed office, furnished with Bukhara rugs and an attractive dark brown mahogany desk with inlaid Brazilian wood. Dressed in his usual crisp army uniform with a full complement of medals, the General rose from his desk to greet his visitors. To his eyes, they looked surprisingly fresh, despite their recent adventure. After a round of tea, the General asked them to evaluate the mission they had witnessed. Speaking first, Roger said he thought it was first-rate and that the elite troops had performed superbly. They also reported that the United States was pleased with the aggressive stance taken against the Taliban and Al Qaeda and hoped that such similar attacks would be carried out on a continuing basis as part of the war against terror. The General said it was the President's intention to do so.

Given the General's importance, Gregory asked him to introduce the ISI personnel in charge of the nuclear bomb theft investigation. He explained that he and Roger had been designated as the CIA point men to assist Pakistan in its inquiry and to help recover the weapons. Delighted that the CIA had dispatched two such competent agents to his country so quickly, the General pledged to assist them. He arranged for his secretary to get Colonel Hasim on the phone. Within two minutes, the Colonel was on the line welcoming them and asking them to join him about 5:00 p.m. that afternoon at the ISI headquarters facility in Islamabad.

Pleased by this response, Roger and Gregory concluded their meeting with the General by complimenting him once more on the army's prowess. They were then escorted back to a vacant officer's suite at the Army base, where their mission first started. After a quick shower and a brief nap, they had a light lunch. Aware that the suite might be bugged, they took a brief stroll outside the barrack's wing to discuss their proposed plan for interacting with the ISI. Knowing that time was not on their side, they realized they had to move the investigation forward quickly and use whatever leads they could glean from the ISI.

CHAPTER 36

ISLAMABAD

January 17, 2007

Under the direct supervision of Colonel Hasim and Major Kassem, the ISI began its intensive interrogation of the captured Taliban and Al Qaeda personnel at one of its detention centers, located in the northern part of the city. Formerly an old warehouse, the center had been converted into one of the most dreaded prison and holding centers. Those brought there who managed to leave alive reported that almost all prisoners confessed– – or else never left.

The interrogating officers were confident they would be able to pry whatever useful information they could from the captured personnel, although they knew from experience that the Al Qaeda group might prove unusually resistant. The Pakistanis decided to start with the 10 captured Arabs first. Because time was of the essence, the Pakistanis used two two-man sets of interrogators, all of whom spoke Arabic, so that two separate, interrogations could be conducted in two adjoining rooms.

The four interrogators were burly, barrel-chested types, sporting heavy beards. These men had done this work for over 10 years and rightfully earned their reputation as the "pryers." If the prisoner had the information, the interrogators would somehow get it. Their technique was simple – – instill enough fear of great pain and eventual death.

The interrogation was held in a room four meters by four meters, dark, damp and ill lit by a single light bulb; there was barely enough space for a small table and two chairs. Since there was no window in the room, the prisoner was unable to tell the time of day, a disorienting feature.

The interrogation followed a typical routine. A friendly interrogator would ask easy, disarming questions to try to gain his target's confidence and soften him up. Then he would ask more searching questions concerning a specific attack and ask the prisoner for details concerning it. If the prisoner denied any knowledge of such a plan or appeared to possess no information about it, the friendly interrogator would continue his probing for a while longer. If still unsuccessful, the other officer would threaten the prisoner, pour cold water on him, kick him and then repeat the tough questions. After several hours, the tough officer would summon two more ISI personnel, who would bring in heavy ropes, make a noose and attach the ropes to a hook high up on the right wall of the room, then grab the prisoner, ostensibly to hang him. Ultimately, the prisoner broke and gave the harsh interrogator the facts he sought.

The Al Qaeda group proved very difficult. For them, a death of honor was an entry to paradise that promised them many delights. They taunted their Muslim interrogators, calling them lackeys of the infidels and questioning their own loyalty to Islam. Many refused at first to reveal anything except first names. Eventually some calmed down realizing that they faced a certain death if they did not cooperate. Only then did they provide answers to many of the questions asked:

"What were you doing in the village?"

"Where did you come from?"

"How many men were in your group?"

"What is your nationality?"

"How long were you in the village or nearby area?"

"What did you plan to do?"

"Who were you going to attack?"

"Did you hear of any plan for a big attack? How was it to be carried out?"

The collective answers gleaned from this line of questioning were somewhat revealing. The Pakistanis learned that there were at least 50 Al Qaeda operatives in the village and the surrounding area. Most of them came from Saudi Arabia, Jordan, Morocco, Tunisia and Egypt; a few came from Pakistan. They had stayed in and around the village for almost four years. Typically, they recruited poor Pakistanis and Afghans to attack the American and NATO forces in Afghanistan, either as suicide bombers or as part of an attacking unit. They offered them far more money than they were eking out. They also ran a small training camp about three kilometers northeast of the village. They were able to buy weapons and ammunition, in the country and in Afghanistan, which they provided to their recruits inside Afghanistan. Often they accompanied raw recruits on their missions, passing through the porous border easily. In addition, they either arranged for transportation or transported the new recruits themselves.

Despite all of their efforts made, the inquisition disclosed little information about the most pressing issue. The Al Qaeda operatives admitted that there were plans to attack foreign troops in Afghanistan to sow further unrest and weaken the Karzai government, but there were no plans for any attacks against the Pakistani Army or against other targets in Pakistan. They knew nothing of a planned major attack on the West, although one senior member heard a rumor about a possible "big bang" against the United States or Europe. Since Al Qaeda compartmentalized knowledge about possible attacks and restricted the flow of information to its participants, the operative was unable to disclose any further details concerning that rumor. While his interrogators pressed the senior member repeatedly on this point - almost to the point of actually hanging him - they developed no further leads.

Meanwhile, three days earlier, the ISI had begun its sweep of known terrorist groups under surveillance in Karachi and Quetta. Mindful of the capture of Khalid Sheik Mohammed, the Al Qaeda Chief of Operations, in Peshawar several years earlier, the ISI personnel hoped for a similar success now. Colonel Hasim had instructed 125 agents in each of the two cities to round up well-known operatives and those suspects they had under surveillance.

In Quetta this time, they focused their efforts on those members of Al Qaeda who had assimilated themselves into the local community. On the first day of their sweep, alerted by an informer about of an important safehouse in a residential neighborhood on the western outskirts, ISI agents took up positions at its location at about 9:00 p.m. Some crouched behind parked cars some 50 meters from the entrance; others surrounded the rear of the house by hiding in the woods behind it. More agents blocked the entrance to the street on either end by using two cars at each end as barricades. The ISI agent in charge of the operation advised his group that there could be as many as 10 men in the house and to prepare for a major gun battle.

Approaching the rear entrance cautiously, four agents dressed in black crawled along the grassy backyard for at least 30 meters. From that position, they were able to make out four men moving on the first floor and several shadows that were visible on the third floor. They reported this quietly to the ISI chief out front using a walkie-talkie.

Their raid leader ordered them to rake the building and the windows in the rear with their AK-47 assault rifles as soon as they heard tear gas grenades fired from in front of the residence. Across the street, in the front of the house, ISI agents rose from concealed positions to fire several tear gas grenades through the front windows on each of the three floors. Immediately following, a steady barrage of fire was unleashed on the rear of the house. Several men inside screamed in pain. On the third floor, two members of Al Qaeda fired their Kalashnikovs and killed two of the agents immediately. Others inside the house began firing at those agents running toward the front of the house, wounding several of them.

Soon, the tear gas took effect and eight men, coughing madly, emerged from the front entrance arms up in surrender. As the ISI agents approached them, one heavily bearded man to the rear of the staggering group pulled two Glock pistols from the back pockets of the member in front of him and killed three agents nearby. Enraged, the ISI agents poured more than 30 bullets into the assailant, killing him instantly, and severely wounding the operative in front of him.

While some of the agents were busily cuffing their captives, others, equipped with gas masks, ransacked the house. They first brought out two more wounded Al Qaeda men, who appeared to be Chechens. Then they brought out two computers, several rocket propelled grenade launchers, two suicide bomber vests and belts and several improvised explosive devices, AK-47s, boxes of ammunition and a sack of U.S. dollars. With luck, the computers might contain the data they desperately sought.

In other parts of Quetta, more fruitful raids were carried out netting 20 more males for questioning.

That same day, the ISI had similar successes in Karachi. In that city of known Islamic militancy, the agents grabbed various known members of Jamaat ud-Dawa (the successor group to the terrorist entity, Lashkar-e-Taiba), from homes, cafes and two mosques. Later that night they raided four known safehouses used by the groups. Surrounding four separate apartment buildings almost simultaneously with more than 20 agents each, they forcefully gained entry to several apartments located in the complex. After several severe gun battles, they subdued the occupants, killing three members of the group, wounding others and capturing propaganda material, explosive devices and several computers. The agents also raided a home supposedly used by Al Qaeda, but found it empty.

This dragnet continued the next day in Lahore, Islamabad and Rawalpindi, other hotbeds of Islamic militancy. These raids resulted in the apprehension of over 150 suspects, including men on a watch list for known or suspected terrorist activities.

Once an urban roundup was completed, the ISI took its captives to a local detention center used primarily for interrogations and as a prison facility. Typically, two suspects were placed in one dimly-lit filthy cell. Because of the importance of the inquiry at hand, interrogation sessions commenced within hours after their arrival at the center.

Colonel Hasim had ordered an officer under his direct control at the main headquarters in Islamabad to oversee the investigations in each of the five cities. His purpose was twofold: as a means to coordinate the nationwide hunt for the bombs and to funnel all vital information to him and Major Kassem. The local ISI head had been instructed to act fast and email a detailed written report to the Colonel by 4:00 p.m. Thursday, January 18th, with a follow-up report by Monday, January 22nd, at 5:00 p.m. Mindful of the fact that these deadlines were not to be missed under any circumstances, the ISI local chiefs ordered their interrogators to use whatever means necessary to get results as soon as possible. Fully aware of the burden imposed on them, the two-man teams of interrogators went to work on the suspects immediately. It was later reported that terrifying screams emanated from many of the interrogation rooms throughout the five cities swept for terrorists.

The interrogations produced mixed results. On the one hand, the ISI gained valuable information about the burgeoning terrorist network in the country aimed at undermining the Musharraf government or continuing the attacks on Indian troops in the Kashmir region. Barely conscious, some suspects volunteered details about the leadership and cells of various terrorist groups, including a new splinter group not previously known to the ISI. On the other hand, those suspects who were not part of Al Qaeda had heard nothing about a big attack planned against the United States or in the West. In short, no leads were revealed leading to the atomic weapons theft probe.

As the email reports accumulated on Thursday afternoon, Colonel Hasim became so enraged that he summoned Major Kassem to his office immediately.

"Major, I can't believe these reports," he shouted. "All this effort, all those sweeps and interrogations, and for what? Look at these reports yourself. They're useless!"

It was impossible to keep his rage under control. He picked up a cup and threw it hard against the wall near the couch opposite his desk.

"Hold on, Colonel," said Major Kassem quietly. "Let me take a look at them."

Stroking his chin, the Major went through each of the five emails quickly. After finishing, he looked up at the Colonel:

"You are absolutely correct," he affirmed. "There is nothing leading to the theft of the bombs." He paused for a moment:

"But these reports are revealing," he went on. "If the weapons were in the country, I think someone we rounded up might have overheard some rumor or private conversation and given us that information."

"I have to agree with you, Major," said the Colonel sadly shaking his head. He took a sip of water:

"What makes matters worse is they scheduled a meeting in less than an hour with our CIA friends," he said, looking at Major Kassem over the rim of his glass. "You know the two men sent to assist us with our investigation? And what useful information will I be able to give to them." He closed his eyes, briefly. "This is shameful and reflects badly on us."

"We'll tell them what we know," said Major Kassem, affecting calm. "That's all we can do."

"And we'll continue pursuing our investigation over the next week to see where that leads," the Colonel nodded.

"Exactly."

Fifteen minutes later, the Colonel's secretary buzzed him over the intercom with the news that his two American visitors had arrived. He instructed her to show them in. As Roger and Gregory entered the office, Colonel Hasim and Major Kassem introduced themselves. Colonel Hasim indicated a seat on the leather couch, which they politely took. The Colonel and the Major sat opposite them. From their drawn faces, the CIA agents could see how tense they were.

"A pleasure to meet you, gentlemen," said the Colonel softly, his recent anger quite dissipated.

"The pleasure is ours, Colonel," said Gregory quickly. "We've heard a lot about you and your staff."

"Only good things, I hope," the Colonel smiled.

"Of course," Roger put in. "There may have been a few negatives items."

"I see. So we're a mixed bag, as you put it. May I call you, Roger? And you, Gregory?" asked the Colonel.

They both nodded. At that point, the Colonel's secretary brought in hot tea and cookies.

"We extended an invitation to the CIA to help us recover those missing weapons immediately and catch those who stole them," said the Colonel, rubbing his hands together. "We did so because you have resources we don't possess. At the same time, we have a well-organized intelligence service in my country. By pooling our resources, we hope to accomplish our two goals."

"I think that sums it up very neatly, Colonel," replied Roger. "There may be other reasons, but we're not here to discuss the politics of this matter."

"I agree," quipped the Colonel, eyeing the CIA agents warily. "Now let me bring you up to date on our investigation. I'll then ask Major Kassem to fill in what I may have missed or what, perhaps, should be restated."

Sipping their tea, Roger and Gregory looked directly at the Colonel and waited for him to continue.

"It is now two weeks since the weapons were last seen at the Ordinance Complex. We learned of the theft on the 10th and called for your country's help five days later on the 15th."

The Colonel reached over to review his notes for a moment and put down his glasses:

"Since then," he continued, "we pursued two separate investigations. One at the weapons factory revealed that a senior scientist of ours, Mamood Ishan, is the most likely culprit. There were others working with him on an upgrade project, but we do not think they were involved. The other investigation took place under our immediate supervision. Major, please bring us up to date on that one."

Major Kassem leaned forward in his seat. "We ordered a roundup of potential suspects from different terrorist groups in five of our large cities."

"With what result?" asked Gregory, shifting in his seat.

"Our interrogations didn't reveal very much on the subject. We think that the weapons are probably no longer in our country."

"How so?" asked Roger.

"Because no one we questioned in our multi-city dragnet ever heard rumors or any news concerning a big attack planned against the United States."

"But that alone isn't enough to lead you to such a firm conclusion," replied Roger firmly.

"I agree with you," answered the Colonel, gazing directly into Roger's eyes. "But in this case, it's our current working assumption. Obviously, we plan to continue our inquiry on all fronts country. Some big lead could still turn up."

The Colonel paused for a moment to allow the impact of this statement to sink in.

"However, we did discover another lead. One of the senior Al Qaeda captives we grabbed in the attack on the border, which you saw, said he had heard that a big attack had been planned against the States or the West."

"Did the prisoner give you any more details?" Gregory asked.

"No, he didn't. We tried to pry it out of him, but we believe he didn't know anything more about it."

"And there are no more leads you can give us?" asked Roger pointedly.

"Yes, we have more," answered the Colonel. "We will give you a brief rundown on the scientist. He was one of the key players at the bomb factory in Wah and worked on most of our major systems. He is an amalgam of East and West. He's an observant Muslim, but he's not married. He has a wild, playboy streak. He likes beautiful women and seeks them out when he has time."

"What else?" asked Gregory, reflecting on what he had just heard.

"We know he was disappointed when he was passed over for the position of Chief Scientist at the Ordinance Complex," the Major interrupted. "Although we raised his salary and added him to our team attending IAEA-sponsored events in Vienna, those perks may not have been sufficient in overcoming his anger and resentment over his rejection."

"So there may be more than one motive here," mused Roger as he rose to stretch his legs.

"Possibly three motives," replied the Colonel quickly.

"What are they?" asked Gregory.

"There's the religious side, but we don't know how seriously he pursues that. At the plant, he showed his secular side. Away from the plant, he may have shown another side. We're still checking with some of the mosques in Wah and within a radius of about 100 kilometers from Wah, including our capital, to see if he came in to pray regularly. I briefly mentioned the other two motives before."

"Could you give us a photograph of him?" asked Roger trying to picture the scientist.

"Yes, here are two we can give you for now," replied the Colonel picking them up from his desk and handing them to Roger. "And I'll have the Major email you several additional photos we have of him, which you can then use or disseminate, as you please."

"Anything more on the scientist?" asked Gregory.

"Yes. We spoke with the other two scientists who attended the IAEA-sponsored meetings with him in Vienna last fall," continued the Colonel briskly. "They said that Mamood attended all the sessions and receptions, and performed admirably. They didn't know what he did at night. They thought he often went to bed early because they overheard him tell the hotel operator that he did not wish to be disturbed."

"Please, go on," said Roger.

"They didn't know if he met anybody unaffiliated with the conference in Vienna - with one exception. On the first night there he met a fellow Pakistani, a businessman, and they went out for some refreshment together, apparently nothing more than that."

"Did they give you a description of this businessman?" asked Roger sitting up more erectly in his seat, trying to concentrate on a possible key clue.

"They could not recall much since they met him for only a few seconds before leaving. They said he was light-skinned with dark hair. That's about all they remember – – and that does not give us much to go on."

"I agree," said Roger quietly.

After a few more questions, the CIA men rose to leave. They both left their cell phone numbers and email addresses with the Colonel and the Major and thanked them profusely for their frankness and for their help.

"We'll contact you soon with an update," said Roger, as he walked toward the door, "and I would appreciate your doing the same with us. Meanwhile, we'll continue our own investigation and see where that leads."

"One last item, Colonel," said Gregory quickly. "We may need your help getting on a flight to our next destination, once we figure out where that will be."

"No problem, gentlemen," said the Colonel smiling. "I think I can arrange that easily. Just let me know."

After leaving ISI headquarters, Gregory and Roger returned to their officer's suite at the Army barracks. They rested for a few minutes, before Roger picked up his secure satellite phone to call Nigel with a report and discuss where they should head next.

CHAPTER 37

LONDON

January 16, 2007

While Gregory and Roger focused on the Pakistani ISI and military front, Anne and Cliff focused on the possible movement of the missing weapons by sea. They were soon joined by Tim, who had been reassigned to their analysis group.

After reviewing Nigel's instructions, they decided that Anne should pore through every available source for the names of vessels that departed from Pakistan from January 4th on. Once that information was amassed, they would begin tracking different routes, ports of call and the final destinations of each vessel. Although a majority of Pakistan's exports went to the United States, they assumed there would be only a small number of vessels to track heading towards the United States already, since only 10 days had elapsed from the presumed date of the theft. They also agreed to keep on tracking vessels leaving Pakistan in the near future.

Anne worked late into the night, a routine to which she had become accustomed. She thrived on challenges and the complex mystery she now faced was daunting indeed. She stayed in her office, ordered a huge seafood salad and remained glued to her computer. On Google, she was able to run down a list of vessels that recently left Pakistan, including those headed to the United States, and those about to leave imminently. Exhausted but somewhat satisfied, she finally left her office after 1:00 a.m. for a well-deserved sleep.

At 9:00 a.m., the next morning the three again assembled in the center's second floor conference room. Anne could not help noticing Tim's haggard look and the fact that Cliff was in desperate need of a haircut. She wondered how she appeared to them.

"Here is what I found," said Anne, munching on a doughnut. "There are 14 vessels that left the country since January 3rd. A freighter, named the *SS Abdullah*, is scheduled to arrive at the Port of Los Angeles tomorrow night. Two others left on the 6th and 7th also bound for Los Angeles." She took a sip of coffee. "Another, the *SS Barooqi*, left on the 8th bound for Jacksonville, Florida. One also left for Seattle on the 10th, and another on the 12th. Lastly, a freighter left for Los Angeles on the 14th and another is scheduled to sail there tomorrow."

"Are any of these ships stopping at other ports before reaching their final destination?" asked Tim.

Anne looked through her notes.

"Three of those headed to Los Angeles are going non-stop," she said slowly. "One is stopping in Singapore and then proceeding non-stop to Los Angeles. Another is stopping in Hong Kong first." She paused and added: "The *SS Barooqi* is slated to stop in Dubai and Kingston before going to Jacksonville. As for the two destined for Seattle, one is stopping in Shanghai and the other in Manila."

"There are also three freighters headed to Rotterdam and one to Hamburg," she continued looking at the pages spread before her. "An additional one left for Dubai. Another is leaving for Alexandria, Egypt on the 17th. That's my brief rundown."

"We certainly have a lot of work ahead of us," said Cliff matter-of-factly as he went to pour himself another cup of coffee. "As I see it, we have to alert the host port authorities to do a thorough inspection of the cargoes unloaded and reloaded on site. And we have to urge them to use whatever available gamma imaging system they have on hand to examine all cargoes being unloaded and loaded."

"That's a good first step," said Tim, leaning back in his chair. "But we must track the smaller fishing boats and other small craft that left, or are about to leave, the country - a far more difficult task."

"That task may be beyond what we, and the ISI and the Pakistani military, are capable of," replied Anne quickly. "We can certainly request that the coastline be monitored, but it's possible a small craft may already be at sea with the bombs."

"Anne, how does your Coast Guard interact here?" asked Tim.

"After 9/11, its mandate was broadened," Anne replied. "Now they can go out as far as 1,500 miles and board a ship, if they sense that it presents a potential danger to the United States. They have been given more funding to increase ship strength and personnel and get additional armaments. They're also expected to patrol more often and more aggressively all along our coastline, and especially in and around our major ports, such as Baltimore and Los Angeles."

"How do you get them focused on our specific bomb case now?" continued Tim.

"I'll have to check on this with Langley. I think that the CIA would contact the Secretary of Homeland Security, or his deputy, the Director of National Intelligence, to put the Coast Guard on a confidential high alert. Of course, the Secretary or the Deputy may already have done so. As you may have heard, there's a whole new bureaucratic set-up to deal with now. And, from what I've learned, they run far from an efficient operation."

"Stop for a moment," interjected Cliff. "Since our group has limited manpower, we have to focus on what we think we can accomplish directly – – and then bring in others to expand our own efforts."

"I think we're all in agreement with that," said Anne. Tim nodded his approval as well.

"Here's where I think we go from here," said Anne in her no-nonsense style. "I'll contact my colleague at Langley, and give him a list of the ships that left Pakistan since January 4th. I will advise him that a search using gamma imaging equipment should be made of all the vessels, most importantly, the one docking in Los Angeles tomorrow night."

"Sounds like a good first step," Cliff nodded.

"I'll also tell him to recommend to the proper authority in the Department that U.S. Customs personnel in Rotterdam, Hamburg, Singapore, Hong Kong, Dubai and

Kingston, together with local officials, make a detailed inspection with the gamma imaging equipment of the cargoes being loaded and unloaded in those ports from those ships, as well as the cargo that remains on board."

She leaned over to pour herself a glass of water.

"Lastly, I'll ask him to recommend that the Coast Guard consider boarding the eight vessels bound for the States a few miles offshore, immediately outside U.S. jurisdiction to inspect their cargoes before they arrive dockside."

"While you work on that angle," said Cliff. "I'll get Nigel's approval to contact the port authority in Manila and Shanghai."

"And I will do the same for Alexandria," Tim added.

They all agreed to meet five hours later, at about 3:00 p.m., to pool their findings and consider what to do next.

Anne immediately got hold of Bud Holliday, at Langley. They had a lengthy conversation about the seriousness of the threat potentially facing the United States and the bureaucratic dance necessary to prompt the Coast Guard into immediate action.

Cliff and Tim met briefly with Nigel, who consented to their alerting the various port authorities in Shanghai, Manila and Cairo.

Several hours later, Anne received her expected call from Langley.

"I was able to meet with our Deputy Director soon after we spoke," said Bud. "After reading your email, he immediately phoned John Punt to recommend that the Coast Guard begin taking immediate action with the eight vessels headed here."

"And?" asked Anne expectantly.

"Punt placed a conference call with us to the Coast Guard Commandant. The Coast Guard got the message. The Commandant said his service would get on it immediately and take whatever steps they deemed necessary." Bud paused briefly and added:

"Next Punt placed another conference call to the head of the U.S. Customs directing him to arrange to inspect the cargoes on the vessels that left Pakistan for Rotterdam, Hamburg, Hong Kong, Dubai, Singapore, and Kingston. The Director of U.S. Customs, too, said he would do so quickly."

"Good work, Bud," Anne said excitedly. "I knew I could count on you to light a fire on the home front."

"I'll remember that, Anne. Those words mean a lot to me."

Anne was pleased that within hours her recommendations were already being initiated in the United States. She recognized, of course, that the parties charged with responsibility might not do their jobs fully. Still, she was encouraged by the immediate response to her request and the role she was playing in this mysterious drama.

Tim and Cliff were equally busy communicating with officials at the three foreign ports. The port authority at Manila readily agreed to inspect the cargo on the vessel destined to stop there. In Alexandria, port authority officials were initially reluctant to undertake such an inspection. They thought it might be viewed as an affront to a fellow Muslim country. However, the authorities relented after receiving assurances that the Pakistani government favored such a step. The Shanghai port authority graciously accepted the request for assistance, but advised that it would decide on its own what to do. Although both Manila and Alexandria were willing to have a U.S. "consultant" present during the vessel's inspections, the Shanghai port authority refused.

At their 3:00 p.m. meeting, Cliff was the first to speak.

"Shanghai gave me a kiss-off," he said briskly. "It's clear that they don't want outside help with this matter. But I think they'll take whatever precaution they think works."

He poured himself a cold root beer and continued:

"Manila was a different story. The authority was thrilled to have us present at the inspection of the vessel arriving from Pakistan on the 18th."

"You will go there, right?" Anne interrupted.

"Yes, I arranged to get a flight there and should be dockside before the vessel arrives," replied Cliff.

"I'm headed to Alexandria," said Tim cheerfully. "I haven't been there for a while anyway. I'll be there on the night of the 19th when the vessel is supposed to dock."

"And I'll be flying to Rotterdam to be on hand for the three inspections scheduled to take place there," said Anne animatedly. "Depending on how long they take, I may make it over to Hamburg. If not, I'll ask the U.S. Customs agent there to brief me on what his group found."

That part of the business settled, Anne told her two colleagues that both the U.S. Coast Guard and Customs had been alerted and had agreed to help hunt for the missing weapons immediately. She added that she would update her list of freighters departing from Pakistan through the end of February.

Leaving for their respective foreign destinations, each felt a little like a gambler betting on a long shot for a possible huge reward.

CHAPTER 38

VIENNA

January 19, 2007

The cool moonlit sky illuminated the pathway in front of the officers' barracks where Roger and Gregory walked out of earshot of interested eavesdroppers. Given the rush to find the stolen atomic weapons, they both realized that any misstep, any unwarranted detour on their part, might be disastrous.

Roger understood the situation. Stationed in Bosnia in the mid-1990s, his Special Forces Unit was assigned the hazardous task of finding and apprehending a ruthless Serbian general who had directed several massacres against innocent Muslim men, women and children. As a Captain, Roger headed up the unit. But the intelligence briefing he and his unit received was puzzling, inasmuch as the General had been sighted at least seven times. To Roger's finely-tuned analytical sense, something was wrong. Believing some key pieces of data were missing, he decided to meet the NATO intelligence officer who had previously briefed him, in an attempt to prioritize the leads given to his unit. When he finally met with his source, and reviewed the available information in depth, he realized that certain hard leads, backed by photo surveillance and firsthand accounts of the survivors of recent massacres, would lead him and his unit to the general, who was captured in a wooded area outside a small village bordering on Albania.

As the two walked quietly for several minutes, Gregory similarly reflected on his experience. When he was with the FBI, he had been attached to the Organized Crime Task Force in New York City. One of his assignments was to break up a major drug cartel that distributed vast quantities of drugs imported from South and Central America. It was a treacherous assignment, which he accomplished successfully. For years, he had honed his own analytical skills and his fluency with Spanish often helped him. Over the years, he had learned to recognize a real from a supposed lead and hard versus soft evidence. He knew he now had to rely on his years of useful experience in deciding what route to pursue.

As they approached the parking lot at the end of the path, Roger gazed at the moon for moment. He stopped walking and turned directly towards Gregory.

"Greg, I've been thinking hard about where we go from here."

"Me, too," replied Gregory immediately.

"As I see it, there are no real leads here in Pakistan," Roger continued. "We have only two clues to go on. The first is that the Pakistani scientist spent a fair amount of time in Vienna. The second is that he met another Pakistani there. That's all the ISI has given us."

"It's not much," Greg agreed. "But remember that when we first met with the Dutch AIVD, we were told about an Arab who boarded the jet in Cairo - the jet with the ransom money - and drove off with the funds in Karachi. I remember that the Dutch agent for the hijacked tanker saw him. It's possible he remembers what he looks like."

"I'd forgotten about that," Roger mused. "But I think the road to unraveling the mystery runs through Vienna."

"So you think we should go there first." It wasn't a question. Gregory already knew the answer.

"Yes," replied Roger firmly.

"I'm on board," Gregory said confidently. He consulted his watch in the moonlight. "It's about 1:00 a.m. now. Let's get a few hours sleep and leave for Vienna."

"Just what I was thinking," said Roger, pushing Gregory playfully in the direction of the barracks. There was a growing feeling of camaraderie between them, the bonding of two self-reliant, confident men bent on protecting the country they served. Each knew instinctively that one would cover for the other in a time of crisis and do whatever was required.

When Roger telephoned Colonel Hasim at 5:15 a.m. that morning, he was delighted to hear the Colonel's deep voice on the other end. Responding to Roger's request, the Colonel said that he would arrange for a private jet to take them to Karachi immediately and that he would delay the departure of the 9:00 a.m. flight to Vienna until his two foreign friends were on it.

Four and a half hours later, they were at Karachi International Airport, whisked through security, and boarded the flight for Vienna.

They checked into the Westbahn Hotel, near the central railroad station, several kilometers from the Donauzentrum Hotel, another four-star establishment where Mamood Ishan had stayed when he attended the IAEA conferences. They dressed casually and ate excellent Wiener Schnitzel at an old quiet Viennese restaurant not far from their hotel. Seated comfortably at a corner table, they began to discussing their plan of action.

"Let's try to put ourselves in the scientist's position when he came to town," said Roger. "If he was merely a workaholic, he might have spent quiet nights in his room. On the other hand, if he was both a workaholic and a playboy, he might have looked for some adventure at night."

"If I were in his shoes," said Gregory, "I would have walked around the city and gone to an excellent restaurant or two. Or I might have gone out with an attractive delegate from the conference."

"True," said Roger. He ran a hand though his hair, thinking. "But, in my younger days, I might have wandered over to some clubs with lap dancers for a night of racy action or even some romance."

"The Colonel did say he liked beautiful women, . . ." Greg said, thinking aloud. "What you say may make sense."

"Step back a moment. We have absolutely no leads to confirm any of these possibilities" continued Roger. "So that really leaves us only one principal route to pursue."

"Not so fast. We could also question the staff at his hotel."

"I think that's a long shot, Greg, but we can check it out."

"Since we can check out the nightclub scene now, why don't we do that first? We can go to the hotel in the morning."

"Questioning hotel staff might be a little iffy," said Roger. "Remember we're not the local police or Interpol. The staff may not want to speak with us."

"O.K.," said Greg easily. "Let's go back to our rooms and get those photos of the scientist. Maybe someone can identify him."

After picking up the photos, they got into a cab idling outside their hotel and asked the driver to take them to the nightclub area for some action. Nodding knowingly, the driver sped rapidly to an area around the Western Beltway. As they approached the old red light district, they saw row upon row of restaurants, small clubs and bars. The streets were full of animated people. Strolling under an elevated subway line, they decided to try a few bars at random before going into some of the clubs.

They had no success at the Ein Krugerl or The Golden Crown - two bars overcrowded with boisterous young people. In both instances, the photo of Mamood elicited no response.

Flushed and tired, they repaired to a nightclub called The New Wave further up the block.

As soon as they walked in, they were quickly ushered to a table to the right of the stage. They both smiled at the bevy of scantily-clad, beautiful young women. Within minutes, an attractive brunette came over offering a lap dance. After several more dances, Roger pulled out the photo and asked her whether she recognized the gentleman. She said no, but pointed to the door entrance, suggesting that they speak to the club manager. They lingered a while longer questioning several other dancers before approaching the manager. He studied the photo closely, but said he did not recognize their friend and suggested that they check out some of the other night clubs nearby.

Moving up the street, they chose The Old Hat, whose neon sign winked wickedly. A curvaceous red-head woman led them to a table in the center of the room with a good view of the stage. Two German girls immediately appeared, asking to join them for a round of champagne. Along with a magnum of Piper Heidsieck, the younger blonde woman performed a lap dance with such erotic grace that it wasn't difficult to figure out why her thong was lined with bundles of euros. Thanking her profusely, Gregory asked the girls if they could help find their friend suffering from amnesia, who had last been seen at one of these clubs. The women shook their heads and even asked several of the other dancers if they recognized the man in the photo, but again, without success.

Exhausted from 24 hours of non-stop activity, the two investigators wearily returned to their hotel, each swearing to sleep until noon.

Fresh from a good night's sleep, they went to Mamood's hotel early the next afternoon. Although its exterior was quite modern, the interior exuded old-fashioned Austrian charm, evident in the well-appointed lobby and bar. While Roger approached one of the registration clerks in the lobby, Gregory sought out the concierge near the bar. Neither provided any help. The concierge checked with the doormen and the bellhops, and again received a negative reply. The concierge suggested they return in the evening when the night shift was on duty. Returning that evening, again they hit a blank wall. No one had any information about their missing friend.

That night, once more, they plowed through several bars and visited three more nightclubs. After many smoke-filled rooms, many drinks, many lap dances and many questions, they received the same negative answers.

Used to handling tough assignments, Roger and Gregory followed this routine over the next three days. Walking around the city by day, they reconnoitered targets they wished to explore at night. The nights of January 21st and 22nd produced no results. Discouraged, they decided to try another part of the city the following evening. The pace was exhausting, but they desperately needed some success.

After another negative foray at a nightclub called der Viennafest, they walked into Der Schwartze Katze. Once seated at a table to the right of the stage, each ordered a Johnny Walker with water. Soon a leggy, curvaceous Swede with long auburn hair descended on their table. After a sensational lap dance designed to arouse even the dead, they asked her to join them. Over a bottle of Moet & Chandon Brut, Tured Nielsen relaxed and Roger showed her the photo. She studied it closely, a hint of recognition on her face. Without saying a word, she rose from the table with the photo and went over to an attractive blonde with terrific legs standing at the bar. Roger looked her over and thought her black sequin tank top and black thong were very becoming and exciting. He watched as they approached the table. Holding the photo in her right hand, the shorter blonde studied the two Americans closely before handing it back. She took in their casual dress, their easy demeanor and their handsome looks. They looked serious, even somber. Nevertheless, despite their air of respectability, she still had her doubts about them.

"You are looking for the man in this photograph?" she asked.

"Yes," answered Roger politely. "We don't know where he is. He may be suffering from amnesia and I think he was last in Vienna."

"Why are you looking for him?" she pursued.

"We think he may be in trouble and we're trying to help him," Roger replied softly, noticing that the woman grimaced at the word "trouble."

"What you say to me doesn't sound right," the blonde said warily.

"If you know him, please sit down with us for a few minutes," Roger implored. "It's important."

She hesitated a moment before joining them. As soon as she sat down, Roger and Gregory introduced themselves.

"I am Inge Seegen from Vienna. How can I help you?" she asked before accepting the proffered glass of champagne:

"Do you know this man?" asked Gregory softly.

"Yes, yes, I know him, but why is that of any concern of yours. What we do here at the club is our business, not yours."

Sensing her resistance, Roger decided to level with her: "This man may be a terrorist. We're not one hundred percent sure, but we think he's deeply involved in a big plot."

Shocked by this accusation, Inge jumped up:

"That's impossible!" she exclaimed. "You guys are crazy. I'm not going to listen to any more of this." Eyes blazing, she rose from her seat and began walking away with quick determined steps. Roger followed her.

"Please," he said, confronting her. "Don't leave. Come back to the table. Just listen to what we have to say. It's terribly important to all of us, even you."

Inge hesitated, not knowing whether to walk away, cry, or join them. On the verge of tears, she gazed directly at Roger and his colleague. Despite her confusion, she sensed they were serious and should at least be listened to. Shrugging her shoulders in a combined gesture of defiance and resignation, she returned to the table.

There was a moment of silence before Roger spoke.

"I don't know what your relationship is to this man, but I realize that what I just said may be shocking," he began.

"It certainly is."

"What I have to tell you is highly confidential and for your ears alone," he went on.

"Go on," she replied.

"You understand?" Roger insisted. "You cannot divulge this information to anyone."

"Yes, yes. I understand. I promise."

"All right," said Roger, somewhat reassured. "We think this man, Mamood Ishan, may have been involved in the theft of atomic weapons from his country. We also think one or more persons may be involved with him, but we don't know who they are."

"Go on," Inge repeated, listening attentively.

"We think this scientist and his collaborator stole the weapons for the purpose of a terrorist attack against the United States or Europe," continued Roger. "We need immediate help in tracking him down."

"This is unbelievable," replied Inge testily. "The man I know is not like that at all. You must be mistaken."

"We could be," Gregory interjected, "but we don't think so. After a detailed investigation, the Pakistani authorities are convinced he's the culprit."

"That can't be," replied Inge in disbelief. "I just don't believe it." She then added. "Who are you?"

"We're with an agency of the United States Government," Roger replied sternly. "And we're afraid thousands of our men, women and children may be killed." He looked directly into Inge's green eyes. "Please help us, Inge."

"It can't be true, and I don't know what I can do to help," Inge replied softly. She rose to leave, but seeing the disappointment in their faces, hesitated.

"I'll be here tomorrow night," she said. "If you want, come back here. At least you'll have a few excellent lap dances," she added bitterly. Moving away, she deliberately raised her voice. "Relax. I'm not running away."

Gregory ran after her.

"Wait! What's your address?" he asked breathlessly. But she just waived a hand and melted into a crowd of people at the bar.

As they left the club, Roger and Gregory decided to take turns following her. Ever the good soldier, Gregory volunteered for the first sleepless night vigil; Roger agreed to take the shift starting at noon the next day, the 24th.

CHAPTER 39

MANILA, ALEXANDRIA AND ROTTERDAM

January 18 and 19, 2007

<u>Manila</u>

Because of the urgency of his mission, Cliff was able to charter an Embraer long-range jet to take him from London to Manila, a distance of some 6,700 miles. Calculating that the flight would take about 12 hours, he threw a few bare necessities into a canvas bag and took off from the private jet service facility at Heathrow at 6:30 p.m. If all went according to plan, he would arrive in Manila shortly after dawn on the 18th, with hours to spare before the arrival of the Pakistani freighter.

Flying over Israel and Saudi airspace, Cliff reflected on his one-year stint in Iraq with the British Special Forces. His unit has been stationed in Basra and surrounding areas after the fall of the Hussein regime. After a brief, peaceful period following its liberation, incidents of violence increased dramatically in the city. Facing death constantly on patrol of that violent city, Cliff developed a heightened awareness of life on the edge. This edge saved his life. As his vehicle turned down a relatively deserted street, his peripheral vision took in the shadow of a rocket propelled grenade launcher sticking out a second floor window in a dilapidated office building. Commanding the driver to swerve right, the vehicle narrowly avoided an incoming grenade saving everyone on board from certain death or severe injury. That trait became part of his character.

Immediately upon arrival, he called the port authority in Manila and confirmed that the freighter from Karachi was scheduled to dock early that afternoon at about 1:00 p.m. Although he had plenty of time to spare, he went directly to the port authority management office, located near the unloading facilities. The officer in charge of unloading and cargo inspection was a dark-haired, wiry Filipino in his mid-40s. Cliff showed him a copy of his email requesting complete inspection of the vessel's cargo on board as well as the cargo about to be loaded. By way of reply, the officer pointed out that a total inspection using the port's gamma ray equipment would probably take many hours. The officer also added that Cliff could personally oversee and observe the inspection, as promised.

Several hours later, the *Lucky Star*, a Panamanian-registered freighter arriving from Karachi, docked at the port. Two Filipino customs officials went on board to pick up a copy of the cargo manifest and informed the captain his cargo on board and about to be loaded would be thoroughly inspected. Shortly thereafter, a red truck pulled a large gamma ray inspection machine into position, some 50 meters from the port side of the shop. Measuring almost 10 meters in height and eight meters in width, the inverted U-shaped machine's imaging technology was capable of detecting the contents of all containers, even those shielded in part with lead panels.

Stevedores descended on the vessel. Each container was lifted by a gantry and placed under the gamma imaging machine. Those bound for the Philippines were scanned first, followed by those bound for the United States, and then those waiting to be loaded on board. Each container was scanned for drugs, concealed weapons and, in this case, powerful bombs. In two instances, the machine's operator thought he saw a foreign object, but it turned out to be a false alarm. One by one, each container was thoroughly inspected. After three hours, the results were in: there were no concealed weapons on board.

The crews overseeing the inspection paid little attention to the tall, pale-faced foreigner, dressed in jeans and a black turtleneck, observing their actions. No one focused on his joining the imaging technician during the inspection for substantial periods. When the foreigner left, few were aware of it.

Cliff congratulated the port superintendent on the professional way the inspection was carried out. Convinced that the bombs were not on board, he sent an encrypted email to Nigel, briefly summarizing the results of his trip. Then he went to a local seafood restaurant near the port entrance for a very late lunch, awaiting further word from Nigel as to his next destination.

Alexandria

Tim landed in Alexandria around 3:00 a.m. on January 19 after an eight and a half hour flight from London via Athens. Checking in at the luxurious Alexandria Hotel, he seemed just like any English businessman, wearing a well-tailored, double-breasted dark brown herringbone suit and a light brown Borsalino hat. After settling into his room, he immediately went to sleep.

When he awoke the next morning, he observed a curious mixture of the old and new - exactly as shown in the tourist magazines in his room - from his fifth floor window. He dressed casually in beat-up khakis and a worn black sweatshirt. After breakfast, he took a taxi and got out one block away from the bustling port. There, he had an overview of the loading and unloading facilities at the Western Harbor, where commercial vessels of all sizes docked. From his perch across from the harbor, he was able to locate the container unloading facility near the center of the harbor and the main administration building. Heavy traffic flowed slowly in both directions on the cornice adjacent to the sea. The city had changed dramatically since he had last visited over seven years ago; many new office buildings, residential apartments and several new casinos had been built.

With several hours to kill, he entered a nearby restaurant, asked for a glass of local retsina and ordered a sturgeon with vegetables. He ate leisurely before embarking on a one-mile constitutional, which led through the city's main entertainment center at the Midan Saad Zaghlul.

At about 4:00 p.m., he arrived at the port administration building for this meeting with the port superintendent, a portly, middle aged man of heavy girth, sporting a virile mustache that proudly show the visitor around. Pointing to the newer gantries that had been installed to make the port more efficient, he also told Tim that the port was equipped with gamma ray technology to detect spectrums of radiation, including those found in plutonium, cesium and uranium.

Marshaling his best stevedores, the port superintendent ordered a close inspection all of the containers aboard the *SS Penta*, a Liberian-registered freighter from Karachi that had docked barely half an hour ago. One by one, each container was processed through the gamma ray inspection station over a several hour period. Initially, Tim and the port superintendent watched the process unfold behind the gantries, but anxious to watch the scans on the containers in progress, they walked briskly over to the gamma ray machine. However, the operator found no telltale traces of uranium, plutonium or cesium present in the cargo on board.

The process was then repeated for the cargoes about to be loaded from the port, since the vessel's next stop was Baltimore. As the inspection continued, Tim heard the muezzins over the rooftops calling the faithful to prayer. Although Friday is the traditional day of Sabbath for all Muslims, the port was in full operation. Again, the container inspection failed to reveal weapons of any kind.

Satisfied, Tim left the superintendent, thanking him profusely. As he rode back to his hotel, he thought about the difficultly involved in inspecting hundreds of thousands of containers that moved through the major and minor ports of the world – – and the state-of-the-art equipment that was necessary and had to be made available for such purposes. Although the *SS Penta* had been rigorously inspected, he was deeply concerned about the terrible risks created by the negligence that prevailed at many ports.

Back in his room, he spoke to Nigel on a special secure satellite phone, advising him that the ship carried no concealed weapons. He also relayed his thoughts about the need to stock radiation scanners and other high-tech imaging equipment throughout the world, a point Nigel seconded heartily. Nigel directed Tim to extend his stay in Alexandria for a day or two. Both wanted to know the outcome of Anne's interview with the Dutchmen in Rotterdam.

Tim finally had a chance to enjoy a relaxing evening, his first in weeks. The feeling was euphoric. He decided to check out the hotel's fitness center before setting down to dinner in the charming hotel restaurant. A Ludlum novel awaited him in his room. He barely read a few pages before going to sleep. Rising at a leisurely hour the next morning, January 20th, he felt refreshed but restless and anxiously waited for Nigel's call.

Rotterdam – January 19, 2007

While Roger and Gregory combed the streets of Vienna, Anne flew to Rotterdam on January 19th hoping for a breakthrough. Her plan was simple. She was to oversee the U.S. Customs personnel as they, together with the Rotterdam port personnel, inspected the entire cargo of three freighters from Pakistan. One was scheduled to arrive later that day, one on the 22nd and another on the 24th.

The rigorous inspection included not only the cargo on board but also the cargo about to be loaded at the port. But she had other tasks to accomplish first.

Walking alone on this dark, rainy day near the port of Rotterdam dressed in a navy blue parka over a warm white sweater and waterproof black slacks, Anne began thinking about her scheduled meeting with Luks Brinhoff and Theo Ringen at the office of Remlant & Sons. They were the only two who saw the participants in the ransom of the *Argus*. Before leaving London, Anne digested the reports the AIVD had prepared on the hijacking and subsequent ransom of the tanker. Blessed with an excellent memory, she vividly recalled the videoconferences with the Dutch intelligence agents. What was missing were further details about the man who boarded the plane in Cairo, the so-called money counter and expert, and his driver in Pakistan. Instinctively, she believed that the Pakistani driver would be of less value if found and interrogated. The individual from Cairo was the more important suspect. She had learned to rely on her hunches, which had proven to be successful in her investigations over the years.

As she covered the last few blocks that led to her destination, she checked the reflection in the storefront windows to make sure she was not being followed. In the field, Anne always experienced a heightened focus, and her pulse rate increased. She was on a high alert, fully aware of her surroundings.

This focus saved her and her CIA colleagues from a deadly ambush in Beirut years ago. She and another agent had been conducting an undercover operation in the city to help Israeli intelligence locate the presence of 130 mile range Zel missiles that reportedly had been shipped to the Hezbollah from Iran. Strolling along a tree-lined promenade overlooking the Mediterranean late at night, she thought she saw a shadow or two dart behind a parked car on the other side of the street. Feigning inattention, she approached a four foot concrete barrier next to a pedestrian crossing 15 meters ahead. Suddenly, she ducked and raced to cover, along with her fellow agent. Just then, she heard the whiz of several bullets pass through the air. Caught by surprise, the attackers stood up for a moment to see where the targets were and that error cost them their lives. They did not expect the woman and her accomplice to be expert marksmen.

Anne smiled as she recalled this incident, one of the many seared in her memory from many years of faithful service to the agency. At this stage, she was unsure of the outcome of the hunt for the weapons. She knew that she and her colleagues at the counterterrorist center would have to use all of their collective smarts to locate the missing weapons. But she was afraid they might not have enough time to do so. She tried hard to erase that negative thought.

Entering the tanker agency's building overlooking the port, she went up to the receptionist, who announced her arrival to Luks. A secretary escorted her to Luks's office on the second floor. As she entered the spacious room, Luks rose to greet her. Shaking her hand, he introduced her to Theo Van Ringen, who was standing next to one of the leather chairs facing a cluttered desk. Van Ringen smiled, shook her hand and gestured to the chair beside him. Anne sat down. Observing the two men, she was struck by Luks's welcoming expression and the confidence he radiated. Theo, on the other hand, appeared outwardly more reserved and, perhaps, less secure. She noted that Luks also had the firmer handshake of the two.

After an exchange of niceties, she got down to business.

"When our friends at AIVD set up our meeting, I assume they explained why I am here," Anne said looking at Luks levelly.

"Yes, they did," Luks answered. "You believe I can help you in your investigation."

"That's right," she said. "Specifically, I know you can identify the man who boarded your flight at Cairo airport. I also hope you may be able to give me some additional information concerning him."

"Okay. What would you like to know?" asked Luks.

"How would you describe him?"

"He's about six feet tall, dark-skinned or swarthy and burly, you know, solidly built. I think he's an Egyptian, but I'm not sure of the last point."

"Can you describe his face and the color of his hair?"

"As I recall, he has a broad face, curly, dark brown hair and no mustache or beard."

"By the way, may I call you, Luks?" Anne smiled.

"Of course!"

"You may call me Anne."

"O.K.," Luks said politely.

"Do you remember what he was wearing?" asked Anne.

"He wore a dark blue, pin-striped business suit, and he definitely looked like a businessman."

"What language did he speak?"

"English. But when we were in Pakistan, I heard him speak Arabic to his accomplice."

"How old do you think he is?"

"I'm not exactly sure. I'd say he was in his late 30's."

"Did you learn anything more about him while you were in Karachi?"

"Not really," replied Luks. "But remember we were followed by some people affiliated with him both when we sought to go to the Dutch consulate, which was closed, and back at the airport."

"Do you have any idea who was watching and following you there?"

"Not a clue. Obviously some people trying to protect the ransom money and him."

"There's nothing that jogs your memory on that last point," Anne pursued.

"Sorry I can't help you on that one."

"Did ABN-Amro tell you whether they were able to track the money you gave the Egyptian?"

"My boss, Peter Remlant, raised that issue with the bank and received a negative answer."

"What happened to the *Argus*?"

Theo, who had been listening attentively, answered quickly:

"After we paid the ransom and recovered the ship, we sent the engineering firm that designed the ship to inspect it thoroughly. They did so shortly thereafter and said the vessel was in first class shape."

"And after that?" asked Anne softly.

"She's back in service carrying crude oil from the Middle East to Europe," continued Theo. "Her crew has been beefed up. Whenever she is at sea, there are now at least three heavily armed security guards on board, Dutch, German or American ex-Special Forces types, and both the captain and first mate have access to an AK-47 or Uzi."

Luks' secretary, an attractive, dark-skinned young woman in a blue pants suit, came in with a pot of strong Dutch coffee and poured each of them a cup. Anne shifted in her seat, took a few sips and looked up again at Luks, who had turned to look out at the harbor for a moment.

"What do you remember about the Pakistani?"

"It was dark at night, and I saw him only for a few minutes, shortly after we arrived when he and the Egyptian left with the money. He was young, maybe about 30 years old; he had a beard which covered most of his face and bushy dark brown hair."

"And what language did he speak?"

"I heard him speak Arabic and another native language, but I'm not sure if it was Urdu or Pashtu."

Anne turned her attention to Theo.

"Anything more you can tell me about him?"

"Not much. He was dressed casually in a T-shirt and khaki pants. He also had a white Toyota van which he drove when they left with the money."

Anne sat back in her chair, wondering whether there were any more questions she wanted to ask. She decided not to probe further.

"I think that's all for now, gentlemen," she said smiling. "You both have been very helpful."

"If there is anything more I can do, please let me know," replied Luks, rising from his seat to accompany Anne downstairs. At the front door, Luks pointed to an oil tanker leaving port. As she watched the vessel slip by, Anne reflected on the unlucky fate of the crew of the *Argus*.

These thoughts accompanied a light lunch of grilled bass and new potatoes at a restaurant a few blocks from the port. Afterwards she returned to her intimate, four-star hotel, the Eden Savoy, located in the center of the city near the Old Harbor. Since she had scheduled a dinner meeting with the Amrit Friesen and Hans Kramer, AIVD representatives, she reviewed her notes again. The three had agreed to eat in the hotel's smaller dining room, where they could have a discussion without being overheard.

The Dutchmen arrived promptly at 7:00 p.m., having traveled from Amsterdam by train. The three ate heartily and shared two bottles of a mouth-watering Pomerol. Over an entrée of grilled prawns with couscous and asparagus, Anne inquired about their progress in the hijacking investigation. By way of answer, Amrit pushed his pommes frites towards her, inviting her to share, and revealed that the AIVD had undertaken detailed investigations in Indonesia (still on-going), Malaysia and Singapore, and had been unable to find any of the pirates or the boat they used in their attack. While devouring his Steak au Poivre, he reiterated that the agency was convinced the piracy was the work of Al Qaeda, primarily because of the bold nature of the incident – – hijacking and collection of a huge ransom – – and the Arabic-speaking Egyptian who had played such a major role in collecting the ransom money. Amrit and Hans knew that the London counterterrorist center agreed with this conclusion as well. As they pursued theories over cheese and espresso, they had to admit they had made little progress in solving the mystery of the hijacking of the *Argus* even though in the ensuing days the stakes had risen alarmingly.

After Amrit and Hans returned to Amsterdam, Anne prepared for the start of the inspection of the vessels that left Karachi. She had carried out two of her three missions in the Netherlands, but developed no new paths to explore so far. Usually an optimist, she hoped the port inspections might bear fruit, although, deep inside, she doubted they would.

Arriving at the U.S. Customs office at the port about 10:00 a.m. the next morning, she immediately looked for with the head of the unit, Ralph Lundgren, a Baltimore native. The *SS Blue Moon*, a Panamanian-registered freighter, was scheduled to arrive at noon. Lundgren told Anne that the port authority planned to make a gamma ray inspection of the entire cargo that originated in Karachi, including the cargo to be loaded in port and that his unit would oversee the operation.

Half an hour later, the vessel loomed into view and, with the aid of an old barge, came dockside. There were over 200 containers on board, but the unloading proceeded quickly. After a container was lowered onto a waiting truck, it was taken for inspection for a radiation and imaging scan. As a participating member of the Bush Administration's Container Security Initiative, the port of Rotterdam was well-equipped to carry out the inspection, having increased its security in recent years. When one container yielded a positive scan, Lundgren and Anne immediately joined two Dutchmen charged with opening it. Anne felt her heart race, hoping that a breakthrough was near at hand. But her excitement soon turned to disappointment. The container, the custom officials learned, had recently been used by a Dutch firm to transport some nuclear isotopes used in medical treatment. The remaining scans revealed no weapons of any kind.

The laborious inspections made on January 22nd and January 24th produced no positive results. The two freighters that arrived from Karachi carried clean cargoes. There were no weapons or any other arms on board either vessel.

Anne returned to her hotel room after the inspection in a foul mood, tossing her bag violently on her bed. She had hoped for a breakthrough and achieved none. Frustrated and upset, she spoke with Nigel early that evening, giving him an update. Nigel told her emphatically that her mission had been helpful. He informed her that the inspection made in Hamburg on a freighter that arrived on the 24th from Pakistan revealed no weapons either. They now knew the weapons, if moved by sea, were not in Europe. Nigel parting words were for her to be on call, since he expected to hear from Roger and Gregory on the outcome of their investigation in Vienna shortly.

CHAPTER 40

VIENNA

January 24, 2007

By the time Inge returned to her apartment, her anger had turned to confusion. She threw her coat on the sofa, stepped out of her heels and began pacing up and down, her mind in turmoil over what to do. The idea that Mamood might be some kind of terrorist - preposterous at first - had begun to take root.

The men at Der Schwarze Katze had said they were looking for an important scientist. Inge shivered. She knew that Mamood came to Vienna regularly to attend IAEA meetings.

Was he involved in some kind of plot?

What should she do?

She felt immense pressure in her chest. She couldn't breathe. She went to the refrigerator to get a glass of water. Chewing on a cube of ice, she tried to think logically and calmly to curb her turbulent thoughts.

Her affair with Mamood had started out innocently and pleasurably. She had taken an instant liking to him the first night they met. As time went by and their romance blossomed, she caught herself thinking more and more about him, awaiting his return, planning things they could do together, shopping for clothes that would please him, for food to cook for him. It was pure happiness. The joy in his eyes when they met after weeks of separation! *Her* Mamood was tender and passionate. He was intelligent and responsible. He was always talking about the future - *their* future. He made her feel important and secure. She trusted him. She was in love.

But there was something about those two gentlemen in the club. They spoke in earnest and were deadly serious. Inge knew that Vienna was a hotbed of intrigue. Could it possibly be true? Could she have fallen into an all-too-familiar trap? A handsome man appearing from nowhere, seeking her out at the club, establishing a relationship with her - could it have been premeditated? Distorted images of their love-making floated before her eyes. Had he been using her?

She suddenly thought of Hamad. Who was he? Why were they always together? What was behind his veiled, seemingly generous offer? Was it simply a gesture of friendship, as she had supposed, or something more sinister? Was it intended to compromise her? She was glad she had never accepted anything from him.

Inge put down her glass and looked at her watch. It was late. Somehow, she had to sleep. She undressed and went into the bathroom. The image that greeted her in the mirror was quite the opposite of her smiling, insouciant self. Her eyes were large and thoughtful; her skin very pale. She appeared grave, almost *severe*. Shaking her head in disbelief, she opened the medicine cabinet and found a bottle of Ambien. A sleeping pill would do the trick - she hoped.

She fell into a fitful sleep almost immediately, tossing and turning throughout the night, finally waking up in the early morning with a cry over the nightmare she had just had. She saw a pulverized city with faceless people limping aimlessly and without hope. A heavy white haze from the ash-filled sky covered the city. Endless bloated bodies lined the streets - mothers, children, men, each wearing a death mask. Rubble was everywhere; a few skyscrapers were still standing, mere empty charred shells.

Stumbling out of bed wearily, she went to the kitchen to make a cappuccino, and decided to cook breakfast. She set down her plate of scrambled eggs and toast carefully before going to pick up the Vienna daily outside her door. After leafing through several pages casually, her eye caught an article on the continuing violence in Iraq and Afghanistan.

She finished her meal, and lay down on the floor on her back to meditate. Fifteen minutes later, she rose feeling refreshed.

All this time, like a musical obbligato, her mind was working steadily. What the Americans said to her the night before brought to mind remarks Mamood had made. He has told her he was involved in an important mission that would change his life and that, once this was accomplished, they could do anything they wanted together. What did that mean? When he returned from a trip abroad, she noticed he had a boarding pass from Dubai. Why did he go there? Could it be that the man she loved deeply might be engaged in some illicit endeavor, one so horrifying that she could not comprehend it? And that dream. Why did she have it now? Was it a harbinger of what her unconscious could see and feel?

Confronted by doubts and questions, she began to wonder whether Mamood, who loved her deeply, had a dark side he never wished to reveal, a sinister aspect of his character that had nothing to do with his love for her. But if he was a terrorist in secret, how, in good conscience, could she live with him, perhaps even become his wife? Could it be that he hated Western civilization? She thought it hardly likely but perhaps there were aspects of it he could not stand. Or maybe he was being paid a king's ransom to commit a heinous act without concerning himself about the awful consequences. Her mind buzzed with "what ifs."

In the final analysis, her conscience determined what she should do. She realized that she would be unable to live with herself if a catastrophe occurred and that she had information that might have prevented it from happening. She decided to meet the Americans. But before she revealed anything about Mamood, she had to have proof from the Americans of their authority.

As she approached the club that night, she felt calmer about her pending decision, albeit with mixed feelings. Even if Mamood was somehow mixed up with the theft, perhaps his role was so minor that those investigating him might decide not to pursue him. Perhaps there was some way of saving the situation - a glimmer of hope. Or perhaps, maybe the Americans were charlatans.

After performing a highly provocative stage act and a few breathtaking lap dances, she took a break and headed to the bar for a drink of bottled water. Inge looked at her watch. It was nearing the end of her shift, a short day for her. As she left the bar, one of the girls nearby said some Americans wanted her to dance for them. Walking confidently, she strode to the table along the right wall and coolly greeted Roger and Gregory, who invited her to join them at their table for a round of champagne. She agreed. Once seated, she faced them directly:

"Before we discuss anything further about last night," she said tremulously, "you must give me proof that you are who you claim to be. If you don't, I'll have the bouncers throw you out of here."

Roger and Gregory knew it was against CIA policy to acknowledge such fact. This lesson was continually drummed into every operative. Roger looked at Gregory and nodded, making the decision for the both of them. It was something they had already discussed and quietly resolved.

"I understand your concern, Inge. If I reveal my identity to you, do I have your assurance that you will tell us all you know."

"There's more," continued Inge warily. "I want you to show me something that says this theft took place or that some investigation is going on."

Anticipating that they might have to reveal the reality of the investigation the night before, Roger and Gregory decided to disclose the contents of an email that Colonel Hasim had sent to their Blackberrys. Little did Inge know that, at the same brainstorming session, the two agents actually considered kidnapping her late at night and spiriting her out of the country, but rejected the idea as unworkable.

"You drive a hard bargain, Inge," replied Roger, moving closer to her. "But we're prepared to show you something highly confidential."

"Okay. First show me proof of who you are," said Inge, looking directly at Roger.

Solemnly, Roger and Gregory took out their BlackBerrys and punched in a secret code that authenticated the user of the Blackberry as a validated member of the CIA. Hesitating briefly, Inge looked carefully at each of the BlackBerrys before nodding grudgingly. Roger then asked her to look over his shoulder at the email he was about to show her which, she did, albeit a bit nervously. The email, which had been decrypted, read as follows:

> "To Roger Dunleavy, CIA,
> Gregory Markel, CIA

January 23, 2007

Our investigation is ongoing. We are still trying to develop new leads. For the moment, our scientist, Mamood Ishan, remains our prime suspect.

Please let me know how your investigation in Vienna is proceeding.

Regards,
Colonel Hasim, ISI."

Roger felt Inge tremble and almost begin to cry before returning to her seat. She gulped down champagne in an effort to control herself. She asked for another glass, which Gregory promptly poured for her. After a few quick sips and a few deep breaths, she looked up at them.

"What do you want to know?"

The CIA agents realized this might finally prove to be a major breakthrough. They knew they had to treat Inge with extreme delicacy. Since preparedness was their lodestar, the two had gone over what information they sought from Inge if she decided to cooperate with them.

"Maybe we should continue our conversation at a nearby café or another place of our choice," Roger suggested quietly.

"That's a good idea," she agreed. "I know a small café about a 15 minute walk from here that stays open late. I often go there to unwind. Since I can leave now, I'll change and meet you at the corner up the block."

"Sounds good," replied Gregory.

Standing at the corner, Roger and Gregory waited nervously for Inge to materialize. Although they were sure her suggestion was not a ruse, each watched the front entrance and side exit of the club carefully. Then they saw a pretty blonde dressed in a black pantsuit under a muskrat fur coat approaching them. Inge quickly led them to one of her favorite haunts.

Settling into a corner table near the back of an old Viennese café called the Hofhaus, they ordered supper and the waiter brought over several bottles of Evian. Inge sat between them. After some polite conversation, Roger turned serious.

"Where did you first meet Mamood?" he asked.

"At the club. I danced for him and his friend."

"Do you know the name of his friend?"

"Yes, I do. His first name is Hamad. I never did catch his last name, but I think it is el Bai or el Baim."

"How long have you known Mamood?"

"Since mid-October, 2006."

"And how would you describe your relationship?"

"We became lovers and close friends. I'm very deeply attached to him."

"Did you spend much time together?"

"Yes, we did when he was in Vienna attending those IAEA conferences. We also traveled a bit too."

"Did he ever mention anything about his work to you?"

245

"Yes, I knew he was a nuclear scientist in Pakistan, but didn't know exactly what he did."

"He is a very senior scientist who worked on many of their most important nuclear weapons projects," Gregory observed, sotto voce.

"If he never told you about the nature of his work, did he give you any hint of what he was doing?" Roger continued.

"Not really. Except once he did say was working on an important mission and that it would change his life. But I had no clue what he was referring to."

"When did you last see him?"

"In November. We took a short holiday trip to Budapest."

"Have you heard from him recently?"

"Yes, he telephoned me a number of times in December and this month as well. I expected to see him in late December around Christmas, but he couldn't make it. He said he was tied up on business and felt sorry he could not come then."

"And have you spoken more recently?"

"Yes, he called about a week ago. He said he would be traveling on business and would get in touch with me soon."

"Do you know where he called from?"

"No, he always uses his cellphone."

"Do you know where he is now?"

"No, I don't."

"Do you recall where he may have traveled recently to?"

"I remember one evening in late-October he returned to my apartment from abroad. We were very glad to see each other. I recall seeing a boarding pass showing that he flew back from Dubai."

"Do you remember the airline?"

"I think it was Emirates Air or British Airways. I forget."

"Did he tell you or hint at a place he planned to go with you once he completed his big mission?"

"No, he didn't say," Inge replied wistfully.

As if on cue, the waiter arrived with their supper. They decided to take a break and ordered a bottle of Bordeaux red. Sensing that Inge was more at ease with them and disposed to help them further, Gregory decided to proceed with his line of questioning over espressos:

"Inge, we would like to learn more about this man, Hamad," he said. "You know, the man you mentioned earlier. Can you describe him?"

"As I recall, he's tall, has thick, dark brown hair, light skin, and penetrating, dark brown eyes."

"Does he have a recognizable identifying mark, such as a scar?"

"No, not that I recall."

"Is he heavy set?"

"No. He's of medium build, but sturdy."

"What language did he speak when you were together?"

"He spoke English with a strange accent. I never heard him speak another language in my presence."

"How long had he known Mamood?"

"I don't know. My impression is that they only met recently but became close quickly."

"Do you have any idea where Hamad is?"

"No, none at all."

Satisfied, the CIA agents stopped their questioning. After thanking her profusely for her invaluable help, they mentioned that her help might be needed in the future and asked her to advise the U.S. Embassy in case of any change of address. Inge hesitated only for a moment, before reluctantly agreeing to do so. In return for her help, she made a request of Roger and Gregory.

"If it turns out Mamood is not the person you seek," she said in a halting, almost choking voice, "promise me you'll help clear the cloud over him." There were tears in her eyes.

"We'll try to do all we can for him on that score," said Roger softly, but firmly.

"One last thing," Inge added. "If he is only held under suspicion in this theft, but there is no proof showing he did it, will you help him?"

"That's a tough one, Inge," he said. "In that case, we'll see what we can do. But we make no promises."

They offered to drop her at her home in a taxi, but she declined, preferring to walk alone. With a heavy heart, she left them, aware that her potential future life with Mamood was probably over. Saddened deeply by that prospect, she nevertheless walked quickly and confidently toward her apartment. Her conscience was clear. She had done as much as she was asked. If they wanted more from her, she was available. She could go to sleep that night knowing that she may have saved many innocent people.

After arriving at their hotel, Roger and Gregory decided to have a night cap in Gregory's room, even though it was 3:00 a.m. Discussing the implications of their meeting with Inge over a Grey Goose on the rocks, Roger could not help but notice the dark circles under Gregory's blue eyes and that he was more tense than usual. He, too, was feeling weary from the unrelenting pace they had been following since they left London almost two weeks ago.

As they sat back on the comfortable easy chairs of the suite, they determined that Inge was their first lucky break. Through her, they had several significant leads to pursue at once. The next stop was Dubai. They also knew they had to give Nigel an update in the morning, which they sensed would surprise him.

CHAPTER 41

VIENNA/DUBAI

January 25, 2007

Early on the morning of January 25th, Roger telephoned Nigel with the exciting news that they had located the scientist's girlfriend who revealed the existence of another Pakistani and Mamood's trip to Dubai. Nigel was delighted.

"I think you and Gregory should go to Dubai immediately," he said. "Meanwhile, I'll arrange with our embassy in Vienna to keep the woman under surveillance. We mustn't lose her."

"I agree. We've done all we can in this city at the moment," replied Roger easily. "It makes sense to follow the next lead, which takes us to Dubai."

"Before you leave Vienna, I want you to give a photo of Mamood and a description of this other Pakistani to the head of our section at the English Embassy there. At my instruction, he'll arrange to have four of his staff on the look-out for these two men just in case they're still in Vienna or decide to come back to the city."

"Good idea, Nigel"

"By the way, I expect to hear from Anne shortly. Depending on what she's learned in Rotterdam, I may decide to have her join you in Dubai."

"That's fine. We may need lots of help there."

"Be careful," said Nigel with concern. "These Pakistanis have lots of friends, and we know they are ruthless."

"Understood," Roger replied nervously fidgeting with the phone. "We'll be careful."

"Keep me posted."

"I will," replied Roger, ending the call.

By the middle of the afternoon, Roger and Gregory were on an Emirates Air non-stop flight en route to Dubai. During the six and a half hour journey, Roger reminisced about his mission in Dubai four years previously when he and another colleague were tracking the movements of several Saudis reputed to be funneling money to Al Qaeda through the Emirates. Working through the embassy's CIA staff and local contacts they had developed over the years, Roger was about to close in on the financiers where they conveniently disappeared, having been tipped off. Roger's fluency in Arabic had proven to be vital, since the locals were more cooperative when dealing with someone who spoke their language. He hoped these contacts were still in place. They could prove invaluable now in unraveling the theft of the weapons.

Arriving late that night, they rented a car and drove to the Dubai Marine Beach Resort & Spa, a four-star hotel along the Persian Gulf. They had devised a plan on the flight and decided to review it the following morning after a good night's sleep.

Although Saturday was not a working day in Dubai, the U.S. Embassy remained open. Bradley Robinson, the CIA head of mission, was in his office expecting company in the morning; prior to leaving Vienna, Roger asked to meet him.

Bradley had been with the agency for over 20 years, spending most of his time in the Middle East and North Africa. Six feet tall and wiry, with cropped, wavy, light-brown hair, Bradley was fluent in Arabic and affable. He had developed a circle of reliable friends and contacts among the international set and had key contacts among the locals. He was a man who loved adventure and usually knew where to find it. He was well brought up and knew how to dress for any occasion.

Roger and Gregory arrived at the embassy at 10:00 a.m. Ushered into Bradley's cluttered five meter by five meter office on the second floor, they quickly filled him in on the nature of their mission. Bradley sat and listened. Occasionally, he ran a hand through his blond hair. The horror of 9/11 had never dissipated and the prospect of an atomic attack within the United States or Europe was almost too terrifying to contemplate. Bradley promptly agreed to cooperate in any way possible.

Roger was impressed by Bradley's easygoing manner and optimistic outlook. A background check revealed he had been a star quarterback at the University of Alabama. The direct gaze from his soft, blue eyes bespoke a confidence emanating from his wealthy, aristocratic family that had made a fortune in the manufacturing business over successive generations.

As Roger described their adventure in Vienna, Gregory slid a photograph of the Pakistani scientist across the desk to Bradley and added that he hoped give him a drawing of the face of the possible co-conspirator very soon. The two visitors asked Bradley to use his resources to try to locate and apprehend the two men quietly. They were wary of involving Dubai intelligence or police units because of a possible breach of security, in the event that Al Qaeda might have already infiltrated those units. It was clear to all that those locals had to be avoided.

One way of tracking the suspects, Roger speculated, was to track the money, which may have moved through Dubai. They had good reason to believe that the scientist had traveled to Dubai en route to an IAEA-sponsored conference. Although they did not know the purpose of his visit, he could have met with additional co-conspirators or perhaps set up a financial arrangement. Bradley said it would be difficult to get the local banks to cooperate with any financial inquiry. The U.S. Treasury counterterrorist unit in Washington might be able to initiate an inquiry, but certainly not the embassy. Even if an initiative was undertaken by the Treasury, it was highly questionable that the local banks would cooperate. Moreover, all three knew that such a probe would take time, perhaps months, before any useful information might be obtained.

As the group sat around strategizing, Roger suggested he could initiate a search for the scientist and his possible accomplice through the reliable network he developed several years ago. Bradley, in turn, offered to start a parallel inquiry using the contacts his current CIA contingent had built up in the country. To avoid a possible duplication of efforts, Roger printed a list of his contacts from one of his encrypted files in his Blackberry and gave it to Bradley. The CIA section head reciprocated. After contacting the English Embassy in Vienna, Gregory found out that a composite of the possible accomplice would arrive the following afternoon. The three agreed to initiate their joint efforts immediately and to keep in touch daily.

Early that evening Gregory and Roger drove to a small café, the Oasis, on one of the streets off Jumeriah Road near their hotel. Since the weather was balmy, they sat down at one of the outdoor tables and shared a plate of grilled eggplant on pita and plenty of hot tea between them. About half an hour later, a bearded, swarthy man of medium height wearing a traditional full-length white outer garment, the dishadasha, and red and white checkered shora as his headdress, appeared. Roger immediately noticed that his friend had aged over the last few years. There was a bulge over what was once a solid midriff and he had dark circles under his sparkling brown eyes. A Dubai native, Yousef bin Adin had lived all his life in the country, witnessing tremendous changes over the years. While engaging in an import-export business of countless products for almost 20 years, Yousef had built an established clientele and an enormous number of contacts, in high and low places. His relationships with such a broad range of people made him valuable to those in need of information, an asset Roger had relied on heavily in the past.

As Yousef approached the table, Roger stood up and the two embraced, kissing each other on both cheeks. Roger introduced Gregory and the two shook hands warmly.

"A friend of Roger's is a friend of mine," Yousef said smiling, showing his gleaming teeth.

"Likewise," said Gregory pointing to a seat between him and Roger. Yousef then sat down between them. Without hesitation, Yousef ordered a plate of grilled spicy chicken kebab with couscous. Clearly, he was a man who knew what he liked and what he wanted. He rubbed the knife wound scar over his left eye.

For Gregory's benefit, they recounted tales from the past, each exaggerating his own exploits. Finally, fork and knife in hand, Yousef looked at Roger with a measured gaze.

"What brings you two to Dubai? I suspect trouble."

"Why do you say that?" asked Roger smiling broadly. "Don't you think I would come here on vacation?"

"Sure, you might just do that," continued Yousef in a deep jocular tone. "But I have a feeling that now you are here for other reasons."

"You always could read me, my friend," said Roger patting Yousef on the back gently. "We need your help."

"What can I do for you?"

Gregory handed Yousef a photograph of Mamood. The Arab studied it closely.

"We'll have a drawing of a friend of his for you tomorrow, as well," said Roger. He took a bite of pita. "We would like you to find out if these men are in Dubai and, if so, where they are. We also want to learn what business they transacted here. If they were here and left, we'd like to know where they stayed."

"That's quite a tall order, my friend," replied Yousef pensively. "Dubai has so many visitors these days. Some stay overnight, others a few days, many still longer. If they were here for only a day or two and left, it would be very hard to find out much, if anything, about them."

"We know it's a tough one, Yousef," Roger nodded. "But will you help us?"

"For you, of course, I'll help. You assisted me in tracking down some of my big overseas creditors who owed me several million U.S. dollars. I owe you. I learned to trust you and you can do the same with me."

"There's some urgency to our situation," added Gregory quietly. "How long might you need?"

Pausing for a moment, Yousef said, "At least several days. I'll have to ask around and make a few personal visits here and there."

"As in the past, Yousef, we must remain invisible, behind the scene."

"Roger, I know how you operate," replied Yousef and he laughed. "You've told me often enough. I've heard all the so-called cloak-and-dagger stories, and in each of them you always keep a very low profile."

"You understand exactly!" Gregory said, smiling.

"Yes, I do."

Once dinner was over, Yousef warmly shook the hands of the two Americans and soon disappeared in his chauffeur-driven Black Mercedes S550.

"He's one of the best contacts I ever made here," said Roger as he and Gregory walked down the street to their rented car. "He has bloodhound instincts, knows where to look and whom to ask. He's also discreet."

"Sounds like a great find, Roger," said Gregory glancing furtively over his right shoulder to see if they were being followed. Many people were out strolling, enjoying the fine weather. Greg patted the Glock in the holster under his left arm.

"I remember when I traveled to Morocco when I was about 22," said Roger, as they returned to their hotel. "That was over 20 years ago. I loved Tangier and Fez and I explored the city by day and by night alone or with a friend or two. I had absolutely no fear when I went into the Casbah at night with an American friend to eat at a restaurant. The place was half mile back in the Casbah, beyond a wide, high-walled alleyway with high-rise apartment buildings on either side. I could literally hear the sounds of families at dinner and kids laughing through their windows. Yet, I saw no one; the alleyway was absolutely deserted and hidden from the streets."

"What happened?" asked Gregory.

"Eventually I found the restaurant I wanted. But the point here is that I felt, as an American, I was absolutely protected. I honestly believed my passport was a good luck charm that would save me."

"And you don't feel the same way today, do you?"

"Not at all. Sure, I'd be tempted to go back to Morocco as a tourist one day, but I don't know how comfortable I'd feel. American citizens have become targets. Remember what happened to that British tourist in Amman in early September, 2006? Some wild-eyed terrorist came out of the blue and killed him and wounded several others."

"Do you think the same thing could happen here in Dubai?" asked Gregory.

"Who knows? Two Americans walking around in the Al Souk at midnight. We might attract too much attention. I think we should keep a low profile in Al Souk when we meet my next contact over coffee in the late afternoon."

Gregory nodded silently. "Let's go over tomorrow's agenda upstairs," he said. "There must be some beer in the mini-bar."

On the morning of the 27th after an anxious sleep, Roger and Gregory hailed a taxi, which took them to the U.S. Customs office at the main port administration facility. Along the way, they marveled at the huge, modern skyscrapers that brilliantly reflected the strong rays of the morning sun. The exquisitely appointed Burj al Arab, a seven star hotel, seemed to rise straight from the dark blue waters of the Gulf. The port area was bustling with freighters from all over the world docking at the port's terminals daily. Trade through Dubai had grown tremendously.

Arriving at their destination, Roger spoke in Arabic to a couple of Arab stevedores sipping mint tea outside the administration building. They told him the U.S. Customs Office was on the second floor and pointed to some windows toward the far end of the building. At the customs office, Roger told the receptionist they had urgent business to discuss with the chief of the office. Several minutes later, they were ushered into a small conference room, no more than four by four meters, with a brown, rectangular conference table and six cheap-looking chairs. Within seconds, Bruce Ramsey came into the room and greeted them. Ramsey had a weather-beaten face as if he spent many years outdoors. He was middle-aged and bespectacled. He hailed from Worcester, Massachusetts and had assumed his present position in Dubai after almost 15 years serving as a customs duty officer in the Boston area. Ramsey was worldly wise and wondered what business these two Americans were about.

"Gentlemen, what brings you here?" he asked, eyeing them skeptically.

"We're on official U.S. government business," replied Roger, looking directly at the customs official. "And we need your help," he said, handing over their passports to Ramsey.

Ramsey studied them perfunctorily.

"How can you prove that you are here on official business?" he asked.

"Call the embassy and ask to speak to Bradley Robinson," Roger answered firmly. "He'll confirm what I'm telling you."

"I'll do just that," said Ramsey picking up the phone and directing the receptionist to dial the U.S. Embassy. Within three minutes, he had his answer. Told to cooperate fully with the two Americans, he replaced the receiver, looked at Roger and produced something resembling a smile.

"How can I help you?"

"We're checking on all freighters from Pakistan that stop here en route to the United States," said Roger almost conversationally.

"What is it you want to know?" asked Ramsey wiping his glasses.

"What type of inspection does the port make when they come through?" continued Roger.

"That depends on the manifest our office in the States receives 96 hours in advance of the ship's loading at the port of embarkation. If they tell us the ship is a potential high security risk, or based on other factors, we inspect it thoroughly. Otherwise, we do spot checks on a small percentage of the cargoes, depending upon where the ship has embarked and other factors."

"Are there many freighters from Pakistan that stop here?" asked Gregory, as he glanced out the window at the bustling harbor.

"We get a lot of traffic from there. Dubai has become an active trading center. Lots of cotton goods are imported here."

"One particular freighter, the *SS Barooqi*, came here around January 10th," continued Roger rapidly. "Could you tell us what inspection, if any, was done on her cargo?"

Ramsey rose from his seat at the head of the table and moved slowly to the Dell desktop computer at a corner work station. Punching in the name of the vessel, he found the information quickly.

"Our records show it was not inspected at all. We received no notification from Washington that there was any high-risk cargo on board."

"Were any containers offloaded here?" asked Gregory quickly.

Ramsey checked his computer printout carefully.

"I see that 25 containers were unloaded on the 11th of January."

"Do you have the names and address of the consignees?" asked Roger, trying to conceal his anxiety.

Returning to the computer, Ramsey reviewed the appropriate file and printed out the requested information, and handed it to Roger.

"This is what our records show," he said.

"I see only 10 consignees listed," said Roger.

"That's right," replied Ramsey. "Anything more I can do for you now?"

"Not at the moment, but we'll be in touch if we need additional help," said Roger.

"I'm generally always available, so just ask for me," Ramsey said, rising from his chair with some effort.

"Appreciate your help," said Roger, extending a hand, as did Gregory. The two men were in a hurry.

Once they were about 50 meters away from the building, Roger began assessing the situation.

"We may have a problem," he said excitedly. If the stolen weapons were on that vessel, they could have been unloaded here. We may have to probe further to find out what goods were actually offloaded to the consignees."

"I doubt these folks have jurisdiction over any of the goods once they leave port," said Gregory in a skeptical tone. "Perhaps they could advise the consignees that there is some irregularity with their paperwork, and ask them to prove what they imported."

Roger stopped, considering this.

"Even if Customs did what you say, the plan wouldn't work. If a consignee received the weapons, he would lie about what was imported and cover up what happened. In other words, if a guilty party said it imported cotton goods, it would find the cotton goods to back up its claim."

"True, but maybe Robinson's staff can check out the bona fides of the consignees and do some additional investigation on that front," replied Gregory, trying to flag down a passing taxi.

"Fine. I'll suggest that approach to Bradley."

They decided to return to the embassy early that afternoon to speak with Bradley and obtain the composite from Vienna that was due to arrive. To Greg and Roger's surprise, Bradley willingly seconded Gregory's idea. In the event that these were certain "irregularities" in the consignees' paperwork, the guilty party might have to take some step or evasive action that, in turn could create a lead. Bradley was clearly turning out to be an imaginative player.

During the meeting, a secretary brought in the composite of the other accomplice, which had arrived via email from Vienna. The three studied two different drawings of the accomplice, the potential mastermind of the atomic theft. His light complexion accentuated the darkness of his brown eyes that stared back icily and frighteningly. Roger wondered when and if they would ever come face to face. Multiple copies of the composite were made to be distributed to hand out wherever and whenever needed. Greg reminded Roger it was time to meet their next contact.

Winding their way through the Al Souk, the CIA agents passed bustling outdoor markets, small shops, cafes and vendors hawking volubly. The atmosphere was permeated by a mixture of scents and spices: lamb kebab baking in barbecues; platters of moussaka and shawarma; the heavy fragrance of jasmine and the odor of fresh fish all combined. By the time they arrived at their destination, the al Jaffa Café on al Raffa Street, they were ready for Turkish coffee and a sweet cake, as they waited for their guest to appear.

Forty minutes later, a young Saudi, resplendent in a white dishadasha and black-and-white checkered headdress, approached their table. Ibrahim al Falal greeted Roger warmly, embracing him and Gregory like a brother. In Roger's eyes, his friend looked just the same: light-skinned, wavy, brown hair, soft, round face and slightly under medium height. Delighted to see Roger and his fellow American, Ibrahim ordered a round of Heinekens and kept his companions laughing heartily for almost 30 minutes. Ibrahim was no fool. This tactic was meant to show all present they were old buddies, good friends having a splendid time. Ibrahim felt very loyal to Roger. The CIA agent had introduced him to important Saudi investors, who, in turn, helped Ibrahim start a successful real estate business in Dubai.

Wiping tears from his eyes, Roger turned to business. Showing him the photo of Mamood and the composite of Hamad, he asked Ibrahim for his help in finding both men, in addition to finding out what business, if any, they carried out in the country. Since Ibrahim enjoyed good banking relationships, perhaps a few discreet inquiries could be made on that front. The Saudi agreed to help, but he was dubious he would find what they wanted. In any event, he would do his best.

Their three-hour rendezvous continued in a festive spirit. After several rounds of beer, they ate a hearty chicken shish kebab dinner with basmati rice, followed by an excellent brewed mint tea. When Ibrahim rose to go, they all embraced warmly.

Late that night back at their hotel, the CIA agents telephoned London to brief Nigel and get an update from him. Leaning back in a comfortable chair in his spacious room, Roger initiated the call on his secure satellite phone, in speakerphone mode, so Gregory, seated nearby, could listen in:

"How're you doing, Nig?"

"I'm fine, Roger. I see it's a bit late for you two."

"True, but, as you know, we believe in duty before pleasure."

"How are *you* doing?" asked Nigel in his usual deep voice.

"We're working with the embassy CIA staff to pursue parallel paths, trying to locate the Pakistani scientist and his accomplice and to find out what business, if any, they carried on here," replied Roger calmly.

"What other steps are you two pursuing?"

"Several of my contacts from the past are prowling around discreetly," replied Roger. "We gave them the photo of Mamood and several drawings of his accomplice. We expect to hear from them within a few days. Hopefully, we'll be able to have some feedback from the embassy contingent here soon as well."

"So you're in a waiting mode," Nigel replied. "Anything else?"

"Yes," interjected Gregory, rising from the bed. "The U.S. Customs office at the port told us it didn't inspect the cargo on the *SS Barooqi*, the freighter from Karachi bound for the States that offloaded goods here on January 11th, about a week after the theft. The officer said Washington didn't advise them to make any inspection. He added that the goods offloaded here were cotton goods, items typically exported from Pakistan."

"Has this vessel reached the States yet?" asked Nigel.

Gregory checked his Blackberry.

"No, it's due in Jacksonville around January 29th," he said.

"Anne gave a schedule of all those pending arrivals to Langley, which, in turn, arranged for the U.S. Coast Guard to inspect these vessels closely, including the *SS Barooqi* you just mentioned," Nigel continued.

"Remember, Nigel, that vessel stops in Kingston before leaving for Jacksonville early on the 28th," Roger said.

"As I said, the Coast Guard will inspect it closely once it approaches the States," replied Nigel in a confident tone.

"Let me update you two on what happened with the other vessels that left Karachi. The Coast Guard advised the CIA at Langley that all vessels coming from Karachi to the United States since January 4th were inspected by them with great care. In fact, they boarded one headed for Seattle and one headed for Los Angeles, a bit outside the 12-mile limit. They were thoroughly inspected with mobile scans and imaging equipment and found to be clean."

"Did anything turn up in Manila, Rotterdam, Hamburg, Alexandria, Kingston, Shanghai or Hong Kong?" asked Gregory.

"Anne told me that the Rotterdam and Hamburg inspections revealed nothing," Nigel replied and paused for a moment before continuing. "Clifford said nothing turned up in Manila. You said Dubai also didn't reveal any weapons. Tim said the inspection in Alexandria was negative."

"What about the Far East, Nigel?" asked Roger, trying to think of all the possible gaps in coverage.

"Langley told us Hong Kong was also negative. As for Shanghai, we received no word yet."

"Where is Anne now?" asked Gregory.

"She's back in London, awaiting my further instructions as to where to go next."

"And Clifford and Tim?" continued Gregory.

"Clifford left Manila and joined Tim in Cairo. They have been there for over a week trying to track down the Egyptian who handled the ransom money for the pirates."

"Any luck on that end?" asked Roger hopefully.

"No, they've run into a brick wall," said Nigel in reply. "They went to our MI6 contingent at our embassy, but they, together with our staff, have been unable to develop any leads so far. They plan to work the case for at least several weeks more. The Egyptian is a key guy to land if we can do it."

There was silence on the line as Roger and Gregory digested this information.

"Let's talk tomorrow in the late afternoon," Nigel said finally. "That will give us a little time to reflect on what to do next."

"Okay," said Roger.

"Okay on my end," Gregory seconded.

Dispirited, Gregory returned to his room. Both men knew they had to get some sleep in order to face another stressful day. Tomorrow, they hoped, would bring some results.

CHAPTER 42

KINGSTON, JAMAICA

January 27, 2007

The white container lay in the port facility in Kingston for only three hours before it was moved that Saturday afternoon. Per instructions given to him previously, Hassan used his cell phone to inform a local freight forwarder, High Transport Ltd., that a cargo for pickup had just arrived. The freight forwarder sent two men and a flatbed truck to pick up the cargo, clear it through Jamaican customs and then transport it to the consignee, All World Trading Ltd., a British Virgin Islands corporation, at its office in Jamaica.

The truck lumbered to the port facility entrance at about 4:00 p.m. The driver, Emmet Richards, an affable, good-looking bachelor of about 30, had worked for the freight forwarder for over eight years and was one of the most recognized persons at the facility. Over the years, he got to know all the local customs officials personally. He approached Percival Henry, an official on duty, slapped him on the back and invited him to join him at the local soccer match two days later - an offer the customs official immediately accepted. After trading a few stories about their respective girlfriends and laughing loudly while doing so, Emmet handed Percival a copy of the bill of lading for the container he had to pick up. Percival glanced at the bill of lading, stamped it as tariff free and gave Emmet a green card, which permitted him to bring his truck into the facility to pick up the cargo.

Craning his neck, Emmet drove his truck alongside a row of containers until he located the white container he sought. It took almost 15 minutes to load the container onto the truck, after which Emmet left the terminal, heading east toward the southeast section of the city where All World Trading Ltd. had its offices.

The trip to the delivery site took about 20 minutes. Emmet was able to skirt the colorful parade to the north and west of his destination. Smiling at the happy sounds of the revelers and tapping his fingers in rhythm to the Reggae beat as he drove, he leaned out to whistle at two girls walking by. They were dressed in white skirts and matching red tank tops with a multicolored sash across their chests and sported decorative straw hats. He was anxious to make his final delivery so he could go to his girlfriend's apartment, pick her up and then go to the festival's park site for an evening of wild entertainment.

Emmet was a bit surprised that the consignee's office would be open at this hour, on a late Saturday afternoon of a festival day. Most offices and other places of business had closed by 1:00 p.m., excepting restaurants, cafes, food and liquor stores and some outdoor markets. He certainly did not question why this office was still open.

When he finally arrived at his destination, a tall, dark-skinned, Egyptian youth, almost six feet tall with a muscular build, greeted him. Emmet had made Saturday and Sunday deliveries to this office before and came to realize that this office seemed to run on Middle Eastern time. The Egyptian, Mohammed Abdel, told Emmet to place the goods in the firm's rear offices, which were large enough to hold the contents of at least two 20 x 40 feet containers. Emmet and Mohammed opened the container's door and lifted out 20 crates filled with spice goods, including the two one and a half by two meter wooden boxes. Since Emmet and his co-worker regularly lifted heavy cartons, they hefted each wooden box, which weighed about 45 kilos, and carried them easily into the rear office. Once the entire delivery was complete, Mohammed signed the freight forwarder's form acknowledging delivery and receipt of the goods delivered. Emmet lost no time leaping into the cab of the truck and eagerly drove off.

Mohammed was one of several employed by the trading corporation in Jamaica. He had worked for one of Mahmoud's trading corporations in Cairo for over seven years and had been promoted to its Caribbean Basin and South American headquarters only a month ago. Mohammed had proved himself many times. Recruited directly from Cairo University by Mahmoud because of his financial acumen, he had risen to controller of one of Mahmoud's largest trading entities. While many of his classmates had been unable to find jobs or, if hired, any jobs that paid decently, Mohammed considered himself fortunate. He felt increasingly beholden to Mahmoud for this position, which allowed him to rent an attractive apartment in one of the more modern residential complexes of the city. A sensitive person, Mohammed had also been drawn to the preaching of the Muslim Brotherhood and had attended many of their clandestine meetings. It was, therefore, no surprise that he was easily recruited to the Al Qaeda cause, after the many hours spent with Mahmoud on that subject. Loyal to the core, Mohammed followed Mahmoud's directions easily and without reservation. He knew his future was inextricably tied to his continued association with Mahmoud and remaining high in Mahmoud's esteem.

Within three hours of the ship's arrival, the crew of the *SS Barooqi* took shore leave for the weekend. The first mate and one seaman stayed on board for the 48-hour layover until Sunday at 10:00 p.m., when the vessel was scheduled to depart for Jacksonville, Florida. After their 13-day voyage, Ashan, Hassan, and the other members of the crew were happy to go ashore, albeit even for several hours. The twosome stopped at an outdoor cafe filled with some of the revelers that were near their destination, the office of All World Trading Ltd. Each has some fried chicken with rice, washed down with excellent cinnamon tea and then honey-filled sweet buns for dessert. The meal took about an hour and they appreciated this brief period of relaxation. When they looked up, they could see pink cumulus clouds tinted by the late afternoon rays of the soon setting sun. The air was balmy, a soft breeze that came from the southwest.

Meanwhile Mohammed awaited the arrival of the two seamen. He knew he was part of an important mission but did not know much about it. He had received an encrypted email from Mahmoud the day before advising him that two seamen would come to the office Saturday night, sleep over in the office's bedroom and leave by early Monday morning. They would help him load two wooden boxes onto a yacht scheduled to arrive near the port of Kingston on Sunday afternoon.

Ashan and Hassan showed up about 6:00 p.m. that Saturday evening. They looked around at the neatly appointed, recently painted all-white office containing four rooms, a separate bedroom and a large storage area in the rear. Before splitting up, the threesome chatted for several hours trading tales of their earlier days and how each became a member of Al Qaeda. Mohammed then left to go to his rented apartment nearby, while Ashan and Hassan prepared to spend the night guarding the offices.

Ashan took the first shift from 9:00 p.m. to 3:00 a.m. while Hassan dozed fitfully in the cramped, but neat, bedroom. He made sure to shut out all the lights to avoid the curious eyes of stray passersby. The neighborhood in the vicinity was quiet, and there were only a few lights on the block where the office was located. Ashan could hear doors opening and closing up the street, as well as the laughing of some Jamaican men who sat on a porch about 200 meters away. The office buildings nearby were entirely silent.

Time passed slowly. Ashan would check the luminescent dials of his watch from time to time. He could hear Hassan snoring rhythmically. An occasional car drove by without stopping. He continued to cradle the Uzi that Mohammed had carefully hidden, together with some ammunition and several grenades, behind a false wall in the back of the bedroom closet. He was certainly ready to deal with any intruder.

At about 3:00 a.m., he then nudged Hassan awake. While Hassan took over the next six-hour shift, the younger Ashan slept easily; he had been awake for almost a full day. The next shift passed without incident. When Mohammed arrived in his new white Nissan van at about 10:00 a.m., he brought them several scrambled egg sandwiches, a thermos of hot tea each and a local sweet pastry. Ashan and Hassan ate their breakfast rapidly; they had little to eat over the last 18-hour period and were ravenous. Over breakfast, Mohammed informed them that a Pakistani businessman would be arriving in Kingston that afternoon. He was expected to join them at the office in the late afternoon.

A bit nervous, Mohammed fidgeted with the keyboard of his laptop computer that lay on his desk, a six foot mahogany table with three filing pullout drawers on its right side. He was expecting another encrypted email, but having checked his emails three times that morning, there was still no message. He knew this type of waiting was typical right before the beginning of an operation. He had experienced it many times before in Egypt and on certain assignments he undertook for Mahmoud in other parts of the Middle East.

When he checked the fourth time, he finally saw what he was waiting for: an encrypted email with further instructions. Once deciphered, the email read:

"Bring additional maritime supplies to the yacht Dream Free at the Duke's Yacht Club tonight between 9:00 p.m. and 10:00 p.m.,

Your Faithful Captain."

Excitedly, Mohammed announced the news to Ashan and Hassan.

At about 5:00 p.m., a yellow taxi pulled up in front of the office. A man in his mid-40s and dressed in a casual business outfit, climbed out of the back of the taxi carrying a black suitcase. Approaching the front door, he rang the bell. Mohammed came to the door while Ashan and Hassan, each armed with an Uzi, took up defensive positions out of sight in a nearby room down the hall. Before opening the door, Mohammed asked:

"Who are you?"

"I come from afar with a message from the Prophet," the visitor replied.

"And what is your message," continued Mohammed in a serious tone.

"I'm a fixer," said the visitor solemnly.

Satisfied by the visitor's use of the secret passwords, Mohammed opened the door. The visitor stepped into the front room, put down his suitcase and hugged Mohammed. The man looked at him directly and said:

"I'm Mamood Ishan. I will join our brothers on the yacht tonight."

Ashan and Hassan put down their weapons and came to greet their new guest with curiosity.

After introductions were made, Mohammed told the group he would go to one of his favorite cafes to bring them dinner. He turned a half hour later laden with food and drink. The group sat around a desk in one of the offices and ate their hearty dinner slowly.

As the time of departure approached, they readied themselves for the task ahead. Before starting with the loading operation, Mohammed walked outside and casually surveyed the street. It was deserted. He returned and nodded at the others. Ashan and Hassan packed the Uzis in a brown suitcase, which they put in the back seat of the van. Then they carried out the two wooden boxes, which they loaded side by side in the rear of the van, covering them with a large blanket. After that, they added several nautical ropes, about 13 meters in length, to the top of the blanket, together with two sets of side bumpers, four mops and cleaning materials. Then they placed two special cans of lubricating oil behind the rear seat. All of these items had been brought by Mohammed in accordance with previous instructions. He got into the van behind the wheel along with the others.

Mohammed checked his watch. It was 8:15 p.m. This gave them plenty of time to make it to the yacht club, which was only 18 kilometers away. He turned into the road that ran along the sea, proceeding cautiously to the rendezvous point. He made sure to drive beneath the speed limit to avoid any police intrusion. It helped, he felt, that it was Sunday night, a quiet night, especially since many partygoers had had a day to recoup from the previous day's activities. The sea road was dimly lit and there were several potholes that he barely managed to avoid.

After 20 minutes, the group could see the lights of the yacht club and the marina in the distance. A half moon illuminated the cloudless night sky and even in the dim light, the constellations, including the Dippers, were easily recognizable. Hassan took out a pair of Japanese binoculars and carefully studied the yachts and other boats docked at the club's marinas. As he looked up and down, he finally found what he was looking for: the *Dream Free* had arrived and was safely secured at a berth in the marina. Moving his binoculars in the direction of the yacht club's entrance, he saw two guards patrolling on duty. As Mohammed drove slowly towards the club entrance, he offered a silent prayer to Allah to let them pass through the gate that led to the marina without incident.

CHAPTER 43

DUBAI

January 28, 2007

Awakening to the sounds of heavy rain the next morning, Roger and Gregory decided to have breakfast in Roger's room and discuss the day's agenda. Over delicious café au lait and an assortment of sweet rolls accompanied by star-shaped pats of butter and miniature jars of fruit preserves (all delectably laid out on a white linen tablecloth), they tried to assess their progress in an ever-changing, desperate situation.

The facts they possessed were few and the clues random.

Twenty-four days ago, a high-ranking Pakistani nuclear scientist stole two suitcase-bombs from the nuclear facility deep in the heart of Pakistan. He then disappeared.

A conversation with his girlfriend in Vienna revealed that sometime within this period he had gone to Dubai and may have had an accomplice.

Thus far, all efforts by the CIA and the ISI had failed to locate either the weapons or the men.

The incredible audacity of the theft and its incalculable danger bore all the earmarks of a large terrorist organization intent on planning a devastating attack somewhere in Western Europe or the United States. Such an attack would result in the deaths and mutilation of hundreds and thousands of people, in addition to destroying the economy of the free world. Despite lack of evidence, it was assumed that the only organization capable of planning such an attack was Al Qaeda.

Was it Al Qaeda?

Roger sighed.

Armed with nothing but a photograph and a composite sketch, he and Gregory had come halfway around the world to track down two madmen intent upon destroying Western civilization with weapons of mass destruction.

It seemed an impossible task.

He finished his coffee. "I've scheduled a meeting with Robinson at the embassy for early afternoon," he said bending over his cellphone. "Let's call Hasim in Islamabad."

"Hello, Mr. Dunleavy. How are you today?" Colonel Hasim's suave voice resounded over the speakerphone. "I hope all is well with you and your colleague. Is he with you?"

"He's with me and we're both fine-"

"Glad to hear your voice again," said Gregory, speaking up.

"That's splendid," Hasim said cheerily. "What can I do for you today?"

"A few questions, "Roger cleared his throat. "Any news about the theft?"

"Nothing yet. But we've continued rounding up terrorist suspects. We hauled in another 80 for interrogation since we last spoke."

"Any leads?"

"Not yet, gentlemen, but we remain hopeful. Our interrogation methods usually produce results," the Colonel said imperturbably.

Roger grimaced. "And no helpful information came out of the initial roundup interrogations?"

"Not really. The initial suspects rounded up from our known terrorist sources said they knew nothing about any big attack or anything related to it. Actually..." the Colonel paused, "I'm a little surprised that we have learned so little."

Roger nodded. "I see."

"But our interrogations have not been wasted," the Colonel insisted, with some pride. "As I told you when you were here, I think the absence of information suggests that the weapons are not in our country. Otherwise, I think someone would have heard a rumor, an overheard phrase from a local source."

"You may be right, Colonel," said Gregory speaking loudly across the room. "We think so too. However, we also know that Al Qaeda operatives compartmentalize their sharing of information so that only the actual participants in an attack know what role they're playing and nothing more. It may be that information is scarce because Al Qaeda is behind the theft."

"I see where you are going," replied the Colonel. "We also have a feeling they could be involved, but we have no hard evidence. Only a rumor about a big attack heard by a senior Al Qaeda operative captured in that military raid you witnessed." He paused. "Any new developments on your front?"

"Yes. We found Mamood's girlfriend in Vienna and now have a composite sketch of a possible co-conspirator," said Roger, pleased to impart something positive.

"Excellent," the Colonel exclaimed. "Please send me the drawing as soon as possible. I'll arrange to have it distributed throughout our ISI network."

"You'll have it within 15 minutes," said Gregory.

"...And we are now in Dubai," Roger went on, "because we found out that Mamood traveled here on his way to Vienna for one of the IAEA meetings." He rose to pour himself some coffee. "But we still don't know why he came here or what he did with whom."

"Sounds like you're in the dark too, gentlemen," said the Colonel. "We alerted our ISI staff at all our embassies, including the one in Dubai. They're all out looking for him. But nothing has emerged, despite our close contacts with our Muslim brother countries. Incidentally, should you want to meet with my representative at the embassy, I can easily arrange that."

"Please do. Let him know we're here and might call," Roger answered. "Many thanks." He felt a surge of appreciation for the Colonel who was trying hard to be cooperative.

"Not at all," the Colonel replied formally.

"Goodbye, Colonel. We'll stay in touch."

"Goodbye, gentlemen. Thank you for the update."

Closing his cellphone, Roger looked over at Gregory, who was standing by the open window staring at the marvelous Gulf. The rain had stopped and a breeze blew in from the sea. Gregory straightened his blue blazer and hiked up his tan trousers.

"I felt a lot of bluster from our Pakistani contact," he said, turning to face Roger.

"But nothing helpful," commented Roger, putting on a light blue jacket that fitted smartly over his wiry frame.

They left the room together.

Although they arrived early for their meeting at the embassy, Robinson's secretary immediately led them to a conference room on the second floor. It was a large, wood-paneled room typically used for important conferences. Making it available suggested that Robinson attached a great deal of importance to the mission. Against the back wall there was a buffet laden with sandwiches, bottles of cold drinks, three large urns (for coffee, decaffeinated coffee and hot water), and an assortment of cookies and Danish.

Roger and Gregory barely had enough time to examine all the goodies before Robinson bounded in, all smiles. He was in shirtsleeves, his tie awry, altogether much more casually dressed than the day before.

"Hey there, buddy," he said slapping both Roger and Gregory on the shoulder. "How's it going?"

They all moved towards the buffet.

"It's going," replied Roger wearily. "Still nothing to report." He bent to examine the plate of sandwiches. "What's this? Chicken or tuna?"

"Tuna, I think. Your sources?"

"Our two contacts are on the lookout. We've got a meeting with Yousef bin Adin later today, and we're meeting with the other one tomorrow afternoon," said Roger sitting down at the conference table.

"Anything more?" Robinson asked, pulling out a chair opposite his two friends.

"Yes," said Roger. He paused chewing his sandwich. For some reason he was ravenous. "We checked further with U.S. Customs. They didn't inspect any freighters from Pakistan that docked here after January 10th-with two exceptions-and, in those cases, they found no arms on board. The Chief of Customs said they swept the two freighters thoroughly; scans came up negative both times." He went to the bar, picked up a bottle of Evian and sat back down. "Did your staff turn up anything?"

Robinson shook his head. "Nothing yet. But we're looking closely at the hotels, especially four and five-star hotels that we recommended to many locals over the years. I have a feeling we may get lucky - but I may be overoptimistic."

"Optimism can't hurt," said Gregory. "When we had tough assignments in the past, it often saved the day."

"...In a few days we'll have a clearer picture," said Robinson, biting into a ham and cheese sandwich. "By then, it'll be four days of intensive effort."

"Yeah," Roger said glumly, looking over at his friend. "You do realize, don't you, that this has been going on for almost three weeks and we still haven't been able to track him down."

"It's over three weeks since he stole the bombs," Gregory pointed out. "But we've been on this case for 18 days."

"Okay, but by now we should be further along than we are," Roger added.

"But if it's Al Qaeda," Robinson remarked.

"I don't care! I don't give a shit if it's Al Qaeda!" Roger cried, banging his fist on the table. "Eighteen fucking days and we don't have anything! Not one fucking piece of concrete evidence! Just the trace of a lead from a Viennese stripper! What if the world blows up? What are we doing *sitting here*?"

"Now, Roger" Robinson remonstrated.

"All these meetings in cafes," Roger railed. "All these lunches and dinners and boozy nights in strip joints just hanging out, waiting for a lead!" He shook his head. "Those bastards are so fucking smart! It's insane!"

"It's frustrating, I know," said Robinson, reaching over to pat Roger's arm.

"Frustrating?" echoed Roger. "It's unbelievable!"

"But there's nothing else we can do," said Gregory.

"No. Nothing." Roger stood up abruptly. "We've got to go. We have a meeting with Yousef in a café on the beach road. Can't be late. So long, Brad. Let's get together in two days, okay?"

"Sure," said Robinson, leading them to the door. "Call if you need anything. Let me know if anything breaks," he shouted after them.

No sooner had they arrived at the Rendezvous Café than Gregory spotted Yousef approaching them. Just like the day before, he sat down, grandly hailed a waiter and ordered a copious meal - complete with an espresso - before turning to smile at his friends. Roger wondered whether despite all the trappings - the chauffeured Mercedes S-550, the sumptuous dress and headgear - he had enough money for food. Or perhaps this was a form of politeness, ritual being what it was in the Middle East: I-trust-you-so-I'll-eat-your-food-and-drink-at-your-table. That sort of thing. Whatever. He leaned forward attentively.

"Nothing yet," Yousef was saying to Gregory. "If the scientist stayed here only for a day or two in October, he may be difficult to track. Even more so if he kept to himself."

"Are there other people you can contact? Any places that might prove potentially useful?" asked Roger.

"For sure," said Yousef confidently, waving a braceleted hand. "Since many of my clients from abroad come here regularly, I've become a fixture at the best hotel bars and restaurants. The hotel staff and concierges all know and recognize me."

"Very good," said Gregory, putting his hand inside his blazer and removing a manila envelope. "Now look here. There is a photo of the scientist and this is a composite sketch of the man who may be his accomplice. Perhaps one of your contacts might recognize them?"

Yousef glanced at the pictures. "It's possible," he said, noncommittally.

"Why don't you take them with you," Gregory suggested, pushing the prints forward. "So that you can pass them on."

"Thank you," Yousef said, as he swept them up quickly. "You must be patient, my friends. As you know, events move more slowly in this part of the world than in yours."

"We realize that," said Roger. "And you know I'm a patient man. But time is of the essence."

Yousef smiled, then turned slightly and waved discreetly.

"He's signaling his chauffeur," thought Roger, with amusement.

Sure enough, three minutes later the Mercedes appeared. As the chauffer stepped out to open the door ceremoniously, Yousef quickly embraced Roger and Gregory and swept away.

The two men smiled as the car sped off.

"I better call Ibrahim and set a date for tomorrow," said Roger.

They returned to the hotel feeling disappointed yet hopeful that something positive might turn up sometime soon. Before retiring, they called Nigel to give him an update.

"Another night out on the town?" cried Nigel in mock reproach.

"The devil finds mischief for idle hands to do," retorted Gregory.

"How are you two playboys making out?"

"We've been busy," Gregory said soberly. "But we haven't been able to develop further leads."

"What about the embassy?"

"Nothing."

"Contacts? Anything useful?"

"No," replied Roger. "We met with one today. He's still working on his contacts but so far hasn't come up with anything."

"It's still too early to know, Roger, what those contacts of yours might turn up," said Nigel soothingly. "Let's keep the stew cooking. Perhaps we'll find some useful information on our own."

"Perhaps," Roger echoed wistfully.

"One last thing," Gregory interrupted. "We spoke to Colonel Hasim in Islamabad earlier today. He said he had no positive developments and still thinks the weapons have left the country. None of the 200 suspects they interrogated revealed any knowledge of the theft or hint of an attack, except for the big attack rumor disclosed by a senior Al Qaeda operative captured at the Afghan-Pakistani border."

"Well, it's clear to me that you boys are the only ones to have developed substantial evidence in the case thus far," said Nigel. "By the way, the Shanghai port authority informed our embassy in Beijing that they inspected a freighter from Pakistan during the third week of January. There were no weapons of any kind on board."

"Gregory and I will continue to pursue our investigation here," Roger stated, by way of answer.

"Absolutely. By all means."

"Oh yes. One more thing," added Roger. "Please give us a report on the inspection of the *SS Barooqi* which is scheduled to dock in Jacksonville tomorrow."

"Anne will contact you about that."

CHAPTER 44

KINGSTON, JAMAICA

January 28, 2007

The *Dream Free* arrived at the Duke's Yacht Club marina at about 2:00 p.m. on Sunday afternoon, completing its last leg from Georgetown in the Grand Cayman Islands. The 38 meter long yacht, was creamy-white with blue trim and was extremely well-appointed. It had four bedrooms on its lower level, two with twin beds, one with a queen bed and the master bedroom, which had a king-sized bed. Each room was furnished in teak with light beige wall-to-wall carpeting. On the main deck, there was a separate dining and seating/entertainment area featuring an octagonal mahogany dining table as its centerpiece. The captain's bridge was in the front of the main deck. The ship was equipped with state-of-the-art sonar and radar equipment and a Scout runaround craft that could hold up to eight people and go at a speed of up to 35 miles per hour. The craft itself had a maximum speed of 22 knots.

All World Trading Ltd. had only purchased the yacht four days previously. Mohammed had contacted High & Co., a well-known yacht broker in Georgetown by telephone and chatted with its owner, a crusty 55 year old Australian who had spent years in the Caribbean on sailboats and motorized yachts that catered to an international wealthy clientele. Ernest Dibbs had established his reputation servicing clients from Spain, France, Saudi Arabia, England, the United States, Egypt and Germany; charter fees that ran from U.S. $40,000-$70,000 per week were paid without a murmur. His experience had earned him intimate knowledge of each ship's workings, as well as a far-flung network of nautical suppliers, crews and vessels.

Mohammed told Dibbs that his corporation was engaged in substantially expanding its business in the Caribbean and in South America and wanted to increase its marketing efforts in the area. The Egyptian added that he could attract lots of additional business by giving some of the firm's key clients and potential customers an all-expense paid free cruise at the corporation's expense. He gave Dibbs specific details about the yacht he sought, such as the desired number of bedrooms, and the need for an entertainment and dining area. He also added that he was prepared to pay up to U.S. $5,000,000 for the yacht and that he needed one very soon.

Within a day, Dibbs scanned his listing of available yachts and contacted several crews. Then he sent Mohammed the photographs and specifications of five yachts that ranged in price from U.S. $3,500,000 to U.S. $5,000,000 via email. Mohammed promptly reviewed details of the *Scott Free*, the *Yalla*, the *Que Sera*, the *Morgan* and the *Dream Free*. After making several calls to Egypt, he telephoned Dibbs a day later and told him that he was prepared to buy the *Dream Free* and would fly to Georgetown the next morning to examine the ship. If the yacht met his specifications, he would sign the necessary purchase documents. Dibbs was delighted with the news – – a fast sale which came out of the blue.

On January 24, 2007, Mohammed flew to Georgetown from Kingston on a two-engine chartered plane and met Dibbs at his office across from the Hyatt Hotel on Seven Mile Beach, so called because of the long stretch of white sandy beaches lined with luxurious hotels. Several cruise ships, which had arrived at the island the previous night, were docked at the nearby cruise terminal. After a quick lunch at the Alligator, an indoor/outdoor cafe near the office, the two drove to the marina to inspect the *Dream Free*. It was a beautiful, sunny, cloudless day and the whiteness of the yacht contrasted brilliantly against the azure sky. As Dibbs took Mohammed around the ship, showing him the various rooms and other well-appointed areas, he outlined the vessel's history. Built in 2002, the yacht was in excellent condition; its Johnson engines roared to life and then hummed efficiently. Dibbs showed Mohammed the maintenance log kept on board and Mohammed was impressed. He had never been on a ship like the *Dream Free* although he had had fantasies of sailing on one as a kid.

While the two reclined on lounge chairs on the outer deck, Dibbs informed Mohammed that the vessel was in first-class condition and was a steal at the lowered asking price of U.S. $4,750,000. Mohammed gave him a bid price of $4,250,000. Chewing on his cigar, Dibbs went aft and placed a call to the ship's owner. After a 10-minute conversation, he returned and told Mohammed that the owner was willing to lower his price to U.S. $4,500,000, if Mohammed signed the purchase papers that day and wired the funds within 48 hours. Mohammed rose up, climbed to the upper deck, looked out over the calm waters and then returned to his lounge chair. He was pleased about bargaining him down a quarter of a million, a fact he hoped his Egyptian mentor would remember. He told Dibbs they had a deal. With that, Dibbs slapped Mohammed on the back, gave him a Cuban Monte Christo and led him off the ship.

After they returned to the office, Dibbs promptly pulled out a purchase agreement form and had his secretary type in the appropriate terms, including his firm's wiring instructions at Barclay's Bank in the Caymans. Mohammed signed three copies of the agreement, gave two to Dibbs and kept one for All Trading.

Dibbs then walked over to the window and looked out over the serene scene as he quietly puffed on his cigar. It was clear he was running through a mental list of additional topics to discuss with his wealthy buyer. After a moment, he smiled and quietly turned to Mohammed. Did he intend to take possession of the yacht here or in Kingston? Mohammed paused and then said he wanted the boat delivered to Kingston. When Dibbs that he could supply a crew of three to take the *Dream Free* to Jamaica, Mohammed replied that would be fine, but that he planned to hire his own crew once the vessel docked in Kingston. In that event, the buyer would agree to fly Dibbs' crew back from Kingston, added Mohammed with an easy smile. Dibbs nodded his approval saying he would add the costs of the crew to the tab.

Dibbs then poured them both a shot of good malt whiskey that he kept on hand for such occasions. They clinked glasses and downed the shot, smiling broadly. After Mohammed thanked Dibbs for his efficient work, Dibbs offered to drive the Egyptian to his waiting plane at the Grand Caymans Airport. At the airport entrance, they shook hands and by 6:00 p.m. Mohammed was airborne, bound for home in Kingston.

Back at the office, Dibbs immediately asked several of his yachting mates if they knew of an available crew for a several day jaunt. Within an hour, he had his answer: Captain Scott Hendricks and two Irish seamen were eager for the job.

At about 9:00 a.m. two days later, after the wired funds arrived, the *Dream Free* raised anchor and left Georgetown with Captain Hendricks at the helm. A bright clear sun glistened over the calm blue waters. Fluffy white cumulus clouds floated by slowly as the vessel departed. Light swells could be seen undulating far into the distance ahead of the craft. It was a perfect day for a sea voyage. The Captain estimated that the trip would take a bit more than a day a speed of about 18 knots. The weather forecast sun for the next three days; no rainfall was expected.

The journey passed by calmly. En route, the *Dream Free* passed many yachts owned or rented by the wealthy, a Royal Caribbean cruise ship, and a number of motley fishing trawlers and freighters. Without lights from the coast nearby, the night sky was brilliant with stars and constellations, literally a planetary feast. When dawn broke the next day, the craft was only six hours away from Kingston.

At about 2:00 p.m., the *Dream Free* neared its designated berth. The marina at Duke's Yacht Club, had berths for close to 200 ships, including at least 25 berths for yachts 25 meters or longer in length. The marina had three parallel U-shaped piers that extended about 100 feet into the sea. The *Dream Free*'s berth was closest to the shoreline at the west end of the pier. The Captain's two crewmen tied the craft to the posts on the wooden pier of the marina and threw rubber bumpers alongside the vessel to prevent any damage to it from its rocking against the pier. While they waited for the arrival of the new crew, the Captain's mates scrubbed the decks, the sides and rear of the vessel. They then added lubricating oil to the powerful engines and came on shore to fill five large gasoline drums. Besides being recognized as an experienced first-rate skipper, Captain Hendricks was fastidious about keeping a clean and properly maintained craft; in fact, he privately was known as "Captain Clean."

Having finished their tasks, they enjoyed some leisure, sitting on the rear deck lounge chairs in the sun. Their white outfits still looked pristine, if a bit sweaty. Shortly after 4:00 p.m., two smartly dressed seamen, each attired in white with black deck shoes, arrived dockside. One seaman wore a captain's stripe, and the other the insignia of a first mate. Both were neatly shaved, had brown hair, olive complexions and were about 5'10" in height. The captain spoke better English than his first mate, although Captain Hendricks could not identify their accents.

The new captain introduced himself and his first mate to Captain Hendricks with a smile:

"Good afternoon, Captain. I'm Ronald Dwayne and this is my first mate, Peter Long. We're here to relieve you."

"Nice to meet you both," said Hendricks warmly. "Giving us a break, are you?"

"Yes, sir," Dwayne replied. "You guys can now take your cushy flight back home to the Caymans. Not a bad life, if I say so myself."

"I agree," Hendricks nodded. "Alright, then, we'll leave this sweet baby with you." He got up. "She's a beauty and runs like a dream, just like her name. We got her all gassed and gussied up for you."

"That's great," said Dwayne. "We really appreciate that. We would have done the same for you if the roles were reversed."

Captain Hendricks and his crew of two left the craft, walked up to the marina's entrance and jumped into a yellow cab idling there. Checking his watch, the Captain saw they had two and a half hours to make their 7:30 p.m. flight bound to Georgetown.

After Hendricks left, the new crew proceeded to inspect the ship from top to bottom. The captain checked the bridge and was pleased to see that the craft had the most advanced radar and sonar equipment as well as excellent radio and computer capabilities. He was pleased that the Scout runaround was in good working condition. He and his mate sat down on a long, brown leather banquette in the entertainment section of the main deck. The captain stretched out for a minute and laughed loudly:

"Awad, you really do look great in that first mate's outfit."

"I must say, Commander, that you could absolutely pass for a captain. But, I think you have more experience with other types of craft than this luxury yacht."

"What you just said is absolutely true, my brother. I have never set foot on a yacht like this. To me, it's just another sign of Western decadence and moral corruption. A mere toy for the wealthy to sun and sin with their girlfriends at the same time."

The Commander straightened up and looked at Awad sternly:

"I think we should relax a little now. We must be very alert for tonight's activities."

CHAPTER 45

JACKSONVILLE, FLORIDA

January 29, 2007

U.S. Coast Guard vessels based in and around Jacksonville, Florida had been on high alert for more than two weeks, ever since the order came down from the Coast Guard Commandant. Jacksonville was one of the largest ports in the U.S. Owing to the important role played by ports in the nation's commerce, maritime security had steadily increased after September 11, 2001, helped in part by the passage of the Maritime Transportation Security Act of 2002. Several additional Coast Guard vessels, with increased armament, now regularly patrolled the area.

This day was slated to be different. The Coast Guard unit in charge of securing the port of Jacksonville had received specific instructions from the Coast Guard Commandant's office in Washington D.C. to board a freighter, the *SS Barooqi*, a freighter from Karachi flying the Panamanian flag and thoroughly inspect its potentially high-risk cargo. Two vessels, the *USCG 817* and the *USCG 620*, each about 35 feet in length, armed with deck machine guns, were to board the vessel beyond the six-mile limit. A helicopter under Coast Guard control, carrying several heavily armed sailors, would assist in the operation by providing additional back-up firepower in support of the interception.

From information received by the local Coast Guard unit, the vessel was scheduled to dock in Jacksonville at about 5:00 p.m. that evening. The captains in command of the intercepting vessels announced that boarding operation would commence that afternoon about 4:30 p.m.

Both Coast Guard vessels left their base early that morning and, by mid-afternoon, were patrolling a mile and a half offshore. On this brilliant, almost cloudless day, visibility was excellent at that hour; the crews could see easily at least five miles into the distance. Surveying the horizon with his binoculars, Captain Tim Johnson, the skipper of the *USCG 817*, a tall veteran with more than 17 years of experience, ordered the vessel to begin heading east-southeast, toward the rendezvous point at a speed of 15 knots. At the same time, the captain of the *USCG 620*, Captain Ray Bulge, a young lanky officer who had been with the Coast Guard for only 12 years, steered his vessel in the same direction, but stayed about half mile behind it. The tension on board each vessel was palpable. While the crew of each vessel had received training on how to board at sea, they never had actually boarded a ship at sea. Moreover, each Captain knew the importance of securing the dangerous cargo they anticipated might be onboard. Preparing for a firefight with a hostile crew, they arranged for a helicopter to be present throughout the operation.

Several miles to the east, the *SS Barooqi*, approached, heading toward Jacksonville. The Coast Guard vessels began to close the distance between them and the freighter – five miles, three miles, one mile. A helicopter hovered over the *USCG 817* as it steered southeast. When the freighter was about 500 yards from the *USCG 817*, Captain Johnson's first mate, Jim Hamlet, signaled the vessel to stop, announcing it would be boarded. The captain of the *SS Barooqi*, a German from Lubeck named Rolf Schmidt, was far from surprised by such maneuvers. About a year ago, he had captained a Liberian-registered freighter that sailed from Manila and had been boarded outside the Port of Los Angeles.

When the *USCG 817* approached within 600 feet of the freighter, its crew lowered a Skidoo containing a boarding party of four men, including the first mate. The light chop, three to four foot waves, undulated evenly into the distance. The helicopter hovered over the freighter. Within five minutes, the Coast Guard party boarded the vessel, moving easily up the rope ladder lowered by the freighter's crew. Two officers in the boarding party carried submachine guns, while the other two were armed with pistols. They were joined by a similarly-armed four-man boarding party from the *USCG 620*, which had closed to about 200 yards from the freighter's starboard side.

Once on the freighter, the first mate informed Captain Schmidt that the vessel had been boarded for security reasons and instructed him to help facilitate the inspection of his vessel's cargo. To the delight of the Coast Guard crew, Captain Schmidt and his men were very cooperative and not at all hostile, a good sign for the inspection teams. Equipped with four mobile scanners, including several small gamma ray machines, the Coast Guard personnel inspected each container on board one by one. Each container was scanned closely; 20 containers were also opened and inspected visually. As the inspection proceeded, an officer checked off each container inspected against the cargo manifest. But despite hours of searching and inspecting over 200 containers, the Coast Guard inspection team found no weapons of any kind. The freighter was now free to proceed to Jacksonville directly.

The first mate reported this finding to Captain Johnson of the *USCG 817*, while the senior member of the boarding party from the *USCG 620* gave the same negative finding to Captain Bulge. Captain Johnson, in turn, related their joint inspection report to the local Coast Guard commander stationed at the port, who had been waiting anxiously for the search results.

Half an hour later, the report was in hands of the Coast Guard Commandant's office in Washington D.C., and disseminated to the interested agencies within the Department of Homeland Security. Copies went directly to the Director of National Intelligence and the Director of the CIA.

While the boarding of the *SS Barooqi* was the most recent in a series made by the Coast Guard, none of the boardings or inspections made on any freighters that sailed from Karachi uncovered the two atomic weapons. Their location remained a mystery more than three weeks after the theft occurred.

CHAPTER 46

DUBAI/JAMAICA

January 30, 2007

Roger awoke early and for a second did not know where he was. It was rare for him to be so disoriented, but he had slept badly. Through a slit in the drapes, he could see that the day was bright. Sunlight poured on the carpet as he pushed them aside, pausing to gaze at the glistening blue gulf below. He had encountered many difficult assignments before, but none had such high stakes. Day two in Dubai. Over two and a half weeks had gone by without a significant break in the case. Years of experience had reinforced his faith in the agency and the men he worked with. Was his optimism misplaced? Was he placing too much faith in his contacts? What information would Ibrahim provide this evening?

He telephoned Gregory and asked him to join him. They discussed the day's agenda over breakfast. Ever the organizer, Roger suggested they first contact Ramsey at Customs, then meet with Robinson at the embassy, follow that up with a meeting at the Pakistan Embassy, and finally meet with Ibrahim in the evening. There was always a last resort: cruising the less prosperous Dubai neighborhoods in the off-chance they might find one or both of the suspects sitting at a restaurant or café. Debating the merits of their drive-by approach, they decided to put the idea on hold, pending the outcome of their scheduled meetings.

Ramsey was waiting for them when they arrived.

"How are things going, gentlemen?" He inquired.

"Did you decide to pursue that 'irregularity' angle with the consignees?" asked Roger by way of answer.

"Yes, we did. Our office knows five of the consignees fairly well, since they regularly import and export goods out of this port," Ramsey replied. "Three have been in business for over eight years; the other two, over five years. We never had any customs issue with them before."

"Did they cooperate with you fully?" Roger prodded.

"Yes, they did. They brought in several boxes of the cotton goods they imported from Pakistan to show that the goods in question matched the bill of lading. They even permitted several of the Customs personnel to inspect their boxes of goods at the warehouses they use."

"And what came of the inspection?" asked Gregory, who was anxious to move the conversation along.

"Everything seemed in order. The goods in the warehouse all matched the bills of lading for the cargoes shipped to the customers and offloaded by the *SS Barooqi*."

"Of course, that inspection does not preclude the possibility that the stolen weapons came in with these cargoes," Roger remarked impatiently.

"That's true," said Ramsey. "We realize the limitations of an inspection once a container has left the port area."

"What's your next step?" Roger asked.

"In the case of the five other consignees, we'll try to inspect the goods imported, hoping that the boxes in which they were shipped have not yet been opened," replied Ramsey. "Maybe something will turn up."

"Keep us posted," said Gregory, as he and Roger departed, thanking Ramsey for his additional help. "We'll contact you soon." Privately, they both suspected that the Customs inquiries would lead to a dead end.

They were also skeptical about the news from the U.S. Embassy. Instinctively they sensed that their personnel were not deeply embedded in the radical Islamic community and, therefore, out of their depth in uncovering the whereabouts of the suspects or their activities in Dubai.

Ushered into the now familiar conference room, they traded stories about their old CIA experiences, which ranged over four continents and three wars. Some were somber, others light. While eating, they listened to Robinson's updated report:

"My personnel on the case chatted with some of their Egyptian and Jordanian contacts, but unearthed nothing helpful," Robinson said pouring himself another cup of coffee.

"They even checked with their friends at the administrative offices of several of the major air carriers, such as Emirates Air and Qatar Airways, as well as with several boat and yacht brokers. But no success."

"What do you plan to do now?" asked Roger, fidgeting with his fork, trying to conceal his impatience.

"We'll continue contacting other friendly sources here hoping to develop a lead," Robinson replied confidently.

"Without any threads to pull, it'll be tough," continued Roger.

Robinson sighed. "Maybe we'll get a break."

"I hope so," interjected Gregory wearily. "Too much time has already passed."

They said goodbye to Robinson, warmly praising him for his efforts.

Outside the embassy walls, Roger checked his watch and saw it was 3:00 p.m., half an hour before their scheduled meeting at the Pakistani Embassy. They decided to keep a low profile and arrive in a taxi, rather than their own car, which they left inside the embassy's garage. As they stood on the corner hailing a taxi, Roger's cell phone rang:

"This is Anne. How are you guys doing?"

"We're fine, Anne. How're you?" asked Roger delighted to hear her voice.

"I'm great. I'm at the London office coordinating our efforts with Nigel." She paused and cleared her throat.

"My colleague from Langley, Bud, called me about an hour ago. He told me the Coast Guard boarded the *SS Barooqi* outside of Jacksonville, inspected her cargo thoroughly with scans and found no weapons of any kind on board."

"That may be the end of our working assumption that the weapons were moved by sea," replied Roger angrily. "Unless of course, the goods were offloaded somewhere," he added.

"That's a possibility we may have to pursue," Anne said briskly. "I'll check with U.S. Customs in Kingston today and let you know."

"Please keep us posted." Roger felt he was clutching at straws.

"I'll call you guys later," Anne replied. "Bye for now."

"Goodbye, Anne."

He turned to Gregory.

"As you heard, our working theory may not have legs," he said sadly. "Anne will get back to us later about what happened in Jamaica."

Their taxi came to a screeching halt near the gate of the Pakistani Embassy. They looked up at the Pakistani flag, prominently displayed, fluttering at the top of the two-storey structure. The embassy was protected by a steel entry gate, guarded by several heavily-armed sentries. Roger sensed that other reserve sentries were on immediate call in case of an emergency. After announcing their arrival, the receptionist took them to a conference room to the right rear of the building, a section reserved for the ISI staff. Curtains drawn over the one window in the room provided a sense of privacy.

"I'm Lt. Col. Mohammed Masur," said a short, stocky officer, extending a hand. He had penetrating brown eyes.

"Captain Abdul Aziz," said the tall wiry officer leaning forward to shake hands almost clicking his heels. Roger and Gregory introduced themselves.

"Tea?" Asked Masur, pressing a button on the intercom. Without waiting for an answer, he said something in Arabic.

Both men nodded watching him.

"Please," Masur waved a hand in the direction of the conference table, "do sit down."

Roger and Gregory obliged, pulling out chairs side by side at the middle of the table.

"It's a pleasure," said Masur walking over to the other side of the table followed by a silent Aziz. Sitting down, he eyed his guests with curiosity.

He knew his branch had a deep relationship with the CIA that started in the late 1980s when they armed and trained the mujahideen to fight the Russians in Afghanistan. After the Russian rout, cooperation had continued. But he, personally, had never had direct contact with the agency's personnel. Although not quite sure about what to expect, they seemed like normal Western businessmen in the region. Each was dressed in a blue blazer and tan slacks, and their bright-colored linen shirts opened casually at the collar. At the same time, he knew that he facing seasoned veterans, men who also were physically fit. Nonetheless, Masur considered himself their equal, having advanced through the ranks over 25 years to arrive at his newly-coveted position, in an embassy and in a country that was rapidly becoming the mecca of the Middle East in addition to a key listening post for events in the region.

After an exchange of polite introductions and niceties, the host smiled warmly at his guests and said:

"It is pleasure to see you both here. Colonel Hasim told me to expect to see you and to extend to you all of our courtesies, of which, I must say, we have many."

"We appreciate your kind words and your gracious invitation. We want to thank Colonel Hasim for arranging our get together," replied Roger politely, as he tried to gauge the sincerity of his hosts.

At that moment, the secretary appeared with a tray of mint tea and almond cookies.

"As the Colonel told you," said Masur politely pushing the plate of cookies across the table, "it is highly unfortunate that this theft occurred. Such a treasonous act by one of our own! We are doing all we can at home and abroad to find the scientist and recover the weapons."

"What success, if any, have you had in Dubai as far as locating him or his alleged accomplice?" asked Roger softly.

"The Colonel forwarded a copy of the drawings of the accomplice to each of our units at our embassies. We have been trying to track both of them down," replied Masur, shifting to a more erect position in his chair. "Here in Dubai we've sent over 20 of our own personnel to search for them. We have gone into almost 100 cafes, 55 restaurants, many of the hotels and their bars, checked the casinos and even visited many mosques. So far there have been no sightings of either of them."

"I'm curious as to how your men check out a mosque," Roger said with interest.

"Our men go inside to pray and blend in with the other Muslims at prayer. One or two of them might kneel in the back row to keep an eye on those entering and leaving. Another agent might kneel on one side of the mosque and also observe the worshippers from that angle."

"Do you think they're still in this country?" asked Roger somewhat skeptically.

"We're not sure," replied the Pakistani calmly gazing directly at Roger. "We think there may be better places than Dubai to hide, such as in bigger cities in the more populous countries of the Middle East. But, on the other hand, they might not trust the police in those places. They may not want to tangle with, say, the Egyptian police who are known to attack the Islamic fundamentalists brutally when they can. This is as honest an answer as I can give you."

"Are you saying, then, you think they could be in Dubai?" asked Roger, trying to understand his host's thinking.

"I said it's possible because they may be able to move more easily here without police interference," replied Masur emphatically. "If I knew for certain that they were here, I would let you know."

"Could these two be keeping out of sight in a safehouse for a period of time?" interjected Gregory.

"Yes, that could very well be the case," replied Masur. "It's not an uncommon practice in our country."

"Did the ISI make any headway in its investigation in Pakistan?" asked Roger continuing to probe.

Colonel Masur walked over to the computer on the desk in the room, checked some of his emails, and nodded.

"There has been no change since yesterday when I received an update from Colonel Hasim," he said turning to Roger and Gregory. "But the ISI is still scouring the country looking for both suspects."

"Do you know if the Colonel still thinks the weapons were taken outside of Pakistan," Roger asked.

"Yes, that's his opinion."

"Is there any more information you can give us?" asked Roger, sensing that their meeting was about to end.

"Not at present," replied Masur. "I'll be glad to help you whenever you call. You have my contact information."

"Yes, we do," said Gregory.

"We appreciate the time you spent with us," Roger said formally. "We'll be in touch. We'll also contact Colonel Hasim to thank him personally and give him our latest report."

The two Pakistanis led Roger and Gregory to the main entrance, shook their hands and watched them leave.

As if by common consent, Roger and Gregory strolled for several blocks before taking a taxi to one of their favorite cafes, the Desert, which was near the beach road. As they sat casually at a table outside sipping Turkish coffee, Roger's cell phone rang.

"Anne, I just can't get rid of you," Roger joked.

"No, you can't."

"What's up in Jamaica?" he asked, as the two men began walking up the street to a more deserted area.

"Hold on, honey," The place was too public and he didn't want their conversation overheard.

He put the speakerphone on.

"O.K. I'm back."

"As I was about to tell you, the Customs official I spoke with said the *SS Barooqi* unloaded 15 containers in Kingston. They were not inspected since cotton goods and spices are not considered a security risk by Washington."

Anne waited for Roger's reply, but heard none.

"Roger, what is it?" she asked. "It's rare for you hold your tongue."

"I'm thinking, Anne. Give me a moment."

"Okay."

"Let me test a hypothesis on both of you," Roger said, looking suddenly very serious. "Let's say you knew about our new tough inspection rules on goods being imported into the States that are deemed high risk. What would you do? Would you take the risk of bringing them into the States on a freighter?"

"Probably not," said Gregory.

"I agree," said Anne.

"What would you do? Would you perhaps decide to offload the high-risk goods en route?"

"Maybe," said Gregory and Anne in unison.

"If you decided to offload them, where would you do it?" Roger pressed forward.

"That depends on the target," said Anne quickly. "If it was Western Europe, you might choose some spot in Africa or the Middle East, such as Alexandria or Dubai."

"But if the target was the States, you'd pick a spot closer to it, say, in the Caribbean or South America," interjected Gregory increasingly excited.

"Exactly," said Roger, feeling almost vindicated. "If you were going to attack the States, you certainly would want to get closer to your target." He paused.

"Okay. Let's think together," he went on. "How could you carry these weapons into the States? Would you try to use a private plane? Or would a boat be preferable?"

Thinking quickly, Anne answered first.

"You could use a private plane to fly near or over the target, or to a remote airport in Florida or some other southern state. However, you'd have to unload your weapons at the airport- which might incur the unacceptable risk of being discovered by security officials, although I believe those boarding a private plane are only subject to whatever security, if any, is provided for private aircraft at the airport. Still, there's a big risk in using a plane for this purpose."

"I agree with your analysis," said Roger animatedly. "So where does that leave us?"

"There's less risk of discovery in loading the weapons onto a small craft or a yacht," exclaimed Gregory. "You can then go by sea to your destination in the States. Your primary risk, initially, will be getting past the Coast Guard before going into port. If the target was inland, a terrorist would have to run all the risks associated with carrying any weapon by car or truck, or even by train, once he got them into the States."

"And what," said Roger, hardly waiting for Gregory to finish, "if your target were a port along the East Coast? You could go all the way by sea to your target."

"Exactly," said Anne.

"Yep. That's right," added Gregory.

"And if, under the scenario we just analyzed, the terrorists were pirates," Roger went on, "they would probably feel most comfortable approaching the States by sea."

"I see where you're going," exclaimed Anne.

"I think the terrorists may have offloaded the weapons in Jamaica," said Roger emphatically slapping Gregory on the shoulder. "Again, it's only a guess, but it would be a smart way to proceed if they wanted to attack the States."

"I think you may be right," Gregory chimed in.

"It's nothing but a hunch," continued Roger, "but I've relied on them often with good success. I think we ought to travel to Kingston and investigate where the goods went after being imported there. We've put a lot of pieces in play here that can continue to move without our personal presence for the next few days. So far, no one has looked into the Jamaican scene."

"Let me bring in Nigel," said Anne. "Hold on for a moment. I'll find him and get him in on this call."

"Fine," said Roger agreeably.

Two minutes later, Nigel's voice came over the wire.

"Anne briefed me quickly," he said. "I agree that you should go to Kingston from Dubai. As a matter of fact, I even instructed Anne to join you. I'll stay here and hold down the home front."

"Great!" said Roger exuberantly.

"It's a deal!" added Gregory.

"We'll check out the airlines and contact you shortly," said Roger.

"O.K. I'll await your call," Anne said. "Bye for now."

"Bye, Anne."

Within minutes, Roger had the information he needed. They would catch a late night flight to London, lay over for several hours and then board a British Airways non-stop flight to Kingston at noon, which would arrive at about 5:00 p.m. the following afternoon. When Gregory informed Anne, she immediately agreed to join them on the British Air flight to Jamaica.

Excited over their new plan of action, Roger and Gregory returned to the café to await Ibrahim. The Saudi appeared within a half hour, jovial as usual. Ordering a round of Carlsberg, he regaled them with funny stories. No one would have guessed that this happy group consisted of two CIA agents and a local informant. It was only after they ordered dinner that their conversation turned serious.

"I've been working hard for you, my friends," said Ibrahim, his smile fading. "I have had separate meetings with several banking associates of mine, but no one knew of any undertaking by the scientist or his accomplice."

"I assume there are more you can meet with," Roger said quickly.

"I certainly plan to do so," replied the Saudi, adjusting his headdress.

"I also asked a good number of my real estate contacts whether they rented an apartment to the two suspects," he went on. "Again, no one had done so, but they agreed to look into the matter further. I have many other friends in the field and will be in touch with them over the next several days."

"That sounds great," said Roger cheerfully.

"As for the hotels, bars, restaurants and cafes, I've made some preliminary inquiries, with many still to go. Again, nothing came up. If these folks were here, they may have been here only briefly or hardly appeared in public."

"Your latter point is well taken," Roger nodded in agreement. "If these terrorists were on a mission, they probably kept a very low profile when they were here."

"In any event, I'll continue to pursue my contacts, and hopefully, come up with good information for you. Remember, Roger, I owe you a lot."

"We appreciate your help," Roger replied earnestly. "We could never get to the places or people you deal with."

"I thank you for your kind words, my friends," answered Ibrahim almost solemnly.

"We won't be around here for a few days, but let's stay in touch," Roger said. "I'll call you to get an update within several days if that works for you."

"Of course," replied Ibrahim smiling. "In any case, I'll need that time to probe further and hopefully develop a juicy lead for you to follow."

They embraced Ibrahim warmly, before taking separate paths into the night.

Once in their hotel, Roger and Gregory packed quickly and lightly, and took the first available taxi to the Dubai International Airport. Despite light traffic on the route to the airport, they arrived at the boarding gate with only 15 minutes to spare. Once they were airborne, they eased into their seats, smiling at the other over stiff Grey Goose vodka. They knew that they would get very little sleep in the days to come, but they were excited at the prospect of a new site to mine for whatever helpful information they could find.

CHAPTER 47

KINGSTON, JAMAICA

January 28, 2007

Mohammed moved his van up to the entrance of the Duke's Yacht Club at about 9:00 p.m. that Sunday night. He told the burly, six-foot guard they were making a late-night delivery of nautical supplies and bringing several additional crewmembers to one of the yachts, the *Dream Free*, which, he said, was scheduled to depart from the Club shortly before daybreak in the morning. One of the guards looked through the window and saw the ropes, bumpers, cans of gasoline and other supplies. Then he looked at the four men closely, eyeing them up and down, before waving them through. It helped that all four were dressed in typical crew attire: an all-white short-sleeved shirts and white pants. Before proceeding, Mohammed asked the guard for the craft's location. The guard stepped back into his booth to check his computer. When he returned, he said they should follow the road down to the right end of the marina and then proceed to a parking area near the ship.

Once inside the gate, Mohammed dimmed his lights to avoid attracting attention to the van as it bounced along an asphalt road, pitted with potholes. Three minutes later, they were within walking distance of the *Dream Free*. Mohammed cut off the engines, shut out the lights and all four men walked toward the rear of the yacht, where two crewmen watched and waited. Approaching the vessel, Mohammed looked up at them.

"What is the password?" he asked.

"Al Andalus," replied the captain.

"It's you!" Mohammed exclaimed. "Days ago Mahmoud said you would be here and be on time."

"You can tell Mahmoud he was absolutely right," replied Hamad laughing softly.

Awaiting his turn, the Pakistani scientist spoke up:

"Hamad, I recognized you easily after all the time we spent together."

"I assumed that you would, Mamood," replied Hamad, descending the ramp to embrace Mamood, then Mohammed, Ashan and Hassan.

"Okay," he said, stepping back. "Let's go and get the goods on board fast."

Quickly Ashan and Hassan went back to the van and grabbed the nautical supplies. Mamood lifted the water bottles. Mohammed picked up the heavy tool kit and the suitcase carrying the Kalashnikovs and other small weapons. Awad had lowered the rear deck ladder so they could board easily. Then he returned with the cans of gasoline. Hamad showed them where to stow the items and Mohammed put the Kalashnikov-filled suitcase in his stateroom. Awad put the heavy tool kit in the Commander's room as well.

Hamad watched as the four men slowly lifted the first large wooden box out of the back of the van. With each person holding a corner, they carried the load onto the vessel, using two separate ladders. They carried the box down to one of the four bedrooms and left it near the door. They repeated the process with the second box, laying it beside the door of a second bedroom. Within the space of 10 minutes, the transfer was complete. Hamad was extremely pleased with his berth's location, since there were no people on the west side of the pier at that hour.

At Hamad's invitation, everybody sat down on the outside deck to drink mint tea, which Awad expertly brewed.

After a few jokes and a second round of tea, Mohammed slowly rose to leave. Hamad stood up and put his hand on Mohammed's shoulder.

"You've done extremely well, my brother," he said. "Everything we asked you to do was expertly accomplished. I will make sure to tell Mahmoud everything. Praised be God. May Allah go with you, my brother."

They embraced warmly.

"My brother, go with Allah and continue to be guided by him," said Mohammed softly.

He left the yacht, walking slowly back to his empty van and drove off. He felt sad at leaving his comrades but knew he had other important work to do, despite that he had just completed a very exciting mission. Feeling a bit let down after the rush of the evening, he decided to return to his apartment reluctantly and settle in for the rest of the night.

After Mohammed left, Hamad began to speak more openly. It was not a question of a lack of trust, but Mohammed was an unknown quantity: Hamad had never served with him in battle or in the training camps, as he had with his fellow pirates. For this reason, he did not want Mohammed to know how the group came to be assembled or what their mission was. He looked at Mamood:

"My friend," he said, sitting down beside him. "I know you took a different route here than Awad and me. How did you do it?"

"I flew directly from Karachi to Dubai and then caught a late night non-stop flight to Gatwick Airport outside of London," replied Mamood quietly. "There was a five hour layover before I took off at noon on a direct flight to Kingston. I got in at 5:00 p.m. today."

"You must be exhausted."

"I am, Hamad. I could use a good night's sleep. But how did you get here?"

"Awad and I posed as wealthy Pakistani businessmen when we arrived in Dubai from Karachi. No one questioned our passports. We entered the country without incident."

"Okay. Then what happened?"

"We decided to charter a private jet, a long-range Bombardier. I knew it was necessary to come and go on a non-stop basis without attracting attention."

"Did you find one on such short notice?" asked Mamood.

"Yes, fortunately, we did," replied Hamad. "A leasing group our Egyptian financier used regularly had just what we wanted. We rounded up the crew on eight hours' notice and came here non-stop."

Mamood got up and stretched. "And, I assume, you had no problem with Jamaican customs officials?" he asked.

"None at all," replied Hamad. "We breezed right through. They didn't even bother to inspect our carry-on bags."

"I now understand why Mahmoud does business here," Mamood said smiling broadly.

"It's very laid back, or, as the locals say: 'No problem, Mon.'"

"Exactly," replied Hamad laughing loudly.

Then his face took on a serious expression.

"I think we should break up now," he said addressing the group. "Mamood, Awad and I will sleep for a while. I want you, Ashan and Hassan, to stay on deck and guard the boat. In about five hours, at 4:00 a.m., you will wake us and we'll take up the watch so you can rest."

"Of course, Commander," said Hassan, bowing his head slightly in a show of deference to his leader.

The three men went to their rooms and fell asleep immediately, exhausted by their long journey from the Middle East and Pakistan.

While they slept, Ashan and Hassan scoured the main deck to make sure there were no loose objects that could damage any crewmember. Then they checked the ropes to ensure that the vessel was securely fastened to the berth and the bumpers were properly in place. When they finished, they sat down in the rear deck and chatted quietly, each surveying the tranquil scene without speaking, lingering on the vistas, not wishing to let go. Constellations glowed brightly in the night sky. A brilliant pale yellow moon illuminated the water, trailing a sparkling reflection on the gently rolling waves. The palm trees surrounding the marina swayed slowly, rustling in the soft breeze that came in from the southeast. This peaceful beautiful scene was an island paradise, a very different paradise from the one they imagined they would soon enter. They both understood that these were the last moments of gentle repose. At 4:00 a.m., they dutifully woke the others and then retired.

At about 5:45 a.m. the *Dream Free* departed. Dawn had not yet broken. The sea was calm and deserted. Initially, they planned to head about 30 kilometers east of Morant Point, the most eastern point of Jamaica, a distance of about 60 to 70 kilometers, before heading toward the calm waters of the Windward Passage east of Cuba. Once the yacht was about 30 kilometers at sea, Hamad checked the radar and saw that there was no other craft within a 60 kilometer radius. Satisfied they were isolated, he turned to Mamood:

"Why don't you open the suitcase bombs now and demonstrate how to detonate them?" he said. "I'll take over while you show the others."

Ashan, Hassan and Awad followed Mamood down the staircase to the nearest bedroom housing a suitcase bomb. After opening the box and removing the protective lead shield, Mamood knelt on the rug and opened the suitcase to reveal its sinister contents. Ashan, Hassan and Awad watched Mamood closely, aware that they had to memorize every detail. Mamood pointed out the three parallel electrical circuit wires each about eight inches in length, each wrapped in different colored rubber tubing, numbered one through six. Slowly, Mamood inserted the positive end of the number 6 wire into the positive end of the number 1 wire and repeated the same maneuver inserting the positive number 5 wire into the end of positive number 2 wire. He went through the same process with the number 4 and 3 wires.

Following this demonstration, he looked up:

"Now the device is almost fully armed," he said to his rapt students. "Only one more step is needed to detonate it."

Slowly he placed his right index finger on a switch near the right hand corner of the suitcase and let it rest there.

"Now watch closely. First, you have to punch in code numbers, 747, into the controller directly below this switch. Once you do that, the switch will be unlocked. All you have to do then is move the switch to the 'on' position - and then the bomb will explode."

Ashan, Awad and Hassan sat quietly for a few moments as they reflected on what Mamood just showed them. The last few words "and then the bomb will explode" reverberated within them. It meant they would cease to exist here and emerge elsewhere. As they sat, Mamood could clearly see the resigned look on their faces and their distant stares, as if each was almost somewhere else, but not quite yet. He understood that the momentous nature of their prospective action had finally penetrated their inner psyche.

Mamood closed the suitcase and, with the help of the others, placed it back into the wooden box, making sure the protective lead shield was securely in place. Remembering Hamad's instructions, he took this step as a precaution in the event they might be swept for explosives by a roving aircraft or naval vessel.

Then Mamood led the group to the next bedroom and partially armed the second suitcase bomb. The only difference between the two was the final code numbers: in this case, 646. He tested each of them twice. They all remembered the final codes easily.

When Mamood went aft, he found Hamad at the wheel, eyes glued to the horizon. Hamad got up, motioning to Awad to take over and steer the vessel towards Morant Bay. The two men went into the dining area, where, once seated at the table, Mamood pulled out a diagram of the bomb and showed Hamad how he had armed the weapon, except for the final step.

"Each bomb is ready to go, Hamad. Your mates only have to remember the final code, which each of them memorized. I even tested them."

"Good," replied Hamad with a sense of satisfaction. "You have carried out all I have asked of you, my brother, and you have done it well. I'm very pleased."

Mamood looked away for a moment, then turned back to Hamad, whose eyes seemed to be fixed on him:

"I told you what I could do – – and now you see it has all come to pass."

"Yes, it has, Mamood. I feel we are on a journey of biblical dimension, mere servants of a higher power, the Prophet. The last key to this journey still remains to be turned, but at this moment we have accomplished as much as we could."

"I agree, Hamad. The balance now rests in the hands of Allah acting through his servants, Awad, Ashan and Hassan."

As they spoke, the *Dream Free* rounded Morant Point, which was visible directly to the west. The craft was heading in a northwesterly direction moving at a speed of about 20 knots towards Port Antonio, about 70 kilometers away. As they passed Morant Point, they saw a fleet of fishing trawlers, some 15 kilometers from land, searching for their daily or weekly catch. Awad steered far from their nets and continued on course. A flock of sea gulls flew overhead, chattering noisily, hoping for some morsels to eat.

Awad surveyed the horizon ahead of him. There were no large vessels of any kind in sight, except for a freighter about eight kilometers ahead of their present position, which was headed toward Port Antonio. After studying the radar closely, he turned to Hamad:

"It looks safe ahead," he said. "I checked our radar and sonar and saw nothing except for the freighter visible on the horizon and those fishing boats to our south and east."

Hamad looked at the horizon as well and double checked the sonar and radar.

"Let me know when we're about seven kilometers from Point Antonio. At that point, Mamood and I will take the Scout runaround and head to shore."

"Okay, Commander."

Hamad motioned Mamood to go below and collect their travel bags. Then he instructed Ashan and Hassan to lower the Scout, a sturdily-made rubber boat with a pontoon on either side, capable of carrying up to eight passengers at a speed of 30 knots.

A few minutes later, Awad yelled they were at their rendezvous point and brought the vessel to a stop. Hamad ran to the bridge and approached Awad:

"Awad, you are my closest friend," he said solemnly. "You have been at my side for many years. It was unbelievably hard for me to ask you to undertake this final mission for us."

"I'm proud, Commander, that you have selected me for this role, the most important we have ever undertaken."

"I knew you would say that, my brother. But I chose you because I believe that you are the most capable and smartest person in the crew, the one most likely to succeed no matter what peril lies ahead."

"I'm deeply honored by your words, Commander. You have shown me a great deal, and made my life so much more productive for our Muslim brothers."

"I'm moved by your words, Awad. I know that you will find the paradise you are searching for, and that Allah will embrace you."

With tears in their eyes, they embraced and held each other close for a moment. Hamad broke the embrace first. He turned to Ashan and Hassan and spoke separately to each of them for several minutes. After his intimate words, he hugged each of them.

Ashan and Hassan steadied the rear ladder as Hamad and Mamood descended onto the idling Scout runaround. From the rear of the Scout, Hamad waved to his three person crew and shouted:

"You are the captain, Awad, and with Hassan and Ashan at your side, you will succeed. May Allah protect you forever."

The *Dream Free's* engine hit full throttle as Awad steered northeast toward the Windward Passage and the most eastern point of Cuba, about 300 kilometers away. Looking south, Awad could see the Scout pick up speed and head towards Port Antonio. He continued to watch, as the Scout became smaller and smaller and, eventually, only a small speck on the receding horizon.

Dressed in his white captain's outfit, sporting a blue nautical cap with a small dark blue peak, Hamad pushed the Scout to a speed of over 22 knots and rapidly approached what appeared to be a marina on the outskirts of Port Antonio. He steered the small powerful craft to a dock on the end of the marina and cut the engine drifting alongside the dock. He and his mate roped the Scout to the dock, then placed their bags on the dock and jumped off. Anyone at the marina would have thought the twosome was taking a break from their routine.

Hamad and Mamood walked briskly through the marina; Hamad looked at his watch and shook his head, feigning impatience at being late. Looking purposeful, they walked toward the main entrance; their demeanor clearly intended to dispel any questions by curious onlookers. The ruse worked; no one came near them. They hailed a new, green taxi and told the driver to take them directly to the Norman Manley International Airport at Kingston. A local man, the driver was reluctant to travel that far. But when Hamad flashed a $100 dollar bill and told him he would receive it on top of the meter, he promptly changed his mind and invited his two seafaring buddies to hop in for the ride.

After a daunting three-hour drive through mountains and winding roads, they arrived at the airport at about 7:30 p.m. on Monday night. Per Hamad's instructions, a six-person crew remained on call at an hour's notice. Hamad made the call to the pilot from the road as they sped southward. Once they arrived, Hamad and Mamood went directly to the Special Services Division at the airport. Within a few minutes, they passed through security without questioning, had their passports examined cursorily and stamped. Their white maritime uniforms aroused no suspicions perhaps because wealthy yacht owners sometimes sent their crew home on private jets. Besides, it made no sense for those on duty to question crewmen or wealthy travelers closely. Now they were free to board their expensive aircraft. Each smiled broadly at the curvaceous, brunette stewardess who greeted them at the stairs to their waiting jet.

Since there was little air traffic that Monday night, the jet was cleared for takeoff almost immediately. Hamad and Mamood relaxed comfortably in their wide, light brown, leather seats. About 15 minutes later, the jet was airborne and headed east on its 10-hour non-stop journey to Dubai. The two attractive stewardesses served them an aperitif - a well-earned Kir Royale. Sipping his fizzy drink, Hamad smiled warmly at Mamood:

"I'm proud of you, my brother," he said. "I trusted you fully and rightly so."

"You were right to do so, Hamad. We spent a lot of time together. I, too, feel that you are a true friend. I knew I could rely on you."

"Yes, you could," replied Hamad almost gleefully. "We've done all we had to do for now. I could not have asked you for anything else." Then he paused. Looking outside the window, he added: "And I'm sure the final part of the mission will succeed."

CHAPTER 48

CARIBBEAN

January 29, 2007

While Hamad and Mamood chatted happily at 36,000 feet, the *Dream Free* continued its journey northeast at a speed of about 22 knots, passing the eastern point of Cuba at about 5:00 a.m. on Tuesday morning. Awad then turned the craft towards the Turks and Caicos Islands. He planned to go from there towards a point about 30 kilometers west of Andros Island in the Bahamas, a distance of more than 550 kilometers. They were now only about 900 kilometers from Miami, their final destination.

Awad made sure to keep a wide berth from the American naval base at Guantanamo. Based on the intelligence reports Al Qaeda had given them, he knew that the U.S. Navy always had several craft stationed there, including one or more destroyers, each with state-of-the-art missile, radar, communications and special tracking gear. Awad knew they had to avoid a search by a boarding party at all costs. He also believed that a huge pleasure yacht under Cayman Islands registry would arouse little suspicion. There were hundreds of yachts registered in Georgetown and they routinely plied these waters en route to any of the numerous playgrounds in the West Indies, including the increasingly popular Turks and Caicos Islands. He smiled inwardly knowing that his fellow Muslims would soon have their revenge for all the injustices done to their lot at Guantanamo and elsewhere.

For this reason, Awad steered the *Dream Free* in the direction of those islands. His radar showed a fast moving vessel about 15 kilometers to his south headed toward Cap du Mole in Haiti. He thought that, based on the vessel's speed, the ship could be a U.S. destroyer headed out on patrol in that direction. He was thankful that it was not heading in his direction.

After passing the most eastern point of Cuba, he made a sharp turn to the northwest heading some seven kilometers away from Matthew Town on Great Inagua, part of the Turks and Caicos. Through his long distance, high powered binoculars, he was able to see many sailboats and small motor boats in and around the harbor. It was a perfect day for sailing. The sun shone brilliantly in a cloudless blue sky. There was a steady breeze of about 10 knots coming from the north. The sea was relatively calm, with undulating waves rising only three to four feet. He stopped there and directed Ashan and Hassan to change into bathing trunks so they could spend several hours fishing, typical of the activity of other yachts in the area.

After a leisurely day, the *Dream Free* proceeded at a slow pace northwesterly, without incident, for almost 300 kilometers approaching Ragged Island in the West Indies. Hassan relieved Awad at the helm for almost three quarters of this leg. At all times, Ashan, Hassan or Awad kept a watchful eye on the radar, aware of the threat posed by any fast-moving vessel, a tell-tale sign of naval craft.

With Miami only 600 kilometers away, Awad began mapping out the route to his final destination. He had debated with Hamad whether to pass to the east or the west of Andros Island in the Bahamas. They were both of the opinion they had to avoid the appearance of coming from the Bahamas since it was a source of immense drug trafficking. With the United States Drug Enforcement Agency regularly intercepting boats believed to be carrying drugs from the Bahamas, Hamad decided against running any risks. On this basis, they concluded it was preferable to go to the west of the island.

However, this choice of route was not without problems. Hamad and Awad also knew that the Drug Enforcement Agency routinely relied on Air Force AWACs to track all flight and vessel movements approaching the United States. While primarily meant to impede the flow of drugs from Columbia, the AWAC's tracking regularly caught traffickers from the Bahamas, Jamaica and other areas of the Caribbean. Thus, once the *Dream Free* entered within about 400 kilometers of the United States, it too would be picked up on the AWACs' screens and possibly tracked. This meant that a roaming reconnaissance plane could routinely feed tracking data to the U.S. Coast Guard, which, in turn, might intercept and board a targeted vessel at sea.

Another risk to their mission was that of U.S. naval patrols. United States destroyers and other naval vessels routinely traveled to and from bases in the States to Guantanamo in Cuba as well as other parts of the Caribbean. While interception of traffickers was routinely left to the Coast Guard, it was rumored that certain destroyers had state-of-the-art technology capable of sweeping a passing vessel and generating radiographic images of their cargoes. The bombs aboard the *Dream Free* could avoid detection from X-ray imagery, but they might be seen by gamma ray imaging equipment. Hamad and Awad were aware that this risk could materialize, but they felt it was more remote.

The Coast Guard, in Hamad's view, posed the greatest threat to intercepting the yacht. Pursuant to United States law, the *Dream Free* had to give the U.S. Coast Guard a manifest of its passengers, their nationalities and passport numbers, at least 48 hours prior to arrival at a port in the United States. Upon receipt of the manifest, the Coast Guard could decide to inspect an approaching vessel and its cargo in the event that the information aroused suspicion regarding a potential terrorist threat to the country.

When the *Dream Free* passed Ragged Island, it sent its required manifest to the Coast Guard via email. Of course, Hamad had instructed Awad to send a list of fictitious names, Ronald Dwayne, Captain, England, Peter Jones, First Mate, Australia, Charles Bainey, crewmember, Cayman Islands, Jessica Sames, crewmember, Cayman Islands, and Frances O'Connell, crewmember, Ireland. The names and nationalities listed were selected to minimize scrutiny by the Coast Guard. Hamad and Awad assumed that it was hardly that likely the Coast Guard would inspect a vessel with that kind of fictitious make-up.

As the *Dream Free* continued its route towards Andros Island, Awad and his men saw what they feared most. About five kilometers to the northwest, a U.S. Navy destroyer appeared, apparently headed to Guantanamo. Awad instructed Ashan and Hassan to don their bathing suits and American baseball caps and start fishing. Within minutes, they were on the upper deck casting for grouper and bass. Hassan made sure to tell Ashan a funny joke, which caused fits of laughter. To a nearby observer, these playboys seemed to be having a thoroughly good time.

Awad continued to keep a watchful eye on the destroyer. The minutes passed slowly and Awad felt his heart beat quicken, as if he were about to go into combat. Fortunately, for them, the destroyer continued on its route and took no interest in the Cayman Islands yacht. The crew on board the *USS Twin* had seen many similar leisure craft on its Caribbean route. There was no reason to inspect this yacht.

The *Dream Free* continued westward passing to the west of Andros Island at a speed of about 15 knots. Again, Awad stopped the craft for another fishing expedition some 80 kilometers from the southern point of the island. Such a move might convince any spotter on an unseen AWAC that the *Dream Free* was on a leisurely excursion with its wealthy clientele. The vessel was now less than 400 kilometers from Miami - or only about 16 hours away if the vessel continued on its course at a speed of at least 15 knots.

As they began their final approach to their target, Awad, Ashan and Hassan observed their ritual of five daily prayers, a show of reverence to the Prophet. Soon they fell into long periods of silence, as each crewmember became lost in his own private thoughts with the final hour approaching. Typically, these periods of contemplation materialized after they had bonded closely, and even laughed with each other.

Devout in their religious practice, they also remained extremely vigilant regarding any vessel that came within a radius of six kilometers of the ship. After all the effort, care and money expended on this mission, these Al Qaeda operatives were ready to do anything required to carry out their orders, regardless of the risk. If they had to make a run from a Coast Guard boat, they would do so. They also had a back-up plan in place: to detonate the bombs if the yacht was unable to carry out its mission at the Port of Miami. Under this scenario, they were instructed to detonate the bombs as close to any shoreline in the States that was accessible, preferably near a heavily populated area, such as Miami Beach.

As they approached within 20 miles of the Miami area, traffic increased tremendously. Many sailboats and other pleasure craft were visible throughout the area. Surrounded by a groundswell of pleasure boating, the *Dream Free* did not arouse any suspicion in the eyes of nearby sailors.

Ten kilometers from the Miami Beach area, Awad looked through his long-distance binoculars and saw that Coast Guard vessels regularly patrolled the Miami Beach shoreline and the entrance to Miami itself. This was no surprise, based on the intelligence briefings Hamad had given to him. Still, he felt calm because he knew that Allah would continue to protect them on their final leg to paradise.

After traveling for hours, the *Dream Free* was only eight kilometers from Miami Beach. Awad looked at his watch. It was 4:30 Sunday afternoon.

CHAPTER 49

KINGSTON, JAMAICA

January 31, 2007

The plane touched down at Norman Manley International Airport at 5:00 p.m. precisely. Traveling with a minimum of hand luggage, Roger, Gregory and Anne cleared Jamaican customs quickly, only to find themselves at the back of a line of passengers waiting for taxi transport into Kingston proper.

"I don't care," said Gregory, breathing in the humid freshness of sea air. He looked around at the palm trees and the grape leaf shrubbery dotted with red and white tobacco plants that lined the airport terminal. Somehow, he felt rejuvenated by the warmth of the climate and the luminescence of the setting sun. Perhaps it was because home was not far away – just across the Caribbean Sea.

"I've made reservations for us at the Kingston Hilton," said Anne, as they climbed into a waiting taxi. "It's the best there is in the city."

"No chance of going over to Ocho Rios or Montego Bay?" teased Roger.

Anne smiled. "Not this time."

An hour later, they were sitting comfortably at a table in the bar downstairs, surrounded by tall tropical drinks and an array of nuts, chips and roasted plantains.

"Let's go over our plan of action," said Roger.

By tacit agreement, the three had eschewed any discussion of the case during their nine-hour flight from London to Kingston. Now, Anne and Gregory leaned forward, looking at Roger expectantly.

"Let's say the bombs were unloaded here," Roger began, speaking very softly.

"Why? Why here? Why not Alexandria or Dubai?" Gregory interrupted.

"Because we're here. We've been through all this before and decided to come here," Roger said irritably. "So let's assume the bombs were off-loaded here. What do we do first?"

"I still say you can't make that assumption," Gregory said, trying to keep his voice down. "The bombs could have been off-loaded at sea."

"Look, Greg, let's not waste time with all sorts of scenarios. Did we or did we not all agree to come here?"

"Yes."

"Did we or did we not agree, in theory, that Jamaica might be the logical place to offload those bombs if Al Qaeda was planning a nuclear attack on the United States?"

"Yes."

"And are we working on the assumption that Al Qaeda is planning to attack the United States, not Europe?"

"Yes."

"Okay. So now that we're here, what's our plan of action?"

"I say we go to U.S. Customs first thing in the morning," said Anne, sipping her pina colada. "I called Bud and asked him to notify the chief of customs – his name is Robert Londine – about our impending visit in regard to the containers offloaded by the *SS Barooqi* on January 25th. Bud assured me that he would cooperate with us fully."

"Bravo, Anne," said Roger.

"So what we'll do, once we get there, is ask him for the bills of lading for each of the containers – I think there were 15 in total," Anne continued.

"And then?" Greg pursued.

"Then we'll check out the merchants who received the goods," said Roger. "Maybe we'll come across a crucial piece of information."

Gregory sighed. "And how do you propose to do this?"

"We'll act like people interested in doing business," said Anne, briskly. "We'll go into the stores and pretend we're interested in importing their goods to the States. It'll give me a chance to do some shopping," she added mischievously.

"Sure," Roger seconded. "Isn't there anything you'd like to bring home as a souvenir, Greg?"

"Some souvenir," Gregory said sullenly.

"Oh come off it, Greg. Look at the bright side," Anne remonstrated. "We're here in Jamaica. It's warm and the sun is shining. At the very least you can pick up a cd by Bob Marley."

Greg smiled. "I guess you're right, Anne. I'm just an old grouse sourpuss. What do you say we all have some dinner?"

They awoke to the warmth of the Caribbean sun. It was already 82 degrees by 9:00 a.m., and the temperature was expected to go higher. As they made their way to the Customs office near the port – just a 15-minute drive from their hotel – they were met by an impressive sight: Huge gantries were unloading cargo from vessels, lifting heavily loaded containers easily and depositing them smoothly on waiting trucks.

The U.S. Customs office was located in a recently built one-storey building. A receptionist led them to a conference room toward the end of the hall. They barely had time to sit down before Robert Londine bounded in, all smiles. A tall, robust Afro-American sporting an unexpected handlebar mustache that complimented his round face and large eyes, he seemed about 50 and bubbling with energy.

"I heard from Washington that you folks would be here today," he said in a bass voice resonating with authority. "How can I help you?" he asked, sitting down at the head of the table.

"Thank you for taking the meeting," said Anne, formally. "Our visit concerns the *SS Barooqi* that docked here on January 25th and unloaded 15 containers. We would like to see the bills of lading for each container and get the names and addresses of the consignees."

"I see," said Londine stroking his mustache thoughtfully. "Would you folks care for some coffee?" Without waiting for an answer, he leaned over the intercom. "Melanie, would you please bring in a thermos of coffee and some biscuits?" He turned to look at Anne. "I need some myself," he said, smiling.

The three agents sat back smiling in turn, waiting for an answer. It was clear that Londine was in charge of conducting the interview.

"And the purpose of your inquiry?" Londine pursued.

"We believe there may be some discrepancies in those bills of lading," Roger answered.

"Discrepancies," Londine repeated, looking at Roger with curiosity. "What sort of discrepancies?" His easy manner belied more than 20 years of service with U.S. customs.

"We're not sure," Gregory cleared his throat. "That's why we want to have a look."

Without ado, Londine leaned over the intercom again. "Melanie, would you please bring in four copies -" he looked at the three agents, mouthing the word 'four' silently. They nodded. "Four copies of the bills of lading from the *SS Barooqi* that docked on the 25th, including the names and addresses of the local consignees? Thanks." Leaning back in his seat, he smiled at Anne. "Fine weather we're having. How long are you staying?"

"Just a day or two," Anne replied, folding her hands demurely.

"You should stay longer. Go up to Montego Bay."

"We'd love to but –"

At that moment, Melanie entered with a tray of refreshments and a sheaf of papers that she placed on the table in front of Londine.

"Thank you, Melanie," Londine said, busily handing out the information.

After reviewing the data briefly, Roger turned to Londine.

"I see that of the 15 containers, 13 carried cotton goods and two carried spices," he remarked. "Are these types of goods typically received here?"

"Yes. From what I've observed over the past two years I've been stationed here, both are typical of the products imported from Pakistan to Jamaica. Freighters from Pakistan come in here regularly with these types of goods."

"Okay," said Roger, lifting a sheet of paper. "I count six consignees, of which four received the cotton goods and two received the spices. Do you know each of these consignees?"

Londine reviewed the consignee list thoughtfully.

"I know four of them well and have been to their outlets or stores to shop for my family and myself," he said. "Three of them are distributors of clothing and fabrics. They've been in business for years. The same is true of one of the spice importers. I know the proprietor, a man of about 60, quite well. He's a close friend of mine and has lived on this island all his life."

"What about the other two on the list?"

"I don't know them well. The cotton goods importer opened a new store in the eastern district of the city about a year ago. I gather his business is doing well, since he regularly gets containers of goods from Pakistan."

"And the other spice merchant? How about him?" Roger asked keenly.

"That's a new outfit. I think they opened up about a year ago. I've heard they sell mainly to customers throughout the Caribbean and South America. I'm not sure if they have a shop in town or anywhere else on the island."

"How often does this new spice merchant receive goods from abroad?" asked Anne.

"Quite often, I'd say," Londine replied. "Maybe eight to 10 containers a month. I'd have to check my records,"

"Please do so," Roger leaned forward, smiling at Londine. "It may be important."

Londine left the room to return to his office. After checking the spice consignee's import for the last 12 months, he printed out a computer record. Deciding to do the same for the five other consignees, he returned to the conference room 15 minutes later and handed the data over to the three agents.

"Your guess regarding the new spice merchant was correct," said Gregory eyeing the information. "He receives eight to 10 containers a month."

"You can see that the new cotton goods merchant also does a fair volume of business, importing over six containers a month," Londine pointed out.

"Like the older established businesses that also import close to eight containers a month," added Gregory.

"Anything more you folks need from me now?" Londine asked softly.

"We have to check out this information in further detail," said Roger. "Could you possibly inform the consignees that there may be some discrepancies in the paperwork for the goods they received from the *SS Barooqi* and ask them to bring some of the goods in question to your office?"

"Such a request goes far beyond our standard protocol," Londine replied. "But if you insist, I'll give it a try."

"You might start with the representatives of the older businesses today and ask the newest consignees to come to see you tomorrow," Roger suggested. "That will allow us to visit the newer establishments today and check out the older ones tomorrow."

"Okay, I'll see what I can do," Londine replied, anxious to cooperate. "Are we finished for today?"

"I think so," said Roger smoothly. "One last thing: When you interview the representatives, watch their demeanor closely. With your permission, I may ask Anne, here, to come in and observe the companies' personnel through the glass window when you meet with them tomorrow. That is, unless we have a change of plan."

"Very well," Londine replied looking over at Anne. He rose from his seat. "If that's all—"

"Thank you for your time," said Anne extending a hand.

"A pleasure," said Londine, shaking it. "I'll see you out."

Escorting the agents to the entrance of the building, Londine again assured them of his cooperation before saying goodbye.

"Well, that's that," said Roger.

"Not much help there," Gregory observed.

Anne shrugged.

"No," said Roger. He had been convinced that his meeting with the chief of U.S. Customs would produce no tangible results. He said as much to Gregory and Anne as they were eating breakfast in the hotel dining room.

"I think our meeting won't last longer than half an hour," he observed, spearing chunks of pineapple with his fork. "After that, we must rent a car."

Now, he looked over the docks, took out his sunglasses and put them on. "Let's go rent a car and check out these new consignees. We'll start with the cotton goods distributor. By the way, I think your plan is great, Anne. While you and Gregory are in the store purchasing items and inquiring about the possibility of buying goods for an importing firm in the States, I'll wait for you in the car around the corner. Afterwards Greg and I will take on the spice merchant while you, Anne, wait for us in the car. Maybe we'll be able to get some leads."

They rented a white Toyota Camry in the southern part of Kingston. Driving through the teeming streets of the city to the first of the consignees, the cotton distributor, Roger hoped that the ruse Anne had devised would prove fruitful.

"Here we are," he said stopping in front of a non-descript storefront. "I'll wait for you around the corner." He bent over Anne, unlocking the passenger door.

Gregory got out and surveyed the street.

"See ya," said Anne sliding out of the car to join Gregory.

Appearances to the contrary, the store Gregory and Anne entered was brand new and quite crowded. Row upon row of cotton goods for adults and children – mostly cheaply priced – were on display.

Anne thoughtfully selected a handful of women's clothing that she brought to the register. A few minutes later, Gregory appeared at the check-out counter with about 10 children's outfits. Arranging the articles on the counter, he asked the clerk if he could speak to the manager. She dialed the manager's office and, within seconds, a Jamaican in his early thirties came over.

Gregory began by complimenting the manager on the variety of his merchandise. He went on to inquire about purchasing larger quantities of goods on a continuing basis for export to the States. The manager listened attentively as Gregory asked about the availability of larger quantities of goods and whether he could guarantee that orders would be filled and arrive on time. The manager nodded affirmatively. His manufacturing source in Pakistan had been in business for many years, was reliable and shipments arrived on a monthly basis.

Professing curiosity about how the goods were shipped at sea, Gregory asked whether he could inspect the boxes, in which the merchandise arrived. The manager quickly complied and led Gregory and Anne to a warehouse next to the outlet. There they were able to see some of the boxes from the shipment that had arrived the week before. Satisfied, Gregory told the manager he was prepared to place a substantial order once his boss in the States approved of the garment samples he had in tow. As he led them back into the store, the manager pressed his card into Gregory's hand, appearing delighted with this news.

Anne and Gregory walked around the block and found the car parked discreetly beneath a shady tree.

"How did it go?" asked Roger.

"I think the place is for real," Anne answered quickly. "There were lots of customers. The manager was willing to show us how the merchandise was shipped."

"Even more important, he was eager for new orders, a sure sign that the business is legitimate," Gregory added.

"Of course those are only our impressions," Anne went on. "We can't be sure."

"Let's take a break for lunch," said Roger. "This is as good a time as any."

They found an outdoor café nearby and ordered sandwiches and soft drinks. Although they were the only Americans there, they felt at home basking in the warmth of the sun. Anne, who had never been to Jamaica before, remarked that it was a great spot for a vacation. Gregory and Roger agreed, smiling wistfully. They all knew that a vacation wouldn't be in the offing for quite some time – certainly not until the investigation ended. As they sat, eating their lunch leisurely, the three friends lapsed into a harmonious silence. They valued each other's company. Privately, Gregory and Roger acknowledged that Anne was a fantastic addition to the team. She was a professional through and through who brought warmth, a sense of camaraderie and great insight to their tedious chore. She also had a good sense of humor and, last, but not least, was a superb marksman.

Moving on to their next assignment, they drove to the spice merchant's premises located in the southeastern part of the city.

After Anne parked the car at a discreet distance a block and a half away, Roger and Gregory got out and began walking east, in the direction of All World Trading Ltd.

They found themselves in front of a long, low building, painted gleaming white, which stood out from its neighboring offices by virtue of its depth.

As they entered the building, they were greeted by a tall, muscular Jamaican who appeared to be in his mid-thirties. A light-skinned young clerk, possibly of Middle Eastern descent, stood behind him. Powerful scents of spices permeated the room. Two of the four walls were stacked with racks of spice jars. Roger and Gregory made a point of studying the jars carefully before asking for help.

"We would like to purchase about half a pound each of some 20 spices," said Roger earnestly. "If our home office in Virginia approves of their quality, we would consider buying large quantities from you, provided, of course, that you could reliably fill and ship such orders."

Pleased by the prospect of receiving substantial commissions from such sales, the Jamaican took Roger by the elbow and led him towards the racks of spice jars.

"You can see the prices on each of the jars," he said. "However, if you buy large quantities, we would certainly give you a volume discount."

"We'll pay the going price for a small order of 20," Roger said coyly. "But we want to be satisfied that you can handle a large order on a continuing basis."

"No problem, mon. The Jamaican waved an arm sporting a silver bracelet with the name "Nigel" on it. "Let's go to the warehouse in back of the shop."

As they followed the Jamaican to the rear of the building, they noticed several smaller offices preceding the storage area.

"This is how we receive our supplies," said the Jamaican, pointing to a pile of boxes some eight feet high. "The spices are kept fresh during shipment in these sealed plastic containers."

"Can you show us a shipment so we can see if the containers are truly waterproof?" asked Roger softly.

"Why not?" replied the Jamaican, pulling down one of the boxes with the help of the Middle Eastern clerk who had quietly joined them. After opening it, Roger and Gregory peered in and felt the containers.

"This certainly seems well protected," observed Gregory. "Where do you get your spices? Can you assure us of a large continuing supply?"

"We've been getting our spices from a source in Pakistan who's been in business for more than 10 years," the Jamaican answered with pride. "He's extremely reliable. We've been doing business with him for over a year already."

"Well, that sounds just fine," Roger said emphatically, as if reassured by this piece of news.

Roger paid for the spices in cash and said he hoped to contact them within several weeks, if not sooner.

"We appreciate your business," the Jamaican said. "We hope you will send us large orders."

"We'll let you know soon," Roger waved goodbye. "See you around."

As they walked out, two customers came in.

"Well, what do you think?" Roger asked Gregory as they walked towards their car.

Gregory shrugged. "Don't know."

Anne was sitting at the wheel of the car reading a mystery novel.

"Well?" she asked, turning on the ignition as they got in.

"The place looks legitimate," said Gregory, adjusting his seat belt. "They buy and sell. They have other customers."

"You may be right, but I had the strangest feeling when I was there," Roger said. "I can't put my finger on it. It was like a sense of foreboding. That other salesman, the one who looks like an Arab, was very quiet. Maybe he didn't want to intrude because we were doing business with the Jamaican. But I had the impression he was observing us. He didn't say a single word while we were there."

"Roger, I know how much you rely on your intuition and generally you're right," said Gregory deferentially. "But there have been times when you've been wrong. The Middle Eastern guy was a bit strange, I must admit. But maybe that's how they behave when they're not directly involved. You know, quiet, respectful. After all, the Jamaican did all the talking."

"Why don't we go back there tomorrow morning, Greg? This time, we'll do business with the Arab. Maybe we'll be able to draw him out."

"Good idea."

When he awoke the following morning to a brilliant, sunny day, Roger felt very tense. An inner voice, born of a well-honed instinct of survival, warned him to be extremely careful and highly focused. He could not say why he was so agitated, but he knew he had to respect his feelings.

CHAPTER 50

KINGSTON, JAMAICA

February 2, 2007

Around 9:00 a.m., in the southeastern district of the city, Mohammed Abdel was enjoying the balmy weather. In fact, he was enjoying Jamaica, period. The laid-back life-style of these island people was a revelation – both wonderful and magical.

He was deeply honored when Mahmoud handpicked him for "deployment" somewhere in the Caribbean. He believed in the cause of Al Qaeda and would have sacrificed himself nine times over. However, he was far too precious to be sacrificed as suicide fodder. His accounting skills and administrative abilities were invaluable to the Egyptian Mahmoud, who had employed him in his company for years. When Mahmoud approached him with this new assignment, he accepted it without question, never thinking that it involved a prolonged vacation in a wonderland called Jamaica.

He did not have much time to adjust to his new life-style when he first arrived. There was the business of setting up shop. Spices were a popular commodity and there was plenty of competition. Luckily, the Egyptian had foreseen this and, in addition to stocking the shop amply, had provided him with a client list of wealthy South American importers. Very soon, he acquired the reputation of a prosperous merchant whose business increased slowly but steadily, month after month.

Of course, some sales – especially those to the natives and tourists – were largely due to Nigel. Ah, Nigel. Nigel, with his carefree Jamaican disposition, his clever way of assessing a situation and, above all, his expertise in martial arts, was a miraculous find. He thanked Allah every day for Nigel.

But Mohammed had no illusions about Nigel. He knew he agreed to work for the money – far more than any salaried employee earned by Jamaican standards. Still, Mohammed took it upon himself to establish a relationship with Nigel, a friendship based upon a modicum of trust and liking. He never discussed world politics or spoke of his past life. If politics came into the picture at all, it was local politics. But he made it a point to socialize with him. The two drank beer together, took out girls and discussed various ways of extending their business further.

His thoughts were interrupted by the telephone.

"All World Trading," said Mohammed.

"Mr. Abdel?" The voice was deep, lacking the usual Jamaican lilt.

"Yes," said Mohammed. He wet his lips. "This is Mr. Abdel."

"Mr. Abdel this is Inspector Londine of U.S. Customs. I'm calling you about the shipment you recently received. We discovered some irregularities in the bills of lading."

Mohammed's heart sank.

"What irregularities?"

"Oh, nothing serious. It may even be a typo – a typographical error, you know. – but it appears consistently and I wonder whether you can come down here with some of your merchandise to clear this up."

"When?" Mohammed was not at all reassured by Londine's blandness.

"How about this afternoon? I could be free, say between two and three. No, wait, better after 3:00 p.m."

"3:00 p.m.?" Mohammed echoed, stalling as his thoughts raced back to the day the shipment was unloaded. What could have gone wrong? What "irregularities" was Londine talking about?

"I guess that would be all right," he said slowly, as if looking through his appointment book.

"Let's say 3:30 in my office," Londine suggested.

"3:30? Fine."

"I'll see you then, Mr. Abdel."

"Goodbye, Mr. Londine."

Mohammed hung up and stared at the telephone.

"Want some breakfast, boss?"

Nigel ambled into the room, without bothering to knock.

"I'm going across the street for some plantains and a doughnut."

"No," said Mohammed morosely, dragging his eyes away from the telephone. "But before you go out, please bring me the bills of lading from our last shipment."

"The bills of lading?" Nigel scratched his head. "Why? What's up?"

"I don't know." Mohammed said irritably. "U.S. Customs just called. They want me to come down there to clarify certain 'irregularities.' "

"'Irregularities?" Nigel repeated. "What kind of 'irregularities?' "

"How should I know? Just get me those bills! I want to go over them before I go down there."

"Sure thing," said Nigel, hopping from one foot to the other restlessly.

"And stop jumping up and down. It makes me nervous."

"Yes, sir."

Nigel left the room quickly and returned moments later with a manila folder.

"Here they are," he said laying them carefully on the desk.

"On second thought, bring me back some coffee," said Mohammed, scanning the papers.

"Milk? Sugar?"

"Black...Wait!" Mohammed cried at Nigel's departing back. "Remember those Americans who were in here yesterday?"

Nigel turned from the door and advanced slowly into the room.

"The two guys who were interested in doing business?" he asked.

"Yes."

"What about them?"

"Do you think they were genuinely interested in importing spices from us?"

Nigel shrugged. "They seemed to be."

"There was something about them…"

"What? You think they were snooping around?"

Mohammed seemed lost in thought. "I don't know."

"Like detectives, doing undercover work?"

Mohammed stared at Nigel. "Detectives?" he repeated.

"You know, like the police or the FBI."

"The FBI?" Mohammed was horrified.

"I said *like* the FBI. I didn't mean the FBI." Nigel paused. "But what would they be looking for in a rinky-dink spice shop?"

"I don't know," Mohammed said, spreading his hands, palms up, in a gesture of bewilderment.

"You're just imagining things," said Nigel, looking over Mohammed's shoulder at the bills of lading. "There's nothing to be suspicious of. Americans love to talk about doing business with us locals. But they rarely make good on their word. "

"I guess you're right. It was just a thought."

"Well, stop thinking. You're tired. You've been doing too much and need a rest. I'll be back in a flash with the coffee."

"Thank you, Nigel."

After discussing their game plan over breakfast, Roger, Gregory and Anne returned to the All World Trading office shortly after 9:30. Again, Anne waited in the car parked around the corner, about 75 meters away.

They entered the office cautiously. Only the Arab was present. The Jamaican who had served them the day before was not to be found.

"Good morning. You're back so soon," said Mohammed, eyeing his customers warily. "Are you interested in buying more spices?"

Roger smiled at him. For some reason, the Arab seemed quite agitated.

"Yes," he said smoothly. "We called our head office back in Virginia and they asked us to broaden our inventory."

"Excellent," Mohammed's thin lips moved in a semblance of a smile. "Please come this way," he said, leading them to an adjoining room where two walls were lined with shelves of spices. "Feel free to select what you like. If you need help, just let me know."

While Roger and Gregory examined the spice jars, Mohammed headed towards the warehouse. Several minutes later, he returned to the front office.

Busily gathering up spice samples, Roger and Gregory did not see the muscular Jamaican running towards them from the warehouse entrance. Suddenly, Gregory felt a karate chop on the left side of his neck, a hammer blow delivered with such force that he fell to the floor crying in pain. As the Jamaican sprang forward to strike Roger, Roger backed away, kicking his assailant hard in the stomach. The enraged Jamaican recovered his balance quickly, whirled, flew into the air and did a dropkick aimed at Roger's head. Moving quickly to his right, Roger dodged the kick deftly. The Jamaican landed awkwardly, drew a six-inch knife and lunged at Roger, aiming for the heart. Instantly, Roger grabbed his Glock, pumped two rounds into the Jamaican and watched as he fell to the floor, lifeless. Blood oozed from a small round hole in his forehead and a wound near his heart, creating a dark pool around him.

Before he could turn around, Roger heard the crackling sound of an Uzi and ducked as several bullets whizzed by. He turned around and saw the Arab, now armed, crouching behind a desk. Only the barrel of the Uzi was visible above the desk. Meanwhile, Gregory, now conscious, was trying to crawl towards the warehouse door. The Arab took aim and fired. Gregory cried out in pain as the bullets hit him in his right leg and right side. Moving towards Gregory, Roger laid down some covering fire, as he dragged Gregory through the warehouse door to potential safety behind a cement wall. But Roger knew his Glock was no match against an Uzi. He also knew they would be cornered within minutes. He pulled out his cellphone and called Anne to come to their aid immediately.

Just then, the Arab fired off at least 30 rounds, barely missing them. Roger heard him load a new magazine in the Uzi, knew he had enough ammunition to keep them pinned down, and eventually kill them. As he surveyed the contents of the warehouse, he realized that the bullets could pass right through the spice boxes. That might slow down their speed, but even if they provided some protection, the Arab would find them because of the trail of blood left by Gregory. Also, Roger feared, the Arab might have friends at his disposal.

As he peered around a corner of boxes towards the warehouse door, Roger saw the Arab aiming a rocket-propelled grenade launcher in his direction. Instantly, he moved to the left, dragging Gregory behind him. He threw himself on top of Gregory in a desperate attempt to shield him from imminent explosion.

Sweat pouring from his brow, he waited. Then a single shot rang out. Roger immediately recognized the sound. It came from a Glock. He heard a body and a weapon fall to the floor heavily. A voice cried out:

"Are you guys alright?"

Anne had rescued them from certain death. With one shot, a bull's eye to the brain, she had killed the Arab instantly.

"Thank God," Roger gasped. "Thank God you showed up in time," he rose unsteadily to his feet and embraced her. "Thank God," he repeated. "I was sure this was it."

Anne leaned over Gregory. She felt his pulse and looked up at Roger.

"He's in bad shape," said Roger. "He's lost a lot of blood. He's unconscious. Call Londine. Tell him to get an ambulance down here fast."

While they waited for the ambulance, Roger paced up and down. "I knew it. I knew I was right about those guys." It sounded like a mantra. "I knew it, I knew it. They were bad."

"Yes they were bad," Anne replied. "You were right. You know, when I called Londine to tell him I wouldn't be coming in to observe his interviews today, he told me he had just spoken to the representative of All World Trading."

"No wonder that Arab looked awfully worried when we walked in! Londine must have called him. "

"Could be. I made that call around 8:30 a.m., just before breakfast."

"Do you think he thought we were Customs agents snooping around?"

Anne shrugged. "Maybe."

"But why did he want to kill us?"

"Because he had something to protect. Something very important," Anne replied thoughtfully. "Somehow I don't think the locals worry much about Customs inquiries. All they'd get would be a fine or a slap on the wrist."

"Exactly," said Roger. "Let's have a look at the evidence."

He walked over the lifeless body of the Arab, eyeing the rocket-propelled grenade that lay on the floor. There were five additional grenades nearby. Roger paused for a moment, inhaling deeply as he reflected on his good fortune. How close he had been to death! He remembered the ominous feeling of dread he experienced when he woke up and shuddered.

Always on the lookout for important evidence, Anne followed close behind, bending down to take note of the serial numbers on the Arab's Uzi and grenade launcher.

They searched the Arab's desk where they found copies of bills of lading, payment receipts, and wire transfers – all the earmarks of a functioning business. They were about to pry open three locked drawers of a filing cabinet when they heard the siren of an approaching ambulance.

The ambulance stopped in front of the building and two paramedics emerged carrying a stretcher and an oxygen mask. Roger went with them to the back of the warehouse and watched as they lifted Gregory gently onto the stretcher, placing the oxygen mask over his face. Walking beside his unconscious friend, he questioned the paramedics closely about Gregory's condition and felt somewhat reassured when they told him he was in critical condition but would live. As they ministered to Gregory inside the ambulance, Roger went to rejoin Anne.

They decided against prying open the drawers of the filing cabinet, but took the most important piece of evidence before leaving the premises: the Arab's computer.

Anne drove back to the hotel rapidly, while Roger spoke to a CIA member on duty at the U.S. Embassy in Kingston. He briefed him about the nature of their visit, explaining that they had come to the island on a secret mission pursuing missing atomic weapons. He further suggested they contact the Jamaican police and outlined a cover story to explain the violence at All World Trading. Amazed by the news and proud to be peripherally involved in a mission of such importance, the CIA representative gladly offered to cover the agents' tracks.

Back in the safety of their hotel, Anne joined Roger in his room.

"We must call Langley," Roger said, easing his bruised body into a chaise lounge.

Anne nodded. "I'll try to get Bud on the phone now."

"I think we should tell headquarters that we think the weapons may have been offloaded in Jamaica, over six days ago."

"I agree."

Anne looked at her watch, amazed that it was just a little past 11:00 a.m. It seemed like a whole day had gone by. She was immensely proud of saving her friends lives, but felt shaken by the terrifying violence she had just witnessed – although her ordeal was nothing compared to theirs. Looking over at Roger, who seemed to be dozing, she opened the mini-bar and took out a large bottle of Evian water.

Roger opened his eyes.

"Want some?" she asked, holding up bottle.

He nodded.

She got out two glasses, filled them with ice and water and walked over to the chaise.

"Thanks," he said gratefully, the cold glass sending unexpected waves of pleasure through his fingers.

Anne sat down on a chair facing him, took out her cellphone and dialed Langley.

"Hello, Bud. Is that you?" she asked, placing her phone in speaker mode

"Yes, Anne."

"Say hello to Roger Dunleavy. I think you two have met several times before."

"Hi, Roger. Glad to speak to you. How can I be of help?"

"We're not sure, but we have reason to believe that the missing weapons may have been offloaded in Jamaica and picked up by an outfit called All World Trading Ltd." Roger said, a hint of excitement creeping into his voice.

"Go on."

"Anne and I feel that this outfit may have helped move these weapons onto the next stage," Roger continued.

"The next stage?"

"At this point we're still speculating," Roger went on, warming to his analysis. "But we think these folks may have put the weapons on a private plane or boat which may already have left, or is about to leave Jamaica for its target."

"That's some theory," said Bud dryly.

"We know that. But we think it makes sense."

"Can you give me something more to go on?" asked Bud.

"Yes, " said Anne. "We think there may be a tie-in between the hijacking of the that oil tanker by pirates in the Strait of Malacca and the theft of the weapons."

"Go on," said Bud thoughtfully.

"Today we came across a Middle Eastern connection in Kingston. An Arab posing as the proprietor of a trading company tried to kill us."

"If pirates are involved at both ends," Roger said, his voice rising, "they would probably feel far more comfortable at sea and may want to use a sea route to bring off an attack. That's our working theory - which has just been bolstered by the Arab's murderous attack on us."

"I get it. What do you want me to do right now?"

"Alert the Secretary of Homeland Security, the Director of National Intelligence and the Coast Guard Commandant immediately," Roger said with authority. "Have them put the Coast Guard on the highest alert immediately. Tell them the weapons may have left here almost six days ago."

"You realize the Secretary and all the others may want a lot more information..." Bud replied, anticipating resistance from his superiors.

"That's all we've got," said Anne emphatically. "We'll continue our investigation on this island for several more days. Maybe we'll come across some more clues. But right now, you've got it all."

"Alright, I'll do my best to arrange everything immediately and keep you posted."

"Thanks, Bud," said Anne, pleased with the call. "We'll keep you informed of any further developments."

"One last item," Roger added. "We took down the serial numbers on an Uzi and a rocket-propelled grenade launcher the Arab had in his possession. Please trace their country of origin," he reeled off the serial numbers.

"I'll run that by our staff," replied Bud agreeably, "and let you know what we find out."

"Great," said Roger.

Several hours later, Roger received a call from Londine. The Customs officer reported that the four consignees produced samples of goods imported by the SS *Barooqi* that matched their bills of lading. Furthermore, he and a staff member had inspected several of the boxes in each of their warehouses and found that they also matched the contents of their bills of lading. No weapons were found. Roger thanked him for his help.

Early that evening, he and Anne went to visit Gregory at the hospital. Upon arrival, they were told he had been operated on to remove the two bullets lodged in his right side and was now in the intensive care unit, still unconscious. His prognosis was considered grave. Roger and Anne left dejected but remained optimistic that their dear friend and colleague would recover fully.

The following morning, February 3rd, Bud called from Langley to let them know that he and his Director had successfully lobbied to have the Coast Guard placed on highest alert status. He added that several additional Coast Guard vessels and aircraft, including Marine Corps helicopters, were being transferred to the East coast and Southeast coast.

Buoyed by the news, Anne and Roger began charting their new game plan for the day.

CHAPTER 51

MIAMI, FLORIDA

February 4, 2007

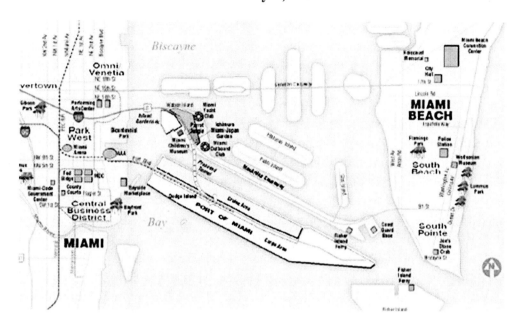

Along the coast of southern Florida, as the black of night faded to amethyst clouds, a narrow pink ribbon appeared on the horizon heralding the promise of a brilliant sunny day. The ribbon widened, spreading into a glow that moved slowly across the glimmering waters of the Atlantic as it approached the scalloped shore of Miami Beach. It illuminated the high-rise buildings that curved along the shore and, seeping through the foliage of barely swaying palm trees, warmed the verandas of stately Spanish-styled mansions. As the sun rose, sprinklers began misting state-of-the-art golf courses, hotel staff began arranging lounge chairs around swimming pools, and men began readying their boats for a sail, while yachtsmen and crew prepared for longer voyages. A sense of happy purpose prevailed as the temperature climbed into the low eighties.

It was Sunday, February 4, 2007.

At the Port of Miami, it was another busy day. Located on Dodge Island, south of the causeway linking Miami Beach to the mainland, and north of Fisher Island – an exclusively wealthy community – the Port was a state-of-the-art facility that serviced cruise liners as well as cargo ships. On the north side of Dodge Island, seven modern passenger terminals maintained seven cruise berths. The south side of the island serviced the loading and unloading of cargo on 6,100 feet of linear wharf where 12 high-speed gantry cranes could capably lift the heaviest of cargos. The Port was also accessible via two channels south of Miami Beach that led to Dodge Island.

At 2:00 p.m. on that peaceful afternoon, the port became a beehive of activity. Three passenger ships were scheduled to leave between 6:00 and 7:00 p.m. that evening. Carnival Cruise Lines, Norwegian Cruise Lines and Celebrity Cruises each had a vessel headed to different destinations in the Caribbean and Mexico. Passengers, most of them families with children, from all over the United States lined up excitedly in the terminals awaiting clearance for boarding. For some it was their maiden voyage.

As passengers milled about the terminals nearest their ship, the staff checked their passports against the cruise manifest and cleared them for boarding. It was a laborious process. In the case of the *Trident*, a Carnival Cruise Lines vessel, there were about 2,700 persons waiting to be cleared; the ship was listed as having a maximum capacity of 2,758 passengers. The other two cruise ships also carried about 1,750 and 2,000 passengers, respectively. The process was time-consuming because both the cruise ship operators and the port authority had to ensure that only those passengers listed on the manifest were cleared for boarding, and to prevent any weapons or other illegal cargo from being carried on board. The port authority security staff also brought specially trained dogs to sniff the passengers and the baggage they carried on their person for drugs and illegal arms.

At 4:00 p.m. sharp, a host of passengers cleared for the *Trident* gladly clambered up the gangplank. Most of them immediately headed straight for their staterooms, while others decided to explore the ship's upper deck with its pool and outdoor dining facilities, its assortment of bars and other recreational areas. The same scene occurred on the Celebrity and the Norwegian Cruise Lines vessels. Guests of the passengers had also come on board for traditional bon voyage parties. Champagne bottles popped on balconies and in many staterooms. Each vessel had a festival in progress on board.

On the south side of Dodge Island, several gantries were busy lifting different colored containers off two freighters that had docked there a day earlier. From the cruise ships, passengers could see hundreds of containers stacked up near the gantries, ready to be lifted onto a trailer chassis or a freight car for delivery to distant places.

Security at the port had been substantially increased in recent years, principally due to the passage of the Maritime Transportation Security Act of 2002, which President Bush signed on November 25, 2002. The act established a variety of security measures that ports and vessels had to adopt in order to protect them from terrorist acts. The Port of Miami maintained that it had a variety of these protective steps in place before the Act became law. The Act demanded personnel identification procedures, screening of vehicles and baggage, access control steps and the installation of surveillance equipment, to name a few items. The United States Customs Service operated a Vehicle and Cargo Inspection System that used a gamma ray imaging system to create images of items being inspected (including vehicles and containers,) and was able to penetrate at least six inches of steel. An additional modernization program was in place to upgrade the security features already in place.

On that day, the Coast Guard in the Miami area and other areas along the southeast, including Jacksonville and Savannah, went on high alert. Late the night before, the Coast Guard commander for the Miami Area, Captain John Sims, a veteran with 15 years of service, received a high security alert from the Commandant's office in Washington. It advised him that the area might be in imminent danger of a major terrorist attack. He cancelled all weekend leaves for those under his command and arranged to place all craft under his control on round-the-clock duty. Upset that eight Coast Guard cutters in the Miami area had recently been taken out of service due to a reconstruction fiasco, he was also aware that reinforcements – – added helicopters and additional boats – – were on the way, but might not reach the Miami area for a few days.

He briefed his senior officers to maintain high vigilance at all times and reminded them they could board any vessel in the area they viewed as suspicious, or were deemed suspicious by his staff based on manifests received by Customs that had been reported to him.

Analyzing what was available, Captain Sims knew he lacked the field resources required to carry out the role assigned to the unit. He had only one 165-foot vessel and four 87-foot coastal patrol boats to blanket the area. The smaller vessels each carried an aluminum hulled in board diesel powered waterjet small boat used for boarding and recovery missions. While he had also requested two HH-65As from the Helicopter Interdiction Unit in Jacksonville, he did not expect them to arrive until the next day or the day after.

As the senior officers boarded their craft, they immediately briefed the crews on their crucial security mission. They knew their mission would be made more difficult as the promise of unusually good weather was expected to bring out weekend sailors and hundreds of small craft and sailboats.

Unaware of the heightened security alert in the area, the *Dream Free* continued on course to its final destination. At about 4:30 p.m. the craft was cruising about 16 knots an hour, five miles off the shore of South Beach, where the bars and restaurants were only partly filled, since night time revelry started later. All three of the crew - Awad, Ashan and Hassan - were on the bridge. As Awad estimated they would arrive on target in about 45 minutes, they began their final mission countdown. Awad, whom Hamad had placed in charge, told his mates that the suitcase bombs should not be brought up to the entertainment area of the main deck until 5:15 p.m. and that they had to be placed directly behind the wooden wall next to the entry of the dining/entertainment area.

"Listen to me closely, my brothers," said Awad. "In that position the suitcases will be hidden from view by passengers on ships or any nearby yacht or vessel."

"And then we would be in a position to go to the final step immediately," said Hassan solemnly.

"Exactly," replied Awad firmly, without hesitation.

Ashan climbed the steps rapidly to the third deck and looked in all directions. Then, he turned and motioned excitedly to his two comrades below:

"I see a helicopter about two miles away headed north along South Beach," he said loudly. "Do you see it over there?"

"Yes I do," said Awad in a cautious tone. "It's off our starboard side."

"That's right," shouted Ashan. They all could hear the sound of the helicopter several miles away; the sound of rapid whirring from the rotor blades and engine carried for miles around.

"I can't see its markings," Awad continued. "But I assume it's a security copter and probably belongs to the United States Coast Guard. So let's keep an eye on it."

"Okay," said Hassan, as his eyes followed the northward route of the copter. "I sure hope it doesn't come our way."

"I doubt it will," said Awad confidently. "As I said, let's continue to track it."

"Look to the north," shouted Hassan, "I see what looks like another Coast Guard vessel, over 50 meters in length."

"Relax," said Awad confidently. "Just keep an eye on it."

Awad and Hassan checked their watches. It was now 5:10 p.m. They had cruised directly south and were now about a half mile from the beginning of the Norris Cut, a channel south of Fisher Island and South Beach that led to the Port area. As the sun had set at about 4:50 p.m., they felt more protected by the approach of evening. Although their craft was clearly visible at twilight, they knew that it was much harder to read the name of the vessel in the dimming light. Awad motioned for his two mates to come close to him.

"Go below and bring the suitcases up. You know where to place them," he said.

"Yes, my brother," replied Hassan.

Ashan and Hassan went below. When they arrived at the master bedroom with its tools of destruction, they first washed their faces, hands and feet as part of a ritualistic cleansing. After that, they both fell to their knees and made a final prayer together in Arabic, rocking back and forth in tandem. Each said in unison:

"May Allah guide us and protect us as his loyal servants always."

Feeling a bit relieved but still anxious, they took each suitcase bomb out of its wooden box with its protected lead shield, carried them one by one up the stairs and placed them at the designated spot below the right rear deck window on the main deck, out of sight. As they looked out over the stern, a strong sea breeze cooled their cheeks.

As the *Dream Free* turned into the Norris Cut channel en route to the port, Awad reduced the engine's speed to 10 knots, since he knew that the speed limit in the channel was lower than that at sea. He could see the MacArthur Causeway and the Marriott Hotel of South Beach off to his north. He steered the craft initially towards the south side of Fisher Island, in a southwesterly direction toward Fisherman's Channel. To his northwest, he could still see the channel that led to the cruise ships, illuminated brightly by stateroom and deck lights. They were now less than two kilometers from their target.

Suddenly, out of the enveloping darkness, he saw a Coast Guard patrol boat, about 30 meters in length with a machine gun on its forward deck, headed northeast toward the open water through the Norris Cut through which he had just passed - no more than 200 meters to his south. His heart raced; he could not believe their bad luck. Steeled from years of fighting and training, he kept his presence of mind and said to his two mates sternly:

"Hassan, take the wheel now. Continue to steer in the southwesterly direction."

Hassan grabbed the wheel and continued to head southwesterly steadily at about eight knots. To an outside observer, he certainly appeared to be a captain of the vessel; his white outfit, with the captain's insignia on it, was visible for at least 100 meters. Although he was heading southwest, the *Dream Free* was still only about 1,500 meters from the cruise ships. As he surveyed the scene around him, he suddenly had to shield his eyes from the Coast Guard's searchlight as it swept over the ship. As instructed, he waved toward the Coast Guard crew and, and to his delight, he could see that several of them waved back at him.

Meanwhile, Awad, also wearing a white outfit with a first mate's insignia, crouched behind the wooden rear wall of the main deck. Sweating, he quickly opened the first suitcase bomb and saw that two of the three arming connections were still in place. He opened the second suitcase bomb and found that its first two arming connections were ready as well. Peering out the open rear deck door, he saw, to his delight, the Coast Guard vessel still headed toward the open channel. He prayed it would not approach for a closer look and was heartened by the sight of the Cayman Islands flag flapping back and forth in the breeze at the rear of his craft. He sensed that the size of the yacht and its known registry would provide the cover they needed. As he reflected on this, he saw the Coast Guard vessel continue along the Norris Cut towards the open sea south of South Beach. He knelt down and prayed aloud:

"Allah, you are still with us. As in the past, I give myself to you from this day forth and forever."

Ashan came over from his position behind the bridge. Awad said to him:

"Help move these suitcases to the middle of the rear doorway here," said Awad.

They moved each one separately so that each suitcase faced the open rear door.

"Ashan, go on deck and get ready to take some photographs of those two cruise ships in the distance we'll be passing in a few minutes. Also, keep a watchful eye on that patrol boat, but don't look at it directly."

"Yes, my brother," Ashan said. He embraced Awad tightly and held him close for several seconds without speaking further. Emboldened in pursuit of a cause, they were like two brothers.

With the Coast Guard patrol boat now well over three kilometers away, he turned the *Dream Free* a full 360 degrees in Fisherman's Channel, west of Fisher Island, heading for the cruise ship channel entrance to Dodge Island, about 400 meters ahead. As the *Dream Free* approached the entrance, a restricted area from which pleasure craft were barred, Ashan yelled excitedly: "Awad that patrol boat has turned around and is headed back in our direction!"

Alerted by this renewed threat, Hassan increased the vessel's speed. Moving at about 20 knots per hour, Hassan steered the *Dream Free* into and up the channel to about 100 meters north of the Carnival and Norwegian cruise ships. In the distance, they could hear the revelry on board, even the high pitched, happy voices of young children. Then, he sharply turned the craft in a southwesterly direction toward the 40-meter gap between the two vessels and slowed his speed to five knots an hour.

The flash from Ashan's camera could be seen by those on the decks of the cruise ships. Some of the passengers on board the nearest vessel, the *Trident*, waved at the approaching yacht. Ashan waved back.

Other flashes could now be seen in the distance. Captain Sims had seen the *Dream Free* head for the cruise ship channel, violating the port's no entry restrictions, and immediately thought of the threat message the Coast Guard sent to him the night before. Alerted to this perceived threat, the Captain had turned his craft around at South Beach and gunned it in the direction of the intruding yacht. The Coast Guard patrol boat entered the cruise line channel, closing to about 300 meters from the *Dream Free*. Bullets from the Coast Guard's machine gun raked the boat. Ashan picked up a Kalashnikov hidden nearby and opened fire on the Coast Guard vessel. A return volley from the Coast Guard craft killed him immediately.

When the *Dream Free* was 50 meters from the cruise ships in their berths, and the Coast Guard vessel about 100 meters away from the *Dream Free*, Awad firmly, and without hesitation, inserted one electrical coil into its holder in each of the suitcase bombs, the last step needed to arm the bombs for immediate detonation, and punched in the codes. He and Hassan cried "Allah Akbar!" The *Dream Free* was now no more than 30 meters from the cruise ships.

The doors to Hell's furnace opened as a 20-kiloton destructive nuclear force was unleashed. The heat from the bomb incinerated everything within two miles. All three cruise ships and their passengers disappeared, obliterated by the blast. There was nothing left of the *Dream Free* or its three suicide bombers. The nearby Coast Guard patrol boat vanished in the firestorm. All of the terminals and the gantries were reduced to white dust. Two freighters on the south side of the island, about a quarter of a mile away, were completely reduced to ashes on the water.

The force of the blast and the immensely powerful destructive concussion flattened office towers, shopping malls and homes for miles around. There were thousands of dead people, with red watery blotches covering their bodies, strewn across the streets within an area of about four to five square miles.

The mushroom cloud continued upward until it reached about one mile in height. A sea breeze from the east began to carry deadly radioactive fallout to the west and southwest. The deadly cloud moved slowly but inexorably; nothing could stop it. Thousands in its path, who were not killed immediately, would shortly die, painfully, from radiation sickness.

Sirens all over Miami wailed. Emergency crews from nearby suburbs headed in the direction of the disaster area—first responders stepping over a threshold into the worst nightmare imaginable—on American soil.

The death toll would ultimately exceed 100,000, not counting thousands who would later die from cancer and other diseases caused by the lethal blast. In addition to the devastating human loss, the economic damage would be incalculable. It would run well over a trillion dollars, with the ensuing collapse of the stock markets. The attack shattered the standing of the United States—bringing to its knees the world's most powerful nation.

Al Qaeda had inflicted the most damaging blow the United States had ever experienced from any one incident in its entire history. Its three suicide bombers would become martyrs and would be worshipped and glorified in many parts of the Muslim world.

America thought it was safe, but it was mistaken.

Breinigsville, PA USA
17 March 2011
257857BV00004B/1/P